A baby-faced cowhand becomes a legend when he unwittingly shoots one of the West's finest gunslingers in **Ed Gorman's** "The Victim."

The men of Virginia City learn a valuable lesson when a breathtaking (and expensive) courtesan comes to town in **Marthayn Pelegrimas's** "Don't Never Fall in Love with No Whore."

In **Louis L'Amour's** "What Gold Does to a Man," a handful of riders discover gold—and that greed can grow between even the closest of friends.

A twelve-year-old tomboy learns life lessons the hard way in Miss Ellie's saloon in **Judy Alter's** "Pegeen's Revenge."

Guns of the West

Edited by
Ed Gorman
and Martin H. Greenberg

BERKLEY BOOKS, NEW YORK

GUNS OF THE WEST

A Berkley Book / published by arrangement with
the authors

PRINTING HISTORY
Berkley edition / August 2002

For information address: The Berkley Publishing Group,
a division of Penguin Putnam Inc.,
375 Hudson Street, New York, New York 10014.

Visit our website at
www.penguinputnam.com

ISBN: 0-425-18573-7

BERKLEY®
Berkley Books are published by The Berkley Publishing Group,
a division of Penguin Putnam Inc.,
375 Hudson Street, New York, New York 10014.
BERKLEY and the "B" design
are trademarks belonging to Penguin Putnam Inc.

PRINTED IN THE UNITED STATES OF AMERICA

10 9 8 7 6 5 4 3 2 1

Contents

Introduction

There are two important historical moments to recall when we're talking about guns of the west.

The first happened in the late seventeenth century. The newly arrived Americans began importing rifles from Central Europe. Reason? Rifles were much more dependable than firearms such as smoothbores.

The second historical moment was in 1846. A guy named Samuel Colt introduced his first revolvers. It took a while, though, before he produced handguns folks considered reliable.

Guns of the west.

Too many western novelists and screenwriters have portrayed those guns as weapons to be used in those legendary snarling gunfights that never actually took place, at least not as they were portrayed in dime novels and on the silver screen.

Guns were used to shoot game for food; as homefront protection against ominous animals; for a myriad of purposes by the military; for competitive amusements at county fairs and holiday celebrations; and as security tools by sheriffs, police officers, and other law enforcement people.

But as for those gunfights in the middle of the street—sorry. Didn't happen.

The lure and lore of guns figured in a million campfire tales passed back and forth by lonely cowhands out on the million patches of rangeland. Some guns were said to be cursed; some guns were said to be blessed; some guns were said to be the former property of this or that legendary outlaw.

We've tried to show you how guns of various kinds were an integral part of the daily life of the old west. We hope you enjoy these authentic looks at historical weapons in their proper historical context.

—Ed Gorman

What Gold Does to a Man

Louis L'Amour

What can you say about Louis L'Amour that hasn't been said hundreds of times before? He dominated the western field as only Zane Grey and Max Brand did before him. His books were everywhere on big screen and small, and by the end of his life, his books went automatically on bestseller lists around the world. Here's one of Mr. L'Amour's best stories.

WE CAME UP the draw from the south in the spring of '54, and Josh was the one who wanted to stop.

Nothing about that country looked good to me, but I was not the one who was calling the shots. Don't get the idea that it was not pretty country, because it surely was. There was a-plenty of water, grass, and trees. That spring offered some of the coldest and best water I ever tasted, but I didn't like the look of the country around. There was just too much Indian sign.

"Forget it, Pike!" Josh Boone said irritably. "For a kid, you sound more like an old woman all the time! Believe me, I know gold country, and this is it. Why should a man go all the way to California when there's gold all around him?"

"It may be here," Kinyon grumbled, "but maybe Pike Downey ain't so dumb, even if he is a kid. He's dead right about that Injun sign. If we stick around here, there being no more than the five of us, we're apt to get our hair lifted."

Kinyon was the only one who thought as I did. The others

had gold fever, and had it bad, but Kinyon's opinions didn't make me feel any better, because he knew more about Injuns than any of the rest. I'd rather have been wrong and safe.

Josh Boone did know gold country. He had been in California when the first strike was made, and I don't mean the one at Sutter's Mill that started all the fuss. I mean the *first* strike, which was down in a canyon near Los Angeles. Josh had done all right down there, and then when the big strikes came up north he'd cleaned up some forty thousand dollars, then he rode back east and had himself a time. "Why keep it?" he laughed. "There's more where that came from!"

Maybe there was, but if I made myself a packet like that I planned to buy myself a farm and settle down. I even had the place in mind.

It was Boone who suggested we ride north away from the trail. "There's mountains yonder," he said, "and I've a mind there's gold. Why ride all the way to Californy when we might find it right here?"

Me, I was ready. Nobody would ever say Pike Downey was slow to look at new country. The horse I rode was the best in the country, and it could walk faster than most horses could trot. It weighed about fourteen hundred, and most of it muscle. It was all horse, that black was, so when we turned off to the hills I wasn't worried. That came later.

Josh Boone was our leader, much as we had one. Then there was Jim Kinyon, German Kreuger and Ed Karpe. I was the kid of the bunch, just turned nineteen, strong as a young bull.

Josh had been against me coming along, but Kinyon spoke for me. "He's the best shot I ever did see," he told them, "and he could track a snake upstream in muddy water. That boy will do to take along."

Kinyon calling me a boy kind of grated. I'd been man enough to hold my own and do my part since I was fourteen. My paw and maw had come west from Virginia in a covered wagon, and I was born in that wagon.

I'd been hunting since I was knee-high to a short beaver, and the first time I drove a wagon over the Santa Fe Trail I was just past fourteen. My rifle drew blood for me in a Comanche attack on that wagon train, and we had three more fights before we came up to Santa Fe.

Santa Fe was wild and rough, and I had a mix-up with a Comanchero in Santa Fe with knives, and I put him down to stay. The following year I went over the Trail again, and then I went to hunting buffalo in Texas. The year after I went all the way to California, and returning from that trip I got friendly with some Cheyennes and spent most of a year with them, raiding deep into Mexico. By the time I met Boone, I had five years of the roughest kind of living behind me.

Boone talked himself mighty big, but he wasn't bigger than me, and neither was Ed Karpe.

We rode up that draw and found ourselves the prettiest little canyon you'll ever see, and we camped there among the trees. We killed us a deer, and right away Josh went to panning that stream. He found gold from the first pan.

Gold! It ran heavy from the first pan, and after that there was no talking to them. We all got to work, but being a loner I went along upstream by myself. Panning for gold was something I had never done, but all the way back from California that time I'd traveled with one of the best, and he'd filled me to the ears with what was needful to know about placer mining for gold.

He told me about trying sandbars and little beaches where the stream curves around and throws up sand in the crook of the elbow. Well, I found such a place, and she showed color.

Wasting no more time on panning, I got my shovel and started digging down to bedrock. No more than four feet down I struck it. It was cracked here and there and, remembering what that old-timer told me, I cleaned those cracks and went back under the thin layers of rock and panned out what I found. By nightfall I had a rawhide sack with maybe three or four hundred dollars in it.

All of the boys had gold, but none of them had as much as I showed them, which was less than half what I had. Jim Kinyon was tickled, but it didn't set too well with either Boone or Karpe. Neither of them liked to be bested, and in particular they didn't like it from me.

Kreuger patted me on the back. "Goot poy!" he said. "Das iss goot!"

We took turns hunting meat, and next day it fell to me.

Mounting up, I took my Sharps Breech-Loader, and I'd buckled on my spare pistol. I had me two Army Colts, Model 1848, and I set store by them guns. I'd picked 'em off a dead Texan down east of Santa Fe.

That Texas man had run up on some horse thieves and out of luck at the same time. There'd been four horse thieves and him, and they had at it, and when I came along some hours later there they lay, all good dead men with a horse for each and six extry. There were their rifles, pistols, and a good bit of grub, and there was no sense in leaving it for the Comanches to pick up or the sand to bury. In the time I'd been packing those six-shooters I'd become right handy with 'em.

They were riding my belt that morning when I rode out from camp. Sighting a couple of deer close to camp, I rode around them. I'd no mind to do my killing close by, where we might need the game at some later time. A few miles further away I fetched me a good-sized buck, skinned him out, and cut us some meat. Down at the stream I was washing the blood from my hands when I glanced up to see two things at once—only one of them was important at the moment.

The first thing I spotted was a full-growed Injun with his bow all drawed back and an arrow aimed at me. Throwing myself to one side I fetched one of those Colts and triggered me an Injun just as the arrow flicked past my face. He slid down off that river bank and right into the Happy Hunting Grounds, where no doubt someday we'll meet and swap yarns.

The other thing I'd glimpsed was upstream just a ways. It was only a glimpse, but I edged along the creek for a better look.

Under a ledge of rock, just above the water, was a hole. It was about crawling-into size, and didn't smell of animal, so I crawled in and stood up. It was a big cave, a room maybe twenty feet long by fifteen wide, with a solid-packed sandy floor and a smidgin of light from above. Looking up, I could see a tangle of branches over a hole, which was a couple of feet across but well-hidden by brush.

When I rode into camp to unload my meat I told the boys about my Injun. "I caved the bank over him," I said, "but they will most likely find him. Then they'll come hunting us."

"One more and one less," Karpe said. "A dead Injun is a good Injun."

"A dead Injun is the start of trouble," I said. "We'd better light out of here if we want to keep our hair."

"Are you crazy?" Boone stared at me. "With all the gold we're finding?"

"We don't need to leave the country." I protested. "But what does gold mean to a dead man?"

"The boy is right," Kinyon agreed. "We're in for trouble."

"We can handle trouble," Karpe said. "I ain't afeerd of no Injuns. Anyway, this just sounds like Pike talking big. I'll bet he never saw no Injun."

Well, I put down the meat I was eating and licked my fingers. Then I got up and looked across the fire at him. "You called me a liar, Ed," I said, mild-like. "I take that from no man."

He stared at me like he couldn't believe what he was hearing. "Now what about this?" he said. "The boy figures he's a growed-up man! Well, I'll take that out of him!" He got to his feet.

"No guns," Boone said. "If there are Injuns, we don't want to draw them nigh."

Me, I shucked my Bowie. Some folks don't fancy cold steel, and Ed Karpe seemed to be one of them. "Shuck your steel, Ed," I told him. "I'll see the color of your insides."

"No knives," he protested. "I fight with my hands or a gun."

I flipped my knife hard into a log. "All right," I said. "It makes me no mind. You just come on, and we'll see who is the boy of this outfit."

He come at me. Ed Karpe was a big man, all rawboned and iron hard. He fetched me a clout on the jaw that made me see lights flashing, hitting me so hard I nearly staggered. Then he swung his other fist but I stepped inside, grabbing him by shirt-front and crotch, swinging him aloft and heaving him against the bank.

He hit hard, but he was game and came up swinging. He fetched me a blow, but he was scared of me grabbing him and hit me whilst going away. I made as if to step on a loose rock and stagger, and he leapt at me. Dropping to one knee, I caught him again by shirt-front and crotch, only this time I throwed him head first into that bank. He hit hard and he just laid there.

When I saw he wasn't about to get up, I dusted off my knees and went back to the bone I'd been picking. Nobody said anything, but Josh Boone was looking surprised and sizing me up like he hadn't really seen me before. "You can fight some," he admitted. "That didn't take you no time at all."

"One time up in Pierre's Hole I fought nigh onto two hours with a big trapper. He'd have made two of Ed there, and he was skookum man, but I whopped him some."

After a bit Ed Karpe come around, and he come back to the fire shaking his head and blinking, but nobody paid him no mind. Me, I was right sorry. It ain't good for folks to start fighting amongst themselves in Injun country. Come daylight I went back to my shaft and taken one look. Whilst I'd been grub-hunting yesterday somebody had moved in and cleaned the bedrock slick as a piano-top.

Sure, I was upset, but I said nothing at all right then. I went on up the creek to a better place and dug me another hole, only when I left this one I covered it with brush and wiped out the sign I'd left.

Kinyon had been hunting that day, and when he came in he was worried. "We'd better light out or get fixed for a fight. There's Injuns all around us."

They listened to Kinyon where they hadn't listened to me, so we dug ourselves some rifle pits and forted up with logs. I said nothing about my shaft being cleaned out.

Next day I went back to my brush-covered hole and sank her down to bedrock and cleaned up. This was heavy with gold, and the best so far. My method of going to the rock was paying off. It was more work than using a pan, and it was more dangerous.

That night when we all came in to camp Kreuger was missing. We looked at one another, and believe me, we didn't feel good about it. Nobody had seen the German, and nobody had heard a shot. When morning came I headed upstream, then doubled back to where Kinyon was working, only I stayed back in the brush. I laid right down in the brush not far from him, but where I could watch both banks at once.

"Jim?" I kept my voice so only he would hear me. "Don't you look up or act different. I'll do the talking."

"All right," he said.

"Somebody robbed that shaft of mine. Cleaned her out whilst I was hunting."

He wiped sweat from his face but said nothing.

"I've some ideas about German Kreuger, too."

"You think he stole your gold and lit out?"

"You know better. Nor do I think Injuns killed him. However, we better have us a look."

"Who do you think?"

"It wasn't you, and it wasn't me. And I'd bet every ounce I have that it wasn't that old German."

Pausing, I said, "You go on working. I'll watch."

He was canny, Jim was. He worked, all right, but he didn't get into a pattern. When he bent down he didn't lift up in the same place, but away from there. He kept from any pattern, so's if anybody planned a shot they'd have to wait until he was out in the open.

As for me, I almost missed it. Almost, but not quite. I'd been lying there a couple of hours, and my eyes were tired. The day was warm, and I'd been working hard the past few days and was tuckered. I must have been looking right at that rifle barrel a full minute before I realized it.

Only the fact that Kinyon was moving saved him. He was down by the water, partly hidden by some rocks, and he was digging sand from the low side of a boulder, preparing to wash it out. That rifleman was waiting for him to come up on the bank where he'd have no doubt.

Me, I didn't wait. Sliding my old Sharps Breech-Loader up, I just throwed a shot into that brush, right along that rifle barrel. There was a crash in the brush, and both me and Jim jumped for it, but the heavy brush and boulders got in the way, and by the time we got there that feller was gone. Nor could we make anything from the tracks except that he wore boots and was therefore a white man.

We tried to track him, though, and found nothing until we slid down among some rocks and there we found Kreuger. He'd been scalped. "No Injun," Kinyon said, and he was right. That was plain as day to any old Injun fighter.

"We've got a murderer in the outfit," I said.

"Maybe," Kinyon said doubtfully, "but there could be somebody else around, somebody we don't know about."

After a pause he said, "We've not much gold yet."

"No one of us has," I agreed, "but for one man it's a healthy stake, if he had it all."

"Injuns around," Kinyon said, that night at the fire. "Today I was shot at."

"I've been afraid of that," Karpe agreed. "We'd better watch ourselves."

Josh Boone glanced over at Karpe. "It ain't Injuns that scares me," he said, but if Ed Karpe noticed he paid no attention.

For the next two days everything went along fine. I worked with an eye out for trouble, and every now and again I'd quit work and scout around the area to make sure nobody was closing in on me. On the bottom of the shaft I'd sunk, I broke up the layers of bedrock where there were cracks, and made a good cleanup. Even me, who'd been doing well, couldn't believe how rich the find was. When I sacked up that night I had more than I'd had in my life, more than I'd ever seen, in fact.

Kinyon met me at an agreed-upon place on the creek bank. "Let's go higher," I suggested, "and sink a shaft together. We'll work faster, and this ground is rich enough for both of us."

Ed Karpe came up to us. He looked from one to the other. "I'd like to throw in with you boys," he said. "I'm getting spooked. I don't like going it alone." He looked at us, his face flushing. "Maybe I've lost my nerve."

"Why do you say that?" I asked.

"I feel like somebody's scouting me all the time."

Boone joined us just then, carrying his rifle in the hollow of his arm. "What's this? Everybody quitting so soon?"

"We're going to team up and work together," I said. "We figure it will be safer. Less chance of Injuns sneakin' up on us. I think we should get what we can and move out while our luck holds."

Josh Boone stared at me. "You runnin' this show now? I thought I was elected leader?"

"You was," Kinyon agreed. "It wasn't any idea of leading that started Pike talking. He figures we'd all do a lot better working together on shares than each working by himself."

"Oh, he does, does he? I don't see he's done so durned well."

"I got more than four thousand in gold. If any of you has over a thousand I'll cook chow this night."

"Four thousand?" They just stared. Jim was the one who said it, then he spat into the dust. "What're we waitin' for? I ain't got five hundred."

That settled it, but it did not settle Josh Boone. He was sore because they all listened to me now. Even Karpe listened, although I was keeping an eye on Karpe. He kept his gun close and his eyes busy, but mostly he was watching me. I saw that right off.

We were edgy, all of us. Here we were, four men out miles from anywhere or anybody, hid out in the Black Hills, but we watched each other more than we watched for Injuns.

German Kreuger was gone, so our little world was lessened by one, our total strength less by twenty percent, our loneliness increased by the missing of a face by the fire at night.

Somebody, either Karpe, Boone, or some stranger had killed Kreuger, and had been about to shoot Jim Kinyon. Only we had found no stranger's tracks, nor even the tracks of any Indian at the time.

Our meat gave out, and Karpe was the hunter. He did not like it very much and he hesitated, about to say something which his personal courage would not let him say. My father, who had been a reading man in the few books he had, often quoted the Bible or other such books, and he was one to speculate on men and their ways. I thought of him now, and wondered what he would say of our situation. Since my father's death I have had no books and read but poorly. It ain't as if the idea wasn't there.

Karpe took his rifle and went out alone, and the rest of us went to work.

It was hot and the air was close. Jim paused once, leaning on his shovel. "Feels like a storm coming," he said, and I did not think he meant only in the weather.

Taking off my guns, I placed them on a flat rock close at

hand while I worked. Folks who've never packed pistols can't imagine how heavy they are. Pretty soon Josh Boone got out of the hole and traded places with Kinyon. Jim, he put down his rifle and went to work.

All of a sudden, and why I turned I don't know, I turned sharp around, and there was Ed Karpe standing on the bank with his rifle in his hands. He was looking down at Boone and I'd have sworn he was about to shoot him.

Boone, he was on his feet his own rifle ready, and what would have happened next was anybody's guess, when suddenly an arrow smacked into a tree within inches of Karpe's head, and he yelled "Injuns!" and ducked for cover.

He took shelter behind the bank while Jim and Boone made it to the fort. Me, I squatted down in the hole where I was, and when the Injuns rushed us I opened up with both Colts. Karpe had turned to fire on them, and what he or the others did I didn't know, but I dropped four men and a horse. Then I caught up my rifle, but they were gone, leaving behind them several horses and some Injuns. A couple of them started to crawl away, and we let 'em go.

Boone went out to gather up what guns he could find and to catch up horses and bring 'em in. Whilst he was collectin' them, I saw him throw something into the bushes. At the time I thought nothing of it. My guns reloaded, I watched the boys come together again. Nobody had more than a scratch. We'd been ready, as much for each other as for them, but everybody was ready to shoot when they showed up, and of course, we had our fort, such as it was.

"Lucky!" Boone said. "Mighty lucky!"

"They'll be back," Kinyon replied grimly. "Our scalps are worth more now that we've shown ourselves warriors."

Nobody knew better than I what a break we'd had. If the Indians had come at us easy-like, slipping up and opening fire from cover, we'd have had small chance. Indians have bad leaders as well as white men, and this one had been too confident, too eager.

Young braves, no doubt, reckless and anxious to count coup on a white man, and wanting loot, too, our guns and horses. But nobody needed to tell anybody what stopped them.

Josh Boone was staring at me again. "You handle them

Colts like a man who knowed how to use 'em."

"Why d' you figure he carries them? I knew he was handy." Kinyon was smiling with some secret pleasure.

Karpe had a wry amusement in his eyes. "And to think I nearly got into a shootin' scrape with you!"

"This does it," Kinyon said. "Now we'll have to go."

Boone started to object, then said nothing. We slept cold that night, staying away from the fire and close to our horses. If they stole our horses and those we had of theirs, we'd never get out of here alive. It was too far to anywhere safe.

We slept two at a time, not taking a chance on having just one man awake, because we didn't know who the murderer was.

At daybreak we slipped away from camp. We'd covered our holes, hiding our tools and what gear we did not want to carry. We kept one pan for taking samples downstream, and then we took off.

What the others were thinking I had no idea, but as for me, I was worried. One of us was a murderer and wanted all our gold. It wasn't enough that we had to watch out for Injuns, but one amongst us as well.

We hadn't gone three miles before Kinyon, who was in the lead, threw up a hand. "Injuns!" he said hoarsely. "Must be thirty or forty of 'em!"

That about-faced us, you can bet! We turned back up-creek, riding fast, and then turned off into the woods. We hadn't gone far before we heard 'em again, only this time it was another bunch already spread out in the woods. A gun thundered somewhere ahead of us, and then an arrow whistled by my head, and as I swung my horse I took a quick shot with the Sharps and saw an Indian fall.

Then I was riding Hell for leather and trying to load whilst we ran.

There was a yell behind us and Karpe's horse stumbled, throwing Ed to the ground. He lit running just as a couple of Indians closed in on him.

One swung a tomahawk high, and I shot without aiming, then shoved the Sharps into the boot and went for a six-shooter. Boone and Kinyon both fired, and Ed came running. He still had his rifle and saddlebags.

"No use to run!" Jim yelled. "Too many of 'em! We've got to stand!"

There were rocks ahead, not far from our old fort, and we hit them running. My horse ran on, but I was shooting soon as I hit the ground, and Kinyon beside me. Boone and Karpe found good places, and they also opened fire. The attack broke off as quick as it began.

Karpe had a bullet scratch along his skull, and a burn on his shoulder. "You boys saved me!" he seemed amazed. "You surely did!"

Our horses were still with us. Mine had run on and then circled back to be with me, or with the horses he knew, I did not know which. We had our horses, but we had Indians all around us and no help nearer than three or four hundred miles. At least, none that we knew of.

"If they wipe us out," Boone commented, "nobody will ever know what happened to us."

"We wouldn't be the first," Kinyon said, "I found a skull and part of a spine and rib cage back yonder when I was huntin' gold. The bones had a gold pan along with 'em."

We sat there waiting for the next attack and expecting little when I heard that stream. It was close by, and in all the confusion I hadn't thought of it. "Look," I said, "if we can hold on until dark, I think I can get us out of this!"

They looked at me, waiting, but nobody said anything. Right at the moment nobody thought much of his chances.

"If we can stand 'em off until dark, we can slip away upstream into a cave I've found. They'll think we've left the country."

"What about our horses?" Kinyon asked.

"Have to leave 'em," I said, although it went hard to leave my Tennessee horse.

"Maybe there's another entrance?" Jim suggested. "Where there's one cave there's sometimes others."

We sat tight and let the sun do its work. It was almighty hot, but we had to put up with it, for there was no more than an edging of shade near some of the boulders. The Injuns tried a few shots and so did we, more to let 'em know we were still alive and ready than with hope of hitting anything.

Boone was lyin' beside me and he kept turning his head

to stare out over the rocks. "Think we'll make it?" he asked me. All the big-headedness seemed to have gone out of him. "I'd sure like to save my pelt."

They came on then. They came in a wave from three sides, riding low on their horses and again it was my Model 48s that stopped them. Not that I killed anybody, but I rained bullets around them and burned a couple, and they couldn't understand that rapid fire. They knew about guns, and had some themselves, but they had never run up against any repeating weapons.

The last Injun was riding away when he turned sharp in the saddle and let go with a shot that winged Josh Boone.

It hit him high but hard, and he went down. Leaving the shooting to Karpe and Kinyon, I went to Boone. His face was all twisted with pain, but when I went to undo the laces on his buckskin shirt he jerked away, his eyes wild and crazy. "No! Let me alone! Don't bother with me!"

"Don't be a fool, Josh. You've been hit hard. You get treated or you'll die sure!"

He was sullen. "I'd better die, then. You go off. I'll fix it myself."

Something in his voice stopped me as I started to turn away. Slamming him back on the ground in no gentle way, I ripped open the rawhide cords and peeled back his hunting shirt.

There was a nasty wound there, all right, that had shattered his collarbone and left him bleedin' most awful bad. But that wasn't all.

There was another wound through the top of his shoulder, which was all festerin' and sore. When I saw that I stopped. He stared at me, his mouth drawn in a hard line, his eyes ugly, yet there was something else, too. There was shame as well as fear.

There was only one time he could have gotten that wound. Like when a bullet comes along a man's rifle and cuts the meat atop his shoulder. It had been Josh Boone and not Ed Karpe who had tried to kill Jim Kinyon, and therefore it had been Boone who killed old German Kreuger.

He stared at me and said no word while I washed out the wound, picked away bone fragments, and put it in the best shape I could manage. I folded an old bandana to stop the bleeding, and bound it tight in place. By the time I finished it was fetchin' close to dusk, and the Injuns had let up on their shootin'.

Kinyon guessed right. There was another hole into that cave, just a big crack, like, but big enough to get a horse inside, even a horse as big as my Tennessee. Once they were inside we pulled a couple of pieces of old log into the gap and then we bedded down to wait it out.

Oh, they come a-huntin', all right! We could hear them looking for us, but we kept quiet and after a while they gave up and rode away. We sat it out for three days in that cave, and then Jim slipped out to scout around.

They were gone, thinking we'd gotten away, and we slipped out, mounted up, and headed back for the settlements. When we had buildings in sight and knew we were safe, I pulled up and turned to face them.

"Josh," I said, "German left a widder behind. She's up at this settlement waitin' for him. With German dead, she will be hard put to live. I figure you might like to contribute, Josh."

He sat his horse lookin' at me, and I knew he was left-handed as well as right. He had a gun, a handgun I'd seen him pick out of the bushes after he'd taken it off a dead Injun. He looked at me and I looked at him. I put no hand to a gun and I knew there was no need. "You just toss me your poke, Josh," I told him.

His eyes were all mean-like, and he tossed me the poke.

"Now the other one."

Ed Karpe and Jim, they just sat watching and Ed couldn't seem to figure it out. Kinyon knew, although how long he had known I couldn't guess.

Josh Boone waited, holding off as long as he could, but then he tossed me the other poke.

Pocketing the pokes, I then took a couple of nuggets and some dust from my own poke. "There's maybe a hundred dollars there," I said. "Its riding money, a loan from me to you."

"I'll owe you for that," he said. "I always pay my debts."

"I'll see no man beggared with a broken arm," I said, "but that's what I named it. Ridin' money. Now you ride."

We sat there watching while he rode away, back square

to us, one arm hitched kind of high. He rode like that right out of time, because we never saw him again.

"Well," Jim said after a bit. "If we ain't campin' here let's ride in. I'm goin' to wet my whistle."

We started riding, and nobody said anything more.

Pegeen's Revenge

Judy Alter

Judy Alter is a modern-day stylist whose work bridges the traditional themes of western fiction with some of the more important contemporary issues of the west. Spur winner, much celebrated by reviewers everywhere, Judy has worked in a variety of styles and voices in both short fiction and long. She is a good example of the female western writer whose time has definitely come, especially with such Spur-winning novels as *Mattie.*

I WASN'T IN the saloon the night Louann got shot. If I had been, I'm sure it wouldn't have happened—or at least, that's what I tell myself. But she had this thing about making me go to bed, so I was upstairs in my room, pretending to be asleep. It was a hot night in August, and I couldn't have slept even if I was tired. The big old hand-me-down man's shirt she'd found for me was so hot it felt like being wrapped in a wool blanket. So I did what I did a lot of nights—I listened to the singing and shouting from the saloon. Usually it was good-natured, but not that night. Somehow as I lay there I sensed a menacing tone in the buzz from downstairs, like low, angry voices were talking.

My name's Pegeen—oh, its Mary Margaret, but everyone called me Pegeen back then. I was twelve years old in 1877 when all this happened. Three years before my mama went to sleep and didn't wake up. I heard someone say the word *laudanum,* and Louann told me she left a note saying I belonged to her now. I missed my mama a lot, but by then I was fiercely attached to Louann. We lived upstairs from Miss Ellie's saloon in Fort Worth, Texas. And no, don't be thinkin' that. Louann wasn't no lady of the night, though Lord knows I know about that. My mama had fallen that low, and that's why she took her life. But Louann, she sang and sometimes she danced on the top of the big grand piano Miss Ellie had bought. But mostly she went around the room, hugging the cowboys, inviting them to have another drink, watching them play cards, and making each one of them think he was the best-looking, most important fellow she'd ever seen.

And some lowlife shot her over a card game!

I HEARD THE shot—it was a loud, muffled sort of a bang, not the clean crack of a rifle shot—and when I threw open the door to the balcony, I saw the smoke, thick and dirty, rising over the poker table. Everyone was yelling and screaming, and I screamed "Louann!" as I lunged down the stairs. I heard someone else yell, "Get Doc McGarrity," and yet another voice cry out, "Find Marshal Courtright."

Strong arms grabbed me and held me. "She's been hit, Pegeen. You can't help her."

"She's not dead!" I screamed.

"No," the voice said, "at least not yet." The voice belonged to Eddie, one of the bartenders. "They've sent for Doc McGarrity. You need to stay out of the way."

I squirmed and wriggled, but he held tight. I was convinced that Louann would be all right if I could just get to her, hold her hand, tell her how much I needed her. Of course, I was wrong. That wouldn't have done a thing to help her.

The knot of people around her parted to make way for Doc McGarrity. He bent over, listened with his stethoscope, seemed to study Louann from several directions. Then he spoke to the men around him. Someone ran up the stairs and returned with a blanket from which they made a makeshift sling, and four of them carried her upstairs.

"Louann!" I wailed again, but I guess even then I knew that she couldn't hear me.

I was still sitting on the stairs, arms propped on my knees

and head buried in my arms, when Randy Spurlock came down the stairs. Without a word, he sat down next to me.

"Who shot her?" I asked, raising a tearstained face.

"Gambler. Fella I'd never seen before. Looked like he came off a riverboat on the Mississippi—you know, creased trousers and a black vest with a big gold watch chain. A real dandy." Randy's voice was bitter. He was sort of Louann's special friend, though I guess both of them would've denied it if you asked them. But I thought Randy was just about the best-looking man I'd ever seen—tall, strong, curly headed with eyes that usually laughed though now they were so sad it hurt me to look at him. Still, he was everything a twelve-year-old girl dreams about.

"Why'd he shoot her?"

"She was . . ." Randy's voice almost broke. "She was tryin' to help me. I was losing bad . . . and you know, Pegeen, I don't lose at poker. She saw the reason. He was dealin' out of his shirtsleeve. When she called him on it, he pulled this little tiny gun. . . ."

"If it was a little tiny gun, then it didn't hurt her too bad, right?" I was figuring all this out in my mind.

He laid a hand over mine. "Wrong, Pegeen. It was a derringer—little but deadly at close range. Big bullet—about this big—" He held up the stubby end of his little finger. "Big and slow, so it hits hard." He was quiet for a minute. "Hit her in the upper arm, aimed for the heart and missed. If it had been her heart . . ." He shuddered.

"Shoulder!" I scoffed. "She'll be all right then. It'll just have to heal."

This time he put a comforting arm around me. "Probably shattered the bone so's Doc can't fix it right. If she lives, she'll never have use of that shoulder again. She won't be dancin' on the piano anymore like she used to."

"What do you mean, 'If she lives'?" I asked indignantly. "Louann's gonna live."

"Sure she is, honey, sure she is."

We sat there in silence, each of us avoiding looking at the other. I studied the saloon, which had been turned into a shambles. Chairs and tables were overturned, and cards and beer bottles were scattered everywhere. I looked toward where Louann had fallen and saw blood on the floor. Not a lot, but it was still blood. I couldn't bear that so I looked the other way.

Suddenly I grabbed Randy's arm. "Look, what's that there on the floor."

Almost relieved to have an excuse to move, he got up, walked to the far side of the overturned table, and bent down. Then came a low whistle. "It's the gun," he said, coming back to where I sat. "He must have dropped it just before he got away in all the confusion."

I reached for it.

"Uh-uh. There's still a bullet in the second chamber." He broke it open and dumped the cartridge into his hand. Before handing me the gun, he looked through both barrels, just to be sure. Then he clicked the gun together and gave it to me.

The derringer was ugly. Stubby and short, like a fat man. I'd seen fancy pistols lots in the saloon. Sometimes men would come in to play and lay their pistols on the table as a show of good faith. I'd seen 'em with gold scrolls and filigrees on them and sometimes brass plates with the maker's name. This one was all black steel, with a rubber grip where you put your hand. And it was so small.

"This little thing?" I asked.

"That little thing is a Remington .41 rimfire double derringer, if you want to get technical. And it's deadly. I can still see the flash when he fired it. Like a burst of flame."

I put my hands over my ears.

A plan began to take shape in my mind. "Randy, how do you fire this thing?" I was pulling the trigger but nothing happened.

"Pegeen, you don't need to be knowing how to fire a derringer."

"Ah, come on, show me."

Reluctantly, he took the gun back. "You got to cock the hammer"—he showed me—"and then pull the trigger."

I tried, but the hammer was too stiff for me, and the gun, small as it was, was awkwardly heavy in my hand. "I could never shoot this."

"Good," he said, reaching for it.

I jumped up and moved away, stuffing the gun into my overall's pocket. "I'm gonna give it to Louann. I think she ought to have it."

"Pegeen . . ." His tone was threatening as he moved toward me. "A girl your age has no business with a gun."

I climbed up a couple of stairs. "You've got the bullets," I pointed out. "I'm just gonna save it until I can give it to her."

I SPENT THE next three days sitting outside Louann's bedroom door. Nobody would let me in to see her. "You'll upset her," they said. "Leave her be," the doc said. "She's having a hard time."

Once as I dozed on the floor, I heard the doc talking to Miss Ellie. "Infection's set in, just like I feared. Those damn derringer bullets are greasy on the outside, and they pick up lint and stuff and carry it right into the wound. Sometimes it's a blessing if they bleed, carry that stuff out. But Louann, she didn't bleed enough. The wound's puffy and red and hot. I dug out the bullet and drained as much pus off as I could, but we'll just have to wait for the crisis."

What crisis? I wanted to scream.

Fortunately Miss Ellie asked, "Crisis? What do you mean?"

I peeked one eye open, hoping they'd still think I was asleep if they even saw me, and saw Doc shrug his shoulders.

"We'll see if the bullet's gonna beat the body or the body's gonna beat the bullet."

"That damn lowlife!" Miss Ellie said vehemently and turned and went downstairs. Doc followed her. They'd forgotten about me, and if I'd kept good track, no one was with Louann right now. I reached into my pocket and held the derringer until it felt warm in my hand. Somehow that reassured me. Then ever so carefully I eased open the door to her room and slid in, gentling the door closed behind me.

Louann lay on her back, so motionless that I thought they were all wrong, and she'd died after all. I crept to the bedside and put out my hand. With one finger, I stroked her cheek ever so softly. She wasn't dead—her cheek was burning hot with fever.

"Louann," I whispered, "there's a crisis coming. You got to fight."

All I got in response was a moan, low and miserable. She

moved ever so slightly. Her left shoulder was all tied up with bandages, I guess to keep her from moving it. Once while I watched she grabbed at the bandages with her good right hand, and I had to take the hand and pull it back down. Had I remembered to wash my own hands, I wondered? I hoped so. Louann was always after me about bathing more often and being more ladylike, and it wouldn't do to carry even more germs to her.

"Louann, I got something for you to fight the crisis with. It's the lowlife's gun, the one that shot you."

She moaned, and I thought her eyes flickered a little. I tiptoed around to the other side of the bed, so's I could put the derringer into her right hand. "There now, you feel that. It'll make you well, 'cause you and me, we got to go for revenge. We got to find that no-good son-of-a-bitch that shot you." Louann would've washed my mouth with soap if she heard me say that! I squeezed her good hand, adding, "And he shouldn't have tried to cheat Randy."

I thought she tried to say "Pegeen," and I quickly whispered, "I'm here, Louann. I'm gonna wait for the crisis with you. We're gonna fight it."

Of course, I slept right through the crisis and never did know it. When I woke up, curled in a ball on the far side of her bed, I heard Doc and Miss Ellie talking. I wanted to stretch my cramped muscles so bad I near cried out, but I sure didn't want them to know I was there.

"Crisis passed," Doc said, relief spilling over in his voice. "She's gonna make it. I don't know how she got the stamina or the will or what, but she's gonna make it."

Well, I knew. It was because I'd given her the gun and talked to her about revenge. Louann was going to get well so we could shoot that scoundrel with his own gun. Now I maybe was only twelve, but I knew that it wasn't something we could do tomorrow or the next day. Louann had a long time of recovering ahead of her, and it was up to me to keep her spirits up by talking about revenge. I could hold out to her a mental picture of shooting that Mississippi gambler in the shoulder, just like he shot her. I guess I was so bent on encouraging Louann that I never thought about the reality of shooting someone. At least not for a while, I didn't.

* * *

IT WAS TWO more days before Miss Ellie officially let me in to visit Louann. By then, she was propped up a little in the bed, and Miss Ellie was feeding her broth. I just thanked her for letting me come in and didn't tell her I'd spent the last three nights sleeping by Louann's bed.

"I can feed her," I offered.

Miss Ellie sniffed. "You'll need to go take a bath, get clean clothes, and wash your hair before I let you any closer to her."

Now I would have been downright offended by that, except I knew that was exactly what Louann would have said. In fact, I think I saw Louann look sideways at me as she opened her mouth to receive broth. But if she could talk, she didn't let me know it.

"Yes, ma'am," I said obediently and left the room. It wasn't no time at all until I was back, freshly scrubbed—well, maybe I'd cheated a little but I really had tried to scrub every inch of my body. And I'd washed my hair—it was still wet. And the most serious sign of my good intentions was that I'd put on that blasted dress that Louann bought me last year. It was too small now, tight across the shoulders, and so short around my ankles that if it was pants folks would have thought I was expecting heavy rain and high water. I may have been uncomfortable, but Miss Ellie thought I was now acceptable.

"You sit here by her, Pegeen," she commanded, "but don't you go to wearin' her out by talkin'."

"Yes, ma'am."

The minute she was gone, I asked, "You got that derringer, Louann?"

She was too tired and hurt too much to laugh, but something told me she would have if she'd had the energy. She moved the covers back with her right hand, and there lay the gun. "Hard to hide when they change the bedclothes," she managed to say.

Well, of course I hadn't thought of that. I just knew it was important that she keep that gun by her . . . I don't guess I knew the words *symbol* or *incentive,* but they were what I meant.

"Can you hide it in the folds of your robe?"

She nodded and took the spoonful of broth that I offered her.

"You know," I said conversationally, "I . . . well, I figure when you're well, we can take a wagon and go looking for this guy. I mean I'm sure he didn't stay in Fort Worth after shooting you. They'd have lynched him."

She nodded as though in agreement.

"But we can't let him get away, so you got to hurry about this mending business."

"Tired," she said, "So tired."

"Well, that's partly the pain medicine Doc is giving you, I suppose. You just sleep and gather your strength. But you be thinkin' about how we're gonna find that guy. And every time you touch that gun, it'll remind you of what we have to do."

She nodded, but she was asleep almost before I could take away the soup and tray.

RANDY CAME INTO the saloon that night. Just as he was about to sit at the poker table, he saw me, sitting in my usual place on the stairs. Eddie had fixed me lemonade and put it in a beer bottle he had rinsed very carefully—he did that for me sometimes, and it was our little joke. I loved to watch men come in and see this young girl in coveralls drinkin' a beer. They gaped and stared and never knew how funny they looked, even when I laughed at them.

"Pegeen, you better not be drinkin' beer!" He knew I wasn't.

"Who's gonna stop me?" I answered like a smart aleck.

"Me! I'll tell Louann on you."

"You seen her yet?"

He shook his head and slumped down beside me. "Miss Ellie won't let me. Acts like I'm gonna attack her or something. I . . . I just want to see how she's doin' and tell her I hope she gets better soon. I'm real glad she's gonna be okay."

"Doc says her left arm will never be much good, but I figure she can still shoot with her right hand."

"Shoot?" he exploded. "Who's she gonna shoot?"

"Oh, I mean shoot pool and do stuff like that. You know."

I thought I recovered very quickly, but Randy was looking at me real skeptical.

"You ain't thinkin' of shooting anyone, are you, Pegeen?" His voice was stern. Then he suddenly remembered. "What'd you do with that derringer?"

"Gave it to Louann like I told you I would. I just thought she should have it. And no, I'm not gonna shoot anybody and neither is she." I tried to treat it lightly. "Well, if that sidewinder that shot Louann came in here, I'd sure shoot him."

"Well, that ain't gonna happen, Pegeen. I guarantee he's in Fort Griffin or Abilene by now . . . or someplace on down the road from there."

"You aren't goin' after him?" I asked, intending to suggest that it would be manly of Randy to seek revenge for Louann.

He shook his head. "Nope. And Louann wouldn't want me to," he said. "If she'd died, I'd have probably helped the law find the guy. But now she's gonna be okay . . . shoot, I don't even know his name."

"You know what he looks like." I was nothing if not persistent.

"Yeah, so does she." He sat for a minute. Then he said, "I got to go play some cards. You see if you can sneak me in there sometime, Pegeen. You do that?"

"Sure, Randy, I'll do that."

BY THE END of the second week, Louann was sitting on the edge of the bed and talking to me almost like her old self.

"Tell me about that guy that shot you," I said. I was sprawled in the one chair in her room, wearing my coveralls again. After that one time, Miss Ellie had quit worrying about getting me into a dress.

"He was mean-looking," she said. "Had the coldest eyes I ever saw. I don't think it bothered him one bit to shoot me. Only thing that would bother him is being hanged."

"Or shot," I offered.

She grinned. "Or shot." She reached into the bedclothes and pulled out the derringer. With her right hand, she rubbed it as though for good luck. "I don't know if I've got the strength to shoot this, Pegeen. These little guns have a kick to them. That's why you have to be right on top of what you're trying to shoot—you can't aim with any kind of accuracy."

I watched her as she raised the gun. Trouble was she couldn't use her left hand to cock it, and it was near impossible to cock and hold in the same hand. "You keep working at it," I said.

RANDY GOT IN to see Louann about that time, and try as I might to sneak in behind him, I couldn't. "Pegeen," he said in his sternest voice, "you stay outside. I want some private time with Louann." He looked at me. "And don't you be peeking through the keyhole or listenin', either one."

I stomped off in a pout.

He must have been in there an hour. I know because I sat at the end of the hall and watched the door. When he came out, his face was red and he was rubbin' his chin, like he was confused about something. He brushed right on by me without saying anything.

When I went into her room, Louann was lying there staring at the ceiling. I thought her face looked kinda red too. "How's Randy?" I asked.

"What?" She was startled by my voice, and it was like I was calling her back from some far place. "He's fine," she said with a shrug. "You know that. You've seen him a lot more than I have lately."

THE FIRST DAY Louann came downstairs in the afternoon, the few men in the saloon stood and cheered. She came slowly, dressed in a cotton wrapper, and clinging to me with her right hand. Helping her was kind of awkward, because you didn't want to touch her left side at all, where her shoulder was bound into a sling. So I just let her hold on to me and hoped that she was steady on her feet.

She was almost winded when she sat down at one of the tables.

"Hey, Louann! Whiskey?" Eddie called from behind the bar.

She gave him a wan smile. "Lemonade, Eddie. And not in a beer bottle."

Everyone was awkward around her, not knowing what to say beyond, "Gee, you're looking good," and "I'm glad you're okay," and stuff like that. I wanted to shout at them that she wasn't suddenly deaf and dumb. She was still Louann who wanted to know what was going on in Fort Worth and who was winning at the poker table. She began to call them by name, ask about this one's wife or that one's child, and pretty soon they loosened up.

Randy came in just by accident, and he was delighted to see her sitting there. He plopped himself down in the chair next to hers and said, "I knew there was a reason I wanted a beer in the middle of the day, just didn't know what it was."

"And what was it?" she asked with a smile.

"So I could see you sitting up and acting like a person instead of an invalid," he said with a grin, and Louann raised her good arm as though she'd swat him.

I wished Randy hadn't come in, and I know that's selfish. But I kind of wanted to be her guardian all by myself. Now she turned her attention to him, and when she announced, after an hour, that she was "wiped out," it was Randy who helped her back upstairs. I sat and nursed my lemonade and my pout.

Louann came downstairs every day after that, each time staying a little longer, and pretty soon she was taking her meals with the rest of us at the table where Miss Ellie had Idabelle serve us. I sometimes had to help Louann cut her meat because she couldn't use both hands, but other than that she was pretty good one-handed.

One day when I walked her back upstairs and followed her into her room, she sat on the edge of the bed and stared at me.

"What's wrong?" I finally asked. "My overalls dirty again? Idabelle just washed them."

"They're too small, legs are too short," she said. "And your hair needs cutting. I haven't been doin' much about taking care of you."

"I can take care of myself," I mumbled, and I wanted to add that I could take care of her too.

"Soon as I get my strength back, young lady, you're gonna start your studies again." Louann, who had more education than you'd expect from a dance-hall girl, had been supervising my reading and arithmetic. I liked the reading all right but not the arithmetic, and missing lessons was about the only good thing I could see about her being laid up.

But the next thing she said really threw me. "Tomorrow I want to go for a walk."

By now it was late September, and that awful Texas heaty had pretty much gone, especially in the early mornings. "You want me to go with you?" I asked hopefully.

She smiled at me. "Well, Pegeen, I don't think I'm quite ready to go alone yet."

That first day we only went a little ways—not even a city block—before she was ready to turn around and go back. "I bet you don't know how hard it is to walk with one hand," she said with a wry smile.

"Why? You don't walk with your hands."

"Nope, But two free arms give you balance. I feel like I'm gonna topple over toward my left, and I can't stop myself. You try holding your arm tight against your shoulder and see."

I tried it but I didn't get the effect she was talking about. We did get some funny looks from people on the street.

When she was back in her room, Louann said with great determination, "I'm going to rest now, but this afternoon I want you to come to my room. There's something I need your help with."

I wasn't exactly looking forward to that, 'cause I knew what she wanted—not my help with anything. She wanted to "help" me with schoolwork. I was so sure of it that I went and dug out the books we'd been using before Louann had declared a summer holiday last July. As I sat there and tried to read *McGuffey's,* I got to thinking about Louann's recovery. She hadn't mentioned the gun or revenge lately, and yet she seemed to be getting a lot better faster and faster. So maybe we didn't need my revenge plan anymore. Maybe she was going to get well just to be well and not to find the man who shot her. A corner of my mind felt a little relieved. I'd enjoy the adventure of setting off to find the man, but I had some qualms about shooting him. And I thought she did too.

Boy oh boy, was I wrong! When I went into her room in the late afternoon, she was sitting up in the chair, fingering the derringer. "I can't do it!" she said in frustration. "I can't cock it. It's too stiff for one hand."

I took it, but I remembered I couldn't cock it when Randy gave it to me. I tried again, nothing. I held the gun with my left hand and tried to pull the hammer back with my right. Still couldn't get it. Finally I braced the gun against my leg and used both hands.

"Try not to shoot yourself in the leg," Louann said. "Even I know that's not how you're supposed to do it."

"It worked," I said, handing her the gun carefully with the muzzle pointed away from both of us. "Can you pull the trigger?" I asked. Randy would probably have shot both of us if he'd been there, because we didn't check the barrels. But I was sure it was unloaded—and it was.

She held the gun away from her, pointed at the wall, and pulled the trigger. "Easy," she said. "But I won't be able to tell that lowlife to stand still while I get Pegeen to cock my gun."

"Maybe you could carry it cocked once you find him and know where he is."

She laughed aloud so hard that I began to laugh too. "What's the matter with that?" I asked, when I could talk again.

"It shows that neither of us knows a thing about guns," she said. "Nobody, but nobody, goes around carrying a cocked pistol."

"Well, this is an unusual case," I said lamely.

"It surely is," she said. Then, "Where are the cartridges?"

"Randy took them."

"Can't ask Randy," she said, "but I know how to get some." I never did ask where or anything, but one day she showed me two cartridges and explained carefully that she kept them separate from the derringer. But I knew this: Louann hadn't given up the idea of revenge, and since it was my idea, I was honor-bound to help her with it.

AS FALL MOVED into October, Louann was pretty much on her feet. Her shoulder was no longer bandaged so tight. Now she could get a dress on both arms, if the sleeves were loose, and then she put a loose sling to hold her wrist and keep pressure off the wounded shoulder. She couldn't use it, of course, but she didn't look as much like an invalid. And could she walk! I was tired sometimes when we came back.

One day as we walked through Hell's Half-Acre, dodging garbage in the streets and turning away the children who offered to shine our shoes or sell us the apples they'd stolen off a vegetable cart uptown, Louann suddenly said, "I won't be able to drive a wagon, you know."

"I can drive a wagon," I said.

She turned to look at me. "Have you ever?"

"No, but how hard can it be? You pull on both reins to stop the horse, the left one to make it turn left, and the right one to make it turn right."

"Well, that's the basic idea," she said. And without another word, she led me to Mr. Standifer's stable, where she brushed away his congratulations on her improved health and said, "I'll need a horse and wagon two days from now, in the evening. I'm liable to need it for some time, maybe even a month."

"Now, Miss Louann, you can't drive a horse with that arm."

"I'll have someone who can," she said crisply. "Meantime, Pegeen here will lead the horse back to the saloon."

Mr. Standifer and I were both astounded, but for different reasons. He looked skeptically at me, but Louann headed him off with, "She's very familiar with horses."

Now that was a slight exaggeration! But what got me was that suddenly not only were we really going to hunt for the gambler, we were going in two days! That made everything much more real. My stomach had just dropped to my feet.

On the way back to the saloon, Louann laid out her plan. We would take two days to put together the things we need to travel. We'd travel light, putting things in her carpetbag. She would secret some biscuits and cheese from Idabelle. Then I'd lead the horse and buggy back to the saloon, where she'd come down the back stairs and meet me.

"Where we going?" I asked.

"Didn't you once say Randy thought the man was probably at Fort Griffin? That's where the hidehunters bring their goods for sale and gamblers wait to get whatever money they get from the sale. We'll start there. Believe me, I can describe him thoroughly."

Well, for two days I lived on pins and needles, jumping every time someone called my name, sure that our plan had been discovered, convinced that Miss Ellie would ask why I all of the sudden wanted all my clothes clean. I was so wound up that I couldn't sleep at night and lay tossing and turning. I wanted this waiting to be over, the way you want the wait to be over before something bad happens—you just want to go on and get it over with.

The night she chose was a Thursday night, which Louann figured would be kind of quiet both in town and in the saloon. It was darker than pitch. Clouds covered the moon, and the air had a winter nip to it. I shivered as I edged along the street, keeping close to buildings so no one would see me. Louann had sent me off with a joyful, "We're going, Pegeen, we're really going. You hurry!" I wanted nothing more than to crawl into my bed and pull the covers over my head.

I sidled into the stable and edged toward the corner where Mr. Standifer had his desk. Actually he had it in an empty stall, so it was sort of hidden when you came in. "Mr. Standifer?" I called.

"Right here," he said. "Come on over here."

I did . . . and there sat Randy! To this day I don't know how he got there, but I guess Mr. Standifer must have told him about Louann renting the horse and buggy. She was going to be furious when she found out, and I didn't want to be in Randy Spurlock's shoes for anything!

"Uh . . . hi," I said.

"Well, Pegeen, what a surprise." He stared at me, his mouth split in a wide grin. "What you doin' here at this time of night." Ostentatiously he pulled a big watch out of his pocket and stared at it. "Nearly ten o'clock. I'da thought Louann would have sent you off to bed by now."

"I came . . . to get something for her."

"Yeah," he said dryly. "A horse and buggy. But, Pegeen, my love, I don't think you can handle that. The horse, maybe yes, but not pulling an empty buggy. You just go on and hop in, and I'll drive the horse."

I heard the *clip-clop* of a horse's hooves and knew that

the stable boy was bringing up the horse and buggy. Looking desperately at Randy, I said, "I'll be all right. I don't want to trouble you."

He stood up. "No trouble at all, Pegeen, none at all. You just go on . . . well, here, let me help you."

And the next thing I knew I was sitting in that buggy, Randy was beside me, and we were parading down Rusk Street. Without asking he turned the horse behind the saloon. He waited until Louann stepped out of the shadows, and then he tied the reins and jumped down. "Hey, Louann, I thought you girls might need some help. It's a far piece to Griffin."

She stared at him without speaking for so long that Randy almost lost his joking good-natured attitude. Finally she said, "Randy Spurlock, I may never speak to you again."

"Yeah," he said, "you will." Without another word, he lifted her by the waist and set her on the seat beside me. Then he heaved the carpetbag into the back of the buggy, walked around, and climbed in. He tapped the reins gently on the horse's back, and we were headed toward the street.

Three made a crowd on the seat of that tiny buggy. Louann and I were tense and silent, but Randy whistled like he hadn't a care in the world. Only thing is, he didn't head west out of town. He headed uptown. Next thing I knew he stopped in front of the marshal's office.

I almost blurted out, "We ain't gonna shoot anybody!" I figured we were gonna be arrested in advance, guilty for having planned a crime even if we didn't get to carry it out.

"Randy . . ." Louann began, but he cut her off.

"Something you need to see in here," he said. "Then I swear I'll take you to Fort Griffin if you still want."

Silently she let him lift her out of the wagon. I scrambled out on my own and followed them inside. Marshal "Longhair Jim" Courtright sat at his desk, his feet propped up on the top, his hat pulled low over his eyes. I thought he was probably asleep and wondered that this was the man that was supposed to clean crime out of the Acre and Fort Worth.

Randy merely said, "Marshal," and headed right past him to the jail cells, pulling Louann by her good hand so fast that I thought she'd trip. The marshal never even looked up, which I thought was odd. In one of the cells a man in rumpled clothes sat on the bunk. His hair was messed, and his eyes were bleary. I had no idea who he was or why we were there, but Louann did.

She screamed, long and loud, and then she buried her face on Randy's shoulder and began to sob.

He put an arm around her and asked, "You got that derringer, Louann?"

She nodded.

"Well, get it out. Here's your chance." When she didn't respond, he reached for her reticule and drew out the derringer, holding it carefully so as not to point it at anyone. In an elaborate gesture, he broke it apart and checked the barrels. "Two cartridges. Good girl. Here."

He handed her the gun, and she took it woodenly.

"She can't cock it," I said.

"Oh," Randy said cheerfully, " 'course she can't. I'll do it." And he did.

The man in the jail cell was getting alarmed. "Marshal! Marshal! You got to help me. This man, he's telling that woman to shoot me."

There was no response from Longhair Jim.

"Now Louann, you get as close as you can, you know, like he was when he shot you."

Then, and only then, did I know for sure who that man was and why we were there.

Louann's hand shook but she raised the gun and pointed it at the man. He began to blabber and beg, even fell down on his knees, crying about how she couldn't shoot a man in cold blood. Louann just stood there, pointing that gun at him. I held my breath and my stomach hurt something fierce. I really thought I was about to see a man die, and I didn't want Louann to pull the trigger. But I couldn't speak. Randy seemed unconcerned.

After what seemed hours but probably wasn't even a minute, Louann lowered the gun and said, "I can't do it."

"I know you can't, honey," Randy said, carefully taking the gun from her. He closed the hammer, broke the gun apart, removed the cartridges, and put everything in his pocket. Only then did he wrap his arms around her, careful always of her shoulder. "Not that he don't deserve it, that lowlife, but I knew you couldn't. Look at him snivel like the coward he is."

Louann turned toward me. "Pegeen?"

I looked at the ground. "I only wanted you to have some reason to get well, Louann. I didn't really want you to kill anybody."

With her good arm, she hugged me fiercely. "But you'd have gone with me all the way to Fort Griffin."

I nodded.

"Now," Randy said, "aren't you glad I saved you the trouble? He never was as far as Griffin, but he killed a man in Weatherford. You don't have to shoot him, Louann. I reckon he'll hang sooner rather than later."

We left, and the sounds of the gambler's sobbing followed us out the door of the office. Marshal Courtright didn't look up when we left either.

Son of a Gun

R. C. House

Of R. C. House's western novels, one critic noted that they will find a place "on everyone's Fifty Best list for generations to come." Dick House has written many fine, authentic traditional western novels and stories that more than live up to this accolade. Look for such titles as *Verdict at Medicine Springs, Ryerson's Manhunt,* and *Requiem for a Rustler.*

WHAT MAKES A kid like that turn sour?

Marshal Hal Geer rattled the question around in his head and still found no easy answers. He had done his best by the boy. At least he thought he had. Geer wearily propped his booted feet on his battered oak desktop and leaned back until only the chair's hind legs rested on the equally battered plank floor: a balancing act. Anything now for relief. He'd have to start out in the morning after Johnny Crimson. Too late to go today. Johnny wasn't the type to run. Give him credit for that.

Geer remembered Johnny as a kid, standing there looking at him with those sunken, oversized blue eyes. Stood right there on that same plank floor staring at Geer, an appeal for help, friendship, love, anything, crying out of those desperate big eyes.

Trying to forget that day years ago, Geer shoved his hat back and concentrated out the back window at the cottonwoods fringing the creek they called Sentimental Branch a hundred yards or more away over scrubby chaparral-speckled hardpan. Good for the eyes to reach for definition in faraway objects, he'd been told; a lawman who had to be a good shot and an expert tracker depended on good eyes.

Besides, Hal Geer needed to think about something else for a few minutes. In spite of himself, his thoughts whirled back to Johnny. What makes a kid like that turn sour?

Johnny Crimson they were calling him now. Huh! Geer's mind talked to itself. How time changes things. The kid had come up here out of the Lone Star State five years ago when he was thirteen, maybe fourteen. Wandered in off the street with that hungry look in his eyes, a beanpole with a shock of unruly red hair. Typically boy, he was coming out of his shirtsleeves at the cuffs—and at the elbows—with a rawboned set of grimy white spindles showing between his big brogans and the ballooning tube legs of faded bib overalls. And toting that piece under his arm wrapped in a hunk of threadbare pink flannel blanket.

The hike up from Texas had taken him four weeks. He'd done it afoot on powerfully short rations. That was plain to see.

Meanwhile, the creek's cottonwoods away off there defied Geer's vision, remaining a greenish blur agitated by random breezes that almost spitefully ignored the town. Outside on the street the air was as still and close as death; inside his office, the gloomy presence of violent death and his need to look into it lay over him like a thick quilted robe on a hot afternoon. He tried to breathe deeply against its suffocation. Any relief only swung his thoughts back to Johnny.

After the kid landed in town and been taken under Marshal Geer's wing, he was known for a long time as Johnny Clumsy. It really did fit, Geer mused without humor. Like a hound pup, Johnny turned all hands and big feet.

Now he was the sleek, swaggering, good-looking Johnny Crimson. Great God, where the years have flown!

"What's your name, son?"

"Clemmons, sir. Johnny Clemmons," the red-topped beanpole answered in a voice that wavered between thin and reedy and a husky bass.

"Any kin to Rich Clemmons, sheriff down Texas way?"

"Son, sir."

"Rich Clemmons's son! I might have knowed. Your dad and me, now, were too thick in the old days to forget. You favor him. 'Specially that red hair."

"Yes, sir."

"Well, sit down, boy, sit down."

Geer was breathless. Johnny Clemmons glanced at the side chair, swung his gaze back to Geer and continued to stand.

"Tell me," Geer said. "How's your dad? How come you're way up here?"

"Dead, sir. That's how I come to be here."

"Rich Clemmons dead?!" Geer paused with a grimace, jarred by the shock and the sourness of the bitter news. "That's hard to take. Ain't seen your dad in, aw, I suppose, twenty years. But I believe we still called each other pard. Aw, hell, that's a damned shame."

Tears started up in the boy's enormous eyes.

"You don't have to tell me how it happened. Gunfight?"

"Paw always told me was anything to happen to him, I was to come up here and look for you." A tear traced a path in the grime alongside his nose; he blinked.

A spear of emotion rattled Geer; he grit his teeth. Good old Rich. The old pact of friendship was strong after all the years. They'd saved each other's chestnuts in more than a few scrapes. He studied the kid. "Then I'm glad you came, boy."

"Told me lots of times after Mama died."

"Lost her, too? Aw, that's too much for a lad your size to have to carry. Never knew your maw. Rich married a year or so after we split up. Wasn't neither of us much of a hand to write. But I heard he had a boy."

Geer knew Rich Clemmons never figured to die in bed. A man good at his law-keeping seldom did. The two of them had come up as deputies under Mose Laramore in Abilene after the war. Rich always gave a good accounting of himself.

The kid's voice had a tremor. "A saloon fight. They ganged up on him, Mr. Geer. He got backshot. But he got the man he was facing, fair and square."

"Before he went down. Damn! Your dad would. I'm sorry, son. Grievously sorry."

"All I got left's his gun here." He lifted the pink-flannel-shrouded package. "Maybe it'll pay my keep for a while, Mr. Geer. I'm right smart out of luck and a place to go to." He unwrapped it. Geer recognized it in an instant.

"Your dad's old Smith & Wesson Schofield." A new pang of grief sent a tremble through him. The blue was still bright, apart from gray around the muzzle from holster wear; any finish on the walnut grips was gone, the wood smooth as velvet from a frequent palm. He picked it up, studying it, remembering.

" 'Lighter, more maneuverable,' Rich used to say. Always bragged on the automatic ejection. I've watched him break this old gun open and kick out the empties right now. He'd fast thumb in six handheld ca'tridges, snap her shut and be back in business quicker'n scat. This old .45 calmed its share of hardcases. Silenced a few others for good. I know. I was there."

He handed it back to the boy. "You keep it, Johnny. Keep it to remember the man your dad was, that he died as he lived . . . on the side of justice. You'll come home with me."

ENOUGH OF THIS living in the past. Geer pulled himself heavily out of his chair. Working his broad-brimmed hat down over his silver-gray hair, he shoved his hands deep in his hip pockets and stepped to the back window; the breeze still ruffled the distant cottonwoods.

The demands of his lawman life kept him lean, leaner than most his age. His tanned, squared-off face had little sag, with only lines around the eyes and mouth to give character to his features. No hint of weakness appeared nor did it in the strong, well-spaced teeth that Geer was inclined to flash; he was good at his work, but also good-natured. Generally, though, like any man, he allowed, he had his point of catching fire.

He was childless; never married. Just as well, he thought. Still, figuring he owed it to the boy's father, he took the kid under his own roof and did what he could about raising young Johnny for the rest of his growing-up years.

Now Johnny was shifting for himself, grown beyond the point where he wasn't accountable for his own actions. Johnny Clemmons, Johnny Clumsy, Johnny Crimson was in hot water. Dude Merriman, foreman out at Bob Ingram's Lazy BI Ranch, lay over at Thompson's Funeral Parlor, dead from two slugs—it seemed—from a .45.

Johnny Crimson had a .45, rare in these parts, and he already had angrily confronted Merriman. Geer's course was clear; bring in Johnny Crimson as a prime suspect.

Geer hadn't heard from Bob Ingram. Ingram would expect Geer to take proper action. It had to be done. Now.

Geer pursed his lips against the trouble brewing in his head. For more than a year, Johnny Clumsy was no longer that. Gone was the overgrown pup, all uncoordinated hands and fingers and suitcase feet.

Back down the line, trying to coax some grace into those straw-slender arms with great bear paws at the ends, Geer had taught the boy one of the few polished skills he knew; proficiency with Johnny's heirloom Smith & Wesson Schofield. The son of a man good with a gun, and adopted by another, Johnny turned sleek and skilled with practice. His draw was flawless.

Now, dammit, Geer thought as he gazed around the crude office that was his headquarters as keeper of the peace, Johnny had to go and use those skills for evil. Or so it seemed. He found it hard to swallow that Johnny had gunned down Dude Merriman; still, the versions he'd heard supported his fears.

With a grim twilight seeping in, Geer dwelled on earlier and certainly happier times, even if Johnny had grown up as graceful as a hog at rooting time.

Johnny Clumsy had earned the nickname soon after Geer, wanting the young man to earn enough, at least, to cover some of his bed and board, found him work in the livery stable, forking hay and manure, and swamping out the local beanery and adjoining saloon next door.

As he backed up with a broom, Johnny's paddle-like feet knocked over a full spittoon in the Last Chance. Recoiling from the sudden, distasteful accident and the shouted jeers of the half-in-the-bag customers, he bumped a table, spilling neatly stacked poker chips and several full glasses of whiskey. It took a long time for him to outgrow Johnny Clumsy.

Geer devoutly wished the name hadn't changed to Johnny Crimson. It spoke trouble. Trouble out of a bullheaded, arrogant upstart getting too big for his britches. Johnny had, in fact, filled out. He no longer went through the elbows and knees of his clothes, but threatened to pop his Levi's through the muscles of his thighs. His shirts took on a tightness across the upper arms and shoulders and chest. His waist didn't change; no one really saw the handsome, well-built young man emerging.

One day Hal Geer looked up and Rich Clemmons's boy had become a man, a knotted cord of man who would no longer kneel to anyone or stand for unkind nicknames. He could prove his point with his .45 Schofield if need be.

Johnny took to wearing his hat on the back of his head, a well-groomed and handsome puff of rusty hair popping out the front. Geer saw him becoming overimpressed with himself; the clumsiness of the body had settled into the head, to Geer's way of thinking. Out of the independent spirit Geer had sought to nurture rose a jughead and a maverick. Geer stewed about it all.

By the time he moved from under Geer's roof, Johnny had graduated from forking manure and cleaning spittoons. He took a room over the freight office; was riding for Marty Gomez, one of the settlers with a small spread out in the valley; and had turned sweet on Gomez's daughter, Helen.

The stew was set to a boil when Johnny came to talk with him. "You know," Geer said, "you oughtn't to call Marty Gomez by his first name. All these years, you still call me Mr. Geer, and Marty and I are of an age. Me and your dad never called Mose Laramore anything but Mr. Laramore. That's the respect you show your boss and your elders."

"That's different. Marty is the boss and we all know it. All the hands call him Marty. He wants it that way."

"He's your girlfriend's father. That ought to make a difference."

"Dammit, Mr. Geer! Don't poke that 'what's proper' down my throat all the time. I'd go back to being Johnny Clumsy again was I the only one in the crew to call him Mr. Gomez."

"Beneath you to be courteous, is it?"

"You never see anything from my point of view. Why do you always take everybody else's side against me?"

"Son, you're like a plow horse with blinders. Only see

what's straight ahead, down the furrow. You settle into the traces, put your head down and go, no matter who slaps you on the hind end. You're the one that don't see."

"Let's don't argue about it, Mr. Geer. I come by to tell you I'm thinking of taking a place to myself. I can make it now."

Geer sighed. "I figured that was coming. You scare me sometimes, boy, with the way you're heading. I know a man your age has got to be given his head. But it scares me you being in so solid with Gomez and that bunch. Things are tightening up between them squatters and the Lazy BI."

"You talk about courteous and then go calling them squatters. Because they want to fence in what's rightly theirs, and protect it? Bob Ingram and Dude Merriman, you know, ain't the only ones in this valley. And you."

"You lumping me in with them so you can really have something to take sides against me with? I want no harm to come to Marty Gomez and his people."

"But it's Bob Ingram that sees you keep this job!"

"Dammit, boy, there's those blinders again. You know I owe no debt to any man."

"Blinders? How about your friends Ingram and Merriman? Them and their kind got blinders on and can't see proper property lines. Last week Buck and Danny and me set posts and wire all along Marty Gomez's south line. Don't you know Dude and some of that Lazy BI bunch come in there and roped our posts, pulled down a good section of fence and run in their beeves. If that ain't askin' for it, I'd like to know what is. And where were you?"

"Aw, hell. I heard about that. I'm a lawman, not a judge. Both sides in that one got their points."

"So I suppose you think it's okay for Ingram. Him and his property rights. It was my work Ingram's hands yanked down. It ain't just Marty. I'm in it now and not going to stand around anymore."

"But don't you see, Johnny? They're hemming Bob in. He's got a big spread that needs open range. When Gomez puts up fences, he blocks Bob off from what he considers rightly his by being here first. Gomez ought to think about stringing his wire so as to give Bob easement to open range and water. That'd probably calm things down and avoid a range war."

"There's an old man talking for sure," Johnny said. "Well then stay in your office and set. We'll take proper care of what's rightly ours and properly worked for."

Geer bristled. "Yeah, and while I was gettin' to be an old man, you turned in your big feet for a bigger mouth!"

"Aw, Mr. Geer, I always tried to respect you and what you done for me. You ought to know that. You've been like the father I lost. But he was my dad. You ain't."

Geer felt the bitter pang of rejection. After all he and Rich had been to each other, and what he'd tried to do for Rich's son. This attitude on the part of the only man who mattered anymore in his life cut deep.

"So you figure to move on out. Forget your dad's good name. And mine. Okay, Mr. Johnny Crimson, you've made your bed, and you're the one's got to sleep in it."

"I was fixin' to do that, yes, sir. I come by to tell you, thinking you'd be pleased. There's a good-sized room over the freight office I can have for next to nothing. Marty's got an old bed frame and a tick he'll let me have. Mr. Farley says I can keep my horse out back in his own stall, long as I help with cleaning the freight office stables. I guess I know how to do that." Johnny tried to muster a grin.

Geer missed the humor. "Got it all set for yourself, haven't you, Johnny Crimson?"

"Yes, sir, I believe I have."

Geer stayed seated as the tower of a man that was Johnny Crimson got up to leave, hat in hand. Geer watched his eyes, remembering the gawky beanpole of a boy who had trudged into that same office five years before.

Johnny stood across the desk from him, still holding his hat, pausing as if there was something more to say. He studied Geer. Johnny's lips moved as if he were about to form some final words. He sighed, crammed his hat onto the back of his head so the puff of red forelock showed arrogantly, and turned to leave.

"Be seeing you, Johnny," Geer called.

Johnny didn't look back. "Goodbye, Mr. Geer." The door slammed behind him.

In the gesture of slamming the door, there was a finality

to something Geer couldn't quite get hold of: the end of one stage of a relationship, and the start of another, perhaps. For better or for worse, and this felt like worse. The threat of it rang around Geer's office like a death knell.

Hal Geer, a man who didn't scare easily, found himself frightened. In the wake of Johnny's visit, he poked into his mounting fears. Despite what Johnny had said, Geer couldn't—and wouldn't—take sides. Only when he could no longer avoid it did he step away from middle ground. He did it then with the assurance that he was operating firmly on the side of justice.

His foster son, in his hotheadedness, thought more and more that Geer had aligned himself with the forces opposed to Johnny Crimson and his squatter friends. On the other side was Bob Ingram, for several decades the only cattleman in the valley. Ingram had a vast spread, with cattle all over the sprawl of open range. Now small ranchers' barbed wire was limiting Ingram's access to sufficient grazing country and to the needed abundant water.

Ingram, Geer knew, was a fair and prudent man: a good man and a good rancher. Bob Ingram was also stern with a streak of bullheadedness straight up the middle of him. Sometimes, he also knew, it demanded all of Bob's skill and determination as boss to keep in line the saddle bums and drifters Merriman found fit to sign on. In a country where gentility had been left somewhere east of Kansas, Merriman provided Ingram with what could only politely be called a motley crew.

Still, prissy little gentlemen from New York accounting offices wouldn't last thirteen seconds against waddies who might be in the saddle from first glimmerings until deep dark in cold rain chousing strays out of country so overgrown and ruggedly hostile as to defy any horse, much less a man. People wore scars in this country—on their bodies and in their heads. And Geer and his boy had a few scars themselves. He sighed again.

MERE WEEKS AFTER the unsettling conversation with Johnny, Geer stood at the window with his hat jammed on, his hands thrust deep into his hip pockets, staring at the cottonwoods away off, sorting out his options. There weren't that many to sort.

This land, indeed, was rough as a cob. So were the people in it. Dude Merriman was dead, and Johnny Crimson was a prime suspect. Geer had tried to stay out the sectional dispute as much for Johnny's sake as for not getting into it until asked. Or forced. *Maybe Johnny was right,* he thought. *Maybe I am getting too old.*

Now the fat was in the fire; Johnny Crimson had gone and done it. Hal Geer was being shoved into a showdown with the only man he loved—a man as good with that Smith & Wesson Schofield as Rich Clemmons himself had been. Maybe better.

Johnny—if it was he—had done his job well. Geer had gone by to see Merriman's body as a matter of a lawkeeper's duty while Thompson, the undertaker, got ready to lay it out. Two bullet holes—could be .45s from a Schofield—showed, one centered at the breastbone, the other square between the eyes. Either could have done the job.

Johnny probably thought he had cause. A hothead would. Geer looked back at the cottonwoods. No, any man would. Any man with guts, and one thing Johnny Crimson didn't lack was guts. Rich Clemmons and Hal Geer had helped put them there.

Ned Bachman, a townsman who had brought in Merriman's body over the Lazy BI foreman's own saddle, provided sketchy details. He'd earlier found Helen Gomez afoot in the trackless prairie, mad enough to bite spikes. He'd put her up behind him and taken her back to the Gomez ranch.

Her story was that Merriman and a bunch of Lazy BI hands had come across her out alone for a morning ride. The cowboys got mouthy and pushy. Helen, spirited like her father—and boyfriend—got mouthy and pushy back. When she attempted to get away, they rode a jeering circle around her; there was some jostling and Helen was rudely unhorsed. The Lazy BI bunch ran off her animal and gleefully left the young woman to make her way home on foot.

Johnny, in a furious rage, rode out to find her horse.

Ned Bachman, riding away from the Gomez ranch, found Dude Merriman's body not far from where he'd rescued

Helen. Ned gave up on his errand and brought the dead man to town.

HAL GEER WEARILY pulled his hands out of his hip pockets. The office clock said it was nearly suppertime. Geer thought about it awhile. He had no appetite. Food, just now, was the least of his concerns. There was a goodly flask along with a clean glass in the bottom desk drawer. He didn't drink much, but when he did, he wanted the best. He got into his thinking chair and measured himself two fingers. The first sip helped. The second was even better. He pursed his lips over the rich, biting taste. It was a good time to be alone. He sipped again.

In the morning, Johnny Crimson might be at the Gomez ranch to answer some questions. Or, he might not.

Still, he'd have to ride out and confront Johnny, or he might have to start roaming the range to run his foster son to earth. Either way, Hal Geer couldn't rest until Johnny Crimson was made to account for his actions. He was sure the town watched and waited to see which way Marshal Hal Geer would jump.

Everybody knew the dilemma he faced.

THE SUN THAT had not yet broken over the ridge to the east behind him already painted long, coldly crisp shadows ahead of fence posts as Geer rode at a canter up the lane to Marty Gomez's place. The house was small, well built, and well cared for. Gomez didn't have a lot to work with, but it was clear that when he built something, he built it to last.

Geer remembered hearing that Gomez had a Mexican father and an Indian mother and had come from somewhere south, maybe Texas, maybe Sonora. It was also said that Helen's mother had died in childbirth. Johnny Crimson's girlfriend, he thought, had a lot in common with Johnny when it came to tragedy. The western country, beautiful as it was, worked that kind of evil on its people. Geer set his jaw and grunted; back to the here and the now.

In a brilliance that can only come in the chilly crisp, clean, wide-open morning air of the West, the sun broke over the eastern ridge, flooding the land with pale light. In but a few minutes, it would increase into full day, bringing a promise of uncomfortable heat by midmorning that might hold until well into dusk.

Geer struggled with a mounting nervousness and tension. Under other circumstances, he mused, this would be a grand morning to be out. Again he set his chin, determined to fulfill the responsibility he had taken for a lifetime—to properly administer the law. A suspected killer had to be brought to bay; it was no more complicated than that.

But it was; godawful complicated.

Riding in, he saw that the front of the house had windows on either side of a centered door over a two-step stoop of split logs. If Johnny was in the house and Geer was forced to call him out, he would have the rising sun behind him, piercing over his shoulders into Johnny's eyes; a gunfighter's edge.

He tied his horse to a fence post where the lane merged with what passed for a dooryard of the Gomez place. He shook his hands from the wrists to calm a trembling. The thought came back. *Great God, where the years have gone! Here I am to take Rich Clemmons's son and my adopted boy to answer to the charge of brutal murder.* And the possibility of gunplay was very real.

Geer's head throbbed with the enormity of it, the incongruity and the outright insanity of it all. *Maybe I ought to quit,* he thought. *Go back to town, leave my badge on the desk, pack a few things and ride on. Hell, I've done it before.*

The confounding thoughts ricocheted around Geer's head as he approached the Gomez cabin. "Yeah, I've ridden on, but never because I turned my back on my duty."

His thoughts were brought up short as his eyes caught movement at the door, centered there and watched an erect, arrogant Johnny Crimson walk off the stoop toward him slowly, arms dangling but ready. He wore the Schofield in the good-quality tie-down rig Geer had given him their first Christmas together. It was in excellent condition, but well used. This, he thought, is getting ridiculous. Duty took precedence.

"Mr. Clemmons!" he barked.

"Mr. Geer?"

"I see you are heeled."

"And you as well, sir."

"Tool of my trade. I have come to take you back in connection with the death of Dude Merriman."

"I had nothing to do with it!"

"That will be up to a judge and jury to decide."

"You got no warrant for my arrest." Johnny's voice was deep and ominous; Geer remembered when it was shrill as a cricket's.

"Suspicion of murder is enough in my jurisdiction."

"I'll not go."

It's come down to that, has it? Geer thought. *You little pigheaded upstart!* Then aloud. "Drop your gun belt, Johnny!"

Helen Gomez appeared in the doorway, distracting both men intent on watching each other's eyes.

"Johnny!" she called. "Go with Mr. Geer. For my sake. And Dad's. Please, Johnny."

Geer hadn't seen Helen Gomez in months. Her face carried the strained, twisted expression of a woman squarely in the middle. She did not want her lover dead. Neither did she want the hand that did in Hal Geer to be that of his adopted son; it would cloud their relationship forever.

"Helen," Johnny said firmly, "I will handle this. Go back in the house." His command was flat, unemotional and definite.

"Johnny . . ." she started.

"Now!"

Geer doubted that Johnny had ever spoken to her in anger. Helen obediently backed a few steps, tears glistening against the sun darting squarely into her eyes. The door closed gently behind her. The air around Johnny Crimson and Hal Geer went silent; the tightness, the heaviness returned.

The intrusion of Helen Gomez was the last interruption. It was now or never. Geer realized that not for a moment had Johnny Crimson taken his steely eyes off his. Memory quickly invaded his thoughts: seeing those eyes from before, large and sunken and pleading. And he remembered the good times in between.

Abruptly he knew what he had to do. Duty and devotion both must be served; it was a chance that must be taken.

He squared himself against the gripping sensation deep

down; a puckering pain like some giant force squeezed at his guts. He took a deep breath. "The gun belt, Johnny!"

"No!"

"If that's your last word, make your play, dammit! When this is over, try to remember your father's good name. Now!"

Johnny's hand flicked for the Schofield like the strike of a snake.

Geer's hand was already filled, the barrel stopped at an angle to the ground when Johnny's gun reached full cock, the muzzle centered on Geer's midriff. Johnny started pressure on the trigger's cold curve. Geer held his gun hand down, staring with stark intensity into Johnny Crimson's eyes. "Do it, John!"

Johnny held his crouched, tense gunfighter's stance, his body trembling, his eyes wide as they were that first day in Geer's office. A boy's voice—not a man's—spoke.

"Mr. Geer, you . . . you held back. You had the drop. You could have killed me."

Geer's emotion burst forth in a rushing torrent that churned through every muscle and nerve. It had to be said. It came out clipped, angry sounding. He forced control into his voice.

"I'd die before I'd hurt Rich Clemmons's son. And mine."

Sounds of a feverish rider up the lane behind them drove an abrupt wedge into the intensity of their encounter and revelations.

"It's Danny," Johnny said, quickly holstering the Schofield. "My pard. You remember."

Danny swung out of the saddle, clutching the reins. "Marshal Geer! They want you in town. They brought in Bob Ingram. He's got a shoulder wound that's mortifying. Gunshot. By Dude Merriman. They had nasty words out on their spread over the way Dude scared Helen Gomez, and it went to a gunfight. You better get back there, Mr. Geer."

Geer's muscles and skin went tight, so tight his face hurt; a shiver ran through him. "Ingram, of course," he thought. "Why didn't I think? Stiff-necked in his dratted pride. Probably drilled Dude with one shot, got hit himself and fired again, taking Merriman in the head."

He realized his own gun was still in his hand. Shaking his head, he holstered it. "And me so worried about Johnny Crimson and jumping to conclusions. I wonder if I'll ever learn."

"I'll be right along, Danny," he said. He turned back to Johnny. "I guess I owe you the greatest of all apologies . . ."

Johnny's eyes were moist. "Would Rich Clemmons's son kill you to get out of taking his medicine? If I'd killed Dude, Mr. Geer, it would've been fair and square. I'd have owned up to it. I would've come right in and turned myself in to you."

"I . . . I suppose you would."

"I'm sorry, Mr. Geer. I should've handled it better. It . . . I just saw red that you'd have so little faith in me. Things just haven't been that good between us lately and I . . ."

"I'm sorry, too, Johnny. I guess I've been shooting from the hip all my life in more ways than one. Can you forgive me?"

"What's to forgive? One thing I'm going to do is shuck that Johnny Crimson name. Like I got rid of Johnny Clumsy. From here on out, I'm Johnny Clemmons."

"Oh, that does make me proud," Geer said, starting for Johnny so relieved he thought he could hug his foster son in this moment of sheer joy. "Real proud. It has a good and substantial ring."

Johnny smiled. "This may sound funny. But so does Helen. Has a good and substantial ring. We're betrothed."

"That's good, son, damned good." Geer did hug the boy, feeling waves of love and relief sweep over him, loosening him, turning him weak. "Your dad would be proud."

"My dad IS proud."

My Brother of the Gun

Gary Lovisi

Gary Lovisi is editor of the popular *Paperback Parade* magazine, a running history of the paperback novel throughout the world. He is also the publisher of Gryphon Books, which publishes novels and collections by authors particularly esteemed by paperback collectors. And when he finds the time, he demonstrates that he has great skill as a fiction writer. The following story is a good example.

IT APPEARS TO me that sometimes in life no matter how you plan things in the beginning, they'll always end up turning out the way they was meant to be in the end.

I guess that's called Destiny. Destiny came into my life back in 1879. I'd been on the run . . . Not only did I have a price on my head but some bad men were after me. I also had an idea I was itching to put to use. It began when I heard from my brother who works at the telegraph. He was a straight arrow, I being the black sheep of the family, but he told me the most interesting story about a town in Nevada called Bonchance that had this vault full of money. Greenback payroll diverted by the railroad for the Virginia City miners.

So I decided to get together with the no-good snaky Cribb Brothers to rob that bank. I told them all I knew about it and they liked the idea, but Buck Cribb, as mean and duplicitous a cuss as ever lived, decided that since he and his brothers now had all the information they needed, they didn't exactly need me no more in the plan, a three-way split being far more lucrative than a four-way one. He was always a greedy bastard; there was no honor among thieves where he was concerned. Of course, I learned that late, almost too late. And seeing as I had a bounty on my head of $100, they decided to get the drop on me and as an added cash bonus turn me in for the reward before they left to cross the state line to rob *my* bank.

Only when they got the drop on me, I was able to escape and hightail it out of town, determined to make my way to Nevada and rob that bank myself. And keep all those greenbacks for myself. Then I'd glory to see the look on Buck Cribb and his brother's faces when they robbed an *empty* bank. Then, afterward maybe, I'd get the drop on *them.*

But, as you'll note, there was considerable complications. I escaped the Cribbs, but barely with my life, weaponless, out of cash and food, with only one canteen of water and my stolen mount having given out miles back.

Now I walked through the harsh and hot Nevada flatland desert on my way to the town of Bonchance, pushing myself forward on pure hate and vindictiveness at my betrayal by the Cribb Brothers. Turn me in for the reward, would they? They'd have another thing coming if I had anything to do about it!

So I walked. Weaponless, without a horse, the heat beating me down. I tried to walk fast, knowing the Cribbs were on my trail, but heading to Bonchance gave me added inspiration. I was fevered with the thought that I'd get to the town before them and nix their plan. Rob the bank—which had been my own damn plan in the first place—then bushwhack them, as they deserved.

I was cogitating on these very thoughts when I walked down a small defile and noticed a gleam of reflected light. It got my attention because I could see that it was reflecting off something metallic. I wondered what it could be and moved closer. Careful. Nervous. It couldn't be the Cribbs, but that didn't mean much. It was something or someone else for sure. Hostiles? A posse? Once I moved closer I finally saw him. Down in the dirt. A man. Propped up, his back against a boulder in a small natural cul-de-sac.

He was in pretty bad shape. Pert-near death if you asked

me, if not dead yet. My eyes were instantly drawn to the gleam of the sun off of his shiny new Winchester rifle. A real beauty. It lay across the man's lap. I noticed a fancy Colt Peacemaker holstered at the man's side. It was engraved with the initials RWG. It meant nothing to me then; all I knew was that the man held his Winchester loosely, weakly. I could see he was wasted, near death, certainly unconscious. A saddled horse stood off a ways tied to a tree grazing on a small bush.

I moved in closer, careful, silent, admiring those guns of his. They were sure pretty. I could sure use a set of weapons like them. I would need them for sure real soon; the Cribbs were on my trail and would catch up with me in a day or so—maybe even in a few hours. But I couldn't just take those weapons off the man. Not just yet. Instead I opened my canteen and approached his unconscious form, lifting his head up as I poured the last few drops of my precious supply of water down his parched throat. I rubbed a bit of water on his face; the man coughed, grabbed at his rifle, and looked at me, reaching for his holstered Colt. Unable to draw it out.

"Take it easy, fella. I just gave you some water is all. Looked as though you could use it," I said, stepping back a bit, plugging up my canteen. It was almost empty now but for a few precious drops.

"You're trying to take my weapons. These here are my weapons! You hear me? Powerful guns, for a dangerous man. Be careful," he warned.

I didn't say anything. I could see the way he was, he didn't have the energy to even lift the Winchester and aim it at me, nor the strength to draw the Colt out of his holster.

He realized it now too, and laughed ironically, "I'm a goner. I know it. No fight left in me at all."

There wasn't much for me to say.

He squinted to get a better look at me, "You're an hombre, I reckon, who has someone after him. No horse, no gun, alone out here in the middle of Nevada's nowhere."

I nodded; he just laughed, thinking something was real funny. I wondered what it was. I just figured the beating sun had gotten to him, or the fact that death's door was open wide and waiting was giving him perplexing thoughts.

"But you did give me water. You tried to help me and by the sad looks of you, you don't have much to give. Why?"

I shrugged, "You looked like you needed the water better than I did. You needed help."

He just laughed at that, "Young fella, I'm beyond water or help. I'm soon to be dead. So why'd you help me, anyway?"

"I don't rightly know."

"I see you can't take your eyes offen my hardware."

"They're beautiful guns."

"*Beautiful* is a word a man uses to describe a woman. When a man describes a gun as being beautiful, that tells me a lot about that man."

"I been around. No doubt, like yourself, a man with such guns might have them because he'd need them, because he'd find them useful in his line of work."

The man laughed, "The brotherhood of the gun, youngster; I been around as you've guessed. Now my time is coming to an end, but I want you to answer me why if you coveted my Winchester and Colt so much, why didn't you just take them from me? Instead you gave me water. It revived me. I could have killed you."

Now I laughed, "No you wouldn't. First, I doubt you've got the strength in you to get off a shot, much less hold your gun steady long enough to aim at me. But that don't matter either, because you ain't the type that would kill me for a kindness even if he could. We's talking like this, makes me know you're some kind of dangerous gunslinger, maybe a killer but not a murderer. There's a big difference. Anyway, you'd best be wary too; I've got a hundred-dollar price on my head."

"A hundred dollars! Do tell! That's a powerful lot of money," he said, laughing now with deep mirth.

"Think it's funny! I assure you it is not!" I bristled.

He just laughed, said, "Not funny, insulting is more like it. Do you know who I am, youngster?"

"No," I said. Then I once more noticed the RWG initials engraved on the rifle and the stock of his Colt. I knew for certain he was some kind of gunslinger, some desperado, a wily coyote on his last legs. I waited, patient. I eyed his weapons. Wanting them.

"Well, I ain't gonna tell you," he said with a cough. "What I'm gonna do is reward your kindness. Giving me water was a natural God-like act uncommon in these parts that I thank you for. I appreciate you talking to me and entertaining me with your dangerous hundred-dollar bounty talk that sure brings back memories. So tell me, just between us, before I kick off, what the hell did you do to have such a grand sum of a hundred dollars in bounty money placed upon your young head?"

"Robbery," I replied, trying to look tough. Feeling like a fool.

"Indeed, you must be one terror of a desperado."

"Don't play with me, I can hold my own."

He laughed, looked at my empty holster. "Son, they're after you hard and you're scared to death. They took your gun, and you rode your horse to death to get away from them."

I said, "I need your guns."

"That you damn well do!" he laughed again, coughing, hacking deeply, but still holding that shiny Winchester to his body like a loving child.

"I could take them from you," I said boldly.

"Hah! But you won't, and you didn't do so yet, so that tells me something about you."

"Well . . ."

"It's okay, son, it's something I like."

"I do need your guns," I said. I was serious now.

"I know you do, son, and that's why I'll never let you take them from me. Instead, what I'm going to do, is give them to you as a gift."

"Give them to me? A gift?"

"Because you need them so bad, and the fact that you didn't take them from a dying man. I'm grateful for that respect so I'm going to make of them a present to you."

I didn't know what to say.

"Come here, come closer. These here are special weapons. They got a secret. I'm going to tell you about them now."

I hunched down beside the man, he looked in my eyes,

hacking coughs with blood on his lips, he was bleeding inside. Busted up and dying slow and painful. He looked in my eyes and then put his rifle in my hands, "Here, take it, it's a Winchester '73, a helluva gun, a dangerous gun for a dangerous man such as . . . you are now."

I held the Winchester like it was Lillie Langtry in my arms.

He made an effort to unholster his revolver and he finally placed it in my other hand saying, "And here, the Colt Peacemaker, a gun for a serious man who no one with a brain in his head would want to stand against."

The Peacemaker, Mr. Sam Colt's pride and joy and the gun that won the west.

"And now, fella, I'm gonna tell you a secret about these here guns. They're both .44-40s, know what that means?"

I said I surely didn't.

"Last year, 1878, was the first year for them; both were special made to be chambered for the same .44-40 cartridge. You know how special that makes these here guns? For the first time a man has a rifle and a handgun that use the same load. With these weapons, son, with *my* weapons, *you'll* be unstoppable. These here .44s blow a hole in a man a yard wide and a mile deep. Might even save your sorry-ass life someday."

I stayed with him and we talked until he died. I buried him soon after. My brother of the gun. I took his guns, his horse, and his name. Robert W. Graves, better known as Bobby Graves. He told me he had a reward on his head in some states, but he wouldn't tell me which ones. Not Nevada though. He made me promise to bury him where he died when he gave me his guns. Made me promise not to dig him up and turn him in for any reward. I kept my promise. Then I rode his painted mare across the Nevada flats toward Bonchance and the bank where I had an appointment. All the time I could feel the Cribb Brothers breathing down my neck. I clutched the Winchester '73 in my hands like it was a lifeline, felt the calm reassurance of the handle of the fancy Colt in the holster at my side. I rode on ready for whatever Destiny had in store for me.

* * *

BONCHANCE, NEVADA, WAS a small railroad town. A mining center. Wild sometimes, I was told, especially back in the old days in the '60s. The First National Bank of Nevada got a shipment of greenback payroll for the Virginia City mines. I rode into Bonchance determined to take that money. I saw the bank down the street, but my attention was drawn away from the bank when I suddenly beheld the most beautiful woman I'd ever seen in all of my twenty-five years. I allowed myself to forget the bank and the Cribb Brothers for a moment. I'm glad I did. She was young and lovely, with fire-red hair, but not all that young I could see, being about my age as determined by the girl child at her side. It was obviously her daughter, four or five years old, a cute kid in her own right; you could see where she'd come by it from her mother.

That woman held my attention. I'd never seen anyone like her before, the way she held herself, the way she walked, gorgeous of form and face. She wore a shapely gingham dress, demure; it just covered her ankles, its puffy sleeves pushed up to her elbows and her hands full of packages. I stopped dead enjoying the view, as she turned to look at me I noticed a small smile play across her lips. I quickly jumped down and tied my horse, then ran over to her.

"Hello, miss, let me help you with those," I stammered nervously, more scared of her at that moment than I was of the Cribb Brothers and all their guns.

She stopped, trying to hoist her bundles, saying "That won't be necessary," but I took them from her just the same. She smiled as she watched me try to manage them all.

I said, "Name's Robert W. Graves, ma'am. Lead the way and I'll be proud to carry these here packages for you and your daughter."

"No, that won't be . . ."

"Mommy," the little girl said, "he looks like Daddy."

I smiled down at the little girl, and then quite unexpectedly she lunged at my leg and hugged it tightly. She wouldn't let go and I stood there awkward with my hands full of packages, wondering if I'd made a fatal error. I didn't need husband trouble right now. Then I realized the truth.

"I'm sorry. It's Mr. Graves, isn't it? Susan's father passed away, she misses him terribly and we . . ."

I nodded, watching the child, silent tears streaming from her eyes. The mother biting her lip, being strong. I really admired her.

"I miss Daddy, Mommy," the little girl said.

"I know, Susan, but come now," her mother urged gently, dislodging the child from my leg, "Let's not embarrass the nice man with our problems. I'm sorry to trouble you so much, Mr. Graves."

"No trouble at all, and please call me Robert."

She smiled, her face a bit flushed, "And you can call me Kathleen . . . Robert. You've already made the acquaintance of my daughter, Susan."

"Susan, it's very nice to meet you," I said.

"You look like Daddy. My daddy was a big man like you. I like your face. You have a nice smile, mister."

I couldn't help but smile when I saw the look on Kathleen's face. My eyes could get lost looking at that face.

We walked on until we came to a dry-goods store that Kathleen owned. She lived with Susan in the rooms above the store. I put Kathleen's packages on the counter; she thanked me for my help. I wanted to ask her if I could see her again and then thought about the reason I was in Bonchance in the first place. The bank. It didn't make no sense keeping company with any woman from this town no matter how pretty she might be nor how pleasurable the company. I excused myself and left.

I walked off to get my horse and took him down to be fed and groomed at the stable at the end of the main street. Then I went to eat a home-cooked meal. Boy, was I starving. I figured I had some time. Then I'd be ready.

At Millie's Eatery I took a lone table in the back. It was a nice homespun place that boasted cheap food and plenty of it. Even at that time of the morning the place was full of men chowing down breakfast with beer or coffee. I sat back, relaxed, enjoyed the food, and listened to snips of conversation, thinking about the bank and the Cribbs. I know I was wasting time; my thoughts kept drifting to Kathleen, her red hair and warm eyes and that smile she'd been so generous to me with. I put the Cribb Brothers out of my mind for the moment.

". . . damn shame about her husband too," I overheard

some old-timer say to a well-dressed gentleman one table up from me. In between mouthfuls of eggs he added, ". . . leaving her a widowed woman and with a young child to boot."

"He was murdered no matter what they say," his well-dressed companion replied, his expensive duds gave him the appearance of a mine owner or the mayor.

"Town's too wild, Jacob, and all that money." He moved closer to the man, adding confidentially, "Jacob, I don't feel comfortable with all those greenbacks in your bank and us with no sheriff."

I smiled.

Just then a kid came into the place and ran to their table, whispering into the well-dressed man's ear. I didn't think much of it then, but when the two men turned to look at me, I grew nervous. I remembered that the boy was the same one I'd seen working at the livery stable where I'd just brought my horse.

I looked back at the two men, said, "Nice town you got here."

"Glad you like it. Passing through?" the old-timer said.

I shrugged, said, "Strange name for a town. French, ain't it?" I was making conversation, trying to see what was on their minds.

The fella I figured to be the mayor said, "Means 'good luck' in French. Good Luck, Nevada, mister. Lotta people could use good luck, we figured it might be good to live in a town with such a name."

I nodded, "Seems as good a name as any." I quickly finished my meal, paid and left the eatery. I felt their eyes on me all the way to the door, but chalked it up to old men with too much time on their hands curious about a stranger. I took a slow walk to the livery stable to get my horse, paid the smithy and walked my horse back down Main Street to the First National Bank of Nevada. I took my time. Thinking. Planning.

As I walked down the street I saw Kathleen and Susan again. I doffed my hat. Kathleen gave me a priceless smile in return.

Susan laughed and said, "Hey, mister, remember me?"

I smiled back and walked on. I had work to do now.

I loosened the trigger guard on my Colt. I moved my right hand on the stock of the Winchester '73, my left holding the reins of my horse. I noticed some people looking at me as I walked by, curious. I figured them for the busybody type. No one said a word. I walked on.

At the bank I tied my horse and carefully looked around. Everything appeared to be quiet. A normal Tuesday morning. I spotted two men across the street at the door to the saloon; one man looked over at me and pointed. The other nodded. When they noticed me looking at them quickly walked into the saloon. I laughed, figured them for early morning drunks.

I concentrated on the bank. It was a moderate brick structure, one of the few such buildings in the town. It sure looked impressive and well-heeled. It'd be less heeled once I got through with it. I left the Winchester with my horse. I walked across the dry dusty boards of the sidewalk, opened the bank door as a little bell tinkled overhead. I closed the door, went inside and looked around. A small lobby, four teller windows with only one teller on duty. A small mousy fellow with glasses. An old lady in the lobby at the window. Another man seated at a desk in the back who looked up when I'd come in.

My hand brushed the handle of my side arm. I knew I'd have to do this fast. But carefully. The old lady was just finishing up her business. I'd wait. Soon enough she said goodbye to the teller, turned and began to walk out. I waited for her to leave. Then the teller looked at me, said, "Yes, sir, can I help you?"

The old lady opened the door, and just as she left the bank Kathleen and Susan entered.

"Look, Mommy, our friend is here!" Susan chimed happily.

I looked over at Kathleen, her red hair, her blazing eyes, that sparkling smile. I saw Susan waving at me. I froze for a moment. My hand moved away from my gun.

I motioned Kathleen to the teller. Then the man I'd seen in the back suddenly got up from his desk and came forward into the lobby.

I turned my back to him, hoping he wasn't coming to confront me.

"Hey, wait! Yes, you! Young fella! I want to talk to you!" he said in a loud voice trying to get my attention. He got it, all right. He was coming toward me fast.

My guts churned. I ignored him and made my way to the door ready to run out when I felt a firm hand on my arm.

"Wait a minute! I said I want to talk to you!"

I turned around, looked in his face and remembered him now; the well-dressed man from the eatery. The man I'd figured to be the mayor. Well, apparently, he was the mayor and the bank manager too.

"You know, I've been watching you ever since you came into town. We've all been watching you," he said simply.

I gulped nervously, "Well, I . . ."

"We've been waiting for you for a long time."

"You have?" I replied astonished, careful, wondering how I could get away from this fellow. Wondering if he knew what I intended to do at his bank.

Kathleen came over with little Susan in tow.

"Certainly," the banker added, surprising me with his accommodating manner. "Now I told everyone you were looking over the town first, looking over the bank—which I tell you I was personally glad to see—seeing it all with the eye of a lawman—or," and he nudged me in the ribs, "of a bank robber, eh?—before you got to work."

I was perplexed. Nervous. Careful now.

"Do you know this gentleman, Jacob?" Kathleen asked the banker.

He smiled, "Only by reputation, Kathleen, by our correspondence through the mail, and the initials on those guns of his."

He reached inside his coat and pulled out a silver star that he suddenly placed in my hand. "Sheriff Graves," he added looking into my eyes, "I'm right proud to make your acquaintance."

I looked at the badge, looked over at the teller cages of the bank, looked into the eyes of Kathleen, and then thought of the man whose guns I wore and whose name I had taken. Robert W. Graves, better known as "Fast Bobby Graves" or "Puts 'em in the Graves Bobby"—sometimes desperado, sometimes law officer. That had to be it.

Kathleen seemed pleased; she looked at me and said,

"Does that mean you're planning on staying in our town, Robert?"

I nodded, trying to catch my breath, looking at the star in my hand, looking into Kathleen's eyes, saying, "Could be, could be, Kathleen."

Jacob Egan, the banker, pinned the badge on my chest. I was too dumbfounded and surprised to resist.

"I can fully appreciate how you wanted to look over the town and the bank before you took the job, Mr. . . . ah, Sheriff Graves. But this town ain't some pig in a poke for needing sheriffing. The citizens are right glad to have you here."

I mumbled some thanks.

Egan, the old coot, noticed that Kathleen and I had taken a shine to each other. He said, "Kathleen, why don't you and Susan take our new sheriff out and introduce him to our citizens and show him where the jail is at?"

The jail, where I now suddenly and foolishly found myself on the lawman side of the bars. I can tell you, it was a new experience for sure.

THE REST OF the day went by in a whirlwind of introductions, handshakes and talk, meeting ranchers and townspeople. I did get a chance to spend some time with Kathleen, and Susan was a charmer as ever. Even Old Egan and the townsfolk turned out to be an okay bunch. I figured, maybe I could stay. There's worse places, worse jobs. Of course I'd forgotten all about the Cribb Brothers until I saw them ride down the main street just after dusk, tie up their mounts at the Royale Saloon, and go inside to get tanked for the evening.

I knew what they were here for. I knew gunplay was their trade and they wouldn't let anything get in their way. Not Kathleen. Not Susan. Not me. So I knew I had to stop them before they hurt anyone.

But there was something else I knew—that while I held Robert W. Graves's Winchester '73 and wore his Colt Peacemaker, and while I wore his name—I was not Robert W. Graves. I did not have his shooting ability. But now I wore his badge.

* * *

I FIGURED THEY'D hit the bank early the next morning just after opening. I planned to take them all tonight, after they left the Royale, in the dark, later on when they were good and drunk. Shoot them in the back if I had to before they could say a word about me and who I really was.

That didn't work out. It appears the Cribbs only took one drink to wet their whistle and clear the dust out of their tonsils, before they exited the Royale and walked down the main street toward the bank. I knew I was in the soup now. With my Colt holstered at my side and the Winchester in my nervous hands, I followed the Cribbs, carefully keeping to the shadows on the other side of the street.

Buck Cribb was the leader of the gang, the oldest brother and as mean a sidewinder as you'd ever meet. Deadly and unpredictable. A killer. He used a Henry repeater to good effect. J. J. was the youngest boy, just out of his teens. He was the one who went along, did as he was told; he always listened to Buck. A poor shot who used a good gun, a single-action Smith & Wesson Schofield .45. Buddy Cribb was the middle brother, big and tough, a pretty good shot.

I watched them standing there in front of the bank, low-talking on the sidewalk. Buck making some kind of plan most likely. Then they all formed up and suddenly looked across at me where I stood in the shadows and Buck shouted out, "Evan! Evan, we know you is here! We been watching you all day with our spyglass from up that hill out of town. I'm calling you out, Evan! You hear me! Come out and meet your maker!"

I stood there astonished. My hand brushed the handle of R. W. Graves's Colt Peacemaker holstered at my side. I raised my Winchester '73, intending to pick me off a Cribb brother, but suddenly they was all gone. They'd fanned out. I saw a blur cross the street down the block over to my side of the street behind me.

Gunfire rang out from across the street. It was Buck Cribb's .44-caliber Henry repeater. He had my position and he was spitting lead all around me.

Lights went on all over town; people came out of stores and homes and went back inside just as quickly. Men came out of the Royale Saloon—heard the shots, saw the Cribb Brothers—and went back inside to the bar and kept on drinking. The streets were dark and empty. There would be no help for me tonight—this was my fight now.

But I had Buck's position now too and leveled my Winchester to get off a few choice rounds in the direction of his fire trail. Then I got out of there as fast as I could. I knew that either J. J. or Buddy Cribb had to be in front of me, and the other was behind me sneaking up. Buck sat across the street waiting for his brothers to flush me out. Once I showed myself, he'd pick me off with that Henry rifle of his and it would be a Boot Hill grave for this Robert W. Graves.

None of which left me with much of a choice with J. J. and Buddy on my heels. I knew I had to make a move against Buck real fast before his brothers were upon me. Easier said than done. I had a position on him though, across the street at the dry-goods store. He was hunkered down in the shadows of the doorway. It was the same store where Kathleen and Susan lived in the rooms upstairs on the second floor.

I looked at the upper windows for a sign of Kathleen or her daughter. There was nothing, only dark shades or curtains drawn tightly. Then I saw the door to the dry-goods store open with Kathleen formed in the doorway holding a candle and looking out at all the ruckus. I almost jumped out of my skin with fear for her. But I also saw my chance with one well-placed shot in the candlelight.

It was all I needed; Buck Cribb outlined clearly in the light. I heard him curse wildly, curse Kathleen and turn to her with his gun. I squeezed off a quick shot on my Winchester. Buck Cribb cursed again, but this time with a rasping voice as he fell to the ground clawing the doorway. I bolted across the street and grasped Kathleen in my arms to be sure that she was not injured. I had Kathleen douse her candle. Then I opened the door and quickly dragged the still form of Buck Cribb into the store. We were alone in the dark in the store now. It was quiet for a moment, and then I heard Susan's voice from above us.

Kathleen shouted at her daughter, "Shush, girl, and stay in bed!" Then to me she whispered, "Robert, what's going on?" She looked at the body of Buck Cribb bleeding on the floor before us.

Cribb appeared to be as dead as dead can be. With no time for explanations I told Kathleen to go upstairs and stay there with Susan. Then I left the store as shots rang out in my direction. I squeezed off two shots at one of the remaining two Cribb Brothers. I think it was Buddy Cribb.

"Buck? Dammit, is that you? I's over here stalking the varmint. Buck?" he shouted.

"Buck can't answer you now, Buddy," I said. Then I saw him weave to the left and I let loose with a couple more shots that I returned in kind as he fled. The brief flurry of shots ended and things were soon quiet again.

I knew Buddy was getting together with his brother J. J. I figured they'd rush me. I readied my Winchester and Colt Peacemaker. I knew the Cribb boys were counting shots. They figured I was low on rounds.

The Cribb boys resumed firing at me. Now I tried to cover myself in the doorway of the dry-goods store. I returned fire with my rifle. When it ran out of rounds I continued with shots from Robert W. Graves's Colt Peacemaker, just to let them know they shouldn't count me out just yet.

That's when they reloaded and came at me from two directions at once from out of the shadows. I fired back. When I clicked empty I heard them laugh and knew they were coming in for the kill. I had just one round left in the Colt. I didn't have time to reload so I pulled the rifle and cocked the lever just as Buddy Cribb rushed me from behind in a mad charge. I quickly turned and fired. A .44-40 slug from my Winchester '73 hit him chest-high. At that close range it blew a hole in him as big as a watermelon. I put the empty Winchester down, immediately picked up my Colt. I had one round left and I would have to make it count as J. J. Cribb snuck up behind me. He cocked his single-action Schofield; I fired my Colt Peacemaker. There were two reports. I saw his body fly back and his gun hand move up. His shot had gone wild. I blinked, saw J. J. Cribb hit the ground behind me dead.

There was commotion from all over the street: people yelling, women screaming, men shouting questions, lanterns and candles lit and glowing. Before the crowd gathered, Kathleen was at my side and in my arms.

"Robert!" she cried. I hugged her tightly, feeling little

Susan beside me, her arms around my leg holding tight, sobbing, "Are you all right, mister?"

"Kathleen," I said, trembling, shock setting in now that it was finally all over. "I'm fine."

And then big bad Buck Cribb was standing there with his Henry repeating rifle leveled at me. The crowd ran off. I pushed Kathleen and Susan away from me. Cribb pulled the lever and I dove for my Winchester, brought it up and fired. I came up empty. I immediately drew my Colt Peacemaker, leveled it at Buck Cribb and fired again. There was a heart-rending click. It was empty too!

"You kilt my brothers, Evan. And you're not only out of bullets, you're just about out of time. I'm gonna kill you slow and long. Make you suffer for what you did," Cribb said, his brutal face twisted in hate, looking down at me and then the dead forms of his two brothers. He kicked my empty Winchester over to the side, made me drop my gun belt and kicked it there too. He picked up my Colt Peacemaker and threw it far over my head behind me.

"Your time has come, Evan," he growled, his rifle pointed square at my heart.

I didn't know what to say or do but when I noticed Kathleen had picked up my Winchester and was quickly putting a round into it she'd taken from my gun belt, I screamed, "No, Kathleen!"

Buck Cribb hadn't missed a thing; he took in the desperate gesture at once, and just laughed. "Your woman friend don't rightly know guns, Evan. You put a .45 load into a .44 rifle and all you get is yourself kilted when you pull the trigger and the damn rifle explodes in your face."

"Kathleen!" I ordered, "Put it down!"

Cribb laughed; he let her load the Winchester, knowing Kathleen was trying to help me and that it couldn't do me no good. He decided to have some fun now.

I said, "Kathleen, put the Winchester down. Buck, you leave her out of this!"

"Stupid interfering woman, she's in it now, Evan," he chided, waving his Henry .44 leveled at my chest, but obviously amused by Kathleen's foolishness about weapons. "Go ahead, little lady, give your man that Winchester. It's got one round in it. That should be enough for you, eh,

Evan? I see you're wearing a badge now, but that don't impress me none, seeing as how it'd be pert-near perfect revenge to see that gun explode on you knowing your little lady done set the trap."

Buck Cribb motioned to Kathleen with his Henry, confused now; she handed me the Winchester. I took the weapon.

"Work the lever, Evan," Cribb said laughing. "Now go ahead, take your best shot."

I cocked the lever of the Winchester '73 .44-40 and took aim at Buck Cribb—he was still bleeding from the wound I'd given him earlier—which was nothing compared to what I was going to do to him now. This time I would make no mistake. I aimed for his heart and pulled the trigger.

The Winchester with that round from my gun belt exploded all right, firing correctly just as it was made to do. My aim ran true and the slug smashed into Buck Cribb's black heart. He flew back with a *woof* of expended air from his lungs, shock and surprise on his face soon overcome by pain, before he hit the wall and died on the spot.

I stood there shocked myself, even though I knew something that Buck Cribb didn't—what the real Robert W. Graves had told me about his Colt revolver and that Winchester being special guns because they both took the same .44-40 load.

Kathleen and Susan ran to me, tearful, crying as we hugged and kissed and celebrated that we were all alive. A crowd formed, shock and wonder from slack jaws, then questions by the townspeople.

I ignored it all and said in wonder to Kathleen, "Tell me, how did you know the Winchester could use the same round as the Colt?"

She just looked at me mildly confused and said, "What are you talking about, Robert? A bullet is just a bullet, isn't it?"

I laughed and hugged her tightly. They say the name Bonchance in English means "good luck" and I sure seem to have had that.

Then Kathleen said, "Now Robert, there's something I want to ask you."

I looked into her eyes and waited.

She said, "That man called you Evan, but you told me and Susan your name is Robert."

I smiled. I'd explain to Kathleen later how Graves's guns worked and how I wasn't the real Robert W. Graves. My brother of the gun. But since I was planning on staying in Bonchance and seeing a lot of Kathleen in the future—and raising little Susan—I figured there wasn't any real hurry now. So I said, "Honey, I'll tell you all about it soon enough. We got time. Now."

She smiled and hugged me, and I put my arms around Kathleen and Susan as we three walked inside away from all the bodies and death around us. A soon-to-be new family. I even forgot about the bank down the street and all those greenbacks, because I knew now that I'd found all the riches in the world in one red-haired woman and one lovely child.

They call it Bonchance, but I'd finally found home. It was good luck for the first time in my life now, and I wanted to live it right for all it was worth.

Faith and the Good Outlaw

Wendi Lee and Mary Kay Lane

Wendi Lee, from Muscatine, Iowa, has collaborated long-distance with Mary Kay Lane, of St. Louis, Missouri, on several stories. This is their first western together. Wendi has written eleven novels, her most current series featuring Boston private eye Angela Matelli. Her latest, *He Who Dies*, is now in paperback, and *Habeas Campus* is available in hardcover from St. Martin's Press. She lives with her cartoonist husband, Terry Beatty; their teenage daughter; and two cats.

Mary Kay Lane has had fiction and poetry published in several small-press publications. She works part-time as a library assistant and lives with her husband, their two children, and their house-trained bunny, Cupid.

FAITH GARY STEPPED into the dimly lit lobby of the Maine Street Boarding House and scanned the room. The walls were covered in velveteen wallpaper and the wood furnishings gleamed in the dim glow of candlelight. Still, Faith was disappointed. Her cursory glance told her that Matthew wasn't inside waiting for her. She had hoped he would be, even though she hadn't seen his horse tethered out front. Maybe, she had thought, he had gotten there early enough to find a stable for it. But no—all her imaginings and wishful thinking came to an abrupt halt. Matthew hadn't arrived.

"Can I help you?" A plump middle-aged woman approached her through a door at the end of the hall. She was drying her hands on a dishtowel. "I'm Mrs. Cuddahy. I own this establishment."

"Nice to meet you, Mrs. Cuddahy," Faith said. "My name is Faith Gary. I'm to meet my husband here and we need a room for the night."

"You hardly look old enough to be married." Faith didn't fail to notice that the woman took a quick glance at Faith's finger, to see if she really wore a wedding ring. At that moment, the big, glittering ruby stone felt like it weighed two pounds and Faith's heart swelled with pride. The ring represented more than just their marriage vows, but also Matthew's new life. He had worked hard to earn the money for that ring honestly. No one would ever be able to call him an outlaw again.

"I'm twenty-two," Faith said. "We've been married for six months, but we've been apart for three. He's been settling in." They had been childhood sweethearts. When Matthew was old enough, he started running with a gang of outlaws and Faith had written him off. Still, although she was courted by several other young men, no one else interested her. And when Matthew came back home one day, they picked up where they left off and were married.

"I have a couple rooms left. Top of the stairs. Take your pick."

"Thank you," Faith said. She began to make her way up the stairs, lugging her valise behind her. It thumped on the stairs as she dragged it.

From behind her, Mrs. Cuddahy asked, "What did you say your name was again?"

Faith stopped in the middle of the stairs and turned. "Gary. Faith Gary."

"Your husband wouldn't happen to be Matthew Gary, would he?"

"That's right," Faith said, feeling her heart swell again. "He's the sheriff of Jackson County."

Mrs. Cuddahy's eyes grew wide. "Oh, I know who he is, all right."

To Faith's surprise, the woman hurried toward her, grabbed the suitcase from her hand and brought it back downstairs.

"What are you doing?" Faith asked.

"I don't want any trouble here, Mrs. Gary. I'm sure you understand."

Faith shook her head. "No, I don't understand. Not at all."

Mrs. Cuddahy's harsh look faded and she wrinkled her brow as though studying Faith carefully. "You really don't, do you?"

"No," Faith said. "Is there some kind of trouble? Is my husband in danger? I know Jackson County can be rough. That's why I waited so long to come out here. He wanted to clean it up a bit."

"Oh, dear," the woman said. Now she was twisting the dishtowel in her hands until it was knotted into a ball. "I just got the worst feeling you're telling the truth."

"What's that supposed to mean?" Faith asked.

The woman opened her mouth to speak, then tilted her head to one side.

"Do you hear that?" the woman asked.

"Hear what?"

"Horses. Lots of horses."

Then Faith heard it—a faint rumbling in the distance, like faraway thunder. She had seen her fair share of violent thunderstorms approaching on the prairies of Iowa, but this seemed much more ominous. Neither woman spoke as the rumblings grew louder and more distinct, so that soon Faith could hear the individual hoofbeats of the horses. Her heart pounded in sync with the horses and she ran to the window to look out just as the first shot was fired.

Mrs. Cuddahy screamed, threw the dishtowel in the air and ran to the back of the house where she came from. Faith ducked below the window. When no shots seemed to be coming in her direction, she peered over the window ledge out into the street. The sun had set only moments before and the street was filled with orange light. The town that had been bustling when she arrived was suddenly deserted except for the men thundering through the town, weapons blasting and horses whinnying.

And at the head of the pack was Matthew. Even from a distance she recognized his tall shape in the saddle and his white hat. It had been a wedding gift from her father to Matthew. Another nod made to Matthew's promise to make a fresh, clean start. It had taken a lot of persuasion on Faith's and Matthew's part to get her father to agree to the union, and Faith had been so proud of Matthew's sincerity, his perseverance, and his success at landing the sheriff job.

Only, now, after three months in the dusty and grimy west, the hat wasn't nearly as white as it had been.

As Matthew roared past the hotel on his horse, Hawkeye, Faith had to fight the urge to rush out to him. She wanted to protect him, to hide him, to save him. He was obviously in grave danger from the band of outlaws pursuing him. Mrs. Cuddahy had had good reason to be concerned about Matthew Gary staying at her house. He seemed to have made a few enemies in his short career as sheriff.

Yet she knew there was little she could do. It would be foolish to run into the street. She had no gun. God, she'd never even fired one before, even though both Matthew and her father had showed her how to operate one. Just in case, they'd said. Though she was sure there would never be a case when she would want to fire a gun. Until now. No, if she ran into the street with some silly notion that she could protect Matthew by virtue of her presence, she would end up getting them both killed. She had enough sense to know that most outlaws didn't let women and children get in the way of what they were after.

Her heart was in her throat as Matthew drew closer to the house. She could see that there was something wrong. He was holding one arm across his stomach, not using it to hold the reins. Even in the dim light, she could see a dark stain spreading from beneath that arm. His face was an ashen blur as he rode by. Hawkeye was covered in foamy sweat and his eyes rolled crazily. The men behind him were drawing nearer and their guns were blasting. Faith covered her ears with her hands and squeezed her eyes shut tight. The air was pungent with the smell of gunpowder.

When she thought she couldn't stand it another minute, the gunfire stopped.

The silence was more deafening than the noise. There was only one reason the outlaws would stop shooting.

Faith sprang from her hiding place as though she were a tightly coiled spring and ran from the house. She ran toward the outlaws, who were standing in a close circle at the end of the street. She didn't care what they did to her. They could kill her, too, for all she cared.

"Matthew!" she cried as she stumbled down the dusty street. People had begun to pour out of buildings and Faith was dimly aware of their eyes on her. Did they know? Did they know their sheriff had been shot? Did they know they were now at the mercy of a band of outlaws?

She tripped over her long skirts and landed in the dusty street. Grime stuck to her tear-streaked face and her hair pulled loose from her traveling bonnet. A nail in the street pierced the palm of her hand, but she felt nothing. She picked herself up and staggered to the men. Amazingly, they parted to let her pass. They didn't try to stop her or touch her or shoot her.

When she saw Matthew on the ground, a thin line of blood trickling from his mouth, she fell to her knees next to him. She laid her head on his chest and felt the shallow rise and fall of his breathing. She tried not to look at the gaping hole in his stomach and what was spilling from it. Instead, she looked into his eyes. Did he see her? Did he know she was there? She kissed his mouth gently and felt a tiny flicker in response.

"Oh, Matthew," she said and brushed his hair from his forehead. The white hat was nowhere to be seen. "Matthew, this isn't how it was supposed to be. You were supposed to meet me at the hotel. We were supposed to have dinner together. You were supposed to take me to our new home and you were going to show me your new office and introduce me to your deputies and we were supposed to start a family. A boy first, and then a girl." Tears began pouring from her eyes. "And then we were supposed to grow old together, Matthew. And we were supposed to have grandchildren. This isn't how it was supposed to be."

"Faith," he whispered, locking his eyes onto hers. She had longed to hear him say her name for the past three months. Yet she found no comfort in it now. "I'm sorry, Faith."

She caressed his cheek. "It's not your fault, Matthew. I'll see that they hang. All of them. I saw it all."

"I want to take care of you," he said.

Faith shook her head. She didn't need him worrying. Not

at a time like this. "You will. You'll be okay. We'll still do everything I said. We'll just have to wait until you're better."

"I'm not getting better." His voice was a hoarse whisper and a bubble of blood appeared between his lips.

"Yes. Yes, you are."

He squeezed his eyes shut for a moment against some terrible pain inside him, then opened his eyes again to focus on her. "As my wife, everything I have will be yours. Hawkeye. The house. The Bible from your ma. There's more."

"Don't do this," Faith said, putting her finger to his lips. "I don't want to hear this." His face blurred for a moment as the tears came too fast, and she blinked to clear her vision.

"It's the only thing I can still do for you, Faith." His voice became as faint as a summer breeze through the prairie grasses. "My darling, Faith. I always loved you." His eyes drifted shut.

"Matthew!" Faith cried.

"Promise me," he whispered so quietly that she had to put her ear to his barely moving lips. Right before she felt his final breath on her ear, he whispered, "Sell it all and go back home, Faith. Sell it all. But keep the Winchester." His head dropped to one side, Faith heard the death rattle—that last breath exhale from her beloved—and he was gone, leaving behind only his mortal shell.

"No!" Faith wailed and threw herself on her husband's still body. Her body racked with sobs.

She had no idea how much time passed as she lay there, but when she raised her head, she was surprised the men were still around her, the townspeople still staring from the dusty sidewalks.

"How could you?" she asked through clenched teeth. She didn't address one man, but the whole group. "How could you kill a man of the law? How could you kill my husband?"

"Ma'am—" one man began as he bent to pick up Matthew's Winchester. The rifle lay in the street, not far from Matthew's body.

"Don't touch that!" Faith yelled. She snatched the rifle

out of the man's reach and cradled it in her arms like a newborn.

All the men took a step back, which, for some reason, pleased her. They were afraid of her suddenly. Because she had the Winchester.

She pointed the weapon around at them, though she would not have known how to shoot it. But that was something they didn't know. "Why are you still here?" she asked. "Aren't you afraid the deputies are coming? Don't you know what's going to happen to you when they get here?"

The man who had first reached for the Winchester held up his hands in a show of surrender. "Ma'am, we *are* the deputies."

Faith's grief was suddenly blanketed by confusion. "What?"

"We are the deputies, ma'am. We used to work for Matthew Gary."

"Then why'd you turn on him?"

No one answered. Every man she looked at averted his gaze. Finally, one voice spoke up quietly. "He turned on us, ma'am. He turned on the whole town of Calhoun. He and his gang tried to rob the bank and killed seven men."

Faith's mind refused to let the man's words make sense. She squeezed her eyes shut tight, but opened them when she heard a footstep. She swung the rifle in the direction of the footstep. "Don't come any closer." The man stopped. She continued. "I don't believe a single one of you. Matthew Gary was a *good* man. I knew him better than any of you. I know the promises he made to me, and he wouldn't go back on his promise." *Would he?* It was a tiny little voice way down deep inside her heart. She started talking again so she wouldn't have to listen to it. "And I'm going to stay out here with him until someone comes and tells me the truth. You're not coming near me or my husband until I know the truth. And I'll shoot anyone who tries. Understand?"

The men looked at each other and shrugged and hemmed and hawed and shifted their weight from foot to foot. But slowly, one by one, they left, drifting off down the now-darkened street to the saloon, to the hotel, to the restaurant, leaving her alone, in the dark and afraid.

She laid her head on her dead husband's chest and let the

tears spill out. Yes, she was afraid. Not of being alone, not of the dark. But that they were telling the truth after all.

WHEN SHE WOKE, it was full dark and she was shivering. Her neck and back and legs were stiff. Inside she felt as drained as a dry riverbed during a drought. Her sleep had been deep and when she woke she felt as if she had been transformed from a young bride to a hardhearted old woman. She had come into town with dreams and hopes and a future. And now all she had was a dead husband whom she didn't even know, who most likely didn't even love her, and who had lied to her.

And his rifle.

She picked herself up off the dusty street and held the gun close to her. The gun was a Winchester Model '73 and had belonged to Matthew's brother, John. The full-nickel plating with gold trimmings was engraved with his initials. John had been several years older than Matthew when he went west to set up practice as a physician in an area that was sorely short of them. John's murder at the hands of a band of outlaws was what had prompted Matthew to turn away from the path he was headed down and devote his life to the law. Matthew had received John's Winchester and it had been not only his prized possession, but his motivation. One glance at it would always steel his resolve to help put an end to the unruly conditions that existed out west.

At least, that was what he always told Faith.

She held the gun to her shoulder and peered down the sight. She could almost feel the power encased in its gleaming wood handle and octagonal barrel. Would she ever be brave enough to actually fire it—this gun that had killed seven men? Yes. She would. And she would kill seven more. Or however many it took to kill the men who had killed her husband.

No, not his deputies. But the ones who had turned him against the law in the first place.

Without even thinking, she walked slowly toward the bar where strains of piano music and raucous laughter spilled out into the night. As she left Matthew's body, she was dimly aware of a wagon approaching, a long wooden coffin overhanging the back.

The driver pulled to a stop beside her.

"If it's all right with you, Mrs. Gary, I'll take care of the body now," the man said.

"Fine."

"There'll be an extra charge since the coffin had to be extended. He was a big man."

"Fine," Faith replied in a brittle tone. She didn't care whether he was thrown in the river or wrapped in silk. She'd pay whatever the cost was. She'd do what Matthew wanted. She'd sell everything. She'd sell her wedding ring. She'd sell everything that reminded her of him. Except the Winchester. She had other plans for that.

She walked into the saloon. She'd never been in one before. If she had entered it only a few hours before, before she knew the truth about Matthew, she likely would have been shocked at what she saw. The drinking; the gambling; the scantily clad, rouged women. But now, nothing surprised her.

No one took any notice of her at first. But little by little, the crowd quieted down and turned in her direction, until the only sound was that of the piano player, who seemed oblivious to the new silence. Then, even the piano music trickled down to a few halfhearted notes and came to a stop. Faith felt a hundred pairs of eyes on her. She looked around the room until she spotted, by the bar, one of the deputies who had pursued and shot Matthew.

She walked over to him. He looked at her warily and she was glad he was afraid.

"I need you to show me how to shoot this rifle," she said.

The man let out his whiskey-laden breath with a slight smile. "Now, why would you want to go and learn a thing like that?" he asked in a slightly condescending manner.

"I don't need to explain myself to you. I'll pay you well."

"You're not going to shoot *me,* are you?"

A few of the other men chuckled.

"No. I promise I'm not going to shoot any of you," she replied in an even voice. "Unless it's by accident because you haven't taught me properly."

The other men laughed and returned to their drinks. The imminent danger over, everyone seemed to quickly forget the threat. The piano player picked up where he left off and the card games resumed.

"Sure. I'll show you. I'll show you real good. How about first thing tomorrow?" He turned away from her and took a long swallow of whiskey.

"Now," Faith said.

"I'm busy now."

"I'm busy tomorrow morning," Faith said. "And then I'm leaving town. If you show me now, you won't have to worry about me all night. You know, distraught widow with a rifle she doesn't know how to operate safely."

The man finished off his drink and sighed heavily. "You win, lady. Let's take it out back. Fifteen minutes is all you got, got it?"

Faith was a quick study. In fifteen minutes, she knew how to load it, settle it against her shoulder, take aim, and squeeze the trigger. Her teacher was impressed and even more so when she paid him enough to send him into a drunken stupor for a week.

IN THE MORNING, Faith said goodbye to Mrs. Cuddahy and thanked her for her kind hospitality. She felt as if she were just going through the motions of etiquette and what was expected of her.

"Where will you go?" the kind lady asked. "Back home to your pa and ma in Iowa?"

"Not yet. I have a little unfinished business."

Mrs. Cuddahy wrinkled her brow and twisted the cloth of her apron. "I think you should just go home. The West isn't safe for a woman traveling alone."

"I'm not alone," Faith said. "I've got the Winchester to keep me company. And Hawkeye."

"Still, I don't think—"

"Please," Faith interrupted, then more gently, "Just fetch my horse. I can't go home until I do what I need to do. I have to take care of Matthew's belongings. Find the house. Sell his property . . ."

"Is that all?" Mrs. Cuddahy was shrewd—she must have sensed that there was more purpose behind Faith remaining in town.

Faith shrugged. "Maybe."

Mrs. Cuddahy left and a few minutes later, returned, pulling Hawkeye by his reins and holding a dishtowel tied around a parcel. "I've packed you some dinner for the road."

"Thank you," Faith said. "You've been very kind."

"Now don't do anything foolish," Mrs. Cuddahy said as Faith mounted the horse.

"I married Matthew Gary, didn't I?" Faith said bitterly. "I think there's not many more foolish things I could do."

She kicked Hawkeye in the sides and directed him down the street.

As she left the town, she could see the fresh mound of dirt on Matthew's grave, and the crude cross that was perched beside it. She didn't stop.

CALHOUN, THE TOWN Matthew had described as home for them, was a full three hours' ride away and when she arrived, Faith was tired and hungry and dusty. The journey had given her much time to think about Matthew and what he had done. She had tried and tried to fabricate an explanation that satisfied her—one that would explain his actions and still offer some solace to her grieving heart. She wanted to believe that he loved her still. But the lies and deceptions made it exceedingly remote.

No one gave her a second glance as she rode into town. Calhoun was even smaller than where she had just left—just one short street in the middle of a sandy desert. She passed the sheriff's office and felt a catch in her throat. Inside she could see a portly bald man seated behind a desk. That was supposed to be Matthew's office, Matthew's desk. She passed the Calhoun Bank and Trust, hulking at the end of the block, a gray concrete windowless building, and her heart beat faster. This was the bank Matthew and his gang had robbed. It seemed impenetrable. How could they ever have hoped to succeed? Then she remembered that one of the thieves had probably been able to come and go where he pleased anywhere in town.

When she came to the general store, she saw a poster attached to a hitching post. In bold letters, it said, "WANTED: For the robbery of the Calhoun Bank and Trust." Beneath was a list of names. She scanned them for Matthew's but didn't see it there. For a moment, her heart lightened. Maybe they had all been wrong. Maybe he hadn't had anything to do with the robbery. Then a voice next to her spoke.

"At least they got Gary already. But it's the other ones that are the real troublemakers."

Faith looked around to find a young woman about her age standing beside her. She was conservatively dressed and carried a book under her arm.

"Did you know Matthew Gary?" Faith asked.

"He was the sheriff. He'd only been here a couple months and everyone thought he was going to be able to clean this place up. But then those other men came into town and I guess they talked him into helping them rob the bank. I could hardly believe it when I found out. He seemed like such a good man. He even has a wife."

"Oh? Where is she now?"

"Well, the sheriff had a house just over the ridge. Built it himself. But she wasn't there. She was coming out soon, I guess. She's all he ever talked about. Just about breaks my heart." The woman put a hand to her chest. "So, are you new in town?"

"Just passing through," Faith said.

The woman's face fell. "I've been hoping for womanly company. It's lonely out here and I don't have much in common with most of the women in town, if you know what I mean."

Faith smiled and nodded. If the woman knew Faith was on a mission of murder, perhaps she wouldn't be so eager to make friends.

"Well, I must be moving on," Faith said.

"So soon?"

"Oh, you'll probably see me again," Faith said.

"Good. What's your name? Mine's Anna."

"Faith. Faith Gary." She pulled the reins and kicked Hawkeye in the sides. Not looking back, she headed out of town over the ridge. She had gotten a little information from Anna that was valuable to her. One—that Matthew had come out here with good intent, but was somehow influenced by the band of outlaws. Had they threatened him or bribed him? Two—that he had talked about her . . . had seemed to love her. And three—that he had indeed built a house for her and that is where she was headed.

Over the ridge she saw it and a lump grew in her throat. It was beautiful . . . small and made of gleaming gold planks of wood. A porch ran the length of the front of the house and real glass windows sparkled in the sunlight. A small stable and corral for the horses stood a few hundred feet from the house.

She rode Hawkeye down the ridge and he broke into a slow trot as he neared his familiar home. She dismounted and pumped him some water from the hand pump beside the trough. Grabbing the rifle, she mounted the porch steps and tried the door handle. It was unlocked and she stepped inside cautiously. It was musty inside, but clean. There was a bed in one corner, with a straw-stuffed mattress. A hand-hewn table stood in the middle. A chest for linens and belongings sat at the foot of the bed. There was even a hardwood floor, a luxury item in many houses. A fireplace with a mantel graced the far wall, and on the mantel was their wedding photo. Faith picked it up and traced her finger over Matthew's face. At that moment, she couldn't believe that he had done what they said.

Suddenly, Faith heard a footstep behind her. She whirled, bringing the Winchester up to her shoulder. She gasped when she saw another gun's barrel only two feet away.

"You're smart to hang onto that rifle," the man behind the gun said. "Though I suggest you lower it before there's an accident."

"I know how to shoot," Faith said. Inside, she didn't feel the bravado she displayed.

"I don't doubt that. But there're still accidents. Like when people are scared."

"I'm not scared," Faith said, surprised that she was telling the truth.

"Then maybe I should be," the man said. "If you promise not to shoot me, I'll put my gun down."

Faith nodded.

The man was young and baby-faced—except for his eyes, which looked old beyond their years. He wore a black hat and a leather vest and a scarf tied around his neck. His hands and his face were filthy, his boots worn, his pants torn.

"Who are you?" Faith said, still pointing the gun at him.

"I thought you said you weren't going to shoot me."
"Maybe I lied," Faith said.
The man laughed. She saw he had crooked teeth and an almost endearing smile.
"Now I see what Gary was talking about. You're pretty *and* smart. It was worth the wait in that damn barn."
"Who are you? And how did you know Matthew?"
"My name's William Bonney. Ever heard of me?"
"No."
"Some people call me Billy the Kid. Ever heard the name?"
Faith's blood ran cold. She swallowed hard. "Yes."
He seemed pleased. He pulled a chair away from the table and slumped down in it. With his legs splayed in front, he eyed her through half-closed lids.
"Where?"
"Newspapers. Books."
"What'd they say?"
"Surely you know."
"Yeah, but I'd like to hear it from you. Since you're so pretty and smart."
"I'm not here to talk about you, William," she replied, swallowing her annoyance. Bonney clearly was proud of his achievements. "I want to know what you have to say about my husband. Are you the one who talked him into robbing that bank?"
"No, ma'am. I didn't have to do no talking at all. He was as eager as anyone."
"I don't believe you."
"I don't rightly care if you do or not."
"Did he really kill someone?"
"Only 'cause they were shooting at him first. He had the cash and when they fired on him, he shot back. He was a damn good shot, too. Got seven men. Just like that. That rifle's a beaut." Billy eyed the Winchester in her hands with appreciation. Then he held an imaginary gun to his face and made seven popping sounds. "Better'n mine even."
"I don't understand. Matthew was the sheriff."
"And he was the most accommodating sheriff I ever met." Billy guffawed loudly and slapped his knee.
"Shut up," Faith snapped. "Why should I believe you?"

"Because I ain't in the lying business." His face became suddenly serious. "I'm in the killing business and the stealing business. And I'm perfectly honest about it." He laughed at his own joke.

But Faith was far from amused. She knew that he was telling the truth. She knew it as strongly as she knew the feel of the cold steel of the rifle in her hands. She knew she was holding the Winchester that had killed seven men. She knew that Matthew hadn't kept his promise to her, to her father, to himself. Her anger at those who had shot him down was replaced by the sick, sad feeling of emptiness that came with betrayal.

"Aw, don't look like that," William said. He looked almost sorry for her. How could a cold-blooded killer have such a feeling for anyone? "It ain't so bad."

"My husband lied to me. He betrayed me. He's a murderer. And he's dead," she said in a flat tone. "How could it get any worse?"

"Well, he didn't lie about the stuff you should really care about."

"Like what?"

"Did he ever tell you he loved you?"

"Yes."

"Well, he didn't lie about that. I never *saw* a man so sick with love. It was pitiful." He was charming, and Faith had to remind herself that she'd already been taken in by one charmer.

Faith slowly lowered the rifle.

"If he didn't have such good connections and wasn't such a good shot, I'd never have kept him with me," Bonney explained. "His reasons was all wrong. His heart wasn't in it, you know, and then he was doomed. You've got to love what you do if you're going to survive. It's how I lasted so long."

Faith looked at him quizzically. What she knew of William Bonney was that he was a cold-blooded killer who could gun down a stranger as easily as look at him. The newspapers and books made him out to be some kind of monster. And maybe there was a monster lurking behind those eyes. But there was also a sincerity and an intelligence in him that Faith found hard to doubt.

"Reasons? What kind of reasons do you need to rob a bank?"

He laughed. Counting off on his fingers, he said, "There's money, of course, and fame and the excitement, and the action, and . . ."

"I mean, why would Matthew? Why would a man of the law rob a bank? He didn't want money or fame—not that kind of fame, or danger or—"

"He wanted me."

"You?"

William sighed and rolled his eyes. "He thought if he could get in good with me, he'd find the opportunity for revenge. He had grand ideas of befriending me, becoming my right-hand man, and then murdering me in revenge. I swear, he should have been writing books. Things don't work that way in real life."

"How did you know? How did you know he didn't just turn bad?"

William nodded toward the gun.

"Finest Winchester '73 I'd seen since . . . well, since I'd seen it last, as it dropped from John Gary's dead fingers onto the dusty road. Would have picked it up myself if I hadn't been in such a hurry to leave, if you know what I mean."

"You knew these plans all along and you still let him rob the bank?"

"I told you—he was good. How else were we even going to get in?"

Faith's mind reeled. Here was the man who had killed John and was, in her opinion, responsible for killing Matthew. And she had the gun William Bonney coveted. She could kill him right now. Finish what Matthew had started. Her fingers tightened their grip on the rifle.

"You'll be dead before you even get it to your hip," William said in an easy tone. He pushed the chair back and stood up.

"Now, if you'll excuse me, ma'am." He tipped his shabby hat, turned his back on her, and walked out the door.

Faith collapsed into the now-empty chair and laid her head on the table. She didn't look up until she heard the *clop* of horse hooves in the gravel. Realizing there were too many horse hooves, she got up and looked out the door. Billy the Kid had taken Hawkeye with him.

"Bastard," Faith whispered. She brought the Winchester up to her shoulder and took aim at William's receding back.

Just before she pulled the trigger, she thought about what William Bonney had said when they first encountered each other: Accidents happened when you were scared.

Faith lowered the rifle and wept.

LATER THAT DAY, as she took stock of the house and belongings, Faith also took stock of her decision to not pull the Winchester's trigger. If she had shot, she likely would have missed. She didn't want to risk angering Billy the Kid. She had found a reason to live again—Matthew was the good man she'd fallen in love with.

She sold the house, just like she'd promised Matthew. She sold everything in it, except the wedding picture. She didn't sell the wedding ring.

And she kept the Winchester.

Broken Windows

Marcus Pelegrimas

Marcus Pelegrimas is twenty-nine years old and a graduate of the University of Nebraska at Omaha with a degree in Criminal Justice. He has written several short stories in the western, horror, and mystery genres and is currently working as a full-time author after serving time as a telemarketer, waiter, busboy, and grocery checker. More of his short fiction can be found in the *Desperadoes* anthology. He lives and works out of St. Louis, Missouri, where he is currently at work on a dark fantasy novel.

TREPASSO, MISSOURI 1867

IT HAD TAKEN Cole Jarriss the better part of the day to pick his spot. He eased himself down onto the ground and took a good, long look at the small town of Trepasso from a grass-covered hill less than a mile away. Summertime in southern Missouri had almost been too much to bear for a man who'd spent most of his life in the Dakota territories. When the heat came, it seemed to roll down from the sky like a wet blanket to settle squarely on his shoulders, getting heavier and heavier as the day dragged on.

The air smelled fresh enough, but it stuck to his skin and stayed there, mingling with his sweat and slicking his thick black hair to his scalp and neck. Back home, it would have been hot, but not like this. No, Cole thought as he settled in among the lush green grass and fragrant blossoms, it wouldn't have been anything like this.

Cole was lucky enough to have dodged the tendency for all the boys in his family to be just as tall as their father. Standing well over six feet and bearing the Jarriss constitution, every one of Cole's brothers was a mountain on legs topped with a summit of shiny black hair. They all used to say that their runt brother was found during Pa's years with the cavalry.

"He stole you from the Injuns," brother Matthew had said.

Over and over, day after day, Matthew would say that. He would say it until Cole couldn't take it anymore. Say it until Cole had no choice but to run back behind the shed and cover his ears. And when Matthew would chase him down and pull Cole's hands away from the sides of his head, the taunting would go on . . .

. . . And on . . . until one day Cole smashed his fist so far into Matthew's face that one of his brother's teeth got wedged into his knuckle.

That was the day when Cole developed his bad temper. It was the day that he realized he would have no trouble killing another man.

He was ten years old.

Cole thought back on that day as a warm, damp wind dragged its feet over the grass and down his back, chilling the sweat on his neck. Rising up above the sounds of the chirping cicadas and the mosquitoes buzzing in his ears, Cole could hear the faint rumbling of wagon wheels as they made their way up from town and toward the ridge that he'd chosen as his vantage point. After a few minutes, he could just make out the sight of the wagon as it was pulled around a stand of trees and slowly worked its way along the main road heading north.

Cole was lying flat on his belly, feeling the moisture from the previous day's rain soak in through his clothes. Slowly, he reached behind him to where he'd dropped his saddlebags and pulled out the Henry rifle that had been stored there. That rifle had been with him since the War between the States, where it had been issued to him during his stint in the Seventh Illinois Volunteer Infantry.

The Henry rifles first started seeing action during the war

in 1862. Two years after that, Cole finally got his hands on one. At first, he didn't think the rifles were anything more than modified Winchesters, but the new rimfire metallic-cased cartridge and new design made such a difference that they became a new legend unto themselves.

Cole had been serving as a sharpshooter after being transferred to the unit commanded by Brigadier General John Corse. They'd been sent down to defend Rome, Georgia, after word got out that rebel troops would be headed that way to take the city. Since Rome was rich in supplies and the location of a major railway pass near Allatoona, Corse dug his men in and waited for the rebs to come.

He didn't have to wait long.

Cole and fifteen others armed with the Henrys poured so much ammunition down on those rebs that his unit was able to hold its position and turn the Confederates back. After that, the Henry rifles became a staple to armies and private citizens alike. In fact, Cole had read some editorial published by a newspaper in Louisville saying that the Henry was the "best weapon of defense that can be obtained."

Needless to say, Cole had kept his gun since the battle of Allatoona Pass and had taken it with him on every job since then. None of those jobs could compare to the exhilarating rush of firing into a mob of oncoming troops as fast as his hands could work the lever, but he'd found that the blood still pounded through his veins whenever that rifle kicked against his shoulder.

Even after Allatoona, Cole and that rifle had ended more lives than he could rightly count. Whenever he could, he would take his time and pluck them off like pheasants that had been flushed from a stand of trees. And if all else failed, he would unleash a storm of lead that could never even have been imagined in the days of muzzle-loading muskets.

The sounds of battle—of gunfire and men screaming—faded slowly away, but would never fade completely. He could still hear the explosions from Allatoona, the drums rattling, and there was the screaming . . . always screaming. Whether raised in victory, desperation, or agonizing pain, those screaming voices were the first thing Cole remembered whenever he thought about his days in the Seventh Illinois Volunteer Infantry.

After the war, he'd been given a chance to collect on a bounty offered for the return of an escaped bank robber. All Cole had to do was sit and wait for the fugitive to ride by on his way to meet up with the rest of his gang. As soon as he'd had his shot, Cole picked off that man with less effort than it had taken him to find the poor son-of-a-bitch.

All he had to do was line up the shot, take a deep breath, and squeeze the trigger. Come to think of it, Cole was usually on his way before their bodies hit the ground. It was a hell of a way to make a living. But then again, it was a hell of a world to live in.

Suddenly, he was back on the ridge in Missouri, lying on his stomach and watching that wagon slowly plod on the trail leading out of Trepasso. A bead of sweat that had been hanging onto the bottom of Cole's eyebrow finally let go and dropped onto one of his cold gray eyes. He blinked it away and swiped at his face with the back of his hand, feeling the sharp sting of the salt against his tear duct.

The wagon was getting closer now and Cole knew that it would only be a matter of seconds before it was in range. Moisture from the grass had soaked all the way down to his guts and even though it was hot as blazes beneath the Missouri sun, Cole felt a chill starting to work its way through his system.

Blinking away a few more stray beads of sweat, he nestled his cheek against the walnut stock with all the tenderness he'd never shown to the few women who'd shared his bed. The side of his thumb rubbed delicately along the brass plate set over the trigger guard, tracing over a spot that had been shined to perfection over the years from all of his delicate attention.

As he shifted his eyes to stare down the octagon barrel, Cole lost sight of everything else besides the intended path of his bullet. Already, his mind was racing to factor in wind speed and direction, the speed of the wagon, the condition of the road, even the slight movements his target might make as he conversed with the other passengers and looked about as though that field weren't the last thing he would ever see.

Cole pulled back on the rifle until it was tight against his shoulder and made sure there was a cartridge chambered and ready to fire. These were the moments he savored the most. It was only at this particular instant, where he was concentrating on nothing but the shot, that the screams in his head truly disappeared.

The drums stopped.

The cannons remained silent.

The pounding footsteps halted.

Even the wind seemed to taper off as though God himself were holding his breath.

When all Cole could see was the shape of the target's head lined up in his sights, he drew in a slow breath . . .

. . . held it . . .

. . . and fired.

The Henry kicked against Cole's shoulder, sending the .22-caliber bullet on its way like a small lead hornet whipping through the air amid a puff of smoke. The next thing Cole heard, even across the distance that separated him from his latest victory, was the smack of lead against flesh and bone, soon to be followed by the pained grunt of another life drawing to its inevitable close.

Cole watched the driver of the wagon sag to one side and then fall heavily to the ground. A woman screamed and another man jumped down from the back of the wagon with a pistol in his hand. Rising up to a one-knee firing stance, Cole levered in another round without taking the Henry from his shoulder. He didn't wait for the man with the pistol to spot him before firing another shot toward the wagon, closely followed by another and another.

Once again, Cole could hear the sounds of those fifteen other Henrys firing all around him in a constant barrage, the men dropping like bottles lined up on a distant fence.

He saw the first target start to move, although it might have been a trick of the sun or another bead of sweat in his eyes. Cole put another round into him all the same.

Still breathing in the leftover gunpowder fumes, Cole waited for the next thing to move down by that wagon. The only thing he saw was a woman kneeling over one of the bodies. Cole couldn't tell which one she was tending to, but the woman didn't even seem concerned about being the next one to catch a bullet.

Instead, she fussed over that corpse and cried out as loud as she could.

Cole gathered up his things and walked back toward his horse rather than take the chance of looking at the blank faces of the men whose lives he'd ended.

SITUATED JUST WEST of the Kansas-Missouri border, Wellston was one of the favored stopovers for travelers heading up north to Omaha. The Hidden Amber Saloon wasn't the biggest such place in Wellston, but it was by far one of the best. It was just big enough to hold a bar and three poker tables set up around a single faro game. The Hidden Amber might as well have been a private club due to the prices charged for its above-average whiskey. Cole liked it there if only because it was usually so quiet.

Six days had passed since his job in Trepasso and already he'd forgotten about such unimportant details as the faces of his target, the names of the men he'd killed and the grief-stricken cries of that woman.

It was just another job now, filed away in the past along with all the rest of them. As soon as he'd collected the rest of his money, Cole had put away enough of that above-average whiskey to banish those memories along with all the others.

Everett Barnaby was the owner of the Hidden Amber; he tended bar and even slept in the back. Whenever Cole stepped into the saloon, Everett was there, even more of a fixture than the smoked-glass mirror hanging on the wall.

"You ask me, I'd say he had it coming," Everett said while swiping away some dust that had settled on top of the bar since the last time he'd cleaned it. "I heard that son-of-a-bitch went to Trepasso after killing three men in cold blood right outside of their own spread down in Texas."

Cole ignored the comment and focused on his drink. Watching the way the brown liquid splashed up against the sides of his glass as he batted it around, he stared down as his mind worked painfully inside his skull.

"Some other fellas tried to bring them in a few weeks ago. Somewheres near Salt Lake, I think. Bastards killed them too. Couple of honest men with families."

"He had a family too," Cole said quietly.

"What's that?"

"I said he had a family too." Cole raised the glass to his lips and tossed the whiskey down his throat. "One of 'em did, anyway."

"You mean that woman you told me about that was with them? Probably just some whore along for the ride. Mills probably had plenty of them in every town he passed through."

Cole felt the whiskey burn its way down his throat and then wind its way through his system like flame through dry sage. "Who?"

"Mills," Everett said. "The man you was collecting the reward on."

"Was that his name?"

Everett laughed with a booming voice that resonated through the entire saloon. Leaning forward with his elbows on the bar, he shook his head and refilled Cole's glass. "How long you been taking these kind of jobs?"

"Since the war was over."

"How many bounties you think you collected since then?"

Rather than hazard a guess, Cole just shook his head and took another drink.

"It's an honest living, you know," Everett continued. "The men you bring in . . . they ain't nothing but murdering trash. Frankly, I think you should kill every last one of 'em."

Everett's words were cold spikes burrowing all the way through to imbed themselves in Cole's spine. They made him realize just how many jobs he'd taken and just how many times he'd felt that Henry rifle kick against his shoulder.

He could remember the feel of the Henry and the sound it made. Of course there were always the screams and moments of divine serenity that filled the spaces between the pull of the trigger and the explosion of gunpowder. But in all those memories, there were no faces looking back at him. All of his targets were just silhouettes and shadows at the other end of his sights.

Everett stopped what he was doing and took a good long look at Cole. "You all right?" he asked when he saw that Cole wasn't looking back.

Shifting back into thoughts of the present day, Cole took

a sip off the top of his whiskey and let it settle on his tongue. He swallowed it down and nodded his head. "Yeah."

COLE STOOD TOWARD the back of Sheriff Kenrick's office with his hands behind his back. The way he turned to face the pair of jail cells set up in the far corner, it seemed as though he were more comfortable looking at the bars than at the man who was counting out his salary.

As always, the cells were empty. Wellston was a big enough town, but there wasn't much of a problem with lawlessness. Some said that was because of the sheriff's diligence and dedication to his duties. Others had a different story. They said that Kenrick was an average lawman who hired exceptional killers to hunt down any criminals that made the mistake of wandering through the area.

Cole had heard those stories, but only in whispered fragments that he'd managed to catch before the ones doing the talking knew he'd come into the room. He knew what they thought. He also knew that Kenrick paid him twice as much as any other bounty tracker.

Sheriff Kenrick sat behind his large oak desk. The battered piece of furniture, rather like its owner, had been a fine piece of work in its day. When they'd first settled into this office, both the desk and the man behind it were fresh and clean with nothing but smooth surfaces to show the outside world. But now, after more than fifteen years, they were both scuffed and worn. They did their jobs well enough, but just looking at them made it obvious that they needed replacing.

A man in his early forties, Kenrick was tall and had a face covered by thick salt-and-pepper hair. The hair on top of his head was well maintained, which, combined with the slight bulge around his midsection, gave him the appearance of a man who'd been comfortably married for quite some time. The gun around his waist was a permanent part of him, although it was rarely drawn.

"Heard this last one got a little messy," Kenrick said as he finished up counting out a stack of bills from a strongbox.

Cole shifted, but didn't turn to look at the lawman. "What do you mean?"

"Mills wasn't alone. Besides his wife, he had his brother with him. At least, that's what I heard."

Even as he thought about the men he'd killed outside of Trepasso, Cole couldn't picture it in his mind. "Isn't his brother what the bonus is for?"

Kenrick's laugh was more of a low-pitched grumble. Shaking his head, the sheriff said, "Just trying to make conversation, is all. You interested in another job?"

"A man's got to eat."

"Hell, with money this next one's worth, you should be able to feed us both for a few months. You'd have to leave today or tomorrow."

"What is it?"

"Man by the name of Pryce. You ever hear of him?"

"No."

"I ain't surprised. I'll bet you heard of what he's done, though. Robbed a few trains outside of Springfield. Been working his way west since then. Been getting sloppy too."

This time, Cole turned around to look at the sheriff. "How so?"

"The crooks were on their way off the train when some locals decided to draw on them in the street. Pryce got nervous and started shooting. He took a hostage and blasted his way out. Killed three locals and the hostage before he made it out. Just got word that he's living over in Illinois. You interested?"

Already, Cole could feel the Henry bucking against his shoulder and could smell the rifle's smoky breath. "Sure. I don't have anything else better to do."

Kenrick nodded as he got to his feet and walked around the desk. Approaching the jail cells, he held out the handful of money he'd counted out. "Mind if I ask you something?"

Accepting the cash, Cole stuffed it straight into the inside pocket of his vest. "Go ahead," he said while starting to head for the door.

"You remember when you first started working for me?"

"I don't work for you," Cole snarled.

The sheriff held up his hands. "Slip of the tongue, is all. But do you remember the first job you took from me?"

"Yeah."

"You said you was saving up to buy some land. Maybe

start a farm or ranch or some such business. Remember that?"

Cole remembered those words as if he'd only just spoken them. During the war and before Allatoona Pass, he'd wanted nothing more than to settle down somewhere quiet where there was nothing more to worry about than bad turns of the weather. It was a dream shared by all the men during those years when combat was broken up only by the occasional stretches of quiet terror.

Back then, a lone house sitting in a deserted field was the closest thing they thought they could get to paradise. It was still in the back of Cole's mind. Nestled right in there among the screams and explosions.

Cole's hand rested on the door handle. His eyes burned a hole through the wood. "I remember," he said.

"Unless you've been spending all your earnings on whiskey and women, you should have that land by now. You want some help picking out a good place to stake your claim? If we get started on that house before winter, we can get you some head of cattle or even—"

"Trying to get rid of me, Sheriff?" Cole interrupted.

In a calm, even voice, he said, "You're getting to be too good at what you do. I just don't want to have to send someone after you someday."

Slowly, Cole turned until he met the sheriff's gaze. There was no threat of violence in either man's eyes, but the words still hung between them like cold, ominous ghosts. ". . . Just tell me where to start looking for Pryce and have my money ready for me when I come back."

SHERIFF KENRICK HAD gotten word about where Pryce was living from one of his deputies who'd spotted the man during a trip to visit family up north. At first, Cole had wondered why the sheriff was even bothering with someone that was so far out of his jurisdiction. But then he remembered they were dealing with the railroad on this one. More than likely, Kenrick would be pocketing close to triple what he was paying Cole for the job.

Not that it mattered. With nothing left to save for and nobody to spend it on, money didn't hold much meaning for Cole. He liked earning it, but once he'd started getting it, the bills just gathered dust in whatever cigar box Cole had picked to stash them.

In the back of his mind, there was still the notion of that house stirring around like a restless little bee. It had been his humble dream during the war, which had become something of a joke to a man who made his living putting others in their graves. How could he ever put that Henry of his over the mantel like some squirrel gun? How could he give up the life he'd dug himself into when it was so obviously what he was meant to do?

The answer was simple.

He couldn't.

Cole shook off those thoughts, since he knew they would just creep further and further into his brain if they went unchecked. Having just ridden into Marville on a brown gelding with white spots, Cole welcomed the chance to get down from his horse so he could stretch his legs.

According to Sheriff Kenrick, Pryce was raising pigs at a small spread two miles outside of town. Cole shook his head as he led the gelding to a hitching post set up outside of a general store. After tying off the reins, he made sure his Henry rifle was hidden beneath a worn cotton blanket that covered the holster on the side of his saddle. Normally, Cole would never leave his rifle like that, but he'd gotten to the point where he just knew if someone was about to lay his hands on the gun. It reminded him of the way men in the war could feel when their amputated limbs were being thrown onto the pile behind the hospital.

The store was only about the size of a single-family home and filled with tables of goods on display as well as various sundries piled up on the floor. A Chinese man in his sixties stood behind a small counter, watching the door as if he'd been standing there just waiting for Cole to come inside.

"Can I help you?" the Chinaman asked.

"Depends," Cole said as he fished a folded wad of bills from his pocket.

The Chinaman's eyes lit up at the sight of the cash.

Cole peeled off two five-dollar notes and held them tightly between thumb and forefinger. "I need to know about a man named Pryce. You ever hear of him?"

"Sure, sure. Mista Pryce in here every week for supply."

"I figured as much." Moving the bills to just within the Chinaman's reach, Cole yanked them away and asked, "Now when do you expect to see him again?"

The small storekeeper didn't even have to think about it. "He be back in one day. Maybe two."

Placing the money in the Chinaman's hand, Cole fixed him with a stare that rooted him to the spot. "You only earned some of this today," Cole said. "The rest you'll earn when Pryce comes back here to stock up. When he does, you don't say a word to him or do a damn thing out of the ordinary. You understand me?"

The Chinaman nodded.

"And you don't tell anyone else about this."

A look of naked fear tainted the Chinaman's face and drained away most of the color from his skin. He tried to say something, but the shakes had taken hold of him and the old man had to concentrate on getting his words out. Cole had seen that look plenty of times, but it never used to be him that triggered the terror in good folks' eyes.

"I . . . I won't . . . ," the Chinaman stammered. "I won't say anything. I promise. Mista Pryce . . . he don't pay most of the time anyway. I . . . I know what . . . he do. Everyone know."

Cole watched as the Chinaman pulled himself together. When the other man cast his eyes down like a dog conceding to the alpha male, Cole let go of the money and turned to leave. "After Pryce leaves," he said over his shoulder, "make sure you stay clear of the street."

ACROSS FROM THE general store, there was a small building that looked to be someone's private residence. That facade was quickly banished, however, the instant Cole walked inside. Instead of a sitting room, there was a small bar and a pair of poker tables just beyond the front door. The tinny sounds of an old piano drifted in from another room, and several women dressed in flimsy slips and nightgowns strutted up and down a narrow staircase facing the entrance.

Cole took a moment to let his eyes adjust to the dim lighting, caused by thick velvet curtains over the windows and not enough lanterns hanging on the wall. At this time of day, the whores seemed to outnumber customers five to one. Plenty of slender young women lounged about the place, eyeing him as though he were being offered up on a plate. There were three people at the bar: two customers and one man tending. Only one of the card tables was being used and that was just for three men playing a quiet game of gin.

The bartender glanced in Cole's direction and gave him a curt nod. "Help you with something?"

Cole stepped up to the bar and fished a coin from his shirt pocket. His left hand was cradling the Henry wrapped in burlap. "Whiskey," he said while tossing the coin onto the bar.

When the drink was set in front of him, Cole downed it in one swallow and turned his attention to one of the girls standing idly near the stairs. One in particular, a short brunette wearing a plain white cotton slip, attracted him more than the others. She wore her long hair pulled to one side, where it hung down in a disheveled mane that reached just past her small, firm breasts. Standing with one hand propped on her hip and the other stroking the banister, the girl gave Cole a sultry smile.

With the Henry still beneath his arm, he walked over to her and slid his free hand over the smooth contour of her hips. "Let's go," he said evenly.

The brunette started to smile affectionately, but when she glanced up into his eyes, the smirk melted away and she turned to head up the stairs. "You can leave your things down here if you like," she said.

"That's all right. I'll keep it with me if that's all the same to you."

She shrugged and climbed up to the second floor, which consisted of a small hallway leading to four small doors. Cole went for the last door on the right and opened it. There was nobody inside, so he walked in.

Eventually, there came the sound of quick, light footsteps scurrying down the hall. When the brunette rushed in behind him, she was breathing heavily and looked mildly annoyed. "My room's at the other end of the hall. Just follow me."

All Cole had to do was let a fraction of his own displeasure blink across his face to break the girl's resolve. "I want this one," he said, knowing full well that he was scaring the petite brunette.

She could feel his eyes digging into her like nails that had been pulled out of a frozen piece of wood and hammered into her flesh. There was no emotion in that stare. Just deadly strength and the promise of violence should that strength be questioned. Rather than try to stir him up, she lowered her head and tried not to think of what had happened to other girls who'd gone with men like this one.

"All right, mister," she said softly while closing the door behind her.

Cole was already turned toward the window, peeling back the clean yellow curtains so he could look down at the street and the general store on the other side. He heard the girl moving around behind him, but didn't pay her any mind. When he turned to look at her, she was kneeling on the bed and sliding the top of her dress down to her waist.

She truly was a beautiful girl. Her skin was pale and smooth, as if it had been bathed in moonlight instead of the sun's burning rays. Her hair brushed against her shoulders like a warm breeze and when it glanced over her breasts, it sent a ripple through her muscles that even Cole could feel.

Although his eyes roamed freely over her naked body, Cole couldn't help but look back into her eyes. "What's your name?" he asked.

"Megan."

"Why are you scared of me?"

She recoiled as if expecting to feel his hand smash against her face. "I'm not scared."

"Yes you are. I can see it in your eyes."

She looked up at him then, defiantly and full of false courage. "You look like the kind of man that likes to hurt a woman. I've been with plenty like you before."

When Cole had first joined the army, he'd wanted to be recognized as a hero. A warrior. Now, seen through the eyes of a young girl, he was recognized for what he'd truly become: a killer. One of the predators instead of a protector. It didn't matter that he hunted down known outlaws and murderers. Not to people like Megan or even that old man who owned the general store. Once they looked into Cole's eyes, they could see all the way down to his core.

What did they say about eyes? Windows to the soul?

Cole thought about this and turned his own windows away from Megan. "You got nothing to fear from me, darlin'," he said. "I just came for the view."

Staring down at the empty street, Cole removed the Henry from its wrapping and went through the process of checking it over to make sure it was in perfect firing condition. Every piece slid with oiled perfection, snapping into place and locking solidly as it had a hundred times before. The rifle was the truest extension of his being. Out there for all to see, not trying to be something it wasn't, the Henry was a tool that served only one purpose.

Just like the man who now loaded it.

A gentle, almost tranquil voice came from behind him. "What do you want me to do?"

"Just sit there, Megan. I'm not gonna hurt you, but I need it to look like we're doing our business in here. How much do you charge?"

"A dollar a time."

"I'll pay you ten to stay here with me until I'm through. You can leave to eat and such, but if anyone asks, I'm just some rich man who's randy as hell. Understand?"

There wasn't another sound, but Cole could just about picture the girl nodding sheepishly to his back. He sighted down the rifle's barrel and peeked from around the curtains. When the hand touched him delicately on the back, Cole nearly jumped out of his skin. He whipped around with the rifle in his grip and saw Megan standing there, her slip hanging loosely off one shoulder.

"You're here to kill someone, aren't you?" she asked.

Cole nodded.

Looking up at him with warm, hazel eyes, she reached out to brush her fingers across his cheek. "I knew it. Even before you took out that gun, I knew what you were here for. I could see *that* in your eyes."

Suddenly, the Henry felt like an anchor in his hands. A sigh of relief slipped out from between his lips as soon as he set the rifle against the wall. Before he knew it, he was holding Megan in his arms and running his hands through her hair. She felt rigid and afraid at first, but soon the trembling passed and she let herself settle into his embrace.

"Who is it?" she asked. When he didn't answer, she added, "Who are you going to shoot?"

The spell broken, Cole felt the weight drop back onto his shoulders and his true nature rear up inside him like a cold fog soaking into his bones. "Forget about who I'm after," he said while picking up the Henry and pulling a chair closer to the window. "Just fetch me something to eat and keep your mouth shut."

THE NIGHT HAD come and gone, footsteps walked back and forth outside in the hall, and Megan had drifted in and out of sleep.

It wasn't until dawn that Cole realized why he'd insisted the girl stay rather than just rent the room outright. She was something to protect. Someone to care for . . . if only for a few more hours.

She rubbed his shoulders and even tried to entice him with her lips upon his skin and her hands in his lap, but as soon as he'd turned to look at her, she backed away.

And he felt it too. Cole had wanted nothing more than to set his gun aside and lie with Megan on that bed, but he couldn't get himself to move from his chair . . . not when he saw the way she looked at him.

Finally, when the sun made its presence known in the murky sky, Cole got what he'd been waiting for.

"Come here," he said to Megan without taking his eyes from the rifle sights. The girl was rubbing tired circles on her face when she stepped up beside him. Pointing down toward the general store, Cole asked, "Do you know that man?"

Megan looked for a second and then nodded. "That's Jim Pryce. He comes in here sometimes."

"Good," Cole said as he pulled ten dollars from the roll in his pocket. "Your job's done. Go find somewhere safe to hide and remember what I told you . . . not a word to anyone."

Reluctantly, she plucked the money from his hand and took a few steps toward the door. "If he's who you're after, then I should let you keep that money," she said while choking back a few burning tears. She wanted to say more, but instead turned and left the room.

Cole listened for a few seconds, but couldn't hear a sound besides her slow footsteps going down the hall. A door opened, then shut, leaving him to his task.

Pryce was a brutish man who easily filled up the doorway to the general store. Even from the window across the street, Cole could hear the train robber barking loudly to the store's owner.

"I told you I wouldn't pay more than that the last time I came here, you little Chink bastard!" he hollered. "Now you get yer ass inside and get the rest of my money!"

Once he knew he had his target, Cole blinked his eyes and took a deep breath. When he looked back at Pryce, he didn't see the bulky man with full beard, chubby face and shaggy brown hair. All he saw was a moving silhouette. A collection of living shadows that formed a target to be shot . . . nothing more.

He moved his finger through the guard and onto the trigger, stroking the sliver of metal as though he were caressing Megan's lips. Slowly, Cole steadied his hand and centered his aim on Pryce's chest. The train robber was stomping back and forth along the boardwalk; a moving target, but nothing too difficult.

Cole sighted down the Henry, tracking the man's movements until he got Pryce's pattern down. Then, with a slight adjustment to his aim, Cole moved his sights ahead of the target and prepared to fire as soon as Pryce was in position.

He waited for his shot . . . got ready to squeeze the trigger . . . allowed his breath to slowly trickle from his lips . . . but Pryce wasn't coming.

Cole waited another second, even though the target's steps should have taken him into the line of fire long ago.

"What the hell . . . ?!" Pryce bellowed from down on the street.

Cole looked up to see the train robber frozen in his tracks and staring directly up at him. For a second, both men simply looked at each other; predator and prey, one killer to another. Then, the street erupted into gunfire.

Pryce was a bit faster on the draw than Cole had been expecting and managed to clear leather half a second before Cole could adjust his aim. His single-action .44 pistol flashed up toward the cathouse's second level and belched out a gout of smoke and sparks with a loud roar.

Splinters flew into Cole's face as a piece of lead slammed into the window frame less than three inches off target. Although he was used to being fired upon, Cole was unable to keep his hands steady as hot wooden chips dug into him like a swarm of invisible bees lancing at his eyes. His instinctual response was to try to blink away the splinters, which only drove some of them deeper and sent sharp, blinding pain through his entire skull.

His next reflex was to fire the Henry and when he felt the rifle buck against his shoulder, Cole pulled himself away from the window just as Pryce sent another shot his way. This time, Cole could hear the slug from the .44 whip through the air and slam solidly into the wall behind him.

"Dammit," Cole hissed as he carefully ran his fingers over his face to try to find the shard of wood that was digging into his flesh.

At first, all he could feel was the warm slickness of blood running over his cheeks. When he moved his fingers higher, Cole came upon a thick piece of jagged wood protruding from the sensitive skin next to his right eye. Cole gritted his teeth, grabbed hold of the wood, and ripped it out with a stifled grunt.

Even with the blood flowing freely over his eye, Cole's vision was getting better since the hunk of wood had been pulled free and tossed to the floor. He wiped at his face with the back of his hand and levered in another round. Cole then leaned out the window, scanning the street below for his target.

"Stick yer head out and I'll blow it off!" Pryce yelled. As soon as he saw Cole through the window, he raised his pistol and took another shot. This one buried itself in the side of the cathouse, missing Cole by a good ten feet.

Blood and rage pumped through Cole's veins like molten steel. He drew a bead on the target and squeezed off a shot, sending a round straight into Pryce's gut.

The train robber grunted once and clamped a hand over his wound, but somehow remained on his feet. Cole took a second to eject his spent cartridge and get a fresh one in the chamber, confident that he'd blasted most of the fight out of Pryce's body. It was that thought that nearly cost Cole his life.

The only thing Cole could hear was the oiled parts of his Henry moving together and the ringing echoes of gunshots. All he could see was the street and the outline of his target at the end of his barrel. Before he could pull his trigger, however, Cole heard another blast from down below followed by the sharp whine of a ricochet.

Sparks flew in front of him and his fingers ignited with a spike of raw, surging pain that raked over his nerves and caused him to pull his hand back and away from the window. At the same time he saw a blackened wound that had torn his knuckles open, Cole realized the Henry was no longer in his grasp. It was at that moment that he heard the *clunk-clunk-clunk* of his rifle skidding down the cathouse's awning and into the street.

Pryce, who was still on his feet, began laughing when he saw the Henry hit the ground. "I'm comin' in there after ya!" he shouted.

Cole watched as the bigger man walked like a newborn calf on unsteady legs toward the cathouse door. On the way, he bent down and picked up the Henry, holding it over his head like a trophy.

There was no more pain in Cole's body.

No more blood in his eyes and no more doubt in his mind.

Without thinking twice, he launched himself out the window and landed with both feet on the wooden awning. Cole's vision still only saw the target in the street, but he could make out every last detail of his rifle in that big bastard's hands. Pryce might as well have been running his hand up Cole's mother's leg.

It only took two steps for Cole to reach the edge of the awning. Once there, he grabbed hold of the structure and swung himself down, landing with both feet planted squarely in the soil. He was face-to-face with Pryce in the next moment, who stared back at him like a wounded, confused animal.

Cole snatched the Henry from Pryce's hands so quickly that the train robber barely noticed it was gone before it was too late. He knew immediately that the rifle had been damaged by the .44-caliber bullet as soon as his fingers found the dents on the firing mechanism. Firing the weapon might possibly jam a round in the barrel or cause the thing to blow up in his hands.

"What you gonna do?" Pryce sneered as his hand twitched on his .44. Blood seeped between his fingers from the wound in his midsection. His eyes were glazed over, but not enough for him to be counted out of the fight. "Goddamn bounty hunter, huh? Tryin' to make a name for yerself by shooting at me when I ain't lookin'?"

Cole could see Pryce's hand moving up, bringing the pistol to bear on him. And still, even from less than two feet away, he couldn't see more than the vague outline of a man. Head upon shoulders on top of a wounded stomach. Parts making up a whole, but still not an entire person.

The .44's hammer clicked back as Pryce raised the gun to Cole's face.

In one sweeping motion, Cole brought the Henry up and across, slamming the stock against Pryce's wrist while twisting his body to the side. The .44 went off, sending a godawful ringing through Cole's ears.

Pryce grunted, his lips turning up in a pained snarl as his fingers reflexively loosened on the handle of his pistol. The .44 dropped a few inches before Cole reached up and snatched it out of the air. With a flick of his wrist, he spun the pistol around to point back at Pryce's head.

It was at that moment that Pryce turned to look directly into Cole's eyes. The train robber had done a lot of things in his life that he would never admit to. He'd killed more people than even the law would find out about, but it was those cold gray eyes that stopped him dead in his tracks. It was Cole's eyes that struck the chord of fear deep within his soul.

It was at that moment that Cole got a good look at the target's face. Standing there, up close—so much closer than he'd ever been to any of the men he'd killed—Cole couldn't help but see the look in Pryce's eyes. He could see right into the windows to that man's soul.

He could see that Pryce was afraid.

Afraid to die.

Afraid of the pain that might come along with his walk to the grave.

Afraid of the blackness that was waiting for him on the other side.

Afraid of having to answer for all that he'd done throughout his life.

Just . . . afraid.

Cole was afraid as well. Afraid that, instead of looking into windows, he was looking into a pair of mirrors reflecting the killer that he'd become despite all his efforts to be a hero.

The gun in Cole's hand began to tremble. It rattled in his grasp and bounced off Pryce's forehead as the blood continued to seep between the robber's fingers. Cole knew he should put the target down in case that wound wasn't going to be enough to finish the job. He should pull that trigger and snuff this target out just like all the others.

But the voice telling him those things was quickly fading away, like the commands issued from a moving train that was pulling out of the station. Cole could hear them . . . even knew what they would say ahead of time . . . but if he just waited long enough . . .

. . . he knew . . .

. . . they would be . . .

. . . gone . . .

Cole took a step back and looked at the pathetic figure standing before him. Rather than a collection of vital spots and targets, he saw a bleeding man trying his damnedest to stay on his feet. Pryce might die and he might just live to see another day. All Cole knew for sure was that the .44 in his hand didn't belong there anymore, so he tossed it to the ground.

Slinging the Henry over his shoulder, Cole turned around and left his old self behind. That part of him wasn't dead. It would live on in the haunting memory carried behind the windows to Pryce's soul. Windows that were broken with the crack of a gunshot that came from over Cole's shoulder.

Cole spun around to see who'd fired the shot that had punched through Pryce's mind and scattered his brains into the air and all over the street. He found that scared little shopkeeper gripping a smoking deer rifle in his hands.

"He dead anyway," the Chinaman said. "Needed to finish the job."

Nodding, Cole said, "Someone had to."

* * *

THE CHINAMAN INSISTED that Cole keep the reward money paid by the railroad for Pryce's capture. Cole put it toward a half interest in the general store and a fund to pay for the Chinaman's early retirement.

Cole stayed in Marville, Illinois, where he could always stay in sight of Megan's beautiful face. He refused Sheriff Kenrick's repeated offers for a job as deputy, just as he refused to so much as touch a gun or even carry a side arm when he traveled.

The Henry was never repaired, but it did get a place of honor over his fireplace. He would look at it sometimes when he thought about the way things used to be. As much as he might have wished for it to be otherwise, some windows simply could never be closed.

The Wisdom of Griffin Stiles

Tracy Knight

Tracy Knight is a psychologist who uses elements of his work to write stories with keen insight into the human mind. Other fiction of his appears in *Cat Crimes Goes on Vacation, The UFO Files, Werewolves,* and *Murder Most Delicious.* He lives in Macomb, Illinois.

IT'S TAKEN TWENTY-THREE years of hard living and slow learning for me to figure out the most crucial difference between brains and wisdom.

As it turns out, it's pretty simple.

Wisdom is quieter.

The man who taught me this lesson was Griffin Stiles. I grew up with Griff, raced him through meadows and over hills on our way to school when we were tykes, and helped him and his pa put up hay most every summer till we were grown. We were inseparable playmates and friends, and I'm sure we both assumed that we'd stay that way for the rest of our lives.

But, as lives will do, ours drifted apart, starting the same day that I drifted away, out of town, to find myself or my fate or my treasure. I forget now what it was I was looking for. What I found were bar fights and unrequited love and pennilessness. And so there were a few years during which I didn't see Griff at all.

The first time I saw him after returning to town made clear that something about my childhood friend had fundamentally changed. It was an important clue that, although we were only three months apart in age, Griff had mastered some advanced lessons in life that had eluded me completely. That was when my real education commenced.

It started at the Rose Bucket Saloon.

THE BARREL OF the pistol pressed Arnold Wylie's nose flat against his face so forcibly that I thought the plump, spider-veined beak would break or explode. Wylie—a barely-washed, unshaved man whose odor preceded him into a room by a full second—tensed every muscle in his body as he lay flat on the card table. A burly man I didn't recognize held him there with only the force of the pistol's barrel.

"I saw you take that card from your sleeve," the burly man growled, his eyes narrowed into something approaching hatred. "I don't cotton to no cheaters when I come to town for a friendly game of cards. You understand?"

Wylie labored to speak but only sputtered, a few flecks of spittle shooting skyward like tiny fireworks. He wrenched his body left and right, but the burly man had all of his weight behind the butt of the gun and it was useless. Wylie was as tightly held to the table with that gun barrel as if he were being crucified through the face.

"Time to die, you lousy skunk!" the burly man said.

Wylie whimpered. I could almost smell his sweat from my place at the bar.

Suddenly the swinging doors of the Rose Bucket flew inward. I put down my whiskey and had a look.

"Stop right there!" a man shouted. I admit I didn't recognize him at first.

He was a few inches over six feet tall and built with tanned muscles. His face was all sharp angles. Long black hair snaked downward from beneath his hat and lay over his collar.

The burly man's pressure on Wylie lessened just enough for Wylie to turn his head and see who entered.

"Help," Wylie squeaked as a patch of wetness spread across the front of his dirty pants. "Help me, Griffin. Please."

I had to rub my eyes. It was my childhood friend Griffin

Stiles—a deputy now, by the looks of his badge—clutching a long Springfield rifle musket.

My first reaction was barely stifled laughter. No one used Springfield rifles anymore. *No one.* They were too cumbersome, especially now, when six-shooters and repeating rifles were so plentiful.

"You heard me!" my old friend Griff yelled. "Let him up!"

The burly man said, "But Deputy . . . this man, he cheated us in cards. Took the last of Chastain's money and he ain't gonna be able to feed his kids. All because of this no-good swindler!"

"That's all well and good," Griff said with admirable composure. "There's ways to take care of that. Shooting him in the head doesn't happen to be one of them."

That moment, the burly man must have noticed that Griff was holding a Springfield. His eyes opened wide and he laughed aloud.

"What is this?" the burly man said, then chuckled again. He nodded toward Griff and, by suggestion, toward the Springfield rifle. "You're gonna stop me with that thing?"

Griff was stolid as a statue. His face didn't change expression at all. His eyes remained locked on the burly man.

Griff set the butt of his Springfield on the floor and commenced the slow process of preparing it. From his pocket he pulled out a paper cartridge containing gunpowder and a round slug.

The burly man raised his gun, holding Wylie's throat to the table with his other hand. "That's a Springfield," the burly man said. "Didn't know anyone used those anymore." He was trying to sound friendly.

"*I* do," was all Griff said in return as he poured the powder down the long barrel.

"Friend, this don't seem fair," said the burly man. "I mean, everyone else in the world has a repeater by now. Hell, I can raise my gun up and you'll be dead before you even have a chance to load that relic."

Ignoring the man, Griff pushed in the bullet with his thumb, drew his ramrod and began tamping the bullet deep into the barrel.

I noticed that the burly man had begun sweating profusely. He let loose of Wylie, who managed to roll off the table and scrabble off into the crowd where he couldn't be seen.

Griff shoved the ramrod back into his belt and looked up to the burly man. He spoke softly. "Sure, I reckon you could shoot me dead before I'm ready to shoot back. I guess that's the truth. But you know something? There's thirty or forty men in here and I'm guessing that at least one would see that you paid for killing me. In fact, I'd be willing to bet that you'd never make it out of here alive. You get to make that call, friend. If the card game was that important to you, I imagine you might as well go ahead and shoot me."

The burly man's face blanched as Griff raised his rifle, sighted down its barrel toward the ceiling, then brought it down and pulled back the hammer.

Everyone in the Rose Bucket went dead silent. Waiting.

Griff continued preparing his Springfield as if he had all the time in the world. He secured a percussion cap on the nib beneath the hammer.

The burly man's hands dropped to his sides, the six-shooter dangling from his fingertips. "Okay, Deputy, okay. You win. I don't imagine that shootin' anyone would be the way to go."

Griff smiled the same warm smile I remembered him smiling throughout our childhood. "You couldn't be more correct, friend," he said. "And don't you worry about losing that money. People around here know Wylie real well, and I'd be willing to bet that at least ten of them will be willing to do the law a favor and get your money back for you."

Rumors of assent issued from the men clustered near the bar.

"Okay, Deputy," the burly man said, holstering his gun.

Griff stepped to the swinging doors, aimed his Springfield toward the fat full moon hanging low in the sky, and fired. The next time he needed to shoot the rifle, he'd have to prepare it anew.

Resting the butt of the gun on the floor like a walking stick, he began to walk out, momentarily turning back to tug at the brim of his hat and give the burly man another one of his smiles.

* * *

THE NEXT MORNING I sat alone in the Rose Bucket having a cup of coffee when Griff entered, lugging his Springfield rifle. In last night's tumult, I was sure he hadn't seen that his best childhood friend had returned to town. Sure enough, when he caught sight of me, his face beamed like a springtime sun. He came over to my table and shook my hand.

"Hell's bells," he said, removing his hat and taking a seat across from me. "Frank Dithers. When you'd get back to town?"

"Just a couple of days ago," I said.

"How long's it been?"

I had to squint my eyes and look toward the ceiling to find the answer. "Four years. Yep, four years. I was just nineteen the last time I was here."

"Where have you been?"

Shaking my head, I said, "All over. Missouri and Kansas, mostly. It's funny, but it seems like a lot of times a man has to travel a long ways just to find out that his hometown is about the best place for him."

He winked. "I imagine that's true."

"Say, Griff, I hope you don't mind me asking, but I was here last night . . ."

"You were?"

"Saw you face down that man who had Wylie pinned to the table."

"I'm thankful it turned out well."

"Me, too. But I'll tell you, it sure seemed curious that nowadays, when everyone has a six-shooter, you came in with only that old Springfield rifle. I thought no one used those anymore. When I see them, they're usually hanging on a wall, like a trophy or curiosity. I don't know if I've ever seen anyone actually fire one."

He leaned back in his chair and braced one leg against its edge. "It was a personal choice. I had to do something. You see, Griff, while you were gone I went through . . . a hard time."

"Hard? How?"

"Lived through a couple of years where I was drinkin' harder than any man should drink. Got myself into some tough spots, too. Nightmares."

It was like he was teasing me, or at least wasn't keen on telling the story any too quickly.

"What kind of tough spots?" I asked.

"Shootings," he said. "And I learned something important, even though—God forgive me—it took a lot of blood to bring the lesson clear. Got drunk one night and killed a man who I thought insulted me, made fun of me. I found out later he didn't. He just had trouble talking, was born that way. But that wasn't the worst of it."

I noticed his eyes shone with tears.

"Nope, the worst was that one night, again when I was drunk, I was sure I heard someone breaking into the house. I grabbed my pistol and shot."

His Adam's apple bobbed in his throat.

"It was my son. My three-year-old son Lester. Wasn't long after that when I lost everything: my wife, my home, my pride, everything. A guy'd have to be blind, deaf, and dumb not to get a lesson from all that."

"That's awful, Griff. It's noble that you got through it all, much less learned something. So what did you learn?"

"Nothing too profound. I learned that my nature was to be impulsive, to act without thinking. You add that to a gut full of whiskey and you got yourself a recipe for a dark, hurtful life. So before I got myself killed, or killed more people who didn't deserve it, I made two decisions. One, I set aside the rotgut for good. Man's gotta have a clear mind to make it through this world and pay proper attention. And I put away my six-shooter and found myself this old Springfield. You see why? Using this gun prevents me from being impulsive. I have to take my time, be completely resolved before I go to shooting anyone."

"I've never heard of such a thing," I confessed.

He shrugged. "I may be the only one who's put a life lesson into practice this way. But it doesn't matter. It works for me. You know, Frank, it's a crying shame that it's the worst times in life that sometimes deliver you the best lessons. I wish life were different, but that's what it's told me. Fact is, if I tried to pick up a six-shooter now, I couldn't do it, not even for target practice. It's no longer even a choice. I'd freeze up. I've changed that much."

We went our separate ways that day, but our brief reunion

brought a lot of ideas to my mind. Our discussion had told me a lot about Griffin Stiles, the man he grew up to be.

I admit, I envied him.

TWO AFTERNOONS LATER, I was walking around town, reacquainting myself with the townsfolk, most of whom treated me fine, as if I'd never left at all. I was sitting on a chair in front of the general store whittling a piece of birch when Griff walked up and tipped his hat.

"Beautiful day, eh, Frank?" he said.

"Just about perfect."

"It's nice to have you back. Makes the town seem more complete."

"Thanks, Griff. That means a lot."

"Got yourself a job?"

"Not yet. Just decided to relax for a few days. But I ain't worried."

"You deserve to relax. But once you're done, you ought to visit with my pa. Hay season's almost here. He's going to need some help."

"That's mighty nice of you, Griff. I might just do that."

He turned to leave. I stood up.

"Wait a minute, Griff."

He turned to me, smiling.

I said, "I been thinking about our talk that morning, you telling me about how you came to use the Springfield. I have to say, I was mightily impressed."

"Nothing to be impressed about," he answered. "It was just the best choice for me. I didn't really have any others, as far as I could see."

"One thing worries me, though," I said. "What if you get in such a dilemma that you can't wait to load your rifle? I heard the sheriff is going to be out of town this weekend. That means you're in charge. I'd hate for anything to happen to you."

"Nice of you to say, Frank. As for what would happen if I couldn't wait to load my rifle, well . . . I guess my fate would be in other hands than mine."

"What troubles me is you said that picking up a six-shooter isn't even a choice anymore, that you'd freeze up. That ain't safe for you, Griff, nor for the town."

"I can only do my best," was all he said.

I reached up to a post where a leaflet had been nailed, and yanked off the paper. "I saw this today, and I think it's a mighty fine idea for you."

The leaflet announced the public appearance that night of Dr. Tillis Houston, a man who had traveled the continent bringing health and happiness to people through hypnotism.

Forehead furrowed, Griff read the paper. "I don't understand. This . . . doctor. What's he have to do with anything?"

"You've heard of hypnotism?" I asked.

"Sure, I've read about it. Doesn't hold much interest for me, though."

"Griff, I saw this guy when I was in Topeka, even met him. This hypnotism, it's almost like magic. Dr. Houston, he puts people into a trance, and they can do things, can change things, that you wouldn't believe. I saw him cure a woman of headaches in minutes, saw him ease a spastic child's nerves, even saw him raise blisters on a man's hand when he was demonstrating the power of suggestion. He told the man he was holding a hot coal and in seconds—*seconds*—his hands became red and blistered. It's the power of the mind, Griff."

"So?"

"Don't you see? He can help you change things."

He was truly puzzled. "What makes you think I want to change anything?"

"Griff, just think of it: If he puts you in a trance and makes it so you don't freeze up when you pick up a six-shooter, well, that gives you another choice should you need it. I'm not saying you need to put away your Springfield but, by God, if you're facing down some murderous man, it'd ease my heart to know that if you needed to you could go back to your six-shooter. A man's stronger the more choices he has. Ain't that right?"

He paused, examining my face closely as he considered what I'd said.

"This hypnotism. It's safe?"

"Safe as milk, Griff."

"And you know this fella?"

"Yep. Introduced myself to him in Topeka. He's an honorable man of science."

Griff scratched his chin. "You know something, Frank? You might just be right. With the sheriff being gone, it'd be pleasing to have a choice should someone decide to take advantage of my . . . situation."

"Great," I said. "When I see Dr. Houston ride into town, I'll talk to him for you, set everything up."

Griff shook my hand. "You're a real friend, Frank."

I MET DR. Houston before his show that night at the edge of town. He said he'd be more than happy to see my childhood friend Griffin Stiles and show him the power of hypnotism. So after the show, 'round about ten-thirty, Griffin met me outside the Rose Bucket and I showed him the way to Dr. Houston's wagon.

Dr. Tillis Houston looked like a magician, all decked out in a shiny suit and glittering top hat. His long hair was silver, and he wore a goatee that came to a sharp point capable of puncturing a balloon.

I helped Griff up into the back of the wagon. He was dressed as a civilian, carrying neither his badge nor his Springfield rifle. He told me I could stay if I liked. In fact, I thought he might have been a little nervous about the whole thing and was comforted by my presence.

Dr. Houston invited Griff to lie down on a plush couch sitting there inside the wagon. Without hesitating, Griff did so, interlocking his fingers over his chest and heaving a great sigh, already relaxing.

Dr. Houston lifted a lamp and held it near Griff's face.

"Griffin," he said in a low, melodious tone, "stare intently at the flickering flame and, as you do, listen carefully to my every word. It is time, indeed, to relax, to drift into the nice warm place of sleep and dreams and, in doing so, to change your life."

Although I'd seen the demonstration in Topeka, it still amazed me to see the power of Dr. Houston's hypnotism. Immediately, Griff's eyelids looked like two weights had been secured to them. They closed decisively; his mouth hung slightly open and not one muscle in his body moved as the doctor continued.

"Deeper," Dr. Houston intoned, "deeper and deeper, until the only thing you can hear, the only thing that truly matters, is the sound of my voice and the words I shall now speak."

It was obvious to me that Griff was in capable hands so, as quietly as I could, I slipped out the back of the wagon and went about my business.

Two hours later I was leaving the Rose Bucket when I ran into Griff. He was smiling wider than I ever remembered, and pumped my hand so hard you'd have thought I'd given him a bag full of gold.

"I don't know how to thank you, Frank," he said.

It did my heart good to hear him say that. "I take it the doctor's treatment worked for you."

He nodded. "Heck, I don't even remember you leaving. In fact, I don't remember anything at all after I started staring at the flame. But I do know this: I feel better, more sure of myself, than I've felt in a long, long time."

SATURDAY NIGHT ARRIVED. The sheriff was out of town on business and the Rose Bucket Saloon was alive with drink and noise and dance. The crops were all planted for the season and it seemed that everyone in town was ready for a celebration. It was a friendly celebration, too, with no eruptions of fistfights or arguments, much less gunplay.

I downed a couple of whiskeys, then decided to get away from the crowd and take a walk through town. The streets were all but empty; the only living things I encountered were wandering dogs. Even they seemed lighthearted, ready for a celebration, prancing and wagging their tails.

About two blocks away from the saloon stood the First State Bank. It was all lit up. Save for the Rose Bucket, in fact, it was the only building downtown from which light spilled.

I stepped closer and heard something.

A muffled explosion.

Wisps of smoke drifted through the windows and were whipped heavenward by the midnight breeze.

From the corner of my eye I caught a glimpse of Griffin Stiles, running from a nearby alley, toward the bank. The first thing I noticed was that he was gripping a six-shooter in his right hand.

Not yet sure of what would transpire, I remained in the shadows to see what unfolded.

He burst through the front door of the bank.

I crept up to the window and peered inside.

"Stop right there!" Griff shouted, pistol at the ready.

Dr. Tillis Houston stepped out of the blown vault, carrying a large bag of money in each hand.

"Drop the bags and put your hands in the air!" Griffin said.

Dr. Houston smiled. "No, I don't think so, Deputy. Why don't you go ahead and try to shoot me."

Griff cocked the hammer back.

Dr. Houston still smiled. "Please?"

Suddenly, all the life drained out of Griff's face. His lips tugged downward, his brows curled. I wasn't sure whether he would cry or rage.

"Ouch!" he yelped, and his six-shooter dropped to the floor. He whipped his hand through the air several times, then blew on it vigorously.

"You see," Dr. Houston said calmly, "when I hypnotize someone, I gain entry into his innermost functions; his soul, if you will. I can make many things happen, manifest phenomena nearly unimaginable."

"What did you do to me?" Griff demanded, right hand tucked into his left armpit.

"Simple. I gave you a powerful post-hypnotic suggestion that in the moment before you would shoot your pistol, it would suddenly become so blazingly hot that you could no longer hold it in your hand. Ingenious, no?"

"You bastard," said Griff, his face a portrait of helplessness.

That was my cue.

I pulled my own six-shooter from its holster and walked into the bank.

"Sorry, Griff," I said, aiming straight at his chest, "I admire you and everything, but things have been awful tough for me the past few years. Got caught for a couple of stagecoach holdups, spent a couple years in jail. I came back here because, simply put, there was no place left for me to go. I met Dr. Houston in jail and he told me everything he could do with his hypnotism. I told him to meet me here and we could collect enough money to go west as far as we decided to go."

Griff stared at me, didn't say a word.

"I'd heard about you becoming a deputy, even about your using the Springfield rifle. Dr. Houston and I hatched the plan: I get reacquainted with my childhood friend, introduce him to Dr. Houston, and make a bank robbery as easy as pie. So here we are. Face it, Griff, you're helpless. So just let us collect the money bags and be on our way. I got no mind to hurt you."

Slowly, Griff reached down toward his six-shooter on the floor.

I cocked my gun.

"No," Dr. Houston said, smirking. "Don't worry about it, Frank. Let him try to pick it up. It'll still be so hot he can't stand it. This may be entertaining."

In a blur of motion, Griff snatched up the six-shooter and plunged toward the floor, simultaneously pulling the trigger.

The bullet hit Dr. Houston in the shoulder. He dropped the money bags and began to moan.

That moment, I wasn't sure whether Dr. Houston's flour-white face was due to the loss of blood, or because he couldn't believe that his hypnotism hadn't done the trick with Griff.

Regardless, Dr. Houston sat down hard on the floor and pressed his hand against the bleeding wound.

Then Griff threw his six-shooter to the floor and turned to face me, hands on his hips.

"You shot him," I said. "Wasn't that a bit . . . impulsive? I thought you weren't impulsive no more."

"It wasn't impulsive at all," said Griff, his voice so soft he might have been reciting a poem. "Just like you knew all about me, Frank, I knew all about you, what you've been through, what kind of life you've decided to live. Sad as it was, I gathered that your coming back to town wasn't a sign of reform on your part; it was a last desperate attempt to make something work that had never worked for you before. Let's face it: You've never been a successful thief. And that's the funny thing about human beings: if they try something and it fails miserably, they inevitably decide that what they should do is try the same damn thing again."

He reached behind a nearby desk and grabbed his Springfield rifle. "I brought this here this morning. Asked the bank president if I could store it for the weekend. I thought I might need it."

"I got my hammer pulled, Griff. I got nothing to lose." I saw that the barrel of my gun was trembling.

He sat the butt of the Springfield on the floor, peered down its barrel then blew into it twice, making a shrill whistling sound. He explored the front pocket of his shirt, then pulled out the small paper cartridge that held the gunpowder and ball. He ripped it open with his teeth and poured the powder down his barrel.

"How come the hypnotism didn't work?" I asked.

He peered down the barrel again. Taking his time. Quiet.

Then he looked me straight in the eyes. "I drifted off when the doctor told me to, all right, but I didn't dream what he wanted me to dream. You know what I dreamed? I dreamed of the times we spent together as children, how we played and laughed, how we saw our lives ahead of us like endless roads, full of sunlit promise. And I wondered what it was that turned you so wrong, why you decided that our dreams didn't matter anymore. You see, they really do matter. And so I didn't take in much of what the doctor said, you see. I was too busy mourning you. Mourning my friend."

I felt a tear in my eye but resisted the impulse to brush it away.

Griff pressed the bullet into the barrel's opening, pushed it in with his thumb. He continued speaking in such a gentle, measured tone you would have thought *he* was a hypnotist. "You know, Frank, you can go ahead and shoot me. Your gun's already cocked and aimed at me. But you need to think this through. I told the sheriff my suspicions about you. I told my friends and neighbors that if I was found dead tonight, it was you who had done it. So you see, you can shoot me dead, maybe even make off with a bag or two of money, perhaps even ride a couple of miles out of town before you're caught and killed. But, as an old friend, I wish you'd consider your choices carefully."

Seeing him pull out the percussion cap, ready to place it on the nib, I said, "Stop. You can stop, Griff. I got no mind to take this further."

I tossed my gun to the floor and held up my hands.

Griff smiled. "That's a good choice you made, Frank. Thank you."

"No," I said. "Thank you. If I'm to be arrested, I'd rather it be at a friend's hands."

I'VE BEEN IN jail a month now and I reckon I'll be here many more. Time like this—empty time—gives a man a chance to think and review, to look back over his life as if it were a story and to see what parts he might like to rewrite. Maybe even think of how he'll fashion the next chapter.

Like Griff said, it's the worst times in life that sometimes deliver you the best lessons.

The story I was living could have reached no end but a bad one. I wasn't much of a criminal, although it took an old friend with an archaic Springfield rifle to teach me that.

He taught me something else, too, though he probably doesn't know it.

I'd been living a life full of noise—drunken shouts, the slap of fists against faces, gunfire—and had come to the conclusion that the noise along with my brains was the formula for a good, smart life.

But wisdom is different than brains.

Wisdom is quieter.

Blacklegs Dancing

Russell Davis

Russell Davis currently makes his home in Maine with his wife, Monica; their two children, Morgan Storm and Mason Rain; and one psychotic cat. In addition to his own fiction and poetry writing, he is the managing editor at Foggy Windows Books. He co-edited the anthology *Mardi Gras Madness* with Martin Greenberg, and his work can be read in numerous anthologies, including *New Amazons, Merlin,* and *Single White Vampire Seeks Same.*

WYOMING TERRITORY, 1883

Part 1
THE CARDS ARE DEALT

JAKE "BLACKLEGS" MCKENNA was sitting at the card table in the Yellow Rose Saloon, Hotel, and Gambling House when the hand was dealt. The dealer, a man everyone referred to as "Skinny," though he wasn't, had sent five cards to each of the five men seated at the table with practiced ease. As was his custom, Jake didn't bother looking at his hand until all the cards were out.

It was his custom, in fact, to wait until all the other players had picked up their cards, which he did, and then he saw the hand he'd been dealt: ace of spades, ace of clubs, eight of spades, eight of clubs, and the jack of diamonds.

He felt a cold shiver run across the back of his neck and make its way down his spine. It was the Deadman's Hand, and every gambler, at least those who were as superstitious as Jake, thought that this particular draw of cards was as unlucky as they came.

In 1876, Wild Bill Hickok had been holding this very same set of cards in Deadwood, out in the Dakota Territory, when he was shot in the back and killed by some tinhorn named Jack McCall. The shiver passed, and Jake took the time to look over his shoulder. There was no one back there that shouldn't have been, and no one looking particularly sneaky, so Jake turned his attention back to the table.

All in all, Jake reflected, the hand itself wasn't so bad. Two pair, with a jack. With a little luck, a man could draw the full house and take the pot pretty easily. Or, he mentally added, a clever fellow could make his own luck.

This was his first night in the small town of Shelby, which had been growing due to a recent mining boom, and which, if Jake were to guess, would be as empty as a bucket with a hole in the bottom within a year or two. He didn't know the men he was gambling with except by their first names, and he scanned his opponents again, trying to decide what his chances for success were. He'd been playing pretty well tonight, and so far was up by about thirty dollars.

On his right, a portly man with a walrus mustache and graying brown hair named Jeremiah sipped his beer and looked sternly at his cards, the other players, or the dealer. He hadn't said much more than "Fold," "Raise," or "Call" all night long. He played pretty well for someone who wasn't a professional gambler, and Jake thought he was probably the biggest challenge at the table. Next over was a lean-faced cowboy who'd introduced himself to Jake as Tommy earlier. Tommy looked to be about twenty years old, though he wasn't completely green, and the way he wagered told Jake that he was just playing with only one real system: hope.

Directly across from him was Skinny, the house dealer. So far, Skinny had dealt like a pro, keeping the cards and the betting flowing smoothly. He didn't play, so Jake didn't concern himself with the man. The two men on his left, brothers by the look of them, were Sam and Wayne. Much like Tommy, they played for the fun of it and in the hopes that they'd get lucky.

No, Jake thought, the only real threat was Jeremiah. But right then, Jeremiah looked to be deep in thought over his hand. The dealer called for bets, and after Tommy checked, Jeremiah opened with an eagle. While the others murmured, Jake raised an eyebrow.

"Must be a hell of a hand to open like that," he said. "But I guess if I'm to satisfy my curiosity, I'd better call." He tossed an eagle onto the table.

Sam and Wayne looked at each other and said, "Fold," in damn near the same breath. Skinny looked over at Tommy who shrugged. "Hell, it's only money," he said, and threw a coin into the pot. "Call," he mumbled.

"Cards?" Skinny asked.

"Gimme three," Tommy said, tossing his discards out.

Skinny peeled three off the deck, slid them over, and looked at Jeremiah.

"One," Jeremiah said. "Just one." He carefully selected a card from his hand and placed it on the table, exchanging it for the one Skinny had dealt him.

Skinny looked to Jake. "Cards?" he said.

Jake shrugged, and decided to see if he could get lucky before making his own luck. "May as well," he said. "I'll take one." He put his discard, the jack, face down on the table, and caught the one that Skinny pulled from the top of the deck.

Three of diamonds. A big fat three of nothing. *Damn,* Jake thought. *Guess it's time for that self-made variety of luck.* He'd taken the nickname "Blacklegs" because it meant gambler, and he was ready to take another risk right now. He glanced at the other players. From the expression on Tommy's face, he knew that the kid had struck out, but he was staring hard at his cards in the hopes of magically transforming them into something better. Jeremiah, on the other hand, was unreadable. He kept his eyes on his cards, arranging them to his satisfaction. Good a time as any, Jake thought, and pulled his sleeve card, an ace of hearts, while making the three disappear.

Which was the exact same moment that the rotten luck of the Deadman's Hand decided to put in an appearance.

It was the simplest of mistakes. He put the three in his sleeve with no one the wiser, but didn't turn it quite far enough to keep it from slipping back out of his sleeve when he reached to take a sip of his beer.

And that was when Jeremiah reached out and clamped down on his arm with a strong grip, pulled the card all the way out of Jake's sleeve, and said, "If there's one thing I can stand, Blacklegs, it's a card cheat."

Two thoughts raced across Jake's mind at that moment. The first one was to draw his other hole card, a small, silver .41-caliber Remington over-and-under derringer he referred to as Lucky that fit up his sleeve as neat as a pin. The second thought, which came immediately after the first, was that it was a damn shame he'd left it with his girlfriend, Shay Deveroux, back in Cheyenne. Most likely, it was at that precise moment his luck had turned for the worse—he just hadn't known it until now.

He shook his head ruefully, and raised his hands. He'd been caught at a cheat, and if he was lucky, they'd take his money and throw him out of town.

Needless to say, the other players were in agreement with Jeremiah's feeling about card cheats. It appeared, however, that Jake's luck was going to go from bad to worse because within twenty minutes of his drawing the Deadman's Hand, Jake Blacklegs McKenna, found himself in jail, awaiting the pleasure of the Honorable Jeremiah Wallace.

Who, as fortune would have it, was the only judge in the small town of Shelby, Wyoming, where the penalty for defrauding an officer of the law (or a judge) was hanging.

Part 2
The Bets Are In

"You must be some kind of idiot, boy," Sheriff Greeley said. "I mean, especially dumb, to go cheatin' at cards with Judge Wallace."

Jake shook his head. "I didn't know he was a judge."

Greeley laughed. "I guess you do now, though, don't you?"

"I guess I do," Jake acknowledged. He looked around his

cell: an iron cot with a tick mattress about as thick as a whisper, a hole in the corner to piss in, and a barred window. Not a whole hell of a lot to work with. He turned back to Greeley, who was still grinning at him through the bars.

"Any chance of someone going to pick up my things at the Yellow Rose?" Jake asked. "I don't want the owner running off with them."

"Why bother, boy?" Greeley said. "You aren't gonna need your stuff anyway."

Jake nodded. "I guess that's probably true. When do I see my lawyer?"

Greeley laughed again, and Jake thought that hanging might be preferable to listening to this blowhard laugh for much longer.

"Lawyer?" Greeley asked. "What the hell for? The judge himself caught you. You aren't going to have a trial. The judge is going to read the charges, find you guilty, and sentence you in the same day." Greeley grinned and spit tobacco juice on the floor. "You'll hang damn quick, probably by Christmas, and other than being talked about as the fool who tried to card cheat the judge, your name will be dust."

"I'm *supposed* to get a lawyer," Jake said. "I've got a right to defend myself."

Greeley chewed and spit. "This here is a little town in the middle of nowhere, boy. Wyoming isn't even a damn state. You've got damn few rights, unless the judge gives them to you."

"Well," Jake said, "isn't that perfect? When do I go to court?"

Greeley smiled. "Tomorrow, boy. We believe in speedy justice." He turned on his heels to leave. "Sleep well," he said over his shoulder. "See you in the morning."

Jake didn't bother to ask about dinner, but crossed the few feet to his cot and took off his suit coat. He didn't want to wrinkle it because he knew that appearance sometimes counted for a lot in the courtroom, but he had the feeling that it wouldn't matter all that much. He folded it neatly and used it for a pillow.

The iron of the cot was cold on his back, but he ignored it as best as possible, and tried to think of a way out of the situation. There really wasn't a good solution, he realized, shifting his body in an effort to get comfortable. The judge here was obviously a hard-ass, if not downright corrupt, and it didn't—based on recent events—seem likely that he was going to give him a break.

He threw an arm over his eyes and thought about Shay. In his mind, he could see her long blond hair, the way her blue eyes had sparkles of silver in them, her gentle laugh. Even though she'd been a working girl, Jake knew he loved her, and thought she felt the same about him. That's why he'd left his hold-out with her. Cheyenne was no place for a woman alone, and she was the first woman he'd ever really cared about. What would she think of him when she found out that he'd been caught cheating at cards? They'd agreed to play it straight when she left off working at Madame Butterfly's Massage Parlor and Home for Wayward Girls. She wouldn't take on any new clients and he wouldn't cheat at cards.

Worse still, what would she feel if he were hung to death right here in the boomtown of Shelby?

He groaned to himself and rolled over, hoping sleep would come quickly.

But sleep didn't come quickly that night. In fact, sleep didn't come at all.

"JAKE MCKENNA, ALSO known as Blacklegs McKenna, you are hereby charged with defrauding an officer of the court. How do you plead?" Judge Jeremiah Wallace asked, staring down at Jake from his seat on the bench.

Jake straightened his lapels and ran through what he was going to say in his mind once more. "What are my options, your honor?" he asked.

"Well, Mr. McKenna, since I was the officer of the court you defrauded, your choices are limited to guilty or not guilty. How do you plead?"

"Not guilty, your honor," Jake said. "And I request the court's permission to hire an attorney and to have a jury trial."

The judge frowned. "Not guilty? I caught you myself cheating at cards!"

"Yes, your honor," Jake said, "but the fact is, that you only caught me cheating at a single hand of cards, and since you caught me, I obviously failed. Therefore, it's impossible that I defrauded an officer of the court."

The judge sighed. "Mr. McKenna, your motions for an attorney and a jury trial are hereby denied, and while I admire the quickness of your mind, the court believes that you had been cheating throughout the game." He glanced down at the papers on his desk.

"But, your honor—"

"No, Mr. McKenna. I don't wish to dispute this with you any further. In Shelby, and this bench in particular, we take a dim view of card cheats, swindlers, and criminals. You are guilty, Mr. McKenna, and while this court has been unable to find any other outstanding warrants for you, it is our further belief that you have no doubt been traveling throughout Wyoming and cheating others." He grinned down at Jake, and in that moment Jake realized something very important: Judge Jeremiah Wallace was not used to losing at cards, let alone losing face, and so was going to have his way.

"Before I pronounce sentence, Mr. McKenna, is there anything you'd like to say?" the judge asked.

Jake shook his head. "No, your honor," he said. "Not really."

"Very well," said the judge. "Then, for the crime of defrauding an officer of the court, I hereby sentence you to be hanged by the neck until dead, on . . ." he looked down at his notes, and continued, "December twenty-fourth, two weeks from today, at noon, in the town square."

Perfect, Jake thought. I'll be dancing from the gallows at Christmas.

"However," the judge continued, "in accordance with the wishes of the territorial government, you are hereby informed of your right to invite close friends or members of your family to your execution, postage to be paid by the town of Shelby, so long as such individuals do not attempt to interfere with the enforcement of your sentence in any way whatsoever."

Jake looked up. "You want me to invite someone to watch

me die?" he asked. "That's . . . that's pretty damn macabre."

"Some folks, particularly God-fearing folks, find that having family members nearby is a comfort when they go to their final judgment, Mr. McKenna." The judge shook his head sadly. "Nonetheless, the choice is yours. Do you understand the sentence this court has passed, Mr. McKenna?"

Jake nodded, his mind racing. "I do, your honor."

"Then this court is adjourned," the judge said, banging his gavel. "Take him back to his cell, Sheriff Greeley."

Sheriff Greeley put the handcuffs back on. "C'mon, boy," he said, tugging on the chains. "I know you're in a hurry to get back to that comfortable cell."

Jake followed him absently, his mind already working on how to word the invitation to Shay. When they got back to the jail, the sheriff put him in the cell and locked it behind him.

"If nothing else," the sheriff said, "maybe word of this will get around and keep the other vultures like you the hell away from Shelby."

Jake turned and looked at the sheriff, rubbing his wrists. "Maybe, Sheriff, but I doubt it. Vultures like me can smell a rube like you and the folks that live in this little town from miles away. This won't keep them away—it'll bring them in droves."

"Keep it up, boy," the sheriff said. "I'm going to enjoy hanging you."

"I'll bet," Jake said. "Now leave me alone."

The sheriff grinned at him. "I've always wondered what the worst part is," he said. "The waiting, or knowing that the last sound you're going to hear is your neck, snapping like a dry twig."

"Sheriff?" Jake said.

"What?" asked Greeley, grinning.

"It's the waiting," Jake said. "Because I've got to spend it enduring your stench."

Greeley's face purpled and his fists clenched. "That's gonna cost you your lunch, today, boy. Have a nice day," he said and walked out of the cell.

"Ah, shit," Jake said, then went to sit on his cot and think about Shay.

Part 3
Call and Raise

THE NEXT MORNING, when the sheriff got around to bringing Jake a breakfast of cold eggs, a biscuit, and a cup of coffee that would strip the bark off a tree, Jake asked him for a sheet of paper and a pencil.

"What for, boy?" the sheriff asked.

"What do you think?" Jake asked. "The judge said I could invite someone to my hanging, so I'm sending someone an invitation."

The sheriff spent a long minute staring at him, then said, "Who?"

"An old friend of mine," Jake said. "You might know him as none-of-your-damn-business."

"Funny," the sheriff said. "In this jail, no such person exists. So now if you want that paper, you'll cut the smart-assery and tell me who it is."

Jake sighed. What difference did it make? "I'm sending it to my fiancée, who's in Cheyenne."

"Fiancée, huh?" the sheriff asked. "It must be a damn desperate woman who'd be interested in marrying your sorry ass, boy."

"Just get the paper and pencil, Sheriff, and leave me to my breakfast."

"You'll get it," the sheriff said. "When I damn well feel like it."

"Sheriff," Jake said, striving to hold in his temper, "I'm going to die in only a few days, and if I've got to spend the remaining time in this cell, I'd just as soon not spend it fighting with you. You don't like me, and that's fine because I don't care much for you. But the good news is that if you do your job even marginally well, then you'll be shut of me before you know it."

"Then what's the bad news?" the sheriff asked.

"Bad news?" Jake said, cocking his head.

"There's always bad news with the good, so what's the bad news?"

"That's easy, Sheriff," Jake said, easily. "If you keep poking at me, then your next two weeks are going to be as nervous as mine, because the first time you slip up around me, I'll kill you." He stood up and crossed to the bars. "I don't imagine that choking or beating you to death will be easy, but I'll try. And I might get lucky."

"You wouldn't dare attack an officer of the law, boy," Greeley said indignantly.

"Wouldn't I?" Jake asked. "Why not? They're already going to hang me, Sheriff. What have I got to lose?" Jake went back to his cot and sat down to eat his breakfast. "Now go get my paper and my pencil, Sheriff, and stop messing with me. The next two weeks will be more pleasant that way."

The sheriff turned on his heels and left without saying a word, but Jake wasn't concerned. Greeley was a blowhard without a lot of grit to back it up, and Jake guessed that he could be bullied. Sure enough, he was back about twenty minutes later with a sheet of paper and an old stub of a pencil.

"Here you go," he said sullenly, shoving the items through the bars. "The judge says usually prisoners are allowed to send out postcards, but since you're only sending the one, you can just make it a part of a letter."

Jake walked over and took the offered supplies. "Thank you, Sheriff Greeley," he said, meaning it. "I'm done with this," he added, gesturing to the half-eaten eggs.

The sheriff nodded. "All right, pass them on through."

Jake knelt and slid the tray through a small slot in the cell door made for just this purpose.

Which was about the time he felt Sheriff Greeley's meaty paw descend on his neck, clamping down tight, and pulling his face forcefully against the bars. "By the way," the sheriff said, "I don't like being threatened. This is a rough town, and I do not tolerate any kind of bullshit." He let go of Jake's neck. "Still, I respect you more than I did because you had the balls to stand up to me. Not a whole lot of the supposed hard-asses in this town do."

Jake struggled to rise, and the sheriff reached through the bars and steadied him. "Thanks," Jake managed, while mentally revising his opinion of the sheriff. Usually when local law talked the way Greeley did, they were just bullies with badges. Apparently, this one was the real McCoy.

The sheriff shrugged. "You're going to be in here for two weeks, boy, so we may as well try to get along. Personally, I think hanging is a bit much for cheatin' at cards, but the judge hates thieves more than anything else."

Jake nodded, rubbing the back of his neck. "I noticed," he said.

The sheriff laughed, "I just bet you did, boy," he said.

Jake had held on to his coffee cup, and he held it out through the bars. "Any chance of a refill?" he asked.

The sheriff shrugged. "Why not?" he said. "Guess I can do that."

"Thanks," Jake said, giving a nod and handing the cup through the bars. When he wasn't playing local badass with a badge, Greeley could be almost friendly.

The sheriff went and got Jake another cup of coffee, and said, "I'm going to be out for a while, so if you need anything else, now's the time to say so."

Jake sipped the coffee and noticed that this cup was substantially hotter and better tasting than the first cup. "No, Sheriff, but thanks again for the supplies and the coffee. I guess I'd better get to writing that letter." He went over and sat down on his cot. "Have a good morning, Sheriff," Jake said.

"Yeah," the sheriff said, and left.

Jake sat on the floor and put the paper on the iron cot. It was a little rough, but it would do the job of a desk, given the alternatives. He licked the tip of the pencil, saw how dull it was, and bent to write.

Dear Shay,

I don't know how to say this, or even what to say exactly. I guess it's better if I get straight to the point. I'm in jail in a small town called Shelby. I was caught cheating at cards by the local judge, who has charged me with defrauding an officer of the court. To make a long story short, he also found me guilty, and has sentenced me to be hanged on December 24th, 1883, at noon. I am allowed to invite whoever I want to the hanging, and though it seems macabre, I'd like to have you here, Shay.

It's probably not worth all that much at this point to tell you that I've loved you from the first moment we met, or that I wanted to marry you as soon as I'd made enough to set us up proper. I don't normally cheat at cards, but the thought was in my mind to make some money quickly so I could ask you that much sooner. Anyway, Shay, I love you and if you could come, and even bring your brother Lucky with you, why, it would mean the world to me. God knows at this point I could use a little luck, and with your presence, I'm sure I'll go to judgment a free man. I hope you will come, Shay.

Love Always,
Jacob McKenna

P.S. Go ahead and bring Lucky. He's seen worse than this, and maybe he should see this, too.

Jake looked over the letter critically and decided it would do. He folded it into precise thirds and settled down to wait. Jake had learned patience at an early age, and this situation was no different. Getting agitated wouldn't change it, and so he chose to relax.

Later in the day, Sheriff Greeley came by and brought him lunch. He noted the folded sheet of paper. "You all done with that?" he asked.

"Yes," Jake said. "If you have an envelope . . ."

"I've got to read it first," the sheriff said. "Judge's orders in case you're trying anything sneaky."

Jake had suspected this would happen and so nodded. "Sure enough, Sheriff," he said, and handed him the envelope. The sheriff scanned it quickly.

"This Shay," he said, "she's your girl?"

"You bet," Jake said. "And pretty as a brand-new double-eagle coin."

"She's got a brother named Lucky?" the sheriff asked, grinning.

"Yeah," he said, "I know it's a silly nickname, but we've gotten to be pretty close."

The sheriff nodded. "Looks all right to me," he said. "I'll bring you an envelope and we'll send it out with today's mail."

"Thanks, Sheriff," Jake said.

The sheriff brought him the envelope, and Jake addressed it

to the rooming house where Shay was staying. The sheriff promised to take it to the post office that afternoon, and Jake again expressed his appreciation. One thing he'd learned was that manners could go a long ways toward keeping a person acting in a benevolent manner.

That night, Jake slept a little better, but the next day and the days after brought no word from Shay, and his hard-won calm and patience began to fray.

Part 4
The Hole Card

It was the morning of December twenty-fourth, and when Sheriff Greeley came in with Jake's breakfast he practically vaulted out of the cot. A thought had occurred to him in the night, and had been eating at him ever since.

"Sheriff," he said, "did you mail my letter? You did, didn't you?"

The sheriff gave Jake a long stare. "Yeah, Jake, I mailed it. Same day you wrote it. If your girl hasn't answered back, don't go blaming me," he said.

Jake hung his head. "I just wondered, is all," he said. "No sign of her in town?"

"No," the sheriff said, "but the morning stage is due to arrive in about an hour. Maybe she'll be on that one."

"Yeah," Jake said, "maybe so."

Was it possible that Shay wouldn't come? Jake wondered to himself. He supposed it was, but he'd thought for sure she would. Jake ate his breakfast slowly and sipped the coffee. If it was going to be his last meal, he may as well savor it.

Around nine or so, Jake heard the stage rattle into town, but didn't have the heart to go to the window and peer out as he had so many times during these past two weeks. Disappointment gnawed at him, and when he heard the sheriff talking in the outer office, he paid it little attention.

Until he heard her voice say, "Sheriff, could I see him?"

Jake sprang to his feet. She'd come!

"I don't see why not, miss," the sheriff was saying. "Guess your brother couldn't make it, huh?" he asked.

Jake winced, anticipating the worst—fearing that she wouldn't remember how to answer.

"My brother?" he heard Shay say.

"Yeah," the sheriff said, rattling his keys. "Lucky."

"Ohh," Shay said, with only a slight hesitation. "Lucky, yes. No, he couldn't come, I'm afraid," she said. "Had to leave on a cattle drive."

"I see," said the sheriff. "Right this way, ma'am."

Jake heard them coming and straightened his clothes as best he could. They were dirty and wrinkled from long days in the cell, but he hadn't been allowed to wash them. When Shay saw him, she ran to his cell.

"Oh, Jake!" she said. "You look terrible, just terrible."

"Shay," he said, reaching for her through the bars and taking her hand. "Guess jail life doesn't agree much with me." He brushed ineffectively at his suit. "I didn't think you were coming," he said, staring at her, and then turned to the sheriff.

"Can she come in?" he asked.

The sheriff shrugged. "All right," he said, "but keep it short. I don't want any trouble."

Jake and Shay nodded. "No, of course not, Sheriff," she said, then turned to Jake. "It just took me some time to face it, I guess," she said.

The sheriff opened the cell door and let Shay in, shutting it behind her. "I've gotta stay here in the hallway," the sheriff said, "in case, you know, but I'll go down there a ways."

Shay blushed and Jake grinned. "As much as I'd love to, Sheriff, it's not really the time or the place."

The sheriff grinned foolishly and walked some distance down the hall, while Jake and Shay indulged in a long, fierce hug.

Finally, he led her over to his cot and they sat down together, holding hands. "Jake," she said. "Are they really going to hang you?"

Jake nodded. "Didn't you see the gallows?" he asked.

"I did," she said, "it just doesn't seem real to me, I guess."

"Me, either," Jake said, then glanced over to where the sheriff was standing. "I heard you say Lucky couldn't come," he said quietly.

"Yes," she said. "He wanted to, Jake, but he had a drive to make." She winked at him, and Jake could see the gleam of mischief in her eyes that had made him fall in love with her in the first place.

Jake nodded. "I understand," he said. "Still, I wish he could've made it. It's going to be quite a show."

"Jake!" Shay cried. "Don't talk like that. It's . . . it's gruesome." She looked down to where the sheriff stood with his back resolutely turned, then slipped a hand under her skirt. Her years as a working girl had taught her how to draw the derringer without the move being seen.

"I know, Shay," Jake said. "But there's no point in being glum about it."

"But Jake," she said, "you sound almost happy about it." She pulled the little derringer from under her skirt and passed it to him.

"In a way I *am* happy about it," Jake said, putting the derringer down the back of his pants. "At least I won't be stuck in this little cell every day."

Shay nodded when he had it tucked in far enough. "I understand, Jake. I just wish I didn't have to see you put into the ground."

"You don't, Shay," he said. "I don't want you to stay that long."

"What do you mean?" she said.

"I want you to go over to the livery and buy yourself a horse, Shay. Hell, buy mine if you want. I want you to sit on the horse next to the gallows and as soon as I'm gone, I want you to ride out of Shelby and never come back. Don't wait for the stage or anything else. Just ride out and head for Cheyenne. It's only a day or two from here anyway, and if you stick to the roads you'll be safe enough."

She tried to conceal her grin and failed. "You want me to ride a horse back to Cheyenne?" she said.

"Better that than see me buried," Jake said. The sheriff was walking slowly toward them. "You better go now," he said, "and get that horse and whatever gear you'll need."

She nodded, and kissed him once, right on the lips. "I do love you, Jake McKenna," she said.

His surprise at her kiss didn't stop his response. "I love you, too, Shay," he said. "I'm glad you came."

"I guess that's long enough," the sheriff said from the cell door.

"All right, Sheriff," Jake said and stood up, offering Shay his hand.

He walked her to the door and kissed her once on the cheek before she slipped out. "Thanks for coming, Shay," he said.

She smiled at him. "Good luck, Jake," she said. "I think you're right, by the way. I don't want to stick around. Guess I'll go buy a horse."

The sheriff glanced at her askance. "Time to go, ma'am," he said, gesturing to the hallway.

She stepped out. "See you around, Jake," she said. "Thank you, Sheriff."

"You're welcome, ma'am," he said, then turned to Jake. "Do you want the padre to stop by?" he asked.

Jake shook his head. "No, I guess I can do my praying by myself."

The sheriff nodded. "I'll be back in a little while."

Jake watched as Shay and the sheriff walked down the hall and out of the cell area, hoping she understood the second part of his plan as well as she'd understood the first.

Part 5
How the Hand Played Out

THE SHERIFF HAD respected Jake's wishes and left him alone for the rest of the morning after Shay had left. Around eleven-forty he showed up carrying a set of handcuffs. "It's about time, Jake," he said.

Jake nodded. "All right, Sheriff," he said. "Did Shay get along all right?"

The sheriff shook his head in bewilderment. "That's some gal, Jake. She went over to the livery and bought your horse and tack, and now she's outside sitting on the saddle and looking every bit like the minute you swing she's gonna ride out of here. I told her she was damn foolish going off on her own, road or no damn road, but she wouldn't listen to me."

Jake smiled. "That's Shay, all right. Stubborn and pretty."

"I guess so," the sheriff said, and opened the cell door. "Turn around, Jake, and I'll put these on you."

Jake did, and the sheriff locked his wrists into the cuffs.

Jake turned to face him. With his hands behind his back, walking was a bit awkward, but he could manage. He tapped his index finger against the waistband of his pants, making sure the derringer was in place.

"How come you're not gonna wear your fancy coat?" the sheriff asked, pointing to where it had been serving as Jake's pillow for the last two weeks.

"I've been sleeping on it for two weeks, Sheriff," Jake said. "It's not much of a coat anymore."

"I suppose not," the sheriff said. He pulled out his pocket watch and glanced at it. "You ready?" he asked.

Jake nodded. "As I'm ever going to be," he said. "Is there a big crowd?"

"Not especially," the sheriff said. "But it's not like you're Billy the Kid or anything, either."

"True enough," Jake said. "I guess that fella would've just shot his way out of that saloon."

"Probably so," the sheriff said. "Course he's dead now. The West is getting more civilized every day. Before you know it, there won't be no outlaws anymore."

Jake laughed. "Oh, I guess there will always be outlaws, Sheriff. Otherwise, you'd be out of a job."

The sheriff laughed. "I reckon you're right, Jake." He gestured. "Let's go," he said, motioning down the hall. "You first."

Jake began walking, keeping his index finger tight against the butt of the derringer. He didn't want it to slip down his pants.

Jake went down the short hallway and out into the front office area, then waited while the sheriff opened the door to the street. He stepped out and what few people there were booed as he appeared. Jake grinned at them pertly.

No point in playing it somber, Jake thought.

The front of the jail faced the town square—such as it was, Jake thought sourly—and the gallows were right in the middle. Jake walked resolutely toward them, resisting the urge to look around for Shay. As he mounted the steps, though, he saw her. She was right next to the gallows, on the back side of them, sitting on his horse.

He smiled at her, and she winked. She'd understood perfectly.

He crossed the few remaining steps, and the sheriff

stopped him. A hooded man waited next to a priest on his left, and at the foot of the gallows was Judge Jeremiah Wallace—the man who was willing to kill him over a lousy hand of cards.

The priest stepped forward, while the judge handed the sheriff a sheet of paper. "May our heavenly Father forgive you your sins, my son," he said. "Would you like to pray with me?"

Jake shook his head. "I've done all my praying, Father, just get on with it."

He felt nervous, knowing that he would have to move soon if he was going to get out of this alive.

"Our Father, who art in heaven . . ." the priest intoned.

Jake ignored him and shifted his body slightly, so his hands were positioned at the top of his waistband.

"Thy kingdom come, thy will be done . . ."

Jake glanced around, and noted that other than the sheriff, who was behind him and to his right, the area to his back was clear. He inched his index finger down inside the top of his pants, and prayed in earnest that no one would notice.

"Amen," the priest said, and stepped back. "May God have mercy on your soul."

"I hope so, Father," Jake said.

The sheriff stepped forward and read the sentence, but Jake didn't pay that much attention. His mind was focused on what he was about to do. The hooded man stepped toward him, holding out a hood.

"Do you have any last words?" the sheriff asked.

"Yes, I do," Jake said, and cleared his throat. "I'm sorry that I *tried* to cheat at cards," he began, glaring at the judge. "And I'm sorry that I didn't get to have an attorney defend me or a jury trial to prove my innocence. Such is justice in the town of Shelby, Wyoming. And I'm especially sorry, Sheriff, that I've got to do this, too," he concluded, pulling the derringer out of his pants and turning his body in that direction.

He fired the first round, which took the sheriff in the belly. Greeley grunted once and went over like a sack of potatoes. Jake spun and planted a boot in the hooded man's stomach, and pushed backwards. The hooded man slammed into the priest and Jake went over the back of the gallows.

He landed, as he'd hoped, right on the pommel of his saddle, and pain shot up his spine. His index finger accidentally tightened in response, and the derringer fired again, the bullet leaving a shallow furrow down the back of his leg. Shay grabbed ahold of his belt and put her heels to the horse, which headed down the street at a surprised gallop.

Jake struggled to get upright, but Shay ignored him, as behind them the yells of the outraged crowd mingled with Judge Jeremiah's screaming for the sheriff to get a posse. The pommel was jamming him right in the lower back, and Jake could feel blood dripping down his leg.

"Shay," he managed to say, "I've got to get off this damn thing."

"Shut up, Jake McKenna," she said. "And hang on." She urged the horse on faster, and Jake groaned.

It was a long time before she stopped, and let him off.

"We've only got a few minutes," she said, helping him to the ground. "Are you hurt bad?"

Jake groaned again. "Let's see," he said, wincing. "I've been shot, and just had a saddle pommel driven into my back for three miles. Nope, I'm fine."

She smiled at him, then looked at his leg. "You were grazed," she said. "And pain is good for you. Humbling of the spirit, you know."

Jake smiled back. "I'm humbled all right," he said, then turned his back. "Are you going to get these off me, or just leave me locked up all day?" He wiggled his hands in the cuffs to emphasize his point.

"I don't know," she said. "I sort of enjoy seeing you this way—helpless and begging." She giggled.

"Shay!" Jake said.

"Oh, all right," she said. "Hold still."

He heard her rummaging in the saddlebags, then she said, "Hold your arms out and away from your body and try not to move a whole lot."

Jake complied up until he heard the hammer of a gun cock behind him. "Shay, get a little closer, would you? You're a lousy shot."

She stepped closer, in fact, so close that her breath was a warm river on his neck. "Then you'd better hope you get lucky," she said and fired the gun.

The bullet shattered the chain holding the cuffs together and he spun and swept her into his arms. "I always do," he said and kissed her.

She kissed him back. "Where do we go from here, Jake?" she asked.

"We'll head south for a while," he said. "Maybe down into Oklahoma."

"All right," she said. "There's just one thing I've got to know."

"What's that?" he asked, adjusting the stirrups, and digging through the saddlebags looking for something to use as a bandage.

"How'd you get caught cheating at cards? You've never gotten caught before."

Jake smiled. "I drew a Deadman's Hand and got distracted," he said.

"Distracted?" she said. "You?"

"Me," he said. He quickly bandaged his leg with a blanket. "We better head out."

"All right," she said. "But when we get to Oklahoma, I want you to try to concentrate better."

He climbed into the saddle and pulled her up behind him. "Why?"

"You almost ended up dancing at Christmas, Jake McKenna," she said. "And that's just got to be bad luck."

"Naw," he said. "There's no such thing."

He put his heels to the horse and they rode south.

Don't Never Fall in Love with No Whore

Marthayn Pelegrimas

Marthayn Pelegrimas is the author of numerous short stories in horror and western genres, including her appearances in *Borderlands 3*, *Till Death Do Us Part*, and *American Pulp*. Her first mystery novel was written under the pseudonym Christine Matthews and is called *Murder Is the Deal of the Day*. She is also an editor, most notably credited with the audio anthology *Hear the Fear*. Currently she is at work on her next novel. She lives with her husband, fellow author Robert J. Randisi, in St. Louis, Missouri.

IT WAS A gray, wet day when we buried Julia. How vividly I recall standing there, alongside the firemen, holding my hat over my heart. Even the heavens seemed to open up and cry for our loss. Rain dripped down my nose leaving a cold trail. The monogrammed handkerchief Julia had given me the Christmas before was tucked in the breast pocket of my good suit and I pulled it out. While I swiped at the wetness I remember hoping no one would see that it wasn't just the clouds that contributed to my discomfort but my own tears as well.

Ahhh, Julia. My sweet, beautiful Julia. How am I ever going to endure living in this world without you?

God, she was a lovely woman. I remember our first meeting so well, even though it took place more than seven years ago, back in the year 1863.

BUSINESS WAS SLOW that day; I was taking the opportunity to relax, sitting on an old splintered bench outside the dry goods. You can see the whole of Main Street from that vantage point. I was absorbed in the morning edition of the *Territorial Enterprise* when I heard hooves pounding and the creaking of carriage wheels. I will never forget—it was a Tuesday. The men were out at the mines and only a few women walked the street, window-shopping or gossiping. At first I was annoyed by the intrusion . . . until I glanced up from my paper.

There she sat, pretty as you please, surveying our town from inside her shiny, painted carriage, which was pulled by two white ponies.

Oh my heaven, but she was dazzling.

Her driver, an average-looking gentleman at least twenty years her senior, stepped down and held up his hand to assist his mistress.

The sun seemed to be shining expressly for her that day. As her delicate feet touched the dusty street of Virginia City, I was filled with an excitement I have not felt since my adolescence.

She was dressed in a long velvet duster. Red feathers of a kind I had never seen before trimmed the collar and caressed the gentle curve of her neck, brushing softly against the deep crease between her breasts. And it was at that precise moment I knew I had lost my heart to her.

I held my breath, hoping she would notice me—afraid she would see me. So torn was I. Wanting her attention and yet afraid that if I got it, I would squander the moment.

"Sir?"

I held the newspaper a little higher in front of my face.

"Pardon me, sir?"

I knew she had to be addressing me and yet I could not move. Out of the corner of my eye I noticed all motion in the street had ceased while the women clucked about the new arrival.

Summoning all the courage I had stored in some great

reservoir in my soul, I was finally able to lower the paper from my face and look up into her clear dark eyes. "Yes, ma'am?"

Then she honored me with the most glorious smile I have ever witnessed. It lit up not only her face but my own as well.

"Can you please direct us to D Street?" Then she looked to her man. "That's where the cottage is located, isn't it, Benjamin?"

The tall man nodded. "Corner of Union and D."

I stood and pointed, hoping she would not see my hand shaking. "Just keep going in that direction. It's about a mile straight ahead."

"Thank you very much . . . mister . . . ?" She waited for me to tell her my name.

I swallowed hard before answering. "Reed, ma'am. Milford Reed."

"Well, Mr. Reed . . ." I detected a slight English accent. "My name is Julia Bulette." She nodded her head slightly. "I thank you for your kindness and hope you will pay me a visit, as soon as I get my home in order, that is."

My heart raced. "Why, yes ma'am, I hope so, too. Thank you."

She pulled the strings on her tapestry bag and fished for a calling card which she handed to me. "This is to serve as a reminder, Mr. Reed."

The paper was stiff and tinted a delicate rose. I accepted it gratefully. "I don't think I'd be likely to forget such a kind invitation, ma'am," I told her.

I have been asked, many times since that first meeting, if I knew then that Julia Bulette was a demimonde and I have always refused to answer.

WORD OF JULIA'S arrival spread faster than a wildfire. Of course, daily stops made by Wells Fargo to her door did draw attention. Fresh flowers, champagne, all sorts of luxurious items had the women's tongues wagging and the men's breathing labored. I am not ashamed to admit, I kept her card tucked inside my Bible, where I could look at it each night. If I had only mustered up my courage sooner, maybe I could have saved her.

I had visited one of the girls down on the row a few years back. And that one visit was brought on by a particularly bad spell in my life. But overall I am very content with my life. I am a solitary man—always have been. I appreciate being left alone. I attend to my business and am proud of the work I do. When the Comstock Lode hit, I knew I could make a good living in Virginia City . . . just as Julia knew.

As much as I tried, however, I could not avoid hearing the gossip. Taking my meals in town left me unprotected from becoming involved, quite unintentionally, with the comings and goings at Number Four D Street.

It must have taken me a good two months before I worked up enough courage to call on Julia Bulette. Of course I had heard about the mayor who had come a great distance to spend just a few hours with her. And there was the report of several bankers, a sheriff, two lawyers, and one actor who was traveling through town on his way to San Francisco. Only the most distinguished and wealthy men for Miss Julia. But she was a lady. A lady who charged one thousand dollars for one night.

It wasn't the money that concerned me, then. After all, we were living in a boomtown. Money was everywhere, flowing all around us like a mighty silver river. But was I equal to the men she was accustomed to entertaining? Would she think me unsophisticated? Dull?

IT WAS LATER reported that there were two thousand of us there to mourn Julia. All of us male. The women stayed hidden behind their curtains, locked behind the shutters. Maybe they thought by separating themselves from our grief that they would not have to witness the outrageous truth. That we loved her. All of us.

A brass band led the way. All those feet keeping time in the mud. After that came the casket. A silver-handled beauty paid for by the fire department. They had taken up a collection and ended up with more than enough money to bury Julia in style. As we walked past the Red Dog Saloon, I remember seeing the *CLOSED* sign nailed across the door. It stood out in my mind because I had never seen the inside so dark before. Its owner, Dallas Dugan, walked ahead of me, holding his head rigid. Beneath his coat I could see his back heaving slightly.

Virginia Engine Company Number One brought up the rear. I walked sandwiched between them and the casket. We were all unified that day. All because of a common respect we held on to tightly. Some of us had physically loved Julia; some had only known her in passing. But no matter what degree of love we had experienced, we were all bound by the same shame. There we were. Capable, strong, healthy men, the whole lot of us. And we had let her down.

Sixteen carriages followed the fire department. It was the most expensive and largest funeral our town would ever see.

WHEN I CALLED on her that first time, I remember being so aware of my stiff collar. It felt sharp enough to draw blood. I could only smile and hope there were no scarlet drops on my starched shirt as she welcomed me into her parlor.

"Mister Reed," she said. "I was wondering how long I would have to wait until you came calling."

I held out a small bouquet to her. She did not seem surprised in the slightest. On my one previous visit to the row it would never have occurred to me to bring flowers to the "lady" of the house. But then she hadn't possessed the charm and grace that came so easily to Julia Bulette.

While she took my hat, I noticed her parlor was furnished with polished mahogany furniture, Brussels carpets, and lace curtains. The room seemed large enough to accommodate at least a dozen visitors. But at that time, there were only the two of us.

"Please, make yourself comfortable." She motioned to a large chair in the corner. "May I offer you a brandy? Maybe a glass of champagne?"

Even though I had never tasted either, I said, "Champagne would be nice."

"Fine." She smiled and I was lost. "I'll be back in a moment."

I could only nod.

It wasn't long before the gentle Julia had me calm and relaxed. Our conversation started off polite but soon turned intimate.

"So, Mr. Reed, tell me . . ." She sat demurely on the settee. "Have you a wife?"

"No," I told her, taken slightly aback.

She laughed to herself. "Oh, you would be surprised how insignificant a wife becomes when a man is in . . . shall we say . . . need of affection."

I could see immediately why her gentlemen callers were members of society's elite. She had charm and a wonderful humor about her.

We shared another glass of champagne. She never made me feel anxious, but rather flattered by her interest in my work and views on life in general. I had been there for more than an hour when she finally stood. Facing me, she slowly began removing the pins from her hair. As the curls fell down her shoulders, she walked toward where I sat, never lowering her gaze.

"Would you like to kiss me, Mr. Reed?"

I could contain myself no longer and rushed to hold her in my arms. Her skin was smooth and scented with lily of the valley. My lips grazed her cheek, her nose, until finally stopping on her mouth. She was perfection in my arms.

"Milford?" she whispered.

"Yes, my darling?"

"Are you staying the night?"

"It is all I have dreamed of."

Without another word, I was escorted into Julia's bedroom.

THE REVEREND WILLIAM M. Martin conducted the funeral. Because a woman in Julia's profession could not be buried in consecrated ground, we had to walk about a mile east of town, two hundred yards from the cemetery. The spot chosen for her grave was on a slight hill. Her steady gentleman friend, the chief of the fire brigade, decided it should be placed where she could be seen from one of her favorite saloons. As a reminder that our Julia was a fun-loving woman. In clear sight so a man could raise his glass in her honor.

THE TIME I spent with her was filled with more happiness and surprises than I have ever known. But the more popular she became with the men in town, the more she was hated by the women. There were threats on her life, damage to her property, and insults hurled whenever she dared show her face in the "proper" part of town.

And that is why I arrived one evening with a special present tucked under my arm. The memory of her excitement that night still brings me such joy.

"You really shouldn't have, Milford. You've already given me so much."

She gushed and I felt the heat of embarrassment flush my cheeks. "Just open it, Julia."

Her disappointment was evident as she removed the revolver from its velvet-lined box. "A gun? Why would you give me such a thing?" She held it between two fingers, away from her, disgusted.

"For your protection." I took the Colt from her. "Here, let me show you . . ."

"No." She turned her back to me. "It's ugly and much too heavy. Besides, I have Benjamin to protect me. I have no use for such a vile thing."

"Benjamin lives three blocks away from here. You hired him to do odd jobs, drive you, not to be a bodyguard. What kind of protection is that? Why won't you just let me show you how this works?" I held the gun in my palm, offering it to her again. "You'll get used to it soon enough."

"But you don't have a gun," she pointed out.

"I haven't had my life threatened."

No matter what I said, I could not convince her. She would have no part of the instrument.

Fearing I would lose her, I relented. "All right, my dear, you win. I will return it tomorrow."

She hugged me around the waist and kissed my neck. "Thank you."

I should have insisted she keep the gun. I should have been stronger. But the idea of upsetting her, possibly never seeing her again was unthinkable.

REVEREND MARTIN WAS quite eloquent that day, or so I have been told. I still cannot remember his exact words but the gist of the ceremony still haunts me. We had lost someone very special. And as I looked around at the faces of the men surrounding me, I knew none of us would ever forget Julia.

The headboard of her bed was used as her tombstone. It had been bronzed and on one side was a plaque engraved with her likeness. It was my job, as the town undertaker, to position it after the casket had been lowered into the ground.

As I wrestled with the large marker, I could hear the departing firemen singing "The Girl I Left Behind."

IT WAS ONLY a few short weeks after my failed attempt to arm Julia that I received a catalogue from Colt Firearms. It announced their new line. There on the third page was what the manufacturer called "The Ladies' Gun." A pretty little .32-caliber pearl-handled pistol. The catalogue stated that the barrel of this particular model was shorter and easier to handle and had more stopping power than a .22-caliber. It also noted that these were considered "hideaway" guns, used as backup for the larger ones.

I knew instantly that I would order one for Julia. And this time I would make her keep it.

THE NEWSPAPER CALLED her murder "outrageous and cruel." My poor darling had not only been strangled and shot, but suffocated and beaten as well. Murder is a despicable act in itself but when teamed up with other heinous crimes it seems to be more the Devil's work than anything thought up by man.

After killing my dear, sweet Julia, the coward ran away with her jewelry and furs, leaving in his wake not only a bloody mess for our town to clean up but wounds too deep to ever heal.

I have often wondered if that brute would have had compassion, left her safe, had he known what a kind heart Julia Bulette had. I have wondered how he could not have been aware of her charitable donations. What if he had been one of those struck down when a fever epidemic struck our citizens? Would his heart have yielded if he had been nursed in her brothel-turned-hospital? And had he known any of these things, then surely he was aware how her possessions did not matter that much to her, or how on earth would she have been able to part with them so easily? Selling off so many of her things for money to buy food for the needy. Why couldn't the bastard have simply stolen from her? But for God's sake, leave her alive! We all needed her so much.

For several months our women—every single one of them—were afraid. Frightened to leave their homes. Insisting their men accompany them on even the most trivial errand. And then finally, the murderer was found. A hated Frenchman by the name of John Millian. Of course he said he was innocent. But Julia's possessions were found in his room. I would have killed him myself, but I wanted the pleasure of seeing him hang.

THE COLT ARRIVED shortly before Julia's thirty-fifth birthday. Of course I knew she would not be happy if I were to present it to her as a gift. So I tucked it away and purchased an emerald brooch. She was giving herself a party that night and only her favorite "callers" were invited.

I felt no jealousy toward those other men. We were connoisseurs of a sort, bound together by the delight we took in our shared interest—Julia.

I arrived at nine o'clock, an hour later than most. She greeted me at the door herself, dressed in a shimmering gown of white silk. Tiny rosettes dotted the bodice. The same small flowers were pinned to her upswept hairdo. She was lovelier than I had ever seen her.

"Oh, Milford." She kissed my cheek. "It wouldn't be a party without you. What took you so long?"

"There was an accident at the mill. We lost Ben Stone."

"That dear man with the ten little children?"

"Yes."

"I'll have to send my condolences to his widow. Maybe some sweets for the children. Of course I know it can't make up for . . ."

"I don't think your gifts will be welcomed," I told her sadly.

She shrugged. "I will try anyway." Then peeking into my pocket, she asked, "What did you bring me?"

When she saw the emeralds, she giggled with happiness.

Not wanting to ruin her party, I decided not to even mention the gun I had purchased. But I vowed I would bring it to her on my next visit.

* * *

JOHN MILLIAN WAS regarded by the gentlewomen of Virginia City to be a hero. Daily gifts of fried chicken and homemade pies were sent to his jail cell. And while he stuffed himself with the fine food, the women pleaded for him to be pardoned—the very same women who had forbidden their men to attend Julia's funeral. What simple-minded hypocrites those creatures were. I grew to hate even the sight of them.

ON MY NEXT visit to Julia's cottage, I tucked the small Colt inside my pocket. I reasoned that maybe if she did not think of the pistol as a gift but rather a necessity, she would realize her need for the weapon. But when I arrived she was in a foul mood and I returned home with the gun still in my coat.

She was planning to visit a friend in Weaverville the following week. Not wanting to spoil her trip, I refrained from mentioning my purchase. The visit after that was postponed due to a piece of bad pork I had eaten. By the time I was feeling better, Julia was dead.

PEOPLE STARTED ARRIVING the night before John Millian was to be hanged. They came from everywhere. On foot, by stage, and on horseback. Once the Frenchman had been found guilty, the whole town began preparing for the event. Never before had such drama unfolded before our very eyes. All the main characters had scandalous backgrounds, and the juicy details titillated men and women alike.

At dawn on April twenty-seventh, John Millian mounted the scaffold. He spoke a few words in his native tongue, kissed the priest, and while thousands of spectators looked on, he was hanged.

I had been praying ever since his capture that once Millian was dead, the pain residing in my soul would be released. But it was not to be.

The crowd slowly dispersed, returning to town. Saloons that had been closed for a second time opened their doors. I wandered along, caught up in the rush of bodies, hoping their gaiety would inspire me to rejoice also.

There was not even enough room to sit, so I stood at the

bar and ordered a whiskey. The man next to me held up his glass as if to toast the demise of Millian. When the bartender slid my glass toward me I picked it up and toasted the gentleman back.

"To Julia," I said. But he didn't hear me.

The air inside that barroom soon became too close. Feeling the need for fresh air, I walked back out into the street. The sun streamed down, promising to deliver a nice day. I only wished for darkness. I was tired and now that the whole mess was over, I wanted only to go home and rest. I had gotten a few feet closer to my front door when I heard a woman call after me.

"Hey, ain't you the man what was married to that Bulette woman?" She nudged her friend. "I believe that's the one all right."

I shook my head. "No, I'm sorry, we were not married."

"Well, look at that, Sally, there is a man in this town with some sense, after all. Mister, I want to shake your hand."

"Pardon me?"

She straightened herself up, all five disgusting feet of her. While she held her hand out, I searched her wrinkled face for some sign of kindness, some softness around her mouth, a glimmer in those dull eyes. But there was nothing.

"I said," her voice rose to an uncomfortable pitch, "anybody with a pinch of sense coulda told you that a whore like that would come to a bad end. These men around here make me sick. And now that poor Mr. Millian had to pay for all their sins."

I turned to leave but spun back around to face her. My anger was so intense that it rattled through me, my eyes seemed to boil in their sockets.

"How dare you," was all I could say.

"Why lookie that, Sally," the woman said to her companion. "We've offended the proper gentleman."

Sally smiled a toothless grin. "Didn't your mama tell you don't never fall in love with no whore?" She cocked her head, waiting for my reaction like a stupid animal.

Julia's gun felt good in my hand. For the first time in months I was happy. Pulling the small pistol from my pocket, I brought it up slowly, considering what part of that woman's piggish body to shoot first.

AUTHOR'S NOTE: In order to stave off criticism from knowledgeable readers, the author would like it to be known that she is aware Julia Bulette died in 1867 and the Ladies' Colt mentioned in this story was not manufactured until 1873. These facts, however, have no real bearing on this story.

Balance of Power

Ronald Scott Adkins

Ronald Scott Adkins makes his professional debut in this collection with "Balance of Power." In his mid-thirties, he lives in Cedar Rapids, Iowa, with his wife, Renee. His poetry and short fiction have appeared in magazines and he's done a good deal of nonfiction for trade publications. He's already at work on his next western story.

DEAD SOLDIERS LAY scattered about the road, their blood turning the dust the color of cocoa. They'd been shot more times necessary to kill any man. Bullet holes pockmarked their chests and backs, arms and legs.

The army had arrived before us. We rode up to find at least a dozen troops from Fort Brown walking about, standing over the bodies, or hunkered down picking through their pockets.

A short little man stood apart. He pointed to corpses, hollered something authoritarian, then pointed to a wagon alongside the road. Men lifted the bodies by their hands and feet and moved them to the wagon.

"Hold on there," I yelled as I dismounted and walked toward them. "Put them down."

The men paused. The little man in charge, a major, pointed to the wagon and they continued on.

"I said stop." I grabbed a soldier by the arm. My deputy—Big Tiny—moved into position behind the wagon. Six-foot-five, shoulders like a bull, he formed a wall to prevent the soldiers from following orders.

I heard the little major come up from behind. He spun me with surprising strength. "I don't know what you're doing . . ." He glanced down at my badge. ". . . Sheriff, but you will desist."

He was at least a half-head shorter than me, with blond hair and skin too fair for the Kansas prairie. His high tenor voice carried a thick, muddy accent I couldn't place.

We stood nearly toe-to-toe. The afternoon sun was at my back. When he looked up at me, his tiny eyes closed into tight squints.

"I'm the law in this county," I said, leaning forward to cast a shadow. "And you're disturbing the scene of a crime."

"This doesn't concern you."

"Put those men down or you're under arrest."

The major chuckled and walked away. He pointed again to the wagon. "Carry on."

I moved toward him, making the mistake of having a hand too close to my revolver. In a heartbeat, a half-dozen weapons were trained on me. I nodded to Big Tiny and he moved away from the wagon.

The major turned to me with a grin. He raised a hand and the weapons lowered. "Come here, Sheriff," he said, his voice relaxed, in command.

The dead men were laid side by side, their arms folded across their chests. When they had all been properly placed, the major removed his hat and bowed his head. "Let us have a moment of silent prayer for these fallen heroes," he said. We all removed our hats and stood quiet.

I looked at the faces of the dead men. Five in all—a sergeant, two corporals, two privates. All but one had their eyes closed, their faces grimacing in death agony. The sergeant's eyes, and mouth, were open wide, as if he'd been killed in midsentence. His expression reflected surprise and confusion, it seemed, not the pain of his wounds.

The major prayed longer than any of us. His lips moved slightly as he spoke to God, but I couldn't understand the soft mumble. In a moment, he stood straight, took a deep breath and opened his eyes, then turned to me smiling.

"My apologies for that earlier awkwardness, Sheriff. It

was a tense moment in dangerous times." He held out his hand. "Major John Falkner."

"Bo Tanner," I said, shaking his hand. "You're in charge of the garrison?"

"I am the commanding officer, yes."

"What happened to Captain . . ."

"Captain Brayton. He was assigned to a unit back east."

"That so?"

"And promoted."

"Good for him."

"You knew him well?"

"Met him once. But I don't know you at all."

Falkner started to say something, then stopped. He paused for a second, then said, "Again, my apologies. I should have made a courtesy call when I arrived. Informed you of the change in command. We are, after all, stationed in your jurisdiction."

Just barely, and not by my choice. About six months ago, Captain Brayton and his men came riding into town. It looked like a circus parade, complete with costumes and shiny brass horns. The only thing missing were elephants and sideshow freaks. Everybody stopped what they were doing to watch them ride by, waving and greeting.

With states seceding, Brayton had said, war was inevitable. This region needed a visible army presence to ensure its security.

"Where were you the last seven years?" I had asked.

Biggest mistake we ever made was listening to Stephen Douglas. His Kansas-Nebraska Act of 1854 had been nothing but trouble. Border ruffians came down to change our minds on the slave issue. Didn't matter what your opinion, there were thugs who disagreed with you, burned your house, and lynched you. Neighbors who used to sit together in church now fought in the street. For seven years, it had been nothing but violence and killing and bad blood. They called us Bloody Kansas, we'd spilled so much of it.

And now it had spilled over the banks of the Mississippi and the Potomac and Bull Run. Brayton was right. War had broken out, but it didn't change things in my eyes. The war was still back east and I wanted the visible army presence just a bump on the far horizon.

They built their Fort Brown ten miles west of town, just inside the county line. We barely knew they were out there. I liked that.

I said to Falkner, "Your comings and goings are your business, Major." I pointed to the bodies in the wagon. "But this is mine."

"This is an army matter and you will not interfere." The smile and courtesy were gone. "We will avenge them."

"This isn't about vengeance. It's about justice. There's murder in my county and I am the law."

Falkner laughed. "This isn't murder, you fool. This is war."

I couldn't argue. I just stood there as the soldiers saddled up.

"Do you intend to conduct an investigation?" Falkner asked.

"Indeed."

"I won't have you looking under stones, getting in our way." He motioned for one of his men to come forward. This soldier looked anything but. His uniform bore no rank insignia and hung on his thin body like a badly tailored suit. Greasy black hair touched his shoulders. His eyes were bright and his whole countenance seemed just on the verge of laughter. Falkner leaned close to him and spoke softly for a minute. The soldier nodded a couple of times. Falkner then turned to me. "This is Mr. James Hickok," he said. "He will act as liaison between our two . . . investigations."

"Do I have a choice?" I asked.

"None." Falkner turned and led his entourage down the road, west to the garrison.

"What do you think, Sheriff?" Tiny asked, when the troops were out of earshot.

"I think he's right, the arrogant bastard. This wasn't from any border ruffians."

"You think it was Rebs?"

"I don't know."

"If it was," Tiny said, "the Union's in trouble." He swept his hand across the open Kansas prairie, flat as a well-made bed to the horizon. "If they can pull off a sneak attack out here."

I nodded agreement. "They saw it coming."

Big Tiny pointed toward the road. "And you see the dead men's guns?"

"What about 'em?"

"None of them had their pistol drawn."

"Damn." I'd seen it the same as he had, but thought nothing of it.

"I think they knew who they were," said Tiny.

"I think you're right." I looked at Hickok, who just stood there, grinning. "There's something to tell your boss," I said. "It's gone back to murder."

THE SUN HAD long set by the time we reached town. The night winds had kicked up, carrying scents of wildflowers off the prairies and supper from the restaurant. I wanted a hot meal and whiskey. "I'm not sure where to put you, Mr. Hickok."

"Call me Bill. If you got a bed in your jail cell, I'll be fine. Wouldn't be the first time I spent the night behind bars."

This Hickok seemed likable enough. He had none of the arrogant swagger of Falkner. "You sound like a plainsman," I said. "Where are you from?"

"Nebraska. I'm on my way to join General Dodge in Kansas City. He hired me to scout for his unit in Missouri."

"Hired you?"

"I ain't regular army. I done some scoutin' and guide work before, then this war breaks out and I thought I'd stick around and see what it's all about."

"How long have you been with Fort Brown?"

"Couple weeks. Just long enough to catch my breath."

"Is that major always such a son-of-a-bitch?" Big Tiny asked.

"Treats his men decent. These folks, at least."

"What do you mean?" I asked.

"Been a lot of comings and goings lately. Transfers, new recruits."

"Like they're getting ready for something. Bracing themselves," I said.

"There is a war on," Tiny said.

"I know." I thought about the dead soldiers. Falkner was right. War was coming to Bloody Kansas.

* * *

TWO SILHOUETTES PASSED the lit windows of the jailhouse. "Company," I said to no one in particular.

Two men faced us as we walked through the door. "General Dodge," said Hickok, who brushed past me to shake his hand.

"Good to see you again, Hickok," the general said, his face without expression. He turned to me. "Are you the sheriff?"

"Bo Tanner." I extended a hand. He was a small man, thin and sickly-looking, with pale, weather-beaten skin. A thick, unkempt beard couldn't shade the deep-sunk hollows in his cheeks. His eyes, bright gray embers, gave off the same strong, nervous energy as his countenance as he gripped my hand hard.

"Grenville Dodge," he said, then turned to his companion. "Dr. Richard Gatling."

"Sir."

Gatling shook my hand without a word. He was taller than Dodge and stout. His face, too, reflected a life spent out-of-doors, but unlike the general, he wore an air of quiet scholarship as well. The gray beard softened the scowl and sad, brooding eyes.

"I'm surprised to see you here, Hickok," said Dodge.

"I'm on special detachment, I guess. I'm supposed to help the sheriff with the murders."

"What murders?"

"Five Union soldiers, west of town," I said.

"We're too late," said Gatling. His head was low and he looked about to cry.

"Steady, Doctor," said Dodge, gripping his arm. Then to me, "Tell me about the killing."

"Like I said, five Union men from Fort Brown. Just lying in the road. And whoever killed them wanted to make sure they were dead."

"How so?"

"Because they were shot to hell and back," I said.

"We're too late," said Gatling.

"Large-caliber weapon," Dodge said, not as a question but a statement of fact.

"You know something?"

"I'm afraid this is an army matter, Sheriff," said Dodge.

"It's murder."

"It's all my fault," said Gatling.

"Doctor," Dodge said as if scolding a child. "Be quiet."

"Sheriff Tanner deserves to know." Gatling pulled a sheaf of papers from his coat pocket. "Those men were killed with this." He spread the papers on my desk, flattening them with his hands. We all gathered round.

I'd never seen anything like it. Mounted on a two-wheeled carriage was the strangest-looking artillery piece.

"Some sort of cannon?" Tiny asked.

"A rifle," said Gatling. "A true repeating rifle."

"The battery gun," said Dodge. "The ultimate war machine."

Gatling winced at that description. He spoke with none of the pride evident in Dodge's voice. "There have been other repeaters before. The Ager Coffee Mill is currently employed with some success. But they all have the same problem. If too many rounds are fired at one time, the barrel warps from the heat and the breech fails to seal. My battery gun utilizes six barrels mounted on a central spindle. Each barrel is rotated into firing position by a crank at the rear. When a barrel moves to the six o'clock position, a cartridge is loaded and fired. And as one barrel is firing, the other five are cooling off. Fifty-eight-caliber cartridges are loaded into the magazine in the rear of the weapon."

"How long can it continue firing?" I asked.

"As long as there are bullets in the magazine, up to three hundred fifty rounds per minute."

"My God," I said.

Tiny whistled through his teeth and muttered something under his breath.

"It's an amazing piece of ordnance," said Dodge. "A gun like this can take the place of dozens of soldiers with rifles. Squads could wipe out battalions. The balance of power on the battlefield could shift in a moment. This war could be over in months."

"Then why is it here?" I asked. "The war is across the river. Until today."

"We're not certain why, Sheriff," said Gatling.

"We just know who is to blame," said Dodge. "Major General Benjamin Butler."

"A real son-of-a-bitch," said Hickok. "I met him once in Omaha. Ugly little man."

Dodge chuckled. It was the first time I'd seen him even crack a smile. "He is, at that." Then, his face resuming that sombre, sickly quality, he said, "Butler has a reputation for unorthodox strategy. When no one else moved to defend the capital, Butler commandeered a locomotive and used it to transport fifteen thousand men through enemy lines. He's also the army's strongest advocate for innovative weaponry. When Dr. Gatling introduced his new war machine, Butler was the first to call for its immediate deployment."

"But the government hasn't been as enthusiastic," said Gatling. "They've ordered extensive field tests before authorizing any manufacture in quantity."

"Apparently, Butler couldn't wait," said Dodge. "He arranged for the prototype's removal from secure storage in Cincinnati and brought here."

"I have to ask you again," I said. "Why here?"

"Kansas might simply be a convenient place to rendezvous."

"I don't understand."

"His fortunes have recently fallen." Dodge showed just a hint of his previous smile. "While his methods have produced results, they're often in flagrant disregard of orders. Upon securing Washington, he abandoned his post to strike at Rebel holds near Baltimore."

"With success?"

"He seized Federal Hill and fortified it with artillery. His actions swayed the Maryland legislature to reject a secession vote. Yes, he was successful. But that's not the point."

"The end doesn't justify the means."

"Precisely. He defied orders, broke the chain of command. And for that he was sent with an expeditionary force to the Gulf of Mexico. Central Command has received no dispatches from his unit in three weeks. We believe he's on his way here to take possession of the weapon, then use it for his own purposes."

"You think he's a Reb?" Tiny asked.

"I don't know," said Dodge. "Until now, I believed Butler

to be loyal to the Union. But he has his own motivations. I'm sure he sees this weapon, as I do, as the future of military ordnance. As I said before, this weapon will change the balance of power. In many ways."

"We know he's willing to kill to keep it," Tiny said. "And he could be long gone by now."

"Doubtful," said Gatling. "For all its potential, the battery gun is difficult to transport. He couldn't have gotten far."

"And it's dark and he's in unfamiliar country. And mowing down U.S. soldiers just brought the wrath of the garrison," I said. "They're probably beating the prairie grass right now."

"I'll need to coordinate with the commander," said Dodge.

"Major Falkner," I said.

"Never heard of him."

"Another son-of-a-bitch," Hickok said.

I TOLD THE general I'd ride with him to Fort Brown in the morning. It was an army matter, he said again, but he didn't argue. It was late and he wanted food and a few hours sleep.

Dodge left, escorted by Big Tiny, to find lodging at the hotel. That left Hickok, who had found his bed and was already asleep, and Dr. Gatling, who sat with me in my office.

He offered me a fine cigar and I accepted, glad to have the taste of sweet smoke in my mouth. I opened a bottle of whiskey and offered him a tall drink. He downed the first glass in two swallows and I filled it again. He nursed this one, staring at the amber liquid through the facets in the cut glass.

"I know a lady in Charlotte," he said, "who owns a topaz that sparkles much like this."

"I've been trying to place your accent."

"My family owns a large farm in North Carolina."

"I pegged you for a farmer when I shook your hand."

Gatling took another long swallow. "You're very observant, Sheriff Tanner."

"Comes with the job, I suppose."

He finished his drink and placed it on my desk. He waved off the bottle when I moved to pour another. He spent a few minutes in silence, savoring his cigar and looking around the room. I'd noticed his eyes kept fixing on the wall behind me.

"You have an intriguing taste in decoration," he said, pointing to the two hangman's nooses nailed there.

"They're reminders."

"Reminders of what?"

"The two sides to my job, I guess."

Gatling tapped a long ash, then poured himself another drink. "Please explain."

"That one on the left," I said, pointing over my shoulder with a thumb, "hung the Reverend Joseph Hampton."

"Heaven prevail," said Gatling, leaning a little closer.

"That's probably what all his victims said, just before he sent them to God. Hampton is proof that it's just a short step from passion to insanity."

"How so?"

"He was a great preacher—compassionate, gentle, fair-minded—on fire for the Lord. And brother, could he light a fire under a congregation on Sundays. Had me feeling like a believer, sometimes. To the people here he was a prophet and a confessor and their deliverance, this meek little fellow who could stop a bar brawl by simply walking into the room. But somewhere along the way, he began to believe it, too, and I think that's what unlocked that dark place in his soul. Killed three people before I figured it all out."

"And you killed him?" Gatling asked, a spark in his voice I couldn't understand.

"I brought him in. He was tried and convicted and sentenced to death. I stood as a witness, then took the noose when it was done. That one," I said, pointing again over my shoulder, "stands for justice."

"And the other?"

"That one was around the neck of Charley Crawford. He runs the dry-goods store and has family in Tennessee. He spoke out once about the slave issue and some abolitionists heard him talking. They dragged him from his bed and strung him up. I got there before it was too late and cut him down. That noose," I said, "also stands for justice."

"So this Charley Crawford sides with the Confederacy?"

"I don't know. I never asked and he's never really said."

"But he's from Tennessee . . ."

"This is Kansas, Dr. Gatling. Everyone's from somewhere else, and we're all tired of standing on one side or the other and throwing rocks across the fence."

"What side of the fence do you stand on, Sheriff?" Gatling asked.

"That's none of your business."

"Forgive me."

I took a long pull off my cigar. "So you're a farmer."

Gatling smiled. "From a long line of farmers."

"Then how does a farmer come to build a war machine?"

"Strangely enough, I first came upon the notion designing a new machine for planting corn. I own a number of patents on farm implements."

"Then your doctorate is in agriculture?"

"Medicine."

"You're a real doctor?"

He laughed out loud. "I've never practiced. I've lost dear family to influenza, cholera, consumption. I studied medicine so I could help, should the need occur."

"You're a perplexing man, Doctor."

"A true paradox," he said, still smiling and puffing his cigar.

"Do no harm."

"I beg your pardon?"

"Isn't that your oath?"

The smile melted and the sadness sunk into his eyes again. I regretted what I said, but the whiskey had loosened my thoughts.

"I never believed anyone would use the damned thing," Gatling said, his voice so low I could barely hear him.

"You built a war machine for the army, you fool. What did you expect them to do with it? Plant corn?"

Gatling stood and leaned over the desk, his face just a few inches from mine. "The army wasn't supposed to have it."

I dug at my ear with a finger. "Must be the whiskey," I said, holding my empty glass between us.

He reached for the bottle and poured me another tall one, then sat back down. "Sheriff," he said, "what does it take to kill a man?"

I blinked hard to focus. The long day and the liquor were taking their toll. "What?"

"What does it take to pull the trigger?"

"I don't know."

"You're a lawman in an often lawless place. Surely you've had to kill for your justice."

"I've killed before."

"Then what does it take?"

"Both times, the other man was aiming at me. I just fired first."

"Self-preservation," Gatling said, nodding his head as if logging the information. "You both had guns, you both had the means to kill. You killed him before he killed you."

"I suppose."

"Would you have killed him if he were unarmed?"

"Absolutely not."

"Why?"

"That would have been murder."

"I had quite a long time to converse with General Dodge on the way here. He talked ad nauseam on the intricacies of this war. He talked about engagements, and armaments, and troop movements. And acceptable losses. But not once did he say, 'Private So-and-So was a good man. I will mourn him.' "

"He's a soldier," I said. "He thinks differently."

"He's a businessman. Butler is a politician. They're in the army because they think it will help their civilian careers. They're generals because they know someone who could grant them a commission. Dodge is friends with President Lincoln."

"I'll be damned," I said, finishing another glass.

"Dodge wants to build a cross-country railroad and war heroes get things done faster."

"What does this Butler want?"

"Power. Generals often become presidents."

"And this battery gun could make him president?"

"Most certainly."

"And what do you want, Dr. Gatling?" I poured him another glass.

"I want this war to end quickly so I can go home."

"Give your invention to the army, says Dodge, and the war could be over by Christmas."

"They can't have it," Gatling said.

"You're not making sense."

"If they have it, they'll use it. We've seen that today."

"That's the point, isn't it? That's its purpose."

"No." Gatling brought his glass down hard. "That is not its purpose."

I rose from my chair, suddenly very tired. "Good night, Doctor."

"Wait," he said. "Hear me."

I sat back down.

"Did you know that families take picnic lunches to the battlefield? It's quite the spectacle. Mother and Father sit on a hilltop while their sons fight below. War is romantic, Sheriff. It's valiant, glamorous. Essentially, war hasn't changed since chivalry."

"Single combat," I said.

"Man against man. One sword against another. Today, one rifle against another." He knocked back the contents of his glass and set it empty beside mine. "It's all a question of balance." He lifted my full shot of whiskey between us. "The Union army is this glass. It is well-armed, is well-fed, and outnumbers its opponent. It is supported by industry that can provide for its every need." He set my glass down and picked up his own. "Now *this* glass, Sheriff, is the Confederacy. It is an army of farmers. Every weapon comes from raided Union storehouses. Every officer was trained at West Point. Their greatest advantage is passion." He put the glass down. "It isn't enough."

"Passion was enough to win American independence," I said. "We faced the same kind of odds against the British."

"Not so," said Gatling, filling his glass. "Americans faced an enemy from thousands of miles away. The ocean was the equalizer. The Confederacy fights for independence against a neighbor. They cannot win."

"Not without an equalizer."

"Precisely."

"Your war machine would make an impressive equalizer," I said.

"It would indeed." Gatling took a drink. "My battery gun

in Union hands merely adds to the juggernaut. If they were to use it on the battlefield, it would be murder."

"I understand."

Gatling rose from his chair. "I must find the hotel while I'm still able to walk. Good night, Sheriff Tanner. You've been excellent company."

I sat alone in my office for some time, thinking and nursing one last whiskey before going home.

THE POUNDING IN my head echoed the pounding on my door around midnight. Big Tiny was outside, about to knock it off the hinges. "Sheriff! We got 'im!"

Tiny tried the door, found it unlocked, and came inside. "He just walked in, easy as you like."

"Who did?"

"General Butler."

I grabbed Tiny by the arm. "Where is he?"

"In jail. I sent word for General Dodge and the doctor."

"This was too easy," I said, running out the door.

DODGE SAT BEHIND my desk, smoking a cigar. "Gentlemen." A smile beamed behind the unkempt beard. "We must celebrate."

"I heard we have a guest," I said, heading for the cells.

"Is that the sheriff?" a voice called out. The accent was thick with Bostonian aristocracy.

General Benjamin Butler was indeed an ugly man. Short, squat, and balding, he had the belly of privilege that stretched his uniform at the buttons. His bulging, baggy, crossed eyes made him look like a greasy bullfrog.

"Are you the sheriff?" he said, approaching the bars as I walked in.

"Sheriff Bo Tanner."

"Release me."

"No."

His bald head turned crimson. "I order you to release me," he shouted, spraying the bars with a rain of spittle.

Dodge and Gatling entered the cell block.

"I can't." I pointed to Dodge. "You're his prisoner."

"You'll hang, all of you." Butler's fat knuckles were white from gripping the bars.

"Why not kill us with your battery gun?" Dodge said.

The crimson drained from Butler's face. "My battery gun?"

"The one you stole," Dodge said, "for God only knows what purpose."

"I did not steal that weapon. I . . . appropriated it."

"*Appropriated it?* That weapon is the property of the United States Army."

Butler released his grip on the cell bars, took a step back, and puffed up like a pheasant. "And I am an officer of the United States Army."

"You stole it like a common thief and were going to use it without orders, you pompous bastard."

"You will not talk to me in that tone, Dodge. I outrank you."

Now it was Dodge's time to puff up. "General Benjamin Franklin Butler, by order of President Abraham Lincoln I relieve you of duty and place you into custody, pending your court martial."

Gone was the fat, posturing blowhard behind bars. Now stood the sweaty, spoiled boy who held his breath and stomped his feet. "Release me."

"Return my property." Gatling spoke for the first time, softly from the back of the room.

"I don't have it."

Dodge took a long pull from his cigar and exhaled slowly, calmly. "You've murdered five men to keep it."

I've seen a lot of guilty men before. I've studied their faces as they profess their innocence. Some have been masters, able to express shock and surprise when confronted by the truth. Others look like clowns, their lies painted on in bright colors. And some rare few are genuinely shocked when accused of a crime. Butler looked genuinely shocked.

"He doesn't know what you're talking about," I said.

"I don't," said Butler.

"I think you have the wrong man, General." I reached for the ring of keys.

"Belay that." Dodge held my arm.

Butler rushed to the bars and reached through. He grabbed Dodge by the sleeves and pulled him forward. "I didn't kill anyone."

"If he was involved," I said, "he wouldn't be here. He'd be hiding from the garrison patrols."

"Why would I hide from the garrison?" Butler asked, calmer now, his voice an octave lower. "That's my destination."

"They knew you were coming?" I asked.

"Of course. Fort Brown is housing the battery gun until I arrive. Captain Brayton understands the need for new ordnance."

"Captain Brayton isn't there anymore," I said. "Major Falkner commands now."

"Never heard of him," said Butler.

I couldn't read the expression on Dodge's face. He would have made a formidable poker player. He stood there, blowing cigar smoke into the crossed, bulbous eyes of General Butler. "We may have a snake in our bed," Dodge said, taking the keys from my hand and unlocking the door.

FORT BROWN SAT silent on the prairie, dark and hulking, as if the whole thing and everyone inside were settled down to sleep. The earth walls seemed like a natural growth from the soil. Only as we drew closer could we see it was built with a deliberate plan—with battlements and sentry towers and reinforced gun ports—built to last as a permanent presence here in Bloody Kansas.

The moon was full and hung low over the horizon. Its ghostlight washed out any stars shining in the clear sky. The night winds had picked up, sending a cold shiver up my spine.

Sentries patrolled the battlements. They leaned forward to spy the riders they heard approaching.

"Attention," Butler called out, surprising us all. "Open the doors."

"Who goes there?" a shadowy figure called back, his rifle pointed vaguely in our direction.

"General Benjamin Butler and party. We've come to speak to the commander."

Two other soldiers ran to the one who had spoken. They huddled together, talking into each other's ears through cupped hands. One of them hurried away.

"Open the door," Butler called again.

"Advance and be recognized," the soldier called back.

We rode closer, close enough that the moonlight brought us into focus through the sights of his rifle. The soldier opened fire. I saw the brief flash before I heard the shot, before I heard the agonized cry of Butler's horse as it reared, careened, and toppled to the ground. Butler was thrown. He landed with a plop and skittered on hands and knees for cover behind the rest of us. The soldier was now joined by others, who fired into the dark, hoping to hit something as we dove for shadow.

"Is this whole camp in Rebel hands?" Butler asked, panting.

"They been moving soldiers in and out for a while," said Hickok. "Could be they've been shippin' the Union boys out and Rebs in."

"A covert stronghold in the west," said Dodge, checking his revolver. "Very clever."

I saw more soldiers on the wall. Some fired blindly into the night. The flash from their rifles lit their faces for an instant. A bullet grazed the rock I hid behind, stinging my face with tiny shards.

Butler and Dodge were to my right. One of them fired. I saw the flash and I cringed.

"You imbecile," Dodge growled, his voice low and angry.

Butler's shot was met with a volley from the garrison.

Big Tiny slid closer and spoke low in my ear. "We have got to get out of here. If they don't pick us off they're going to come out and find us."

"I know."

"Fall back," Dodge whispered.

We crawled to a patch of tall prairie grass maybe ten yards back. The garrison fell quiet again. They tired of wasting ammunition.

"You're a menace," Dodge said.

Butler reloaded his pistol. "We can fight like men, like soldiers, Dodge. Or we can lie in the grass and be picked off like prairie chickens. Only the bold die with glory."

I had to hand it to the little bullfrog. He showed true courage, grunting to his feet, taking aim without so much as a quiver, firing and piercing the heart of a Rebel. The soldier let out a short, gurgling scream, then fell to the ground clutching his chest. He was lost in the deep shadow of the night.

The Rebels responded with fury. Rifles blazed orange-red, peppering us with shots that buzzed by our ears and ricocheted off the hard ground. In the moonlight, I could see Tiny looking at me. He was a good man and a fine deputy. But he was no soldier. He would never survive on a battlefield. He would do his duty, fight alongside all the others. But he would hesitate for that one second while his enemy took aim and fired.

As his enemy took aim now, finding his shadowed form in the half-light of the moon, and fired. Tiny yelled out, clutching his left arm. Blood ran dark through his fingers.

Out of the corner of my eye I saw Dodge and Butler stand, take aim and fire five rounds rapid at the Rebels on the wall. Like good soldiers, they had taken advantage of a situation. The Rebs had their attention on Tiny and the generals attacked their open flank.

And I, hoping to survive this night, followed their lead. I stood and emptied my pistol into a shadowy figure against the nighttime sky.

I crawled to where Tiny knelt hunkered down. I helped him tear his shirt for a tourniquet.

"I'm fine, I'm fine," he said, pushing my hand away as I touched the skin around the wound. "That hurts worse."

"I don't think the bullet went in."

"Just grazed the wing, is all. Hurts like hell, though." The shot had torn a wide gash across the meat just below the shoulder.

"Can you move it?" I asked.

Tiny winced, but he moved his arm up and down without much trouble.

I felt a hand pull at my shirt. It was Hickok. "The general says to pull back," he whispered in my ear.

We took refuge in the gully of a trickle stream. We sat back against the dirt slope, caught our breath, and reloaded.

"We're dead." Tiny stood and looked toward the garrison. "They'll be out looking for us any time now."

"No, they won't," Hickok said. "They have the high ground. "They'll sit and wait until we're gone, then skin out. Our best hope is now. Under cloak of darkness."

"And they won't expect us to attack again," said Butler.

"Frontal assault is suicide," Dodge said.

"Agreed." Butler squat down and traced outlines in the dirt. "Here are your orders."

Dodge said nothing as Butler laid out his plan of attack. He was an arrogant, fat bastard, but his idea seemed sound.

Tiny, Dodge, and I would swing around the garrison and position ourselves at the south face. Butler and Hickok would find cover near the main gate and open fire. The attack at their front door would draw the Rebs' attention, we hoped, leaving us to scale the wall and attack from inside.

The wind died and the night grew quiet. Our footfalls sounded painfully loud. I was certain the Rebs on the wall heard every step and waited for a clear shot. Gunfire sounded from inside. I could hear laughing and singing.

Closer to the wall, I could hear Major Falkner shouting. His muddy accent was gone. In its place was the tenor drawl of a southerner. He cursed at somebody. Glass shattered and he cursed some more. I pictured him hurling a whiskey bottle some arrogant Rebel had used for a toast.

We stood flat against the wall as the attack began. I heard the bustle inside, as startled Rebs scurried to find their weapons and join the battle.

Big Tiny stooped low and cupped his hands around the sole of my boot. He stood with a jerk and catapulted me to the top of the wall. I hunkered down, looking for trouble. There were no sentries. I could have stood full upright and not have been noticed.

I waved for Dodge to follow. Once up, Tiny jumped, grabbed the top of the wall, and hoisted his bulk with a soft grunt. The yard was empty. We dropped down inside without notice.

I took one step and tripped over something. It was the body of a Union soldier. Two more were lying close by. The shots we'd heard through the wall were probably these poor souls being executed. Falkner hadn't had time to transfer all the real Union men and needed to silence these three when our surprise attack began.

The air was warmer and close. The smell of gunpowder hung like fog. Thin moonlight gave everything a spectral glow or cast it in deep shadow. The only movement was along the front wall. Maybe two dozen men stood at the battlements and fired into the night. A handful of others scurried up ladders to join them. Some stayed on the ground, hoisting up boxes of ammunition or more weapons.

Dodge tugged at my arm and pointed to the center yard. The battery gun stood there, its six brass barrels gleaming. It was larger than I imagined, perhaps five feet long. It looked more artillery than rifle, mounted on its two-wheeled carriage, and impossibly heavy. Even resting silent, it was a powerful, intoxicating thing to behold.

I watched Dodge eye the prize. He walked toward it, trance-like, revolver lowered, as Falkner stepped from the shadows across the compound.

He was still dressed as a Union officer and it gave Dodge pause. He hesitated long enough for Falkner to raise his own pistol and fire. The shot missed and Dodge scurried for cover. He rose to return fire but Falkner was already at the battery gun, turning it with effort and taking aim at our position.

We heard the bullets blaze by before we heard the report, like so many fierce bees about our ears. Short bursts of flame erupted from each barrel as it rotated into position. Every round served to shred what little cover, besides darkness, we could find.

Dodge hit the ground. Tiny and I hunkered behind wagons and barrels. Falkner kept turning the crank, sending more shots toward us than I ever thought possible.

The men on the wall ceased fire. They turned to see Falkner blasting the ultimate weapon into the shadows, cutting the night air with round after round after round.

Two or three more soldiers fell from the wall as Butler and Hickok took advantage of their distraction. It was enough to turn Falkner's attention. Dodge stood and fired.

He missed.

I don't know how Dodge survived. Bullets pockmarked the ground at his feet and the wall behind us, but he lived through it to dive for cover beside me. "I won't die huddled behind a crate of rations," Dodge said, wheezing slightly. He pointed for Big Tiny to make his way down the wall to our left. "You move right," he said to me. "When I signal, we stand at once and holler out loud."

"He can only shoot at one of us," I said.

Once in position, Dodge gave the sign and we jumped up shooting and shouting. Falkner hesitated, uncertain where to turn.

Dodge's shot hit Falkner in the shoulder, knocking him back a step. Blood ran from the left breast of his tunic. His chest heaved as if he couldn't catch a breath.

My bullet struck his head. He recoiled for an instant, then a broad smile covered his face. He stuck his tongue out to taste the blood that poured down his cheek. He laughed and fell to the ground.

Dodge and I reached the battery gun in a second or two. Tiny crouched just outside the line of shadow, giving us covering fire.

"Help me," Dodge said, straining his thin arms to aim the weapon against the front wall. It was a monstrous thing to move, but we shouldered it into position. Dodge's face held no expression as he grasped the crank.

The reports were louder than I imagined, like lying on a piece of lumber as someone pounded nails just beside your ear.

The Rebels were dead in seconds. Some cried out. Some merely collapsed to their knees, then fell to the ground ten feet below. Some had the strength to take aim but Dodge fired again and the battle was over.

The battery gun gave off a pungent odor of heat and spent powder. Shining in the moonlight, I found it strangely beautiful.

"LOYAL AMERICANS," GENERAL Butler said, pointing to the battery gun now sitting in the center of town, "I give you peace, through superior firepower." His boast was met with modest cheers from the townspeople gathered in a circle. They stood around it, studied it from all angles, as the escort from Kansas City mounted it to a team of horses.

Butler and Dodge took turns speaking to the crowd. Gatling and I stood back quite some distance, passing a flask between us.

"What are they saying about it?" Gatling asked me.

"Some are scratching their heads, wondering how such a funny-looking thing could win a war."

Gatling chuckled. "I'm sure they doubt the damned thing works."

"It works," I said. I took a long pull from the flask.

Butler patted the barrel of the war machine as he might pet a dog.

"Upsets the balance, doesn't it?"

"Not yet."

"How can you stop them? It's in their hands."

"Just the prototype."

"They'll order more."

"They'll never get them. I'll burn the factory down if I have to. That should preserve the balance."

I handed the flask back to Gatling. "Your fatal error, you know, was offering it to the army in the first place."

Gatling's face turned red. His hands shook as he took a drink. "I had no choice."

"But you opened yourself to people like Butler. And Falkner."

"Major Falkner was a good man. A patriot. He would have restored balance if I couldn't." He raised the flask, as if in toast. "You're a good man, as well, Sheriff. A man of partiality and discretion?"

"The balance has been tipped, Doctor. Indiscretion now would do nothing."

"Thank you," said Gatling with a relieved smile. He offered me one last drink from his flask but I refused. "To your safety," he said, "in dangerous times."

We shook hands and parted. The entourage left town a few minutes later. General Butler led the parade. General Dodge and Hickok brought up the rear. They were content, it appeared, to converse over cigars.

I SAW TO it that all the fallen men, Rebel and Union, were given a Christian burial. The dirt walls of the garrison helped fill their graves. Prairie grass soon covered the bare patch of earth that was Fort Brown, restoring the balance of an unbroken Kansas plain.

The Victim

Ed Gorman

Spur-winner Ed Gorman notes that he came to the western form when he was four or five years old. "This was back in the war years when Roy was becoming King and Gene was starting to fade. Thanks to Republic and Monogram movies on Saturday afternoons and an obsession with Masked Rider comic books, I was hooked for good. Then in the fifties I discovered Luke Short; *Gunsmoke; Have Gun, Will Travel;* and *Maverick.* Hooked for life at that point."

I SUPPOSE EVERYBODY in this part of the territory has a Jim Hornaday story to tell. See, you knew right away who I was talking about, didn't you? The gunfighter who accidentally killed a six-year-old girl during a gun battle in the middle of the street? Jim Hornaday. Wasn't his fault, really. The little girl had strayed out from the general store without anybody inside noticing her—and Hornaday had just been shot in his gun hand, making his own shots go wild—so, when he fired . . .

Well, like I said, the first couple shots went wild and those were the ones that killed the little girl. Hornaday managed to kill the other gunfighter too, but by then nobody cared much.

There was a wake for the girl, and Hornaday was there. And there was a funeral, and Hornaday was there, too. He even asked the parents if he could be at graveside and after some reluctance they agreed. They could see that Hornaday was seriously aggrieved over what he'd done.

That was the last time I saw Jim Hornaday for five years, that day at the funeral of my first cousin, Charity McReady. I was fourteen years old on that chilly bright October morning and caught between grieving for Charity and keeping my eyes fixed on Hornaday, who was just about the most famous gunfighter the territory had ever produced. When I spent all those hours down by the creek practicing with my old Remington .36—so old it had paper cartridges instead of metal ones—that's who I always was in my mind's eye: Jim Hornaday, the gunfighter who always carried a Colt Dragoon revolver with the silver stars on the grips, just the way he'd had it specially made at the factory. He believed that having a custom-made gun was good luck.

I killed my first man when I was nineteen. That statement is a lot more dramatic than the facts warrant. I was in a livery and saddling my mount in the back when I heard some commotion up front. A couple of drunken gamblers were arguing about the charges with the colored man who worked there. You could see they didn't much care about the money. They were just having a good time pushing the colored man back and forth between them. Whenever he'd fall down, dizzy from being shoved so hard, one of them would kick him in the ribs. For eleven in the morning, they'd had more than their fill of territory whiskey.

Now even though my father proudly wore the gray in the Civil War, I didn't hold with anybody being bullied, no matter what his color. I leaned down and helped the colored man to his feet. He was old and arthritic and scared. I brushed off his ragged sweater and then said to the gamblers, who were all fussed up in some kind of Edwardian-cut coats and golden silk vests, "You men pay him what you owe."

They laughed and I wasn't surprised. The baby face I have will always be with me. Even if I lived to be Gramp's age of eighty-six, there'll still be some boy in my pug nose and freckled cheeks. And my body wasn't any more imposing. I was short and still on the scrawny side for one thing and, for another, there was my limp, dating back to the time when I'd been training a cow pony that fell on me. I'd have the limp just as long as I'd have the baby face.

The taller of the two gamblers went for his Colt, worn gunfighter-low on his right hip, and before I could think about it in any conscious way, I was drawing down on him, and putting two bullets into his chest before he had a chance to put two in mine. As for his friend, I spun around and pushed my own Colt in his face. He dropped his gun.

I asked the colored man to go get the local law and he nodded but, before he left, he came over and said, nodding to the man dead at my feet, "I don't think you know who he is."

"I guess I don't."

"Ray Billings."

Took me really till the law came to really understand what I'd done. Ray Billings was a gunfighter mentioned just about as often as Jim Hornaday by the dreamy young boys and weary old lawmen who kept up on this sort of thing. The law, in the rotund shape of a town marshal who looked as if he were faster with a fork than a six-shooter, stared down at Billings and then looked up at me, smiling. "I do believe you're going to be famous, son. I do believe you are."

He was right.

Over the next six months I became somebody named Andy Donnelly, and not the Andy Donnelly I grew up being—the one who'd liked to slide down the haystacks and fish in the fast blue creeks and dream about Marian Parke when he closed his eyes at night, Marian being the prettiest girl in our one-room schoolhouse. This new Andy Donnelly, the one that a bunch of hack journalists had created, was very different from the old one I'd known. According to the tales, the new Andy Donnelly had survived eleven gunfights (three was the true number), had escaped from six jails (when, in fact, I'd never been in a jail in my life), and was feared by the fastest guns in the territory, Jim Hornaday included.

All of this caught up with me in a town named Drago, where I had hoped nobody would know me. I was two hours past the *DRAGO WELCOMES STRANGERS* sign, and one hour on my hot dusty hotel bed, when a knock came and a female voice said, "I'd like to talk to you a minute, Mister Donnelly."

By now, I knew that a man with a reputation for gunfighting didn't dare answer a knock the normal way. Propped up against the back of the bed, I grabbed my Winchester, aimed it dead center at the door, and said, "Come in."

She was pretty enough in her city clothes of buff blue linen and taffeta, and her exorbitant picture hat with the fancy blue ribbon. She was wise enough to keep her hands in easy and steady sight.

"Say it plain."

"Say what plain, Mister Donnelly? I'm Patience Falkner, by the way."

"Say why you're looking for me. And say it plain."

She didn't hesitate. "Because," she said, all blue, blue eyes and yellow hair the color of September straw, "I want you to kill him."

"Him. Who's him?"

"Why, Jim Hornaday, of course. Isn't that why you came to Drago? Because you knew he was here? I mean, he killed your poor little cousin. You're not going to stand for that are you, an honorable man like yourself?"

I smiled. "You don't give a damn about my cousin. You're one of them."

"I think I've been insulted. 'One of them' . . . meaning what?"

"You damned well have been insulted," I said.

I swung my body and my Winchester off the bed, went over to the bureau where I poured water from a pitcher into a pan. The water was warm but I washed up anyway, face and neck, arms and hands. I grabbed one of two cotton work shirts and put it on.

"You know how old you look, Mister Donnelly?"

I turned, faced her, not wanting to hear about my baby face, a subject that had long ago sickened me. "What did he do to you? That's why you want me to kill him. Not for my little cousin . . . but for you. So what did he do to you, anyway?"

"I don't think that's any of your business."

"You don't, huh?" I said, strapping on my holster and gun. "He shoot up your house last night or something, did he? Or maybe you think he cheated your little brother at cards . . . or insulted your father at the saloon the other night. Last town I was in, somebody wanted me to draw down on this gunfighter because the gunny wouldn't pay his hotel bill. Turned out the guy who wanted to see me fight was the desk clerk at the hotel . . . figured I'd do his work for him." I shook my head. "Lots of people have lots of different reasons for us gunnies to shoot each other. Now, are you going to tell me your reason or not?"

I didn't make it easy for her. I slid on my flat-crowned hat and went out the door.

She followed me down the stairs, talking. "Well, I probably shouldn't tell you this but . . . well, he won't marry me. And he gave me his word and everything."

I smiled again. "And you want me to kill him for that?"

"Well, maybe my honor doesn't mean much to you," she said, out of breath as she tried to keep up with me descending the steps, "but it means a lot to me."

Down in the lobby, a lot of people were watching us. I said, "You're right about one thing, lady. Your honor doesn't mean one damn thing to me. Not one damn thing."

I walked away, leaving her there with the smirks and the sneers of the old codgers who sit all day long in the lobby, drifting on the sad and worn last days of their lives.

PATIENCE FALKNER WASN'T the only one who told me that Jim Hornaday was in the town of Drago. There was the barber, the bootblack, the banker, and the twitchy little man at the billiard parlor—all just wanting me to know he was here, just in case I wanted to, well, you know, sort of draw down on him, as they all got nervously around to saying. Seems this fine town had never been the site of a major gunfight before and—just as Patience Falkner had her honor at stake—Drago had honor, too. They'd be right proud to bury whichever of us lost the gunfight. Right proud.

I was on my way to the saloon—being in dusty need of a beer—when a man said, "Wait a minute. I want to talk to you when I'm done here." He stood on the edge of the boardwalk. He had been busy jabbing his finger into another man's chest. He was a stout man in a white Stetson, a blue suit, and a considerable silver badge. After he got my attention, he turned back to the man he'd been arguing with.

"Lem, how many damned times I got to tell you about that horse of yours, anyway?"

Horse and owner both looked suitably guilty, their heads dropped down.

"You know we got an ordinance here . . . any horse that damages a tree, the owner gets fined one hundred dollars. Now, I've warned you and warned you and warned you . . . but this time I'm gonna fine you. You understand?"

The farmer whose horse had apparently knocked down the angled young sapling to the right of the animal looked as if somebody had hit him in the stomach. Hard. "I can't afford no one hundred dollars, Sheriff."

"You can pay it off at ten dollars a month. Now you get Clyde here the hell out of town and keep him out of town."

"Don't seem right, folks fining other folks like that. God made us all equal, didn't He?"

"He made us equal, but He didn't make all of us smart. Fella lets his horse knock down the same tree three times in one month . . . that sure don't say much for brains . . . horse or man." He had an impish grin, the sheriff, and he looked right up at the horse and said, "Now, Clyde, you get that damned dumb owner of yours the hell out of here, all right?"

The farmer allowed himself a long moment of sullenness, then took the big paint down the long, narrow road leading out of town.

"Looks like you were headed to the saloon," the sheriff said. "So was I." He put his hand out. "Patterson, Deke Patterson. I already know who you are, Mister Donnelly." Then the impish grin again. "You look even younger than they say you do."

Inside, I had had two sips of my beer when Patterson leaned and said, "I need to be honest with you, Mister Donnelly."

"Oh?"

"I grew up with Jim Hornaday over in what's now Nebraska. He's my best friend."

"I see."

"I wouldn't want to see him die."

I smiled. "Then you're the only one in Drago."

He laughed. "I saw Patience headed over to your hotel.

She tell you they were engaged and then he broke it off?"

"Uh-huh."

"And she asked you to kill him?"

"Uh-huh."

"She tell you why he broke it off?"

"Uh-uh."

"Because he walked along the river one night and there on a blanket he found Patience and this traveling salesman. Sounds like an off-color joke, but it wasn't. Old Jim took it pretty hard."

"Don't blame him," I shrugged. "But it's no different in any other town. People always have their own reasons for wanting you to fight somebody."

The grin. "You mean, in addition to just liking to see blood and death in the middle of Main Street?"

"Sounds like you don't think much of people."

"Not the side of people I see, I don't." He had some more beer and then looked around. On a weekday afternoon, the saloon held long shadows and silent roulette wheels and a barkeep who was yawning. Patterson suddenly looked right at me. There was no impish grin now. All his toughness, which was considerable, was in his brown eyes. "He's hoping you kill him."

"What?"

Patterson nodded. "He's never been the same since he accidentally killed that little cousin of yours. For a long time, he couldn't sleep nights. He just kept seeing her face. That's when he took up the bottle and it's been downhill since. He keeps getting in gunfights, hoping somebody'll kill him. That's what he really wants . . . death. He won't admit it, maybe not even to himself, but the way he pushes himself into gun battles when he's been drinking . . . well, somebody's bound to kill him sooner or later. And I know that's what he wants because he can't get your little cousin out of his mind."

"I didn't come here to kill him, Sheriff. My reputation is made up. I got forced into three fights and won them, but I'm not a gunfighter. I'm really not."

He regarded me silently for a long moment and then said, with an air of relief, "I do believe you're telling me the truth, Mister Donnelly."

"I sure am. I didn't even know Hornaday was here."

"Then you don't blame him for killing your little cousin?"

"Some of my kin do, but I don't. It was accidental. It was terrible she died but nobody meant for her to die."

He asked the barkeep for two more beers. "One more thing, Mister Donnelly."

"You could always call me Donny."

"One more thing, then, Donny. And this won't be easy if you've got any pride, and I suspect you do. He's gonna try and goal you into a fight, but you can't let him. Because the condition he's in . . . the whiskey and all. . . ."

I stopped him. "I don't have that much pride, Sheriff. I don't want to kill Hornaday. Sounds like he's doing a good job of it himself, anyway."

We talked about the town and how it probably wasn't a good thing for me to stay much past tomorrow morning, and then I drifted back to my hotel and my room and there he sat on my bed, a man with an angular face marked with chicken pox from his youth. These days, he resembled a preacher, black suit and hat and starched white shirt. Only the brocaded red vest hinted at the man's festive side. He'd never been known to turn down a drink, that was for sure.

"You're her cousin?"

"I am."

"And you know who I am?"

"Yes, I do, Mister Hornaday."

"I killed her."

"I know."

"I didn't mean to kill her."

"I know that, too."

"And I'm told you came here to kill me."

"That part you got wrong, Mister Hornaday."

"You didn't come here to kill me?"

"No, I didn't, Mister Hornaday."

"Maybe you're not as good as they say, then."

"No, I'm not, Mister Hornaday, and I don't want to be, either. I want to be a happy, normal man. Not a gunfighter."

"That's what I wanted to be once." His dark gaze moved from me to the window where the dusty town appeared below. "A happy, normal man." He looked back at me. "You should want to avenge her, you know."

"It was a long time ago."

"Ten years, two months, one week, and two days."

If I hadn't believed he was obsessed with killing poor little Charity before, I sure did now.

"It was an accident, Mister Hornaday."

"That what her mother says?"

"I guess not."

"Or her father?"

"No, he doesn't think it was an accident, either."

"But you do, huh?"

"I do and so do most other people who saw it."

He got up from the bed, the springs squeaking. His spurs chinked loudly in the silence. He came two feet from me and stopped.

The backhand came from nowhere. He not only rocked me, he blinded me momentarily too. He wasn't a big man, Hornaday, but he was a strong and quick one.

"That make you want to kill me?"

"No, sir."

He drove a fist deep into my stomach. I wanted to vomit. "How about that?"

I couldn't speak. Just shook my head.

He took a gold railroad watch from the pocket of his brocaded vest. "I'll be in the street an hour and a half from now. Five o'clock sharp. You be there, too, you understand me?"

He didn't wait for a reply. He left, spurs still chinking as he walked heavily down the hallway, and then down the stairs.

The next hour I packed my war bag and tried to figure which direction I'd be heading out. There was always cattle work in Kansas and right now Kansas sounded good, a place where nobody had ever heard of me, a place I should have gone instead of coming here.

I was just getting ready to leave the room when I heard the gunfire from down the street. A nervous silence followed and then shouts—near as loud as the gunfire itself—filled the air. I could hear people's feet slapping against the dusty street as they ran in the direction of the gun shots.

I leaned out the window, trying to see what was going on. A crowd had ringed the small one-story adobe building with *SHERIFF* on a sign above the front door. A man in a brown suit carrying a Gladstone bag came running from the east. The crowd parted immediately, letting him through. He had to be a doctor. Nobody else would have gotten that kind of quick respect, not even a lawman.

I was turning back to the door when somebody knocked. Patience Falkner said, "Did you hear what happened?"

"Why don't you come in and tell me."

She didn't look so pretty or well kempt anymore and I felt a kind of pity for her. Whatever had happened, it took all her vanity and poise away. She looked tired and ten years older than she had earlier this morning.

"Jim killed Sheriff Patterson."

"What?"

She nodded, sniffling back tears. "The two best friends that ever were." She glanced away and then back at me and said, "I should have my tongue cut out for what I said to you this morning. I don't want Jim dead. I love him."

She was in my arms before I knew it, warm of flesh and grief, sobbing. "I wasn't true to him. That's why he wouldn't marry me. It was all my fault. I never should've asked you to kill him for me. And now he's killed the sheriff. . . . They'll kill Jim, won't they?"

There was no point in lying. "I expect they will. Why'd he kill him, anyway?"

She leaned back and looked at me. I thought she might say something about my baby face. "You. You were what they were fighting about. Jim told Patterson that he'd called you out for five this afternoon. Patterson told him to call it off but Jim wouldn't. Jim was drinking and angry and Patterson gave him a shove and . . . Jim took his gun out and they wrestled for it and it went off. Jim didn't mean to kill him but . . ."

"Where is he now?"

"Nobody knows. Ran out the back door of the jail."

I shook my head. This was a town I just plain wanted out of. I eased her from my arms, picked up my Winchester and war bag, and walked to the door.

"You're leaving town?"

"I am."

"Then . . . then you're not going to fight him?"

"No, ma'am, I'm not."

"Oh, thank God . . . thank you, mister. Thank you very much."

"But if you're going to say goodbye to him, you better find him before that crowd does."

Even from here I sensed that the crowd was becoming a mob. Pretty soon there would be liquor, and soon after that talk of lynching. The territory prided itself on being civilized. But it wasn't that civilized. Not yet, anyway.

I'd paid a day in advance so I went down the back stairs of the hotel. The livery was a block straight down the alley. I paid the stocky blacksmith with some silver and then walked back through the sweet-sour hay-and-manure smells of the barn to where my mount was waiting to be saddled.

I went right to it, not wanting to be detained in any way. Kansas sounded better and better. I had just finished cinching her up when somebody said, "You probably heard I killed the sheriff, Donnelly. He was my best friend."

The voice was harsh with liquor. I turned slowly from the mount and said, "Little girls and best friends, Hornaday. Not a record to be proud of."

"I didn't say anything about being proud, cowboy. I didn't say anything about being proud at all."

The men in front had overheard our conversation and had walked through the barn shadow to get here quickly. There were three of them. They were joined moments later by Patience Falkner.

"Jim . . . " she started to say.

But his scowl silenced her.

We stood in the fading light of the dying day, just outside a small rope corral where the six horses inside looked utterly indifferent to the fate of all human beings present. Couldn't say I blamed them. Hornaday eased the right corner of his black coat back so he could get at his gun quick and easy.

"Even if you don't draw, cowboy, I'm going to draw and kill you right on the spot. That's a promise."

"I don't want this fight, Hornaday."

"What if I told you I killed that cousin of yours on purpose?"

"I wouldn't believe you."

"I killed my best friend, didn't I?"

"That could have been accidental, too."

By now there were twenty people filling the barn door, standing in the deep slice of late-afternoon shadow.

"You've got to fight me," Hornaday said. "A reputation like yours . . ."

"You need to get yourself sober, Hornaday. You need to take a different look at things."

"I'm counting to three," Hornaday said.

"Like I said, Hornaday, I don't want this."

"One."

"Hornaday . . ."

"Two."

"Jim, please . . ." the Falkner woman cried. "Please, Jim . . ."

But then he did just what he'd promised. Feinted to his right, scooped out his six-shooter, and aimed right at me. What choice did I have?

I was all pure instinct by then. Scooping out my own gun, aiming right at him, listening to the shots bark on the quiet end of the day. His knees went and then his whole body, a heap suddenly on the dusty earth. Nobody moved or spoke.

I just stood there and watched Patience Falkner flutter over to him and awkwardly cradle him and then sob with such force that I knew he had just died.

The blacksmith went over and picked up Hornaday's Colt Dragoon, which had fallen a few feet away. He picked it up, looked it over. He'd probably talk all night at the saloon how strange it felt holding the same gun Jim Hornaday had used to kill all those men.

Then he said, "I'll be dagged."

"What is it?" I said.

The blacksmith glanced around at the curious crowd and then walked the gun over to me.

"Looks like you performed an execution here today, mister," the liveryman said.

He handed me the Colt Dragoon. All six chambers were empty. Jim Hornaday had fought me without bullets.

They got the Falkner woman to her feet and led her sobbing away, and then the mortician brought his wagon and they loaded up the body and by then the deputy sheriff had finished all his questions of the crowd and me, so I was up on my roan and riding off. I tried hard not to think about Hornaday and how I'd helped him commit suicide. I tried real hard.

Slicing Through Ninety-Two Pages of New Testament

Tom Piccirilli

Tom Piccirilli is the author of nine novels, including his first western, *Grave Men.* His short work has appeared in the anthologies *Best of the American West II, Desperadoes,* and *Boot Hill.* Tom lives in Estes Park, Colorado, where he's currently at work on a second western novel entitled *Coffin Blues.*

A BRIMSTONE PREACHER named Deed had decided to make trouble for Miss Patty.

He'd been out there in front of the parlor house for an hour already in the late-afternoon sun. Priest had been watching him the whole time, enjoying the show. Deed wore a black frock coat and flat-top Stetson, and actually did thump his Bible now and again. His voice carried to the rooftops on the burning wind, and he knew how to position himself just right so that his exhorting would echo up the street and catch the attention of passersby. His words had a slight twang and snapped hard against his teeth. Oklahoma. Maybe Kansas.

Deed's fury over such open vice worked him over like the current of a river, jouncing and flinging him down in the dust. Sometimes it was like dancing, and his bony knees nearly reached his chin. Other times he kneeled and swung an accusing finger around, pointing out faces in the crowd, laying shame and doom. Once he pointed at Priest, and there were some mutters and whispers. It was nothing new.

Lamarr loved Miss Patty, and many other ladies of the house too, but he couldn't help himself from joining in. Singing high unto the Lord and listening to the ministry in the fields had been about the only thing that had kept him and his people alive on the plantation. Even with Miss Patty scowling at him through the front window, every so often Lamarr kicked in with a "Praise Jesus!"

All the Christian Ladies' Coalition needed to fire them up was a protest against some form of wickedness in Patience. Soon twenty-five women marched with Deed in front of the whorehouse. They scurried across the street and made prune-faces, reciting scripture and peering gravely at their frightened husbands, who cowered outside the ring.

Watching Lamarr swinging about and swaying, you'd never guess he was closing in on fifty. He looked a little dangerous jumping around like that with the red sash tied around his waist and the two Navy .36 revolvers tucked at the small of his back, but nobody else appeared to mind much. His hair was fringed with a touch of gray but his smooth, shining dark face and beaming white smile made him seem like a child. Priest was twenty-three and had a shock of silver hair in front that hung in his eyes, and he looked older than Lamarr.

Several patrons still tried to make it inside, but no man likes to be pointed out and railed at. Miners, merchants, cowpunchers, hardheads, and harlot-chasers frowned at Lamarr. Some crossed the street anyway.

Lamarr stood abashed. "Hold on now, I was just giving some love up to the Lord. I didn't mean for Miss Patty to lose any business."

Priest said, "Looks like a lot of fellas are going to have to give up their love tonight too."

"Now that just makes me feel bad."

"Bet it makes them feel a lot worse."

"Can't see any help for it now."

Priest couldn't see any either. "If you had any intention of spending a few late-night hours with that Lorelei you've been mentioning, I'd say you can forget it."

"Well, that just ain't fair! I done took me a bath today."

"Damn waste of water."

"At least I didn't go and squander any soap too." Pawing his chin, Lamarr came up with an idea that brightened his face. "You go on in there and get Miss Patty to simmer down some."

"Hell no!"

"Just remember, she leads with her left. Keep your hands up."

"She always gets in under my guard."

"She's got good footwork too. And watch out she don't kick you in your personables."

Shadows crept forward as evening came on. Patty glanced out the window again and Priest caught her eyes. Her draping black hair framed her face in a way that made him think of the lost mornings when she'd turn over in his arms and smile up at him just after dawn in back of the livery. The memory almost chased him down but he came back to himself when he realized she was actually fogging the pane, panting, worried. She played with one curl, twisting it through her fingers. He hadn't seen her like this since they were kids.

There was a new buzz up at the corner. Heads turned and folks drifted away. Deed moved toward it angrily as if he wanted to fight whatever was stealing his audience. Priest stepped toward the latest commotion, knowing what it was, what it had to be. He'd been expecting Gramps for a week now.

Somebody laughed and others stared at Priest as he shouldered his way through the throng. That was all right. Many thought he was cracked; the rest were afraid. Most of the time it worked out.

Gramps was back from White Mountain. He'd been up there with Chicorah's people for a couple of months now. But he could only handle it so long, pretending to be somebody else, and then the rest of his whole white life pushed back through. When he started calling out his long-dead wife's name, Chicorah knew it was time to get him off the rez and send him back home before the old man started scaring their children.

Gramps had started to go white again, but he hadn't gotten all the Apache out of himself yet. He still wore his breechcloth, curled under the trough. Deed kneeled beside him, placed his palms on Gramps's forehead, trying to get Jesus in or the *Ga'ns* mountain spirits out. Priest was hoping that maybe it would work. Gramps moaned in Apache and occasionally groaned Grandmother's name, "Ethel, Ethel." But after about twenty minutes Deed got tired of laying his hands on Gramps, and Priest couldn't blame him for that.

Another hymn began and he heard Lamarr's bass kick in. Priest lifted Gramps into his arms and carried him back down the block and up Miss Patty's steps.

Deed had followed. He reached out and grabbed Priest's shoulder firmly, digging in the hard and cracked yellow nails. "Brother, your soul is in jeopardy."

So, it was going to be like that. "Thanks for the warning."

"If you want the old man's demons cast out you need to bring him into a church, not a house of ill repute."

"They're not demons."

"What?"

"According to Chicorah, the son of an Apache subchief, my grandfather is blessed with *Ga'ns* mountain spirits."

"And you?"

"Yes, me too."

"No, I meant, do you actually believe what a heathen savage might say about your immortal souls?"

"Sure," Priest said.

Deed's gaze had taken on a flinty inflexible edge, with the hint of a smile lacing his lips. A ripple passed over his face and Priest got a glimpse beyond the sermonizing act. He didn't like what he saw in there.

For the first time Priest considered the preacher closely. Deed had large cloudy eyes with a trace of fire and lightning in them. His fingers were long and the color of bone, and he still hadn't let go of Priest's shoulder. Tufts of white-blond hair stuck out from beneath the hat at ugly angles. Shadows continued to twine among the porch railings and across the men's legs. Lamarr and the ladies were halfway through "My Heart to Thee, My Shepherd." Lamarr was good at harmonizing and really hit the low notes well. The ripple stirred along Deed's face again and brought on an appearance of concern. His eyes had already reverted to the holy, grim love of a fanatic.

"Well, well," Priest said. "So, what's your game?"

"Now, brother, the righteous path is difficult to find, and even more arduous to walk, but the path can be shown to you. Let me guide—"

"No use back-stepping at this point."

The hint of that mischievous grin came back. "I suppose not." Deed didn't much mind being seen through at this point, and that worried Priest. He kept searching for the flame in Deed's eyes, but it was gone now. He wanted to know what it meant. Priest knew it was going to get somebody hurt and he tried not to sigh.

Gramps gave a snort in his sleep, and finally Priest remembered he was holding the old man. Deed clucked his tongue and said, "Tell Patty that Cousin Josiah says hello."

"Sure."

"And I'll be around to pay a call on her soon."

"I see."

The smarmy expression came out then, oozing like oil, and Deed tilted back his head, squinting. "I know about you and her, from way back. I suggest you keep out of this one affair."

"Thanks for that warning too."

"Call it what you like," Deed said. "Just so you listen."

"Uh-huh."

"Or suffer the outcome."

"By the way," Priest told him, "have all the fun out here in the street that you want, but if you give her any trouble, just so you know, I'll have to put you down."

"My pards and I might take you up on that challenge."

"Call it what you like."

Priest turned to go and Deed tightened his grip, about to say something else, opening his mouth to put on a real show and call Jehovah out of the sky. Priest spun and let one of Gramps's knobby knees rap Deed in the jaw, knocking him back down the steps with a snort.

It gave him some satisfaction, and his grandfather seemed to like it too. In his sleep, Gramps smiled. Deed's long coat had opened. He wore a long-barreled Schofield in a greased, open-end swivel holster on his left hip. Slick and sly, he liked the trick shot. Deed wiped blood from his bottom lip, buttoned his coat again, and backed off into the street where the Christian ladies fluttered around him, cooing.

Priest stood in the doorway another minute, thinking on what had just happened, before he grabbed the handle. Lamarr quickly followed him inside and said, "Baby Jesus seen what you done to that preacher, and I bet he ain't too happy 'bout it."

"Me and baby Jesus haven't been on speaking terms in years," Priest admitted as the whores and their men wheeled past him, shrieking with laughter.

FAT JIM WAS playing the piano wildly, bouncing up out of his seat as usual. He weighed a hundred and five pounds and barely came up to the shoulder of most of the girls. His cigar spewed ash all over and tobacco juice ran down his stubbled chin. He looked a little touched banging at the keys like that, trying so hard to drown out Deed and the Christian ladies outside as the night came on.

The main parlor was just beginning to clear as the folks retired upstairs for baths and a final glass of wine before the finer points of the business began. A lot of other men were just leaving, having begged off work an hour or two early and now needing to return home. Those remaining shuffled backwards out of the way as Priest carried Gramps in. Lamarr found Lorelei tending bar and he proceeded toward her, cutting off a bank manager who was explaining principal, interest, and dividend exclusion to anybody who might listen. The banker cocked his chin when he saw the two Navy .36 revolvers tucked into Lamarr's sash but he kept right on talking.

Wainwright, the houseman, stood six feet five, in the neighborhood of three hundred pounds. He had a natural inclination to hunch forward a little, with those massive arms hanging at his sides. There was something of the animal in him, but he always remained respectful, polite, and quiet. Priest had never heard him speak above a whisper, not even when he was breaking somebody's arms. When Wainwright sat in his enormous wrought-iron chair, he seemed as much a part of the house as the walls or the ceiling. The houseman said, "The old man's room is occupied at the moment. There will be clean sheets on the bed in about a half hour."

Priest put Gramps down on a divan. He expected Patty to still be holding vigil at the front window, but she wasn't there anymore. That bothered him too. "Tell Patty I need to talk to her now."

"I'm not sure she wants to see you."

That stopped him. "Say again?"

"It has something to do with the preacher. And you. She's stared down marshals, judges, ministers, angry wives, and mothers-in-law without so much as turning a shade of pink. Today's about the first I've ever seen her unnerved."

"Go find her, and tell Fat Jim to lay off the action so we can clear the parlor."

"Your sweaty naked grandfather pretty much did that on his own." Wainwright shambled off in search of the mistress of the house.

Already this wasn't working out too well. Priest didn't completely understand why he'd given orders or why Wainwright had taken them. A very ugly image lay just out of sight, and he felt that if he kept moving fast enough he might avoid having to ever look at it.

Lamarr overheard Wainwright talking to Fat Jim and allowed Lorelei to usher the banker upstairs. He gazed after her as she glided up the steps, trying hard not to leer or grimace as her curves came out in full, and failing on all accounts. He glanced at Priest and said, "And you thought you felt bad before."

"My misery deepens but I shall endure."

"You and me both."

The big room was empty and the chandeliers had begun to sway.

IT TOOK FIVE minutes for Wainwright to return with Miss Patty. They both appeared angry and hurt. Patty also looked tired and nervous. The beautiful lines extending from the corners of her nose to the corners of her mouth were dark trenches. She seemed to be sneering even though she wasn't.

Priest felt as if something or someone—perhaps the teenage boy he'd been—stood just behind his left shoulder trying to get his attention. He purposefully ignored it.

"Go on home," Patty told him. In this light, with the sun nearly gone, her hair caught the color of her blue petticoats.

She backhanded a curl off her forehead, showing off the cool pale angle of her neck and perfect rose O of her lips. The burr in her voice scratched at him. It sounded almost like resentment, except Patty didn't have it in her to ever get jealous.

"What's the matter with you?"

"Nothing I can't handle." She poured herself a bourbon and didn't offer any around. Wainwright receded into the shadows at the far end of the room, sat in his iron chair, and didn't appear to be listening. Patty had another drink, sinking into a chair, and Priest understood what she was attempting to draw out of the bottle. He'd tried it for five years. "Now do what I said, Priest McClaren. Go on home."

"Sure," he said. "Just answer me first."

She hadn't so much as set eyes on him yet, so Priest slid his hand out across the black lacquer-top table until it rested beside the shot glass. She set her lips and looked into his face. "That bastard's my cousin. Wired me for money a couple of weeks back."

"Maybe you should've given it to him."

"I did, just so he'd keep away. Now he's grudging that I'm flush, and he wants to cut himself into my business. Claims it's the least I can do for the last living member of my family."

Priest's chest continued to tighten. He was certain she wasn't lying, but there was a lot more there he wasn't being told, and he felt surprised and a little betrayed that Patty had never mentioned this cousin before. When they were sixteen they'd planned on marrying—before her miner father had been blown up at the bottom of a shaft while checking dynamite charges, and before Priest's parents had been murdered and he'd taken to the bottle.

Lamarr did his best to lessen the friction. "He'll have to do a whole lot more'a that hellfire preaching to close your doors, Patty!"

"That's what's got me worried. He's planning something. He wants to rob the ladies from the pulpit on Sundays and get a kicker from the house every week." Then she realized who she was talking to and the red anger flooded her cheeks. "And you! Don't you dare say anything to me, you dancing turncoat Judas!"

"But, Miss Patty! I was just singin'!"

"I'll come over there and give you something to sing about!"

"Not my personables!"

Priest said, "Deed wears an open-end swivel holster. Schofield."

Lamarr smiled, letting it out inch by inch as his teeth flashed. He liked the idea of taking Deed down, now that God had been betrayed. "Tricky, this voice of the Lord. Goes for the sneak shot when he's sittin' having a parlay. Schofield is too long to draw quick, but easy to aim out the bottom."

"He mentioned having partners," Priest said.

Patty had rallied now. She set the bourbon aside and had overcome, at least for the moment, whatever it was that had been trying to shove Priest away. "The only ones he ever ran with were two swindlers named Lane Gruber and Foley Longstreet."

"Gruber?" Lamarr lifted his chin a little and nodded to himself, clucking a little, as if he'd just gotten a long and involving joke told a while back. "Gruber. Lane Gruber. If it's the same one, and why would there ever be two, I ask, then he was a captain during the war."

"I don't know about that," Patty said, "but I suppose he'd be the right age."

"He ran under Bragg. Met some of his men in late November '63, in Chattanooga. They had the heights commanding the supply lines, but in three days we drove 'em out. His tough times must've only started there if he's runnin' with a swindling preacher nowadays."

The action would keep to a minimum until midnight, when the poker players and drunks would begin to steadily stroll in. Deed and his pards would show up sometime before then.

"He'll come tonight," Priest said. "To sniff around."

"I don't owe him a thing," she said. There was a tremble in her voice that resonated within him, far down where she was still a girl lying in the shadow of the saguaro with him, where they'd made love in the dust. Priest glanced up and stared into her eyes and knew with a cold and precise knowledge that he was going to have to kill Deed. "He owes me."

He'd never heard anything like that come alive within her before, not when her mother ran off, not even when her father had been blown to pieces. Priest could feel the aching under his heart come alive again with a ridiculous swiftness. The image started to catch up to him again. He was slowing down, he had to move.

From the divan, Gramps said quite distinctly, "Put your knife away."

Priest looked down to check. He wasn't holding his knife. Priest turned to say something back to the old man, but Gramps was already asleep again, breathing in bites and sweating heavily, hissing in Apache.

He carried his grandfather upstairs and put him to bed in a room that Patty kept set aside for the old man. The sheets were clean. A heated breeze brushed against his throat. Priest leaned against the open window and watched the traffic in the street. There was a shouting in the distance. A full moon tonight burned over the desert. Gramps's frail bronze, leathery chest had a sheen on it that glinted like blood. His clothes were in a suitcase under the bed. In the morning he'd probably be white again, get dressed and light his pipe and flirt with the girls, forgetting that he'd ever been up on the rez scaring the hell out of the Indian children.

There wasn't anything else to do but wait. Priest was almost out the door when Gramps whispered, "Give me your knife." Then he muttered something else in Apache.

Priest looked down.

He was holding his knife, blazing insanely in the moonlight and in his mind.

NO USE FIGHTING it any longer. The pictures caught up with him and kicked around the inside of his skull, and it felt better letting them in than it had keeping them out.

Priest wasn't sure why he wanted to be left alone with Deed. Why he wanted him and Lamarr to be left alone with Deed and his pards, but for some reason it was important even if it made the job harder. Since the day that the hulking Wainwright had become houseman, he'd never left his post. He'd never taken a vacation or asked for time off or not shown up when he was supposed to. Priest wanted him to leave now.

And Patty too. He kept looking at her across the table, and she at him. She'd suddenly quit avoiding his eyes. Their gazes locked and tangled and fluttered aside. Perhaps they were both embarrassed by feelings and events that were already five years gone. He couldn't shake off the sense that his ego, in some way, had been wounded. Before today he hadn't thought he had much pride left anymore, but there it was.

The tension kept growing within him, and the familiar frenzy and pain was almost comforting in a way. It calmed him down. One of these days he'd have to dwell on that some and figure out just what was wrong with himself.

In the meantime he decided to ride it out. He turned to Wainwright and said, "I want you to take her upstairs."

"Now, wait—" Patty protested.

Wainwright had heard everything and understood it all. "Certainly. If you need any help, just holler."

"Sure."

Priest was again amazed that a man who looked so much like an animal could be so clear in his thinking. Wainwright knew blood was coming, and it was his duty to protect Miss Patty and the ladies. As a friend, he allowed Priest to follow his course.

"You want I should go too?" Lamarr asked, trying to be helpful. "I fear Lorelei ain't being quite as satisfied as she might be, that poor darlin'."

"Are you men talking about me as if I'm not here?" Patty asked, her voice breaking down the middle. She grabbed the neck of the bourbon bottle until her knuckles cracked, ready to smash it into somebody's nose. "I've got to say that you boys have shown me a fair amount of discourtesy so far today. I reckon I won't put up with any more of it."

He stood and she did too. Patty stepped closer, her shoulders dappled with sweat. She brought her lips nearer, and nearer still until he almost leaned in toward her, expecting that familiar taste again. That's how it once was.

She flashed him those dimples that, as always, made his entrails buck. He spun to one side, hoping she didn't notice how he flinched.

"Go upstairs."

"This is my place, Priest McClaren. Nobody tells me what to do in it."

They could go around like this for a couple of hours, but Priest didn't have it in him. "Just go," he said.

"Why?"

"I've got a thing or two I'd like to talk to Deed about."

"His real name isn't Deed, it's—"

"I don't care."

She touched the side of his face, and he turned his mouth to her palm but didn't kiss it. "You pick the damnedest times to play the fanciful romantic, you headstrong fool."

Priest thought about it for a moment and realized it was true. He wanted to add something but there wasn't anything else to say, so he simply watched as she stormed up the steps followed by Wainwright, whose bulk filled the stairway and blotted out the lamplight.

LAMARR AND PRIEST sat in the parlor, playing cards. Three stragglers wandered in over the course of the next hour, all pretty drunk, and Priest didn't need to do much more than turn them around and give a push to set them back on their way again.

Someone directly overhead on the second floor let out a high-pitched cry of jubilation that surged into a shriek. It sounded very painful. Lamarr said, "That'd be the right proper work of Lorelei we're hearing."

"Any chance that banker she's with will live through the night?"

"Don't think she's lost one yet. Take an ax handle to beat the smile off that jasper's face tomorrow. She got natural God-given talent, Lorelei does."

The banker let out another shrill squeal that was met by an undulating feminine scream. The screeching went on like that for a while until it made Priest wince.

"She sounds pretty satisfied to me," he said.

"Goddamn. And here I was feelin' sorry for her."

"I've got a question."

"No," Lamarr told him. "I ain't never got her to make that there noise, and there's no need to rub my nose in it."

"That's not my question."

"Oh, well, all right then."

"Why do you carry a Confederate gun?" Priest asked.

"I'm from Georgia, after all."

"You fought for the Union."

"Well, I was a slave, after all."

Lamarr drew his revolver and handed it to Priest.

Although it had been converted, the pistol was a real 1851 Navy .36 and not one of the Southern Navy revolvers with brass components produced by the Confederacy when steel became hard to obtain. It was light, less than three pounds, and well-balanced. It was the first time Priest had ever held the gun, and he enjoyed how it sat in his hand. No wonder it was the most common model used during the war. Southern arms manufacturers copied them more easily than the .44.

"Cavalry horsemen favored it," Lamarr said. "Worn by General George Custer hisself."

"Didn't help him much at Little Bighorn."

"I reckon I won't argue that particular point. Also worn by the Prince of Pistoleers, ole Wild Bill. He never did convert to cartridge, though."

Priest almost didn't want to let the gun go, but he handed it back as the aggressive noise of heavy boot steps filled the porch. Deed came with his pards. Two hardcases in almost the exact same serge frock coats and brocade vests, carrying bibles and strapped with pistols, also playing the preacher game but nowhere near as good as Deed did. It was now late enough and dark enough that they could come to the house without arousing any real suspicion from the rest of the town.

They fanned out and silently checked the alcoves and peered up the stairwell, ignoring Priest and Lamarr at the table. When they were satisfied there would be no ambush the three closed ranks again and approached.

Lamarr didn't drop his smile but looked at Deed with a genuine hatred. "At least they ain't dressed like Spanish monks. Now that would've just been plain blasphemous."

"I don't talk to underlings," Deed said. "Call Patty down or I'll go look for her."

Priest went to the bar and got four glasses. He set the bottle of bourbon in the center of the table and handed the glasses out. "She's here, but you can deal with me for the moment."

"Like I just told you—"

"Sit and have a toot first. Then we'll take care of business. If we can't struggle through to an understanding, then she can work out the finer details with you."

Deed considered the proposal and let it ride. He noticed Priest didn't have a glass and said, "You're not having one? I'd have to say that's mighty unfriendly of you."

"Don't take it personal," Priest said. "I spent five years smelling like mash liquor and crawling naked through pig shit."

"It's true," Lamarr said, and it was. The first time they'd met had been when Lamarr had pulled him out of a hog sty. "Even the pigs used to keep away from him. You never seen such scared hogs."

Priest watched the three newcomers sit and drink. They were lookalikes. They had the same sort of hands—long, bony, and pale-fingered. Deed kept hold of his Bible, tight to his chest, but the others had put theirs down. All three had near-white blond hair worn way too short, cut with a dull straight razor, prison-style. They'd run together for so long that they'd taken on the same stern expressions and mannerisms. Captain Gruber stood out a little more because of his age, maybe twenty years older than the other two, but sun and chain gangs had evened them all out some.

"Where's all them girls you been telling us about?" Longstreet asked.

"Busy, I hope," Deed said. "Making money."

Gruber had a saber scar that twisted out from beneath his collar and up to his left ear, surely a memento of his days riding under Bragg. By chance he'd happened to sit beside Lamarr and it clearly bothered the hell out of him. Lamarr kept the smile eased out, really putting his all into it, even showing off his back teeth now. Gruber tried not to shy away as he frowned. "You in the war?"

A soldier could pick a soldier out of a room full of men. "For a fair while," Lamarr said.

"Kill lots of Rebs?"

"Only the ones who whistled Dixie at me."

"Let me tell you," Gruber said, facing into the brilliant

white of Lamarr's smile. "My granddaddy was a plantation owner."

"That right?"

"Yep. Owned fifty slaves. The goddamnedest herd of black folks you ever done met. Animals, really. Some straight from Aferca."

"Never been there myself."

Gruber had a practiced glare and he tried to wither Lamarr with it now. Gruber's breath hissed from his nose, with his back teeth clicking as he settled deeper in his seat. He kept the glare going until the edges of his eyes began to water.

Lamarr kept beaming and said, "What was your granddaddy's name? Maybe I knew the man."

Lamarr had been born and grown on a Georgia plantation owned by a man called Thompson, his mother only fifteen years older than him. Lamarr worked the fields until he was seventeen and finally strangled Thompson, and he took his time doing it, first choking the master with his left fist and then his right, making it last a good long while.

"You know what the trouble with niggers is?" Gruber asked.

"I'd be beholden to you if you told me."

"They don't know when they got it good."

"That might be true. When I used to get whipped and salted, I almost never realized how good I had it."

"Yep, that's the way of it."

"Bet you striped a black back or three in your time."

"To be sure I done that some too. Right down to the bone."

"Enough of the good old days," Deed put in, leaning forward toward Priest. He still clutched the bible tightly to himself. "Let's talk business. Patty and I are kin, the only kin we got left."

"That's important," Priest said, and he meant it.

"We're blood. There isn't anything as important as blood."

"I agree with you."

"She owes me and I'm here to collect what I've got due."

Priest knew a lot about the significance of family. But hearing Deed sound so sincere even while the greed dripped in his voice made Priest's scalp prickle.

"I'm coming back every week for half the house profits. She either pays me or I'll preach each day out front, all day long, and gather my congregation and drive her out of town."

"Seems to me blood wouldn't do that to blood."

"Don't you believe it."

Priest tried not to sigh and said, "I don't, really."

"If she doesn't give me what I want then my righteous wrath will descend on this house."

Priest's hand flashed out. He grabbed the Bible so quickly that Deed continued to hold his hand to his chest as if he were still carrying the book. It wasn't until Priest flicked through the pages that Deed realized it was gone. Deed thrust his seat from the table and sat there blinking and sort of growling. His pards joined in. Gruber and Longstreet drew their guns on Priest and Lamarr, who waited calmly. Gruber carried a Smith & Wesson .38 pocket model. Longstreet held an ugly little revolver that looked hammered together from junk.

"What kind of gun is this?" Lamarr asked.

Longstreet didn't answer so Priest said, "It's a Pepperbox."

He'd seen one before, a long time ago. A .31 five-shot revolving percussion Pepperbox pistol. It had five tightly ringed rifle barrels, with a ring cocking trigger lever and a separate trigger for firing. Double-action bar hammer. All five barrels pulled forward on a hinged breech. The walnut grips had an engraved floral scroll. It was a screw barrel pistol, much more powerful than muzzle-loading ones. It looked like the kind of pistol snappy civilians would favor until it blew up in their hands. It was a stupid gun for stupid men.

Gruber held the .38 almost to Lamarr's temple. "I could put a bullet in your eye but I'd rather see you swing on a tree. That's what we do with uppity niggers where I come from."

"Well, I come from that same place, and I 'spect you ain't seen nary any uppitiness yet."

Deed's swivel-holster was greased but he hadn't used it in a while. There was a tiny squeak as he moved it on his hip, aiming under the black-lacquer table at Priest's belly.

He was so sure the trick would work that he reclined a little lazily in the seat now, stretching out.

Overhead, another cry undulated, keening wildly like a vulture's screech. The banker must've woken up and still been randy enough for another go. Lorelei moaned and wailed herself, making some heart-wrenching sobs.

"What's that?" Longstreet asked.

Lamarr turned to Priest and said, "Damn, maybe that poor bastard ain't gonna make it till mornin'. That Lorelei, sometimes she don't know when to stop."

"Maybe you ought to be glad you never got her to make that noise. Sounds like it could be one's undoing."

"She got this little wriggle she uses."

"That right?" Priest asked.

"It is. She sorta gets snaky."

"It saddens my heart to learn I might've gone my whole life without knowing that fact."

"Shut up!" Gruber shouted. "You two get on your knees and crawl. When that whore finds what's left of you she'll know not to fool with us no more."

"It's just a cheap show!" Longstreet said. He kept looking toward the ceiling. "They're scairt! It's a trick. There's gotta be somebody else here watchin' us."

"That'd be baby Jesus," Lamarr said, "and he don't like what he sees."

Priest said, "You three can leave town and play your game elsewhere. If you go now."

"It's no game for me," Deed said, grinning. "Nor for you, son. You got the hurt look of a man who comes home and finds out his wife's been keeping the bed warm with somebody else. Patty owns a cathouse—what've you been thinking, that she's got a lily-white pure heart?" Deed let the venom out, spewing it. "You want to know, don't you? You got suspicions but you want me to say it, don't you?"

"No," Priest said.

"Well, I'll tell you anyways—I had her! I had her good. I was her first. Long before you, boy! So I took her in a shed when she was twelve, she still would've been set on this course. I started her on her way, and you helped her further along down the path."

Those cloudy eyes lit with that lightning once more.

Maybe it was madness, maybe just a reflection off one of the pistols. But again Priest understood with an intense clarity that he had to kill Deed. It sharpened his vision to such an extent that he felt as if the world had abruptly gone black and white.

Priest felt the moment coming, but he had to wait for Gruber to move his pistol from Lamarr's head. Lamarr knew he had to do something and said to Gruber, "If you're really set on a lynching, I got some rope out back. Wait here and I'll go get it." He stood and Gruber actually did a little hop to get out of the way. And there it was.

The trick shot was nothing without surprise. Priest hurled the Bible at Deed's face. The book caught Deed flush in the nose and sent him falling over backwards in his chair. He managed to get a shot off with the Schofield, but Priest was already gone. Longstreet had been looking at the ceiling, listening to the cries, and only now lowered his eyes. Gruber didn't know who to watch anymore and hesitated in pointing the Smith & Wesson anywhere. Lamarr drew both of his Navy .36s from his sash and fired directly into each of Gruber's thighs.

Longstreet was coming around, aiming the Pepperbox at Priest's chest. That was all right. Priest had the knife out and held it by the blade, swinging the pommel down into the hinged breech of the Pepperbox. He struck it as hard as he could. All five shots went off at once in a tinny burst of metal and smoke. Longstreet screamed as the shrapnel tore his fist wide open and blew off two fingers. He took one look at the shards of burst knuckles sticking up through his flesh and passed out.

Deed wanted to take another shot from the floor but he couldn't get the swivel to swing to the correct angle, and he'd played the trick for so long that he didn't even think of actually drawing the gun. Gruber thrashed in agony and rolled over the preacher, leaking and splashing blood everywhere.

Lamarr said, "See there, Captain. Now that's uppity!"

Whatever else he might be missing, Gruber didn't lack for scorn. He managed to swallow down enough of the pain to get some words out. "You're a damn fool, nigger," Gruber said. "If you don't kill me I'll just keep coming back, and one of them times I'll get you on the hanging tree. And I'll be whistling Dixie when I do it."

"The nasty fact is that I believe you, Captain," Lamarr said, and shot him in the head.

Deed took it in stride, perhaps the way a man who actually believed in heaven might. He stood and didn't even bother to glance at his fallen pards. "I want to see Patty."

"Sorry, Cousin Josiah," Priest said. "But she doesn't want to see you."

"I'll get what's mine!"

"Sure."

"I shall be—"

They both looked up together to see a shadow unfurling from the darkness at the head of the stairs, rising now and lunging forward. Gramps gave a coyote wail war cry. He came down the steps three at a time and snarled at Priest in Apache. Priest had a pretty good idea what Gramps wanted. He flipped the knife up, and the old man caught it in midair as he leaped upon Deed. The preacher let out a cry to God and hit the floor hard, with Gramps crouched over him grunting and wheezing, as the blade wove gently against the flesh of his throat.

They waited like that for a while. Finally Deed whispered through his clenched teeth, "What's this crazy bastard want?"

Priest said, "I think he's mad that you tried to get rid of his *Ga'ns* spirits. Or maybe it's just the spirits themselves that are angry."

"Jesus, you're as sick in the head as he is."

"Maybe you should apologize to him and the mountain ghosts."

"You and your ghosts can all go to hell."

Gramps backed away, hissing and gesturing with his hands. He even pointed at Lamarr, who had tossed his guns on the table and sat there drinking with his feet up. Like Lamarr, Gramps or the spirits had decided to leave whatever vengeance was left to Priest.

Deed understood it too, and chuckled as he got up and brushed himself off. Here he was, facing a man armed with only a knife. Over there, a buck drinking in a chair without his guns. An insane naked old man barking and yelping.

There was righteous wrath to be had. Deed spun the long-barreled pistol in its swivel holster.

Priest hurled the Bible in the same instant as Gramps threw him the knife. The book flapped open as it hit Deed's chest, and the soft crinkling of pages was like a whisper of forgiveness in the night. The book wasn't open to the center, but further toward the back where the New Testament taught absolution and mercy, none of that eye for an eye. Time was running out already, the book about to fall, the open-ended holster angling up toward Priest's belly. The black mouth of the barrel appeared through the bottom of the leather.

Priest remembered his mother's prayers, the eulogy for Patty's father, the lectures and brimstone accusations, and the torrent of grief that followed him into and out of church. The book was moving now, beginning to drop. Deed's lips started to creep, maybe into a smile, maybe not. Priest didn't really care.

He drove the blade cleanly through the Bible, and continued to thrust it deep into Deed's heart.

A WEEK LATER, Patty found him preaching in a hog pen to a sounder of pigs about to be butchered.

Wainwright carried him back to the house and put him to bed upstairs in Gramps's room. She stayed with him the entire time wiping sweat out of his eyes, spoon-feeding him stew, and cleaning up his mess until he could keep some food down. He didn't remember talking to the sheriff or having spent a couple of nights in jail until everything had been cleared.

Gramps came to visit him once, dressed in a nice suit with a bow tie and suspenders, smoking his pipe. They didn't talk about much, and wound up just sitting there enjoying each other's company for a bit.

After two full days in bed Priest still hadn't completely dried out. He awoke late in the night, the room almost completely dark, and Patty was there beside him.

"There wasn't a reason in the world for you to have done what you did," she said. He didn't know if she meant killing Deed or preaching to the pigs, so he kept quiet.

"You don't love me, you know. Not anymore."

Priest's voice was still raw from the whiskey, and he didn't recognize it as his own. "You and I, we're as good as blood."

"Yes."

"That's all that matters then. The rest—it'll sort itself out or it won't."

"I heard him shouting. He told you awful things. They were true, but they were awful."

"Worse for you than for me."

"I'm not sure about that. I locked what happened—what he did—away from me. You couldn't."

"No."

She whirled away then, her petticoats flapping, hair a jumble of shadow in a deeper darkness. He heard the tears falling from her chin and striking the floor. As she drifted out the door she said, "Thank you."

It wasn't until he threw the sheets aside that he realized she had laid a bible on his pillow, alongside his knife. He picked them both up, weighing each carefully, one in each hand, and stayed like that until the sun's rays began to light up the pages, and the edge of the blade shone back at him with his own face.

Deadlock

James Reasoner

James Reasoner is the bestselling author of the *Civil War Battles* series, published by Cumberland House, and the World War II series *The Last Good War*, published by Forge Books. A professional writer for over twenty years, he has authored many western and historical novels and twice has been nominated for the Spur Award by the Western Writers of America. He lives in Texas with his wife, western and mystery writer L. J. Washburn.

THE MOBS STARTED from opposite ends of the street. The thickset man on the Appaloosa was in the middle, having entered the town on a cross street. He looked one way, then the other. A few men in each crowd carried torches. Angry muttering filled the air.

The stranger's right hand brushed aside the long duster he wore. He unhooked the rawhide thong over the hammer of the LeMat revolver holstered on his hip. Then he swung down from the saddle, not hurrying, and looped the Appaloosa's reins over the hitch rack in front of the sheriff's office.

The office door opened, and a white-haired man stepped out onto the boardwalk. He had a shotgun in his hands and a tin star pinned to his vest. He pointed the Greener at the stranger and said, "Who the hell are you?"

"Name's Earl," the stranger said. He was middle-aged,

medium height, with a neatly trimmed salt-and-pepper beard that was tending more to salt these days.

The mobs were still on their collision course, each of them only a couple of blocks away from the sheriff's office. The lawman asked the stranger, "You got any part in this?"

"Nope," Earl said. "I just rode into town."

"You'd better take your horse, then, and get out of here, mister. Lead's going to be flying pretty soon."

"After a prisoner, are they?"

"That's right."

Earl reached up to his saddle and slid a Winchester from its sheath. "I'll side you, Sheriff."

The lawman's eyes were bright with fear, even in the shadows of the awning over the boardwalk. "What?"

"I stand with the law," Earl said as he stepped onto the boardwalk. He moved so that he was at the sheriff's left shoulder as he turned to face the street.

Each of the mobs came to a stop, leaving the space directly in front of the sheriff's office open. If they opened up on each other, the street would become a killing ground.

Earl heard the sheriff swallow, then the lawman raised his voice and said, "You boys might as well go on home. Thorp's locked up good and tight, and that's where he's going to stay."

"You can forget that, Sheriff," one of the men in the forefront of the mob to the left called out. "The boy's comin' with us!"

"The hell he is!" That shout came from one of the leaders of the other mob. "That murdering little bastard's going to hang! We're going to see to that right now. He won't cheat the gallows again!"

Earl's eyes went from one group to the other, studying them. The men to the left were cowhands, dressed in range clothes and broad-brimmed hats. Those to the right were townspeople: a mixture of businessmen, storekeepers, and the like, including one burly fellow who was probably the blacksmith.

Everybody on both sides had a gun, or at least so it seemed.

The sides were drawn evenly. The cowboys probably had more experience with their weapons, but the townspeople couldn't be discounted. A man had to have sand in his craw to live out here on the frontier, even in a settlement.

"Nobody is taking the law into his own hands!" the sheriff said. "The Thorp boy's going to get a fair trial. There's a circuit judge on his way here right now."

"We don't need to wait for a judge," the spokesman for the townspeople said. "Everybody knows Thorp is guilty. We say string him up right now!"

The man who spoke for the cowboys said, "You do that and you'll have a war on your hands, Calder. The old man'll wipe this town off the face of the earth if anything happens to his boy! He's comin' back to the ranch with us."

The two sides surged a little closer together, and a faint whiff of powder smoke seemed to be present in the air already, as if to warn of what was about to happen. The sheriff glanced over at Earl and asked, "You sure you want to be part of this?"

"Don't have any choice now," Earl said. "I'm standing in the middle."

The sheriff made one more attempt to reason with the mobs. "If you boys will just listen to reason and wait for the judge—"

"To hell with the judge!" one of the cowboys yelled.

That was just about enough, Earl decided. He stepped forward, surprising a startled "Hey!" out of the sheriff. He shifted the Winchester to his left hand and used his right to pull the LeMat. It was a .42-caliber revolver that packed nine shots in its cylinder instead of the more common six. In addition to that, the cylinder revolved on an axis that also functioned as a smooth-bore barrel where a shotgun shell containing buckshot was loaded. A flick of the thumb against the hammer pivoted the striker to fire the buckshot. A favorite weapon of Confederate officers during the war, the LeMat was known as the grapeshot revolver, and at close quarters the load from the shotgun barrel would blow a man almost in half.

Earl had carried this LeMat for years. It was like a part of his hand. Everyone saw it plainly as he stepped to the edge of the boardwalk and said in a loud, clear voice, "You don't have to wait for the judge. He's already here."

That quieted some of the muttering and blustering from

the crowd. The spokesman for the townspeople said, "What?"

"I'm Judge Earl Stark."

Disbelief was tangible in the air. In duster, Stetson, bib-front shirt, denim trousers, and well-worn boots, Earl Stark looked more like a grubline rider than a jurist. But then, from the back of the crowd, someone said, "Damn! He must be the one they call Big Earl."

The sheriff looked over at him with slitted eyes. "Is that true?"

Stark nodded. "I used to answer to that name, all right." He turned his attention back to the opposing mobs. "If you're all bound and determined to shoot each other up, wait until the sheriff and I go back inside to do it. But no matter what happens out here, the prisoner stays in his cell, and he goes on trial tomorrow morning at nine o'clock. Anybody who tries to interfere with that will be held in contempt of court."

He lifted the LeMat slightly.

The sheriff added his voice to Stark's. "You heard the judge! Break it up! Rance, you take the boys back out to Thorp's ranch. Calder, you send your people home."

A lot of grumbling and complaining came from the crowds, but Stark saw men on the edges of each mob start to drift away. He knew that was all it would take. In a matter of minutes, both groups had dispersed like smoke in the wind, heading back toward their respective ends of town.

The sheriff heaved a sigh. "I thought there'd be gunplay for sure." He looked at Stark. "Are you really the judge?"

"That I am," said Stark. "Let's go inside and bolt that door."

THE SHERIFF'S NAME was Dave Fulton. He had worn a badge for a long time, in a variety of Western towns. This was as prickly a problem as he'd ever faced, though, he told Stark over cups of coffee from the battered pot staying warm on the cast-iron stove in the corner of the office.

"Jud Thorp's been the he-wolf of this country for almost thirty years," Fulton said. "He came out here before the war, when there wasn't anything except prickly pear and Comanche and Apache. Naturally, he thinks the whole valley is his, including the town."

"But the settlers don't see it that way," Stark said. He had taken off his hat, revealing thinning dark hair, and hung up his duster.

"No, of course not. They figured when they moved in and started the town, there'd be law and order. The West is tamed, to hear them tell it."

"I wouldn't go so far as to say that."

"Me neither, and I'm the one they elected to keep the peace. I've done a pretty good job of it, if I do say so myself. But then Billy Thorp grew up and decided he was going to be a gunman."

Stark shook his head. "Kids."

"Yeah. There's a hand who rides for old Jud, name of Bennett. It's said Bennett used to be good with a gun. Billy got him to teach him how to draw and shoot."

Stark thought that over, then said, "Devlin Bennett?"

"I've heard him called Dev, so I reckon it's the same man."

"Bennett fought in several range wars up in Wyoming and Montana. He's good, all right. Past his prime, maybe, but he wouldn't have lived this long if he couldn't take care of himself."

"Well, I wish he'd stayed the hell out of West Texas," Fulton said. "He got Billy Thorp believing that he's a gunfighter, too, and it wasn't long before Billy had to go out and prove it."

"He killed a man?"

Fulton shrugged. "Fair fight, so they say. Billy prodded the fella into drawing first, though. Otherwise it wouldn't have happened. Then it happened again, and again after that. That time, folks got after me to arrest him and put a stop to it. Before I had a chance to, Jud Thorp came in with that girl of his and Ranse Albin, his foreman, and Jud told me all of Billy's killings had been self-defense. Said he wouldn't stand for Billy being arrested." Fulton's hands wrapped around his coffee cup and tightened. "Thing of it is, technically all those fights were fair. I might've had a talk with Billy and tried to put the fear of God into him, but I couldn't have arrested him. The way Jud made it look, though, by coming into town and lighting into me like that, everybody thought he'd laid down the law to me and that I was knuckling under to him. Billy must've thought that, too. He went too far next time."

"Who did he kill?" Stark asked.

"A young fella named Sam Woodson. Clerked over at Calder's General Store. As nice a youngster as you'd ever want to meet, and he had a pretty young wife and a baby, too. He was loading a bag of flour into a wagon for a customer, and Billy Thorp came along and tripped him. Sam fell down and busted that bag, got flour all over him. I guess he looked pretty ridiculous, all right. Folks on the street were laughing at him. He was mad, but I reckon he would have got over it. Then he reached under the apron he was wearing—and Billy Thorp pulled a gun and shot him. Claimed he thought Sam was going for a gun." Fulton looked down at the desk, and his voice shook a little as he went on, "Turned out Sam had a little pinwheel in his pocket, a toy he was going to take home to his kid. Best I can figure it, he was checking to see if he'd broken it when he fell down, and that's when Billy Thorp shot him. Drilled him plumb center. Sam was dead when he hit the ground."

Stark let the hush set in the room for a moment after Fulton finished speaking. Then he said, "So you arrested Thorp this time."

"Of course I did. It was nothing but cold-blooded murder."

"Did you take him peaceable?"

"No, I had to lay a gun barrel alongside his head when I found him in the Spur Saloon a little while later. He wasn't expecting it. I reckon his pa had told him he didn't have anything to worry about from me."

Stark heard the anger and pain in Fulton's voice. The sheriff prided himself on being a good lawman. He had to be asking himself if he really had knuckled under to Jud Thorp. He had to wonder if Sam Woodson would still be alive, had he taken a harder line with Billy Thorp earlier.

Stark couldn't answer those questions, but he could see that justice was carried out legally. That was what he intended to do. He stood up from his chair and said, "I'd like to take a look at the prisoner."

"Sure." Fulton got up and snagged a ring of keys from a nail in the wall. He went over and unlocked the door to the cell block behind the office.

Fulton lit a lantern that sat on a stool in the aisle between the two rows of cells. Only one of the cells was occupied at the moment. The young man lying on the bunk inside it was maybe twenty years old, with curly brown hair and a wisp of a mustache. Just a kid, thought Stark, and he had already killed four men, the last of them in cold blood.

Billy Thorp swung his legs off the bunk and sat up. He stared at Stark and said, "Who're you?"

"Judge Earl Stark. I'll be presiding at your trial tomorrow."

Billy's eyes widened. A muscle jumped in his jaw. He was scared, Stark saw. He had reason to be.

"I heard a commotion outside a while ago. What happened? Was it a lynch mob?"

"Part of it. A group of townspeople wanted to string you up. But your father's foreman and a bunch of the ranch hands came in to take you out of jail. Neither side got what they wanted. You're still standing trial in the morning."

Billy leaned his elbows on his thighs and put his head in his hands. "I thought Woodson was reaching for a gun, I swear I did. I swear it!"

"Court's the place to talk about that," Stark said. "Better get some sleep." He turned and walked out of the cell block. Sheriff Fulton blew out the lantern and followed him. The cell block door shut with a solid, heavy sound.

"It's a hell of a deal," Fulton said when he and Stark were back in the office. "I wish somebody had taken that kid in hand besides Bennett."

"Right about now, he's probably wishing that, too," Stark said.

STARK RECOGNIZED THE man waiting for him in the lobby of the hotel. Not by name or by face, but by type. The man was a newspaper reporter. Stark had seen the same eager expression on the faces of countless other men over the past few years, ever since he'd been named a circuit court judge.

"Judge Stark," the man said as he got up from the chair where he'd been sitting, "my name is Simon Foster. I'm the editor and publisher of the *Star.* Do you mind if I ask you a few questions?"

"I had in mind renting a room and getting some rest."

"This will only take a few minutes."

Stark knew it never did any good to argue with the press. They'd just print whatever they wanted to, whether it was true or not. It was better to at least try to get the facts straight.

"All right," he said, "but let's sit down. I've had a long ride to get here."

He had made sure the Appaloosa was bedded down properly in the livery stable, then come over here to the hotel. Now he sat down in one of the lobby's upholstered armchairs and placed his hat on his knee.

Foster drew up another chair and took a pad of paper and a pencil out of his coat pocket. "You *are* the judge they call Big Earl, isn't that correct?"

"No, they call me Judge Stark. I answered to Big Earl back in the days when I was working as a shotgun guard on the old Butterfield stage line."

"That was before you became a lawyer?"

"A mite," Stark said, his tone dry.

"If I remember the story correctly, you educated yourself in the law by reading a set of books left behind on one of the stagecoaches."

Stark nodded. "Well enough to pass the bar, anyway."

"And you had a successful career as an attorney until you were appointed to the judgeship you now hold?"

"That's right."

"Yet you still . . . no offense, your honor . . . but you could still pass for a stagecoach guard."

"I'll take that as a compliment," Stark said. "Out here on the frontier, Mr. Foster, dispensing justice doesn't require some fancy get-up, just a good working knowledge of the law along with plenty of common sense and some grit. I like to think I've got all three of those things."

"Yes, of course. What do you think of the case that brings you here?"

Stark's eyes, permanently squinted by a life lived mostly in the open, narrowed even more as he said, "That's a matter for the trial, not for a newspaper article, Mr. Foster." He put his hands on his knees and pushed himself to his feet. "Now, if you'll excuse me . . ."

"Just one more question, Judge. Emotions are running very high on both sides of this dispute. Do you think there will be any violence connected with Billy Thorp's trial?"

Stark put his hand on the butt of the holstered LeMat. "Not in my courtroom," he said.

Then, as he turned away and the newspaperman could no longer see his face, he rolled his eyes. He was getting too damned good at making such dramatic pronouncements, he told himself. But those scribblers had to have *something* to put in their stories.

DESPITE WHAT HE'D told Simon Foster about not needing a fancy get-up, Stark *did* have a suit stowed away in his bedroll. He shook out the wrinkles in it the next morning and put it on, along with a white shirt and a string tie. He supposed he looked about as respectable as he was capable of looking as he walked into the town meeting hall where the trial would be held.

Sheriff Fulton had already set up a table to serve as the judge's bench, along with a table each for the prosecution and the defense. A dozen chairs along one wall provided seating for the jury. The rest of the room was filled with benches where the spectators would sit.

Quite a few of those benches were full already. Stark saw the man who had been leading the group of townspeople the night before. Fulton had called him Calder, Stark recalled, which probably meant he was the owner of Calder's General Store and had been the employer of the late Sam Woodson.

Stark strode to the front of the room and joined the sheriff behind the table. "Where's the prisoner?" Stark asked.

Fulton inclined his head toward a door in the back of the hall. "Got him locked up in a little room back there."

"Any windows in it?"

"Nope. And Thorp's got his hands cuffed and shackles on his legs. He's not going anywhere."

"Any problems last night?"

Fulton shook his head. "No, it was quiet. I reckon you put the fear of God in those folks, Judge. Or at least the fear of that LeMat you carry. I never saw one of those streetsweepers up close before."

Stark grunted and took the LeMat from its holster. He placed it on the table, then took a gavel from his coat pocket and laid it down beside the heavy revolver.

A commotion at the door of the hall made him look up. He saw a man being pushed into the building in a wheelchair. The man was broad-shouldered and had a rugged, weathered face topped by a shock of white hair under a broad-brimmed Stetson. He had an Indian blanket draped over his legs. Pushing the wheelchair was Ranse Albin, the spokesman for the group of cowboys that had come for Billy Thorp the previous night. Stark knew without asking that the man in the chair was Jud Thorp.

"That's the kid's pa," Fulton said, leaning close to Stark to confirm the judge's assumption.

A young woman came into the courtroom behind Jud Thorp and Ranse Albin. She was tall and slender, with hair the color of a sunset.

"Donna Preston," Fulton said. "The old man's ward. She was set to marry Billy Thorp, until he went wild."

"So young Thorp's not only on the verge of losing his freedom and maybe his life, but that girl, too. All for the thrill of pulling a gun."

"Damned foolish, ain't it?" said Fulton.

The room finished filling up. Stark nodded to the sheriff, who called out, "All rise!" Everyone came to their feet, with the exception of Jud Thorp.

Stark dropped his Stetson on the table, sat down, picked up the gavel, and rapped it sharply. "Court is now in session," he said. "Be seated." He looked at Fulton. "Bring in the prisoner, Sheriff."

Fulton went to the back room, unlocked the door, and went in to fetch Billy Thorp. The young man shuffled out. Fulton put a hand on his arm and kept it there until Billy was seated at the defense table, where a goateed man in a swallowtail coat was talking to Jud Thorp.

The man rose to his feet and said, "Everett Thurber for the defense, Your Honor."

"From Dallas?" Stark asked.

Thurber smiled, clearly pleased that Stark had heard of

him. "That is correct, Your Honor. I have the privilege of representing this fine young man."

That brought some grumbling from the side of the room where most of the townspeople were seated. The benches on the other side, behind the defense table, were filled with cowhands from Jud Thorp's ranch.

A slender young man with brown hair, spectacles, and a noticeable birthmark on his face sat at the prosecution table. He stood up and said, "Your Honor, I'm Franklin Lester, the county attorney. I'll be handling the prosecution."

Stark nodded. He had never heard of Lester and wondered just how many years the young man had been out of law school. Not many, Stark thought. He might have trouble with an old legal wolf like Everett Thurber.

It took only half an hour to swear in a jury, which, not surprisingly after the allotted challenges of the attorneys were used up, was composed of six men from the settlement and six cowboys. None of them worked for Jud Thorp but rode for smaller spreads in the area instead. Still, Stark didn't have a good feeling about how this was going to work out.

"I'll hear opening statements," he said when the jury was seated.

Franklin Lester came to his feet first and spoke for five minutes, briefly outlining the short, violent history of William Thorp and concluding with the killing of Sam Woodson. Then Lester sat down and Everett Thurber stood up. Thirty minutes later, Thurber was still on his feet, haranguing everyone within hearing distance about how poor Billy Thorp had been the victim of a tragic misunderstanding. His comments about how the town and its citizens mistreated the ranch folk who were responsible for the settlement's very existence brought cheers from the cowboys and catcalls from the townspeople, until Stark gaveled them all into silence and swept his stony glare across the room. Finally, Thurber wrapped up his opening statement and sat down with a sweep of his coattails.

"Call your first witness, Mr. Lester," Stark said.

The trial proceeded quickly. There had been half a dozen witnesses to the shooting of Sam Woodson. Franklin Lester called all of them and had them tell their stories. The testimony agreed on all the important points: Billy Thorp's tripping of young Woodson, the laughter, Woodson's anger, the reach under the apron, the shot . . . Everett Thurber's cross-examination couldn't shake any of the witnesses.

The prosecution rested. Stark was impressed with the job Lester had done, despite the county attorney's youth. Of course, it helped a lot to have the facts of the case on one's side.

To start the defense, Thurber pulled a small surprise. He called Sheriff Dave Fulton to the witness stand. Under Thurber's questioning, Fulton had no choice but to admit that all the other killings in which Billy Thorp had been involved were fair fights. Thorp had been able to claim self-defense in each of them, and he had never been arrested or charged with a crime.

Then Billy Thorp himself took the stand and testified that none of the previous incidents had been his fault. He had been picked on, he claimed, because he was the son of the wealthiest, most powerful rancher in the area and the townspeople took out their resentment toward his father on him instead.

"They kept drawing on me because they don't like us," Billy said, a catch in his voice. "They wanted to hurt my pa by killing me. But I was too fast for 'em. When . . . when Sam made his move, I thought he was going for an iron, too, like the others. I didn't have any choice. I had to defend myself."

The story almost rang true, Stark thought. Maybe Billy had even convinced himself that it *was* true. But the plain fact of the matter was that Billy Thorp had gunned down an unarmed man. There was no getting around that.

But when Thurber rested his case and the jury withdrew for its deliberations, Stark knew what was going to happen next. Sure enough, the jury came back in just after noon.

"The defendant will rise," Stark told Billy Thorp as the jury members settled down in their chairs. Stark looked at them and said, "How do you find?"

Two men popped up, one of the cowboys and one of the townies. They glared at each other, and the cowboy said, "I'm the foreman of this here jury."

"He is not, your honor," the townsman said. "I am."

Stark sighed. If they couldn't even agree on a foreman, he knew what to expect regarding the verdict. He pointed to the townsman and said, "You sit down." To the cowhand, he said, "You tell me the verdict."

"Well . . . we ain't got one, your honor. We chewed it over for a while, and fact is, nearly come to fisticuffs amongst ourselves, but we just can't decide. Half of us says Billy ought to be let go, and t'other half says he ought to hang."

Stark looked at the townsman who had stood up. "That agree with the way you see it?"

The man came to his feet again and nodded. "Yes, your honor. We're hopelessly deadlocked."

So, Stark thought. He had a hung jury on his hands. He picked up the gavel and said, "I hereby declare this a mistrial. The defendant will remain in custody of the sheriff, pending a new trial."

Which would likely come out the same, Stark thought, as long as the community was split down the middle as it was. He hesitated, waiting for Franklin Lester to jump up and move for a change of venue, a motion that Stark would have granted. That was probably the only way Billy Thorp would ever receive a fair trial.

But the county attorney remained seated, no doubt due to his inexperience, and finally Stark had no choice except to rap the gavel on the table and signal the end of the trial.

Before he could do that, Jud Thorp bellowed, "No! There ain't gonna be no new trial! The jury didn't find my boy guilty, so you got to let him go."

"It doesn't work that way, Mr. Thorp," Stark said. "This was a mistrial. It didn't actually find your son guilty or innocent."

"I don't care." Jud Thorp's hand came out from under the robe that was thrown across his withered legs. His fingers clutched the butt of a Colt revolver.

The instincts Stark had developed as a stagecoach guard were still there. The movement of his hand was almost too fast for the eye to follow as he dropped the gavel and snatched up the LeMat. As the barrel of the LeMat came up, Stark eased back the hammer, and suddenly he and

Thorp were staring at each other over the barrels of their guns.

"You let my boy go, Judge, or by God I'll kill you!"

"No!" Donna Preston said as she came to her feet and tried to move over toward the wheelchair. Ranse Albin caught hold of her arm, stopping her.

"Put that gun down, Mr. Thorp," Stark said. "You're just going to make a bad situation worse."

"The hell I will." Thorp's voice shook a little, but his hand was rock-steady. "I come into this country when there wasn't a blasted thing here worth havin', except for the grass. I made it so's folks could live here. I did! By God, this pissant little town wouldn't even be here if it wasn't for me, and now they say they're going to hang my boy!"

"He's a murderer," Calder said. "He's a cold-blooded killer, and you know it, Thorp."

"No!" That cry came from Billy Thorp. "I had to do it!"

Thorp ignored all of it. He had his gaze fixed on Stark, and there it stayed. "You let my boy go, Judge," he said again.

Slowly, Stark shook his head. "Sorry, Thorp. I just can't do it."

"I'll shoot!"

"So will I." Stark paused, then went on, "And so will the sheriff, and likely there's some other folks in here who have guns on them, even though they're not supposed to. There'll be bullets flying all over the room, Thorp. Could be your son will be hit, or Miss Preston. Is that what you want?"

"I want my boy!" Thorp said, but his voice shook even more now. "He's mine, damn it! He's all I got left of my wife!"

The tension in the hall was thick. Stark couldn't take his eyes off Thorp, but he knew that given the slightest chance, chaos would erupt in the room. The mobs from the night before were right here, ready to clash again. Stark had headed off one such riot, but it wouldn't be so easy this time. Emotions were running too high.

"All right," he said. "You're the bull of the woods, Thorp. You're used to getting your own way. We'll settle this, you and me. How about that?"

Thorp frowned. "What do you mean?"

"I mean everybody else gets out of here except the two of us. We'll have it out. If you win, you get Billy. If I win, the law gets him."

"That's crazy!" Sheriff Fulton said, belatedly adding, "Your honor." He went on, "You can't do that."

"I'm the judge here," Stark said. "I can do whatever I damn well please."

He could tell that Thorp was thinking about it. The rancher licked his lips.

With her arm still in the grip of Ranse Albin, Donna Preston said, "Pa Thorp's a cripple! It wouldn't be fair."

"Hush up, girl," Thorp said. "My legs may not work anymore, but my gun arm sure does."

"You put that Colt in your lap," Stark said, "and I'll put my LeMat on the table here. When the room's clear, we'll go for our guns. What do you say, Thorp?"

Thorp used his free hand to rub his white-stubbled jaw, then said, "Ranse, get Donna out of here. Take the boys with you."

Albin began, "Boss, you can't mean to—"

"Do what I told you! Get out!"

Donna Preston started thrashing and fighting as Ranse Albin pulled her toward the door. A couple of cowboys had to help the foreman get her out of the hall. The rest of them started filing out.

Stark said, "Sheriff, see that the townspeople are escorted out."

Fulton leaned close to Stark. "Judge, are you sure you want to do this?"

"I don't see any other way to settle it, do you?"

Franklin Lester cleared his throat. "Your honor, I object to this irregularity—"

"Overruled," Stark said. "This is the West, Mr. Lester. It gets a mite irregular every now and then."

Sheriff Fulton shook his head, then raised his voice to say, "Folks, you heard the judge. You have to get out of the courtroom now."

Calder tried to argue, but Fulton shushed him and prodded him out of the hall. The other citizens went after him, as reluctantly as the cowhands had done before them. The whole time, Stark and Thorp sat there staring at each other, guns leveled.

Everett Thurber put on a silk top hat, gave Stark a wry look, and said, "These are some of the oddest instructions from the bench I've ever heard, your honor, but I'll follow them." He went out.

Sheriff Fulton came back inside after all the townspeople were gone. Stark said, "Dave, I'm counting on you to keep the peace out there, no matter what happens in here."

Fulton nodded. "I sent Mr. Thorp's men down to the saloon, and Calder's bunch is gathered at his store. I'll do my best to keep 'em apart, Judge." He gestured at Billy Thorp, who still sat at the defense table, his arms and legs shackled. "What about him?"

"Take him back to the jail. Either Thorp or I will be over there in a little while."

"Judge . . ."

"Just do it, Sheriff," Stark said.

"Pa, please don't do this," Billy said as Fulton hauled him to his feet. "Don't get yourself killed on my account. I'm not worth it! I'm no good, Pa! You know that. I've never been any good."

"Shut your mouth, boy," Thorp said. "You're my son. That means you're worth any ten of these no-account, soft-handed townies. You go on with the sheriff now. I'll be over to get you in a little spell."

Fulton left the hall, taking the protesting Billy Thorp with him. That left Stark and Jud Thorp alone. Stark sighed. At least no one else would get killed in here. With any luck, now that they were alone, he could talk some sense into Thorp and prevent any bloodshed at all.

"All right, Thorp," Stark said. "We said we'd put our guns down."

Thorp's face was gray with strain. He lowered the Colt into his robe-covered lap. Stark followed suit, placing the LeMat on the table next to the gavel.

"Wait a minute," Thorp said. "I'm a mite short of breath."

"Sure. We can wait as long as you want, Thorp. In fact, we don't have to do this at all."

"I can't lose my boy," Thorp muttered.

"You already have." Being so blunt might not be the best

idea, Stark knew, but it was his nature. "You lost him when Dev Bennett showed him how to pull a gun. And you lost him when you taught him that he was better than anybody else around here and that the law couldn't touch him."

"It's my right! This is my valley, my town! If it wasn't for me, there'd be nothin' out there, nothin'!" Thorp leaned back in his wheelchair and drew a deep, ragged breath. "But what do they do? They buzz around me like a bunch of damned gnats, tellin' me how my day is done, how I got to fence my range and follow their rules and put up with their damned civilization! They figure because they're meek, they've inherited my earth!"

"You're not God," Stark said.

"In this corner of West Texas I am!"

A floorboard creaked behind Stark, and suddenly he knew why Thorp had wanted to wait. He hadn't heard the back door of the hall open. Whoever was behind him could move quiet-like.

"Bennett?" Stark said.

"That's right," a cold voice replied. Stark had seen him earlier with the other cowhands, lean and hawk-faced, dangerous despite his age.

"Dev, be careful," Thorp said.

"Don't worry, Mr. Thorp. I ain't afraid of the judge here. He might've been a hell-raiser once, but that was a long time ago."

Stark looked at the LeMat. His hand was only a couple of inches from it, but he knew that Bennett had to have a gun pointed at him. And Bennett wasn't slow. Never had been.

"I thought we had a deal, Thorp," Stark said.

"I'm sorry," Thorp said, and he sounded like he meant it. "But I got to have my boy back. I know he maybe ain't worth it, but . . . he's my boy."

Stark took a deep breath. "You and Bennett'll have to kill me to take him."

"I know that. It's a shame, but if that's how it has to be . . ."

Stark saw Thorp's eyes flick toward Bennett, saw the tiny nod of the old rancher's head.

Saw, too, the flash of movement at one of the windows

and heard the glass crash as a shotgun boomed. Stark's hand slapped down on the butt of the LeMat as he went out of his chair in a rolling dive. Above and behind him, a rifle cracked wickedly as Dev Bennett fired.

The load of buckshot fired through the window had distracted Bennett, and a couple of the pellets had nicked him, but not seriously. He was swinging the Winchester around as Stark came up on one knee and triggered the LeMat's shotgun barrel. At that range, the buckshot tore into Bennett's midsection and shredded it, the force picking him up and throwing him backward.

Stark went sideways again as Jud Thorp's Colt began to blast. He sprawled on his belly and tipped up the barrel of the LeMat, but before he could fire, Dave Fulton loomed up behind Thorp and brought the butt of his shotgun down on the rancher's right shoulder. Thorp howled in pain as the gun slipped from his fingers. He hunched around in the wheelchair and clutched at his shattered shoulder with his left hand. Fulton stepped around the chair and kicked away the fallen gun.

"Thanks, Dave," Stark said as he climbed to his feet. "I should've known an old law dog like you couldn't stay away from trouble."

"Bennett had the drop on you, didn't he?"

Stark nodded. "He would've killed me if you hadn't fired through the window when you did."

Fulton gestured toward Jud Thorp. "What do we do with him? Arrest him for shooting at you?"

Stark considered, then shook his head. "Might as well arrest the wind for blowing."

Clearly not understanding, Fulton shrugged. "It's up to you, Judge. I'll go fetch the undertaker for Bennett."

As Fulton left the hall with the shotgun tucked under his arm, Stark went over to stand in front of Thorp's wheelchair. "You lost your gamble, Thorp. I'm declaring a change of venue in this case and taking Billy over to Fort Stockton for a new trial."

"You . . . can't do that."

"Yes, I can, and I'm going to. And if you interfere, you'll either go to jail or wind up dead, the way you nearly did this time." Stark paused, then added, "And if that happens, the townies really will have won, Thorp."

The rancher looked up at him for a moment, eyes filled with pain. "At least you . . . understand. You know . . . how it used to be . . ."

Stark holstered the LeMat. "I understand. I was there."

A CHEER WENT up from the townspeople as Stark left the hall a few minutes later. Calder came up to him and put a hand on his shoulder, saying, "You did it, Judge. You showed that old relic that he can't fight progress."

Stark looked at the merchant and said, "Get your hand off me."

Calder jerked his hand away as if he'd been touched with a hot iron.

Franklin Lester was waiting on the porch of the sheriff's office. "You just made a motion for a change of venue, Counselor, and I just granted it," Stark told him.

"Thank you," Lester said with a sigh of relief. "I thought of that, but it was too late by then."

Stark looked back at the town hall, saw the hunched-over form of Jud Thorp being pushed out of the building in his wheelchair. A worried Donna Preston was hovering over Thorp while Ranse Albin pushed the chair.

"It's too late for a lot of things," Stark said, then he went inside the jail.

IN A TRIAL presided over by a different judge, William Thorp was acquitted by a jury of his peers in Fort Stockton, Texas, on July 27, 1894. On September 3, 1894, he was killed as the result of a gunfight in the Oriental Saloon in Pecos, Texas. The man who shot him was not arrested, since it was a fair fight and the man claimed self-defense.

Judson Thorp died on March 7, 1895. His last will and testament left his ranch and the rest of his estate to his ward, Donna Preston. On July 29, one year and two days after Billy Thorp's acquittal at Fort Stockton, Donna Preston and Ransom Albin were married. They lived on the old Thorp ranch for many years and raised six children there. In the 1950s, their great-grandchildren leased the land to an oil company and eventually sold it to the same company.

Judge Earl Stark put on his duster, saddled the Appaloosa, and rode on to his next case.

The Gunny

Bill Pronzini

While Bill Pronzini is best known for his suspense and crime fiction, such western novels as *The Hangings* have made him an important voice in the development of the modern western. He has experimented with just about every subgenre, too, from high comedy and western-mystery even to a fine example of the Northwestern, the excellent *Starvation Camp*. He continues to grace our field from time to time.

THE OLD MAN sat smoking his pipe in the shade in front of Fletcher's Mercantile, one of the rows of neat frame buildings that made up the main street of Bitter Springs. It was midafternoon, the sun brassy hot in the late-summer sky, and he was the only citizen in sight when the lanky stranger rode into town from the west.

Horse and rider were dust-spattered, and the lean Appaloosa blew heavily and walked with a weary stiffness, as if ridden long and hard. But the stranger sat his saddle tall and erect, shoulders pulled back, eyes moving left and right over the empty street. He was young and leaned-down, sharp-featured, a dusty black mustache bracketing lips as thin as a razor slash. Hanging low on his right hip was a Colt double-action in a Mexican loop holster thong-tied to his thigh.

The old man watched him approach without moving. Smoke from his clay pipe haloed his white-thatched head, seeming hardly to drift in the overheated air. He had a frail, dried-out appearance, like leather left too long to cure in the sun; but his eyes were alert, sharply watchful.

As the stranger neared Fletcher's Mercantile, he took notice of the old man sitting there in the shade. He turned the Appaloosa in that direction, drew rein, and swung easily out of the saddle.

"Hidy, grandpop," he said as he looped the reins around a tie rack. He stepped up onto the boardwalk.

"Hidy yourself."

"Hot, ain't it?"

"Seen it hotter."

"I been riding three days in this heat and I got me a hell of a thirst. You know what I mean?"

"Don't look senile, do I?"

The stranger laughed. "Loaded question, grandpop."

"Saloon up the street, if a cold beer's what you're after."

"It is, but not just yet. Got some business to attend to first."

"That a fact?" the old man asked conversationally.

"Where can I find Sheriff Ben Chadwick?"

"Most days you could find him in his office at the jailhouse, down at the end of Main here. But he don't happen to be there today."

"No? Where is he?"

"Rode out to the Adams place, west of town. Some fool's been running off their stock."

"When's he due back?"

"Don't rightly know. What kind of business you got with the sheriff, son?"

"Killing business."

"So? Who's been killed?"

The young stranger laughed again, without humor. "Nobody yet. Ben Chadwick ain't here, like you said."

The old man took the pipe from his mouth, staring up at the youth. Downstreet somewhere, a dog barked once like a gunshot in the stillness. There were no other sounds except for the faint rasp of the old man's breathing.

"That mean what I think it means?"

"What d'you think it means?"

"Like you're planning on murder. Ben Chadwick's murder."

"Murder ain't the right word. Payback's what I'm fixin' to give."

"Payback for what?"

"Sheriff of yours shot up a couple of men on the trail to Three Forks two weeks ago. You heard about that, grandpop?"

"I heard."

"Well, I was in Arizona Territory when I got word. Else, I'd of been here long before this."

"What was those two fellas to you?"

"One of 'em, Ike Gerard, was my cousin."

"Well, now," the old man said dryly, "looky what we got here. Johnny Goheen, ain't you?"

"That's right, grandpop. Johnny Goheen."

"Your cousin and his sidekick robbed the bank in Three Forks. Killed a teller. But I reckon that don't cut no ice with the likes of you."

"No, it don't."

"A damn gunny," the old man said, and spat on the worn boards alongside his chair. "Quick on the shoot, are you?"

"Quick as any there ever was."

"Braggart, too. How many men you shot down, Goheen?"

"Four. All in self-defense."

"Uh-huh." The old man spat again. "Ben Chadwick's a duly appointed law officer. You kill him, it'll sure enough be murder."

"Will it?"

"They'll hang you for it."

"No warrant out on me. Chadwick draws first, sheriff or no sheriff, I'm entitled to defend myself."

"And you aim to prod him into drawing first."

"If needs be."

"Suppose he don't?"

"He will. Bet your boots he will."

"Maybe he's faster'n you."

"He ain't," Goheen said.

"He's got friends in this town, Ben Chadwick has. They won't let you get away with it."

"You one of 'em? You figure you can stop me?"

The old man said nothing.

Goheen laughed his mirthless laugh. "Tell you what,

grandpop. You sit right here in the shade and rest your old bones. No use gettin' all worked up on such a hot day."

Again the old man was silent.

"Pleasure talkin' to you," Goheen said. He tipped his hat, turned, went upstreet to McQuaid's Resort, and pushed in through the batwings without a backward glance.

The old man sat for a minute or so, staring downstreet to the east—the direction Ben Chadwick had ridden out earlier in the day. The road and the flats in that direction appeared motionless except for shimmers of heat haze, unmarked by the billows of dust that foretold the arrival of a rider or wagon. Then he knocked the dottle from his pipe, stowed it inside his shirt, and got to his feet. He shuffled over to the mercantile's entrance.

Howard Fletcher, elderly, balding, his bow tie loosened and his cuffs unbuttoned, looked up from behind the counter and smiled. "Well, Jeb, you get tired of setting out there and decide to come in for a game of cribbage?"

The old man didn't return the smile. "I come in to ask a favor, Howard. You still got that Remington .44-40 under the counter? The one I sold you?"

"Course I do."

"Cleaned and oiled recently?"

"I'm not one to mistreat a side arm, you know that. Why?"

"I need the use of it."

The curve of Fletcher's mouth turned down the other way. "Now what would you be wanting with a six-gun?"

"I got my reasons."

"Mind my asking what they are?"

"Howard, you and me been friends for a long time and I ain't never asked you for much. I'm asking you for that .44-40 Remington now. I'll get me another handgun somewheres else if you got objections."

"No objections," Fletcher said. "I just don't understand what's got your hackles up."

"You will soon enough. Let's have it."

Fletcher shrugged, reached under the counter and then laid the blued-steel weapon on top. The old man picked it up, hefted it. Its worn walnut grips fit snugly, familiarly against his palm. Most men he knew, Sheriff Ben Chadwick among them, preferred Colt's single-action army revolver, but the old man had always sworn by Remington's Model 1875 despite the remnant of the old percussion loading lever under the seven-and-a-half-inch barrel, the side ejector rod, the handle some found clumsy. Colt, Forehand & Wadsworth, Hopkins & Allen, none of 'em made a better or more accurate shooting iron than the Remington single-action—if a man knew how to use it.

He flipped open the gate, made sure all six chambers were filled, and snapped it shut again. "You'll have it back before long, Howard," he said. "One way or another."

"Meaning?"

"You'll find out."

The old man went outside again, the Remington held down along his right leg. The street, and the road and desert flats to the east, were still empty under the hard sun glare. He hesitated, then walked slowly upstreet toward McQuade's Resort.

But when he was two buildings from the saloon, he veered off at an angle, stepped onto the boardwalk, and took a leaning position against the wall of Henderson Brothers Feed & Grain. He spat onto the planking at his feet, watching the entrance to the saloon with narrowed eyes. Goheen might do all his waiting inside there, but then again he might not. Be better if he made up his mind to come outside again, If the old man had to go in after him, some citizen might get hurt.

Five minutes he stood there. Ten. Frank Harper drove by, his wagon loaded with fresh-cut lumber. Harper waved, but the old man didn't wave back.

Another five minutes vanished. And then the saloon's batwings popped open and Johnny Goheen appeared, rubbing the back of one thin arm across his mouth and squinting in the direct sunlight. He moved down off the boardwalk, past the hitchrails into the dusty street.

"Hey, boy!" the old man called sharply. "Come over here, boy!"

Goheen's head jerked up and around; he stopped in midstride with his hand poised over the handle of his revolver. His face registered surprise when he realized who had called him.

"Grandpop, you better not take that tone of voice with me again. What d'you want?"

The old man shoved away from the Henderson Brothers wall, bringing the Remington up in a level point. When Goheen saw the weapon, his expression changed to one of slack-jawed amazement.

"What I want," the old man said, "is for you to unbuckle your shell belt, slowlike, and drop it."

"You gone crazy?"

"Not hardly. I'm making a citizen's arrest, taking you to the jailhouse."

"The hell you are. On what charge?"

"Threatening the life of a peace officer."

"You can't make a charge like that stick!"

"Circuit judge is a hard man. He don't like a gunny any more'n I do."

"You ain't arrestin' me," Goheen said. "Be damned if you are. Put that iron away, grandpop, or else—"

"Or else what? You'll draw on me?"

"That's right. And I'll kill you dead, too, before you can squeeze off a round."

"Welcome to try, if that's how you want it." The old man lowered the Remington, slowly, until he was again holding it muzzle downward. "Well, boy?"

Seconds passed—long, dragging, tense. Goheen's gaze didn't waver; neither did the old man's. Then Goheen said, "All right, by God, you asked for it," and his hand darted down, came up again filled with his Colt—but when he pulled the trigger it was only in belated reflex. The Remington roared first and a bullet kicked up dust from his shirtfront, drove him half around; his slug went harmlessly into the street. His legs buckled; he dropped to his knees. The double-action slid from his grip; he made no move to pick it up. His face wore the same expression of slack-jawed amazement as before, tempered now by shock and pain.

The old man stepped off the boardwalk and kicked Goheen's side arm to one side. Men were spilling out of buildings along the street, and from behind him the old man could hear Howard Fletcher calling anxiously, but he kept his eyes fixed on the fallen youth at his feet.

Goheen tried to stand, couldn't, and fell sideways clutching at his bloody chest. Grimacing, he twisted his head to stare up at the old man. "Damn you, grandpop, you hurt me bad. Why? I didn't figure you for no . . .. no hero."

"I ain't one. I'm just a retired gunsmith that learned how to shoot fast and straight before you were born."

"Then why? Why?"

"Sheriff's got a bad arm, Goheen. Hurt it when his horse shied at a rattler three days ago. I couldn't stand by and let you kill him. I'd lay my own life down, and gladly, before I'd let that happen."

"What're you talkin' about?"

"My name's Chadwick, too," the old man said. "Sheriff Ben Chadwick's my son."

Rio Blanco

Gary Phillips

"Rio Blanco" is the first western story Gary Phillips has written. Over the years he has watched every western movie Anthony Mann, Sam Peckinpah, Sergio Leone, Richard Brooks, and Budd Boetticher made—some of them more than once. He also writes in the crime and mystery genre. *Shooter's Point*, the second Martha Chainey crime novel, was published in October (2001).

THE *BRUJA*, THE witch woman, pinched her thin lips and eyes closed in her craggy countenance. She rocked back and forth on the chair, kneading her hands together and reciting her incantation in a low, whispery voice like powder on the wind. Her trailing white hair hung straight from her head, and was almost to her waist. While her clothes and shack were unkempt, that hair seemed to glimmer with inner lights as if in receipt of a source of nourishment separate from its owner.

"What is it, you old devil, what do you see?" Her questioner leaned forward across the table, his sinewy forearms causing the poorly made item to creak. The flame of the lump of a candle between them licked at the bottom of his graying van dyke.

Her agate mestizo eyes crinkled open. She stopped rocking and sat upright, letting her hands grasp the opposite shoulder as she sat sideways to him. "Boots and ropes," she declared in Spanish.

In his Tennessee-accented Spanish he said, "What the hell are you talking about, bitch?" He gripped the sides of the table, his arms shaking with the effort.

The old woman, stout and shapeless in her faded black dress, rolled her head toward him, spittle bubbling on her bottom lip. She laughed hoarsely, spraying the man and the candle. "Where is my money, *puta?*" she asked, mostly in English, then laughing again at him.

"I ought to snap that evil Mex neck of yours," was his reply. But he didn't take his hands away from the sides of the table. His knuckles stood out like bleached ridges.

Those eyes, flat and unknowable like a raven's, remained on the man before her. They dared him to strike her, aware he would do nothing. "A black rider on a black horse is coming to White River." She smiled a cruel child's smile. The *bruja* flopped a hand, palm up, on the table between them. Her fingers were curled open, a plant of flesh waiting for its meal.

The man stood and angrily knocked the candle away. "You've got to tell me more than that, you goddamn harpy." The candle had been snuffed out when it struck the buckled floorboards. In the nether light that engulfed the cabin, their forms seemed to be carved from the pitch itself.

"Is he coming with others? How many ride with this man?"

"Many," she said. "Many *sombras.*" She snickered at her own joke.

"You fucking crazy witch," he bellowed. He put his hands to his face and momentarily it seemed as if the earth were moving out from under him. "What's his name?" he demanded.

"Does it matter? When did it ever matter to you?" She stuck out her hand again, letting it slowly rise toward him.

He scowled at her contented expression and it seemed he'd just as soon cut that hand off as satisfy the greedy cow. But he did what he always did after insulting and threatening her to mask his need for her. He reached into his pocket and doing a hollow laugh of his own, tossed twin double eagle gold pieces on the floor.

"How about that, you snake-skinned hag," he spat in English.

The seer let her tongue slide over her lower lip again. If she had been younger, it might have been sensuous; as it was, there was a lurid, deviant quality to her action. Then a column of light flared. The candle was back on the table, and its wick burning hotly. She rubbed her bony hands on her upper thighs, arching her head and shoulders back. The candle sizzled and popped like hot grease in a skillet and he balled his fists up as he pressed his back against the wall. Next to him was one of the dried animal heads she'd tacked up. This one was a jaguar and its orbs had been replaced with jade.

"What the hell," he panted. Sweat was boiling off the top of his head. More than anything he wanted to feel his big, knotty fists colliding with the horrors she was calling up inside him. "You better quit messin' with me. I paid you your goddamn money, you red nigger."

"What's wrong, Captain Stoddard? Are you seeing those boots dangling from the leaves?" She held her hands aloft, the fingers pointing downward as she fluttered them. The candle's light coruscated around her long fingernails.

"Shut up, or old woman or no, I'll beat you into the ground."

"He knows about those boots," she advised.

The light subsided to its usual glow. The thumping of his brain ceased. His face and shirt were clammy from sweat, and he breathed hard as if he'd been running after a wayward horse. "When will he be here?" He wiped at his forehead with the flat of his hand.

"When he gets here."

Stoddard turned to leave. He was through with her games, at least for now. But as he tugged on the latch of her door he couldn't resist asking. "You say he'll be wearing all black?"

Her peal like an hyena made the back of his neck go cold. "It's not even a real horse," she said boisterously. He stepped out of her cabin into the sticky night. Down below, the village was a tomb. And even the laudanum he drank later couldn't grant him sleep for more than ten or fifteen minutes at a stretch.

Two days later, two men had themselves tucked away under an outcropping on a rise overlooking the village of Rio Blanco. One wore a heavy woolen coat and the other a jacket made of horsehair. This second garment gave off the unpleasant aroma, in summer and in winter, of its unwashed predecessor. The man who chose to wear this particular garment, seemingly inured to its gamy smell, took a perverse pride in his nickname.

"I sure wish your grandma was here, Horseshit."

"Yeah, why's that, William Lee?"

"She can suckle on a man's balls like no other woman I ever met. And nasty and windy as it is this here night, I sure'in could use the attention."

Horseshit was busy sealing a cigarette he'd just rolled. He snuggled his tobacco pouch in his vest. "Help me light my smoke, funny man."

"My good pleasure." William Lee Sykes rested the Sharpe's with its scope against a rock, and cupped his hands close to his friend's mouth.

The other man had a match poised and waited until there was a lull in the wind that had been gnawing at them all through the starless evening. On his third match, the fire held and the cigarette was lit. Horseshit blew a thin bluish stream around his head. "Maybe your sister could come along too. I like the way she lets you poke her from behind while she holds on to the hitchin' post."

"Yes sir," the other man said agreeably. "She learned it good from Ma."

Both men laughed in their throats. They didn't want to make too much noise and give their position away.

"Hey," William Lee said abruptly.

His companion was busy trying to blow triple smoke rings like he'd seen this fairy actor do in Kansas City once. "What?" he uttered languidly after William Lee said something indiscernible.

"Shhh, you hear that?" William Lee admonished Horseshit.

The *clip-clop* of shod hooves was faint but growing in clarity. The animal would be coming along the main trail that led into town. That's why the men had been posted where they were.

Horseshit looked closely at the pocket watch he kept on the other side of his vest. "It's nigh on three-thirty."

"Must be the one Stoddard's all a-twitter over. Hardly nobody else comes this way, and it sure ain't no trail hand waltzing into here this time o' the morning."

"We sposed to bushwhack this billy goat?" Horseshit got himself set. He took the glove off his right hand, and blew on the ball of his fist before unlimbering his Colt .44.

William Lee plucked his Sharpe's from where it was leaning, and sighted through the scope. The moon was flat and bright like a fresh-washed china plate and afforded light on the trail. "Cap'n says he wants us to bring whoever it is to him if'n we can." After a moment, the ambusher declared, "That cain't be."

"Huh?" Horseshit, whose real name was Remmy Nolan, not only needed advice on clothing but was in sore need of glasses. The one vanity he indulged was going without an aid to his vision. He felt spectacles made him look too old. He leaned over, ready to fire, then saw what the other man had seen. "Huh," he said again.

"Come on," William Lee. The two got out from underneath the outcropping and went to their horses tethered to a sickly jacaranda on the blind side of the hill. The pair rode down onto the main street—that is, the trail that led into town and became the central artery through the village.

"A donkey, by hisself." Horseshit pointed at the beast that had seemingly wandered into Rio Blanco. The creature was now standing at a puddle, lapping at the water before it all turned to mud.

"It's a mule," William Lee corrected. "Big too." He dismounted and approached the creature. He put his hand on its side, examining its flanks and sniffing at it.

"You want me to leave so you two can git better acquainted?" Horseshit chided.

"This ain't no plow mule," William Lee pronounced. "I can see where the saddle's been cinched on him, and his hair has been washed and groomed not too long ago."

"Yeah, he sure is a-pretty," Horseshit concurred. "He's so black and glossy like one of them paintings."

"So where's the cowboy that was on him?" William Lee wondered aloud.

"Maybe he got thrown. The saddle come loose and he fell and cracked his head open."

"What about the bit and the reins?"

"How do I know?"

"Let's take him to Stoddard."

"Are you loco, William Lee? He wants us to bring him a man, not a goddamn donkey."

"Mule."

"Shit."

William Lee put his rope around the animal's neck and led him to La Reina Cantina. The establishment was located at the other end of the short main street. Eli Stoddard kept a large portion of the second floor of the cantina for his personal quarters. They tied up the mule and went to inform the boss.

Stoddard wiped at sleep in a corner of his eye. He'd come downstairs and the three of them stood near the cantina's bar.

"No markings or nothin' on it?" Stoddard fooled with the belt to his robe but decided to let the thing hang open over his long johns.

"Walked into town easy as you please." William Lee thumbed in the direction of the door, where the mule was tied outside.

Stoddard scratched at one of his lambchop sideburns. "It's been regular fed?"

"Yep," William Lee confirmed. "It damn sure belongs to somebody, Cap'n. The question is what happened to the hombre that were a-ridin' it."

Stoddard shifted his vision to the door as if he were going to walk out to see the animal for himself. But he merely turned his gaze back to his men. "And black?"

"Like coal," Horseshit added.

"That's very unusual for a mule," William Lee contributed. "They mostly run to variations on brown or even gray." He set his hat back from his crunched brow. "Fact, I don't believe I've ever seen one this dark. Nope, cain't say I have."

Stoddard ran a hand over his dry mouth. "I want you two

to go back out of town the way this mule came, and find the man jack that was on it."

"Now?" Horseshit whined. He'd been envisioning slipping into his bed after two days and nights catnapping among the rocks.

Stoddard's graveyard stare told him the answer. "And take the breed with you."

"Okay." William Lee made to go, then said, "What about the mule?"

"Shoot it."

"I was hopin' to keep it."

"Why, it cain't mate," Stoddard answered irritably.

"But it's a fine animal, Cap'n. We could get some money for it."

Stoddard was too tired and too keyed up to sustain an argument. And extra income was always welcome. "Let's see about it when the sun is up and you've brought me the man who owns it."

"Okay," a pleased William Lee said. It would be a shame to destroy the mule, he mused. He liked animals, found their company generally to be much more suited to his temperament than humans. Men he could kill with no qualm. But even wringing a chicken's neck for Sunday dinner gave him pause. Oh, he'd do it all right, it would just set heavy with him some was all.

They collected the one Stoddard had called "the breed." His name was Alfonso Rey, and he was half Mexican and half Comanchero. His cascading hair was bleached of color after so much time in the sun, and he wore calfskin boots and a matching flat-brimmed hat. Thereafter, the three set out from town once they'd gotten a few supplies.

It didn't take them long to come upon the smoke from a small campfire. Rey and William Lee had smelled the singed air before seeing the anemic smoke.

They were about a hundred yards away, and could see the slight plume rising from what once had been a Spanish mission. One of many selfless attempts by the conquerors to bring the one true faith to the savages—to not only show them the way, but ingrain in them to be more complacent subjects. The mission had been partially destroyed by cannon fire during a junta by Mexican independence forces during the Plan of Iguala in 1821.

"I'll come in from that way," Rey said quietly, pointing to the south. Absently he adjusted his gun belt, then sidled away.

"We'll come at him through what's left of that archway." William Lee indicated the path he and Horseshit would take.

The men got off their mounts and headed to where they assumed they'd find a man asleep or passed out from his injuries. What remained of the rough-hewn floor of the mission was rent and its stones strewn about as if a great force had bubbled from underneath. Weeds and small cacti sprouted everywhere and they had to watch their step so as not to trip. William Lee had left his Sharpe's in its scabbard on his horse. He had his pistol out, a Smith & Wesson that he favored over the more popular Colt of the same caliber.

They got the archway, one on either side of the opening. The campfire was to their right, a saddle and unwrapped bedroll nearby.

"Does this fella really exist?" Horseshit craned his neck in several directions.

"I know. It's like he's—" William Lee stopped at the sound of a foot scraping over the dry ground.

"It's him," Horseshit breathed excitedly.

"Maybe," a cautious William Lee said.

A figure walked from the south. He stopped, then came forward again. The other two showed themselves, their guns on the man.

"All right, mister, there's somebody wants to meet you." William Lee cocked the hammer of his pistol to show the stranger he wasn't foolin'.

The figure gurgled, then they could see it wasn't the rider at all. It was Alfonso Rey, and he had a large skinning knife imbedded off-center in his chest, in his heart. William Lee and Horseshit started forward as Rey uselessly tried to remove the knife from his dying body. But doing this caused the blood to pucker from around the wound. He stopped trying to take the knife out, gasped, and dropped to the ground like a life-sized puppet whose strings had been cut. He sat slumped forward, one leg folded under him.

"Goddamn," a frightened Horseshit exclaimed.

William Lee was already in motion. "Come on." He started for the relative cover of the mission, Horseshit at his heels.

The crank of a rifle's repeater lever, just as a silhouette filled the archway, caused Horseshit to collide with William Lee in a comical way. But nobody was laughing.

"What'll it be?" the shape challenged. It didn't seem he was offering much in the way of choice.

William Lee got off a shot before several rapidly fired rounds fatally aggravated him. He stumbled back, tripping over Horseshit's leg as the latter ran for safety. "Goddamn is right," he bellowed, and died.

Horseshit dove into a clump of brush that included some thick bramble. His arms and face were cut, and a thatch of his cheek came away on a hooked thorn. Not bothering to dab at the wetness seeping into his whiskers, he peaked through the foliage. "Hey, mister, we just wanted to talk, that's all." It was blind luck that Horseshit had managed to stay alive during the war. He'd been at the slaughter of Chickamauga and had come through with only a little toe shot off. Yet here he was, scooting behind cover that couldn't keep the wind out. And he was hollering, giving his position away. But the certain anticipation of losing his life was more pressing on him than good sense.

"Sure," the no-name man said, "let's talk."

There was flint in his voice and a down-home quality Horseshit recognized. "Sound like we from the same part of the country, I mean, you know, up north but down south, am I right?" The man didn't answer.

It wasn't clear to Horseshit what to do next. Minutes limped by and he lay there, sweating and fretting. "Mister," he said again. And again there was no response. Not even the owls hooted. "Look, mister," he began, "this here quarrel you got is with Cap'n Stoddard, ain't that so?" He hadn't expected the man to say anything and went on talking. "So, how about this? How about I toss out my gun and you let me git to ma horse?" He got up on a knee. "I ride the hell out of here to Texas, and don't look back. Don't that sound fair to you?"

"Sure."

Where was he? Horseshit threw his six-shooter onto the ground. "I'm coming out now, okay?"

"Grab some air while you're at it."

He did as he was told. Horseshit remained standing behind the low shrubs. The man who'd killed his friend and the breed was tall but not overly so. He had a wrangler's gait that was evident as he walked closer. The rifle he possessed was unusual. Though Horseshit couldn't tell what kind it was, he could see that its barrel had been shortened. Why, he didn't know. But that's not what finally possessed his interest.

"You're a burrhead." He then remembered that this man could send him to Kingdom Come. "I, uh, say, how about letting me git to ma horse? I promise I won't be no trouble to ya."

The man stepped even closer. His features were haggard and there was a crescent of a scar starting up on his brow that curved like a scorpion's tail under his eye. "You got to sing for your supper, reb."

Horseshit's stomach clenched involuntarily. This colored boy knew about them. "What do you want?"

"How many men does the captain have?"

"You done kilt the best ones," he replied.

"That's not what I asked, is it?" Casually, he struck the man in the stomach with the stock of the sawed-off rifle.

Horseshit teared up, firecrackers exploding inside his head. He had enough presence of mind not to insult the black again and make him really mad. A sullen "Five, not counting me," issued forth.

A menacing "You sure?" was his reply.

"Yeah. I mean yes."

"You lost another two in that last robbery your outfit did on the Santa Fe train out of Tulsa."

"You tellin' or askin' . . . mister?"

"What about my mule?"

"William Lee," he gestured over the taller man's shoulder, "liked that animal. He saved it for you."

If the other man had regrets about killing him, he didn't show it. "Turn around."

"What are you plannin' on doin'?"

"Gettin' my mule back."

Horseshit got a chill, and it wasn't from the cold weather.

Not long afterward, the dawn leaked gray into the underbelly of the early morning. And a horse and man came riding fast through town to the surprise of early-morning risers.

"Jesus, Mary, and Moses!" Horseshit screamed in agony. The kerosene soaking his clothes fed the flames that swarmed him. His gaping features matched the terror of his horse's as the two careened through town.

One of the villagers ran for the cantina to tell Stoddard. But two of his men were already out in the street, trying to halt the runaway horse. The horse ran into the side of the Flores Gran Almacén just as one of the men, called Blue, reached the two. He was grabbing at Horseshit, who was now loosened from being tied to the saddle. As he did so, two rifle shots cracked over the horse's whinnying, and the top of Blue's head was gone forever.

The other man, Casey, saw this and ran toward the doorway to the tannery. But this being before business hours, he found the door locked. He was about to shoot it open when another shot sounded, and a bullet entered his back and traveled downward, shattering his spine. He collapsed on the planked walkway, alive but unable to move.

"He's on a rooftop," one of Stoddard's remaining men concluded. He strained to see, crouching under the cantina's swinging doors.

"Who is this bastard?" Stoddard demanded of no one and everyone.

"Let's skin him first and ask him later," one of Stoddard's four remaining gang members announced.

"How you figure to do that, Oakley?" One of the other men, a one-eyed individual named Fenton asked. "This gravedigger is colder'n a virgin drinkin' ice water. He seems awfully intent on killing all of us."

"Yeah, he does indeed," the third one, Harris, an Irishman originally from Cork added. He exchanged a conspiratorial glance at Oakley. The two, like Blue, had not been in the Confederate army with Stoddard and the rest. They were distant cousins, and had joined up with the gang after hearing about the sweet setup the ex-captain had down here. Neither had any illusions about blood spilled in battle making them brothers and all that rot Stoddard would give speeches about—particularly after several glasses of mescal.

"We've got to flush him out," Stoddard said, pounding a fist on the bar.

There was a sound and the anxious men pointed their guns at the entrance. Horseshit's stallion walked aimlessly in the main street past the cantina and on toward the end of the road and a bunch of hibiscus.

"Get on the roof, you two." Stoddard pointed upward at the rafters.

Oakley and Harris pretended like they were setting off to do as told. One stood at ten o'clock to the other's three o'clock to their leader. "It ain't us that boll weevil is after," Harris, who did most of the talking for the two, said.

"Goddammit, Stoddard, is there a bunch of Texas Rangers out there or what?" Josefina, the owner of the cantina, hastened down the stairs. She was a handsome woman large in the hips with gray creeping like vines through her black hair. Her dressing gown was loosely tied, and its rosy satin complimented her tawny skin.

"Get your hogleg." Stoddard had his gun out, languidly pointing it in the direction of Harris.

Josefina went behind the bar and freed the sawed-off shotgun hidden there. She rested the weapon on the bar top. One of her heavy breasts poked out, her nipple hard with excitement. "I just had some flattened pesos cut up too." She patted the shotgun like it was a pet.

Stoddard asked unnecessarily. "What you got to say, Fenton?"

"I'm with you, Cap'n, you know that." To prove it he got up and relieved the two cousins of their pistols.

"Now git," Stoddard commanded.

"Git where?" Harris balked.

He wheezed, "Don't be cute."

"That's cruel, even for you, Stoddard. Give us a chance."

"Like you were going to do for me, Harris." He slapped the man with the barrel of his Colt. "Now you two better hotfoot it up there or we'll cut you down here and now. Come on, Fenton."

Oakley and Harris shared resigned grimaces and began up the stairs, their two captors, men who they'd rode and stole with, behind them.

"All right," Stoddard said, at the top, taking hold of Oakley's collar. He jammed the gun into his back. "Get over there, Harris."

Harris seethed. "If I get out of this, I'm going to rip you open, Stoddard."

"Big man. Let's go, Oakley."

Oakley went in, Stoddard pushing him while Fenton kept his gun on Harris on the landing.

Harris faced Fenton. Stoddard had his back to the men. Harris wiggled his index finger, indicating for Fenton to shoot Stoddard. "Do it," he mouthed, hoping the other man, scared and confused, would catch on.

"Come on, Fenton, bring that turncoat in here."

Harris took advantage of Fenton's indecision and jumped him. The two went against the wall, knocking a painting of a bullfighter loose. Stoddard turned and fired, his bullet chipping into the flocked wallpaper. Oakley lunged but Stoddard was too fast. He pivoted around and used the butt of the pistol to club the man.

Harris and Fenton were entangled, thrashing at each other as they crashed against the banister several feet from the landing. Josefina rushed up the stairs, her shotgun poised. Stoddard stepped back into the hall to shoot Harris, but Oakley wasn't done. The blow made him woozy, but he managed to latch his arms around Stoddard's legs, upsetting his balance. He went forward just as Josefina reached the top and she had to sidestep his falling form.

Simultaneously, Harris slammed the heel of his boot into Fenton's forehead, and tore off in the opposite direction along the hall. Josefina let a blast loose that clipped the fleeing man in the side and dusted part of the banister. Harris kept running, then stumbled and crawled around a corner. She took off after him.

Stoddard was on his back and Oakley was on him, his arm holding the gun hand of the man down on the floor. "Fenton," Oakley called, "this is our chance."

"Don't be a fool, Fenton," Stoddard bellowed. "You think that gunhawk out there will just stop with me?"

A dazed Fenton was groggily getting to his feet. Oakley used Stoddard's neck for leverage with one hand, pressing his weight on it as he lurched his body upward. "Fenton," he pleaded. Stoddard bucked but couldn't get free.

Fenton scooped up his gun where it had fallen on the carpet. He brought it up as the two men continued to struggle, taking aim. Whatever his decision was, he took with him. The shotgun echoed again. Instantaneously his guts were festooned on the walls and the faces of the two on the floor. Slivers of the peso halves glistened among his entrails.

Josefina had already jacked in the new shells she'd taken time to place in her gown's pocket, also from underneath the bar. The double barrels bore down on Oakley. "Let him up."

Oakley did so.

"Where's Harris?" Stoddard asked.

"He got out on the roof through my room and rolled off." She came closer to him. "Now what?"

"We get this son-of-a-bitch," he snarled.

"In case you haven't been counting, we're a mite shorthanded, *mi amor*."

"Then what's your idea, woman?"

"What does any man want?"

Stoddard gave her a cockeyed look. "You think you can sport Lea or one of your other girls out there naked on a horse and he'll be satisfied?"

"Besides pussy."

Then he understood, and looked at Oakley.

Soon, Oakley, bare-chested and barefooted, with his hands in the air, marched out the front of La Reina Cantina. Josefina and Stoddard held their guns on him, crouching from the doorway.

"Mister," the frightened man yelled into the unnaturally still morning. "Mister, they want to make a deal." He kept walking, turning his head and grinding his teeth as pebbles crunched into his feet. "Mister, can you hear me?"

"What kind of deal?" came a voice. Because of the gunplay, the villagers had wisely remained indoors. The main street was deserted. From the side of the Flores Gran Almacén, the general store, the man stepped out.

Oakley was so nervous, he was only momentarily surprised to note the man's race. "Stoddard's got money, he figures that's what you want."

"How much?"

Oakley frowned. "I cain't rightly say, but since me and my cousin joined up we've done several jobs, you know, takin' down a train shipment and even a bank over in Nogales. Hell, must be ten, twenty thousand. That'd be a pretty good stake, wouldn't you say?"

The man jerked the odd rifle he was holding for Oakley to step closer to him. He did.

"Fancy shooting iron you got there," he said, trying to ingratiate himself with the stranger. "That's a Henry, ain't it? How come you had the barrel cut down?"

"How do I get the money?"

"Stoddard says he'll load your mule with it and then you can ride out, just that simple."

"Nothing's that simple." The man adjusted his hat, the rising sun starting to slant across the buildings. "You gonna bring my mule back to me with the money?"

"I guess," he said, unsure of the procedure.

"Tell him the price is ten thousand. You bring my mule back to me with the money in an hour or it's no go."

"Okay." He didn't move, didn't want to anger the man. But the man didn't say anything else, so Oakley turned around and started back. "I'm going to tell him now, okay?"

"Where is my mule?"

Oakley stopped, his back to the man. "William Lee took him to the hacienda we bunk at. It's just outside the village, by the dried-up riverbed."

The man with the rifle didn't say anything, and Oakley felt as if his watery knees were going to give out any second. He chanced a look round but the man had already made himself scarce. Quickly he returned as fast as he could.

Back at the cantina, Stoddard concluded, "He's going to gun us at the hacienda." He glared at Oakley, who was sitting, dabbing at his feet with a wet cloth. "This buck was wearing cavalry boots?"

"Yep," Oakley said.

"What else?"

"Nothin'," Oakley said. "Except his rifle like I told you too. We wasn't exactly havin' no palaver, Stoddard. He wants the money, and he wants it now."

"Then that's our chance to get him," Josefina said.

Stoddard paced, rubbing his hands. "This nigger is smart,

we have to be smarter. He's got to be guessing we'll dry-gulch him here, but we won't."

"You're going to let him ride out with all that money?"

"Yes. But when he leaves, that's when we get him."

"The ambush idea didn't work too good the first time," Oakley reminded him.

Stoddard shouted. "He's not going to go back through town, you idiot. He's going to go over the mountains, that's what I would do. You didn't tell him about Harris?"

"Nope. But he must have heard the gunshots from in here. He saw me walking out with no gun and no shirt. He knows something's up."

Stoddard waved his comments away. "But he doesn't know how many of us are left," he surmised. He pointed at Oakley. "You get his mule loaded, He's going to be riding one of the men's horses, and use that animal to pack. I'm going to give him all the gold pieces in with the paper money. That load would slow him down too much to ride just the mule."

"That makes sense," Josefina concurred.

"So what about me?" Oakley stood,

"What about you?" Stoddard laughed. "You do what you're told, and you get to live a little longer."

Oakley threw the cloth down with force, but there was nothing he could do. Yet.

The hacienda had once belonged to a landowner named Ortiz. He'd had a vision of Rio Blanco becoming a bustling town of commerce and crops, and he its titular king. But the nearby river that the town had gotten its name from had dried up. And Ortiz had become involved with the losing side in the treacherous arena of Mexican politics. Ortiz was murdered by his rivals on a cattle-buying trip to Guadalajara, thus further precipitating the decline of the town—but making it the ideal hideout for Stoddard's gang.

With Josefina keeping guard on him, and helping take the money over by horse, Oakley got several haversacks filled and tied onto the mule. The two waited another hour, but the stranger, who in less than a day had totally disrupted the way things had been, was not around.

"What do you want me to do?" They stood outside the hacienda, the smell of mesquite strong. Stoddard had hidden himself up in the hills, waiting for the man to ride by.

The woman scanned the area as she had been doing. She was dressed in patent-leather boots, riding pants, and a man's shirt. "Take the mule back to where you first talked to him." She switched her shotgun to her other hand, used her right to get on her horse, and grabbed the reins of the other horse. "Get along. And don't you try to get away; we'll track you down."

Sighing, Oakley got on the mule and headed back through the village. Josefina rode hard in the opposite direction to get Stoddard. As Oakley passed what had once been the livery, his cousin stepped out from inside. He'd tied part of a blanket around him, which was dark from the wound on his side. Hungrily he eyed the bulging canvas bags.

"Forget it," his cousin warned him. "We got that bloodthirsty nigra on one side, and Stoddard and Josefina on the other. An we ain't got no gun a'tween us."

"That's a lot of money." Harris touched one of the haversacks as if it were a mirage. "So much money."

"You must be fevered, Colin. I've got to drop this off. You go back and hide and then I'll come back. Together, we can get out of this mess we got ourselves into." He tapped his heels against the mule's side and started off again. Harris trailed after him. "We can kill the nigger, then hole up in the stable. When Stoddard and his whore come back, we take them too with his gun," he chortled gaily. "This is our only chance, Luther."

"No." Luther Oakley wanted to gallop away, but mules don't gallop. His cousin grabbed his leg and yanked. Since he was riding bareback, it was easier to make him slide off his mount. The two fell into the dirt of the street.

"Don't be crazy, Colin. We can't do this." He hit his cousin in the jaw.

"No, we worked for that money. I ain't givin' it to no black boy who just happens along." Harris grabbed his cousin round his middle and the two men wrestled and scratched, dust billowing around their bodies. The mule kept going.

"Colin," his cousin appealed. He got to a knee. "You're not thinking right." He wiped at his bleeding mouth with his sleeve. Stoddard had let him put on his shirt and boots.

Harris's desire for the money was worse than any desire he ever had for a woman. But he said, "Yeah, yeah, what am I doing? We're family, for God's sake." He stood and came forward, holding his hand out as if to help him up.

Oakley took the hand, and was pulled hard, his cousin kneeing him in the face. This was followed by him being clubbed senseless after Harris clamped his fingers together.

"You'll thank me later," he muttered, taking off for the mule. He was surprised to find the animal alone, near the Flores store. Warily he approached the creature. "Mister, mister?" he said. There was no response and he smiled broadly.

At the other end of town, Stoddard and Josefina rode in. Stoddard said, "That eight ball surely done this." They'd halted, looking down at Oakley, who was groaning. "Come on, we can catch that clever boy."

They got their horses going and caught site of the mule and its rider up ahead. "There he is," a gleeful Stoddard cried, taking a bead with his pistol.

"I'm not sure," Josefina started, but didn't finish as Stoddard rode ahead, shooting and hollering. His faster horse closed the gap and he shot Harris from behind—who had intended to retrieve his cousin until he saw the two coming. But now he lay on his back on the edge of town, looking up at the cloudless sky.

"Where is he?" Stoddard stood over him, his gun pointed at the dying man's skull.

Harris's response was to cough up blood. Disgusted, Stoddard blew his face off.

The mule munched on a berry bush. Stoddard took the beast's reins and headed back to the cantina.

"Stoddard," Casey called out as he rode past, "Stoddard, help me, I can't feel nothin'." Stoddard looked down and kept on.

"Hey, Josefina," he said, stepping through the swinging door. Oakley was sitting at a table, a lopsided grin his expression. Josefina was sitting next to him, her hands on the shotgun, staring straight ahead.

"Josefina," he began, then saw the dark stain spreading from beneath her left breast. One thrust from his knife was all the deed had required. Stoddard had his gun out and spun toward the banister but he wasn't there.

"Who are you?" He had his back to the door, but he didn't have to look around to know that that black rider was standing there.

"Somebody who's taking you back."

"For the bounty? There must be a nice price on my head by now."

"That's ri—"

Stoddard had hoped to catch the man unawares as he turned, flung himself flat, and fired. But the shooter was greased lightning with that trick rifle of his. The .44-40s perforated his upper body viciously. In battle, the Henry could easily put a man down at two hundred fifty yards. This close, the damage was savage. Lying amid the sawdust of the cantina, his essence sagged out of him. One of his last glimpses was of the boots of the man as he stepped over to kick Stoddard's Colt away.

They were cavalry boots all right. "You were a blue belly, huh? Fighting to free your people," he said contemptuously.

His killer didn't answer. But he stood before him, saying something Stoddard couldn't hear clearly to Oakley. He shuddered. It was bitter cold, like that night, so long ago, when his men had captured four Union soldiers. They were blacks, of the Twenty-Fifth Regiment. Buffalo soldiers, the Indians had called them, because of the texture of their hair like that of the namesake's fur.

They'd had a good time that night, drinking corn liquor and teaching those tar babies a lesson, then they hung the four of them. Only now, with his life spilling out of him in a village not on any map, it didn't seem so goddamned funny. Those boots dangled before him, the faces of the men they'd slaughtered no longer features he could call up. One of those pair of boots had a plug missing from its toe. The soldier had fixed it with a piece of rough brown hide he'd sewn into place.

Stoddard gulped; he saw that boot like it was now, then realized, just as he began to slip away, that he was looking at that same boot right before him. It was on the gunman's foot. "That can't be," he said. "That can't be, we burned those bodies," he wailed hoarsely and the fog enclosed him for good.

Oakley looked over at Stoddard. "What he say?" But he was asking himself. The stranger was out in the street, having hitched his saddle back on his mule. Oakley stepped out into the street too, as did several of the villagers. The money sacks were draped over a horse. On the lower part of the saddle was branded the name O. H. Mimms.

"Mimms," Oakley said aloud. "In Galveston I heard of a black bounty hunter with a specialty in tracking down Confederate war criminals. That you, Odet Mimms?"

"Give me a hand with Stoddard." The two wrapped him in a couple of serapes and placed the body across the horse with the money. There was something funny about that, but neither man chuckled.

"I wish I knew what to say." Oakley hunched his shoulders.

"Looks like you got a few graves to dig." Mimms adjusted his hat. Riding away, he passed by the *bruja*'s cottage on the butte. She was sitting on the porch, watching him. After a while, the black rider, his mule, the money, and the fresh corpse disappeared in the sun's haze.

Death on D Street

Kristine Kathryn Rusch

Kristine Kathryn Rusch was a double Edgar nominee for 2000, once in the short story category and once in the novel category (under her pen name Kris Nelscott). Under her bestselling romance pen name, Kristine Grayson, she has won the Romantic Times Reviewer's Choice award. She is an award-winning science fiction author as well (and has just sold two science fiction mysteries to Roc Books) and is now branching into the western genre.

GINNY HAD JUST blown out the lamp and snuggled against me, her slender arm across my chest. The house still held too much of the day's warmth for us to be cuddled so close together, but I didn't move her. I liked the touch of her skin against mine, even when we were both too tired to do anything about it.

The baby was quiet for the first time in two days. She was teething and not happy about it. Ginny'd been rubbing my brandy against the baby's gums and it didn't seem to be doing anything except wasting good liquor. Still, Ginny swore that was a teething trick and I figured she'd know. She had gotten Sam through it, and on her own. By comparison, this couldn't be as bad.

We should have expected the knock on the door—or something—to break the quiet, but the knock surprised both of us. The baby wailed. Ginny must have already been asleep because she rolled over fast and reached for the gun she kept in the top dresser drawer.

I caught her arm and soothed her awake. I'd seen this reaction before and knew its source. A woman traveling alone across country had to be adept at protecting herself and her child. Nothing I could do convinced her she was safe. I'd stopped trying a year before.

I jerked on my pants as the knock came again. The baby's wail grew into a scream. I grabbed a shirt and said, "See to the kids." Then I headed down the stairs.

The knocking started a third time. I yanked the door open. Travis stood outside. He'd set his lantern on the porch. The yellow light illuminated his mud-stained pants and scuffed boots. The stench of cigars and cheap booze wafted inside.

"Sorry to wake ya," he said, "but Doc sent me. We got a holy hell of a mess on D Street."

D Street was the closest thing we had to a red light district. Three whorehouses and a few independents all lined up in a row. When I was sheriff, I restricted the hookers to that area. I'd learned that getting rid of them was impossible, not to mention unpopular. When men got time away from the mines, they wanted some affection, even if they had to pay for it.

"Where's Sheriff Muller?" I asked.

"Couldn't roust him."

"Drunk again?" I glanced up the stairs. The baby was still crying. The floorboards creaked as Ginny walked with her, trying to quiet her.

"Smelled like it," Travis said.

"What kind of mess?"

"Somebody killed Jeanne."

I stepped onto the porch and pulled the door closed. "While she was servicing him?"

"Jesus, Will, how'm I supposed to know?"

I shook my head and strode down the street. The dust was caked thanks to the summer heat, the wagon ruts treacherous in the darkness. The air was cool now, almost cold—one of the benefits of being in the mountains—but by dawn the heat would be creeping back, oppressive and overwhelming.

D Street was three blocks over and two down. I walked along Main Street. Most of the saloons were still open.

Music filtered out of O'Halleran's—someone was banging on the town's only piano. A few drunks were collapsed on the wooden sidewalk, leaning against the building, and I knew who they were.

I'd lived in Hope's Pass since it was founded, eight years before. I'd stumbled through here, looking to make my own fortune mining for silver. I lasted a month underground in the dark, candle burning away the oxygen, cave-ins a constant threat. Even though the pay was pretty good, I realized there were other ways to make money.

The town needed a sheriff and I volunteered, setting my own pay so high that no one in their right mind would meet it. But in those early days of what would become known as the Comstock Lode, no one was in their right mind.

They paid me more than I was worth for six years. Then Ginny came to town with little Sam and enough money to set up a dressmaking business. Four months later, we were married and I had resigned as sheriff. I felt it wasn't right to be dragged out of bed at all hours to calm down drunken miners or settle disputes over one of the town's whores. I ran for mayor and won; then I appointed Johann Muller as the new sheriff which was, I think, the worst decision I'd ever made.

D Street was down two blocks from Main, at the very edge of the mountainside. The ground was treacherous here—subject to floods in heavy rains. The buildings had washed away more than once. There were other problems as well. Mine shafts had been dug underneath this entire area of Hope's Pass, and more than one man had fallen through the street to the emptiness below. One of my campaign pledges had been to shore up the South Town area, but no one was really pushing me to fulfill that promise.

Lights were on in all the houses, and laughter filtered down from one of the porches. The men here weren't drunk—or at least weren't obviously so. A lot of them stood outside, smoking and talking as they waited in line. It must have been payday for one of the mines. I'd gotten so caught up in my daughter's teething drama I hadn't been paying attention.

I walked to the very last house. The street trailed off into nothing here, just scraggly grass and dust. Light poured out of this house as well, but the door was shut tight. As I approached, I saw a man knock and get sent away.

I didn't bother to knock. I tried the knob but it didn't turn. I glanced over my shoulder. Travis hadn't followed me. Apparently his only task had been to fetch me. That completed, he was able to go back to one of the saloons and see if he could finish the task of getting drunk.

So I rapped on the big picture window, closed despite the coolness of the evening, and shouted, "It's the mayor!"

The door opened just a crack.

"Doc sent for me," I said.

The door opened the rest of the way. I didn't recognize the girl behind it. She was blond and buxom, wearing a cheap satin wrap that tied at her waist and left nothing to the imagination. I didn't recognize her, but that wasn't a surprise. Girls came and went at these places so fast that sometimes I was surprised anyone knew who they were.

Her face was ashen and she didn't even bother to greet me. She just stepped aside, waited until I crossed the threshold, then pulled the door closed.

Six girls were in the parlor. A few were wearing dresses. The rest had on stained wraps just like the girl who had opened the door. Lucinda Beale, who'd opened this house six years before, sat on the edge of a chaise longue.

She waved a hand toward a door. "In there."

The room smelled of sweat and perfume. One of the girls sat on the ornate staircase leading to the second floor. She held her face in her hands, her legs slightly spread, revealing everything.

I walked through the women. They all moved away from me, something I'd never experienced in a whorehouse before.

The door led to the back parlor. It was usually reserved for the girls and "family," anyone involved with the house. I'd been there half a dozen times before, mostly for a drink after getting rid of unruly customers. I hadn't been inside since I married Ginny.

I swung the door open and stepped inside the room. It was hot and had the copper odor of blood.

"Watch where you step." Doc Clifton leaned against the wall, arms crossed. His open medical bag sat on the ornate red sofa. His face was puffy from lack of sleep. He'd been up the night before helping one of Rena's girls down the way through a particularly difficult birth.

I gave him a sideways look. Doc nodded toward the floor.

Jeanne lay there, legs splayed, wrapper open. Her torso was undamaged. The only visible wound was around her neck. It had been cut so deeply that her head had nearly been severed. Her hands, flung back beside her face, were cut as well.

I crouched beside her body. Her eyes were open. Her expression was one of great fear. I'd seen that expression on her face before. Her ebony skin brought a certain kind of clientele to Lucinda's—one with exotic tastes. But some of the customers objected to Jeanne's presence. Most of the fights I'd stopped in his last year as sheriff had started over Jeanne.

"Someone got her this time, huh?" I asked.

"It's not that simple." Doc pushed himself off the wall. He pointed to her hands. A single matching slit ran across both palms.

"So he surprised her, cut her throat, and she grabbed at the knife at the last minute."

Doc nodded. "But he killed her in here."

I rocked on my toes and looked around. Blood spattered the rug and a nearby table. It had clearly spurted. "He spun her."

"Yep."

I sighed. Murder in a small town was always difficult. I hated the cases when they involved someone important. Investigating one with a prostitute—and one who wasn't even white—would be even harder.

"We knew it was only a matter of time, Doc," I said. "If someone didn't get her here, they would have got her when Lucinda sent her to service the boys in Shantytown." I'd escorted her back a number of times and that was when I'd seen the fear on her face. The men usually ignored her, but the town's women—even my usually tolerant wife—gave her looks filled with hate.

Doc's eyes narrowed. "You gonna let this slide, then, Will?"

Of course I was. Solving murders wasn't my responsibility anymore. "That's for Sheriff Muller to decide."

"Sheriff Muller's a drunk and you know it. You gave him the job so someone would take the midnight calls and you could continue overseeing everything else."

I stiffened. "The girls get hurt. Sometimes they die. It's not a safe or particularly joyful profession. If anyone knows that, it's you, Doc. How many times do you get sent to D Street to tend to someone who'd had it too rough or was dying in childbirth and didn't know who the father was?"

"So we let this go."

I looked at Jeanne. She'd been pretty in a quiet sort of way. And she had been soft-spoken, almost shy. The prettiness was gone now, leached out of her with the blood. "It might be better to forget about it."

"Will you say that when this same maniac slits some other girl's throat? Or what if he attacks a real citizen, someone you care about? What then?"

There was an edge to Doc's words that I had never heard before. "You got a personal stake in this, Doc?"

His gaze slipped away from mine. "I don't ever want to see a mess like this again."

"Chances are it was a drifter."

"Who got invited into the back parlor?"

"All right. Maybe it was someone who knew her. Maybe even a relative. Lord knows Lucinda wouldn't want a colored man in her waiting room."

Doc looked at me. His gaze was clear and direct. "Is this about Jeanne's profession, Will? Or her color?"

My cheeks heated up. "I'm just trying to take care of this with a minimum of fuss."

"Fuss? We got a dead woman lying at our feet. Someone damn near sliced her head off and you're worried about fuss?"

"Yes," I said. "It's my job to keep things calm in Hope's Pass."

Doc's cheeks were an ugly red. "You ignore this, Will, and I'll kick up a fuss like you never seen before."

I turned to him, careful to keep my feet away from the blood smeared on the floor. "What was Jeanne to you, Doc?"

"A person," he snapped, and walked out of the room.

* * *

I'D NEVER BEEN shamed into an investigation before, and truth be told, it didn't make me enthusiastic about it. Still, I'd prove to Doc that I could solve this—or at least make sure whoever'd done this was long gone.

First, I gave the scene one more once-over. A silver tray lay near the kitchen door. Two glasses lay on the rug. One still had a bit of whiskey inside. The smell of blood overpowered the smell of alcohol, which was why I hadn't noticed it when I'd first come in.

The couch's cushions were untouched, except for Doc's bag, which he had left behind. I peered in it and saw nothing out of the ordinary. In fact, except for the body and the blood, the room was neat. Lucinda always had a penchant for clean.

There were no footprints in the blood on the floor, no handprints on the wall. Whoever had done this had been careful. There was also no break in the spatter, so he hadn't gone at her from the front.

Already I could hazard a guess on how the attack happened. He'd been sent to the back parlor and waited there, standing near the empty fireplace as Jeanne came out of the kitchen, carrying a silver tray. She'd clearly expected to entertain him, but whether that entertainment would lead to a trip upstairs, I couldn't yet tell. She'd planned on drinking with him, though, and she hadn't even gotten to the place where she could set the drinks down.

He grabbed her from behind, slit her throat quickly and viciously. She'd realized what was going on—she probably had a hell of a self-preservation instinct—and grabbed at the knife as he pulled it along her throat. But she hadn't had a chance to scream—he'd been too fast for her—and the method he chose wouldn't have allowed it.

Her life sprayed out of her fast, but she'd still struggled, forcing him to spin around because he was having trouble holding her. But she'd stopped pretty quick, going limp in his arms. Then he dropped her and ran out the kitchen—arms and hands bloody, but otherwise unscathed.

Knife wasn't there. Nothing else was there, except a downed silver tray and the body of a woman Doc felt important enough to take time from my family.

I pushed open the kitchen door and went inside. The kitchen was clean and everything was in its place. No dirt on the sideboards, tin canisters lined up against the walls. No fire burned in the stove, even though this room was hotter than the parlor. The only thing out of order was the whiskey decanter on the long kitchen table—and the bloody handprint on the back door.

I DECIDED TO talk to the girls individually. Most of them couldn't tell me anything—they'd been upstairs with a client. Only Lucinda and Elly had seen anything at all.

Elly'd been between customers when the front door opened. A blond man, his hair falling ragged over his collar, came inside. Despite the day's heat, he'd had on a gray coat. It was worn, almost a part of him. His hands were tucked in the pockets, pulling it down, messing up its shape.

At first she thought him old because he was so thin and he walked with a limp. Then she looked at his face and realized he couldn't be thirty yet. He spoke with a southern accent and his eyes were haunted. She figured him to be a Reb who'd been wandering since the war ended. She didn't remember seeing him before.

She'd sidled up to him, put a hand on his chest, and thrust herself against him. "I'm just what you need," she'd said.

"Maybe so, darlin'," he'd said gently, "but you ain't what I want."

She'd backed away from him then, and Lucinda'd come forward. Elly went to the kitchen where Jeanne was cleaning the sideboards. She hadn't had a customer all night and she was restless, feeling trapped in the house, unable to go outside.

They talked for a while, about nothing, Elly said, and then Elly rolled herself a cigarette and took it out back so Lucinda wouldn't catch her.

Not that Lucinda was trying. She was talking to the stranger, finding out exactly what it was he wanted.

He'd heard, he said, she had a colored girl in the house. Then he'd lowered his voice so soft she had to strain to hear. "Growin' up the way I did, I got me a special hankerin' for colored girls."

"We do have a girl," Lucinda said. "Her name's Jeanne. I'm sure she'd be happy to see you."

He glanced at the front door then, and she could sense how nervous he was. "I'd like to talk first, but if my friends find me with her . . ."

He didn't finish the sentence. He didn't have to. Lucinda had heard that request dozens of times.

"Why don't you go to the back parlor?" Lucinda said, pointing the way. "I'll have her join you in just a few minutes."

He'd smiled then. She'd thought it a particularly gentle smile, grateful really, and she'd smiled back. She hadn't thought anything of it, not even when she'd heard the tray and the thud. Jeanne knew the rules—clients should be taken upstairs once the transaction was to begin—but sometimes men were too eager. That was a rule Lucinda was always willing to bend, as long as the man paid in full.

It was when the hour was up and then some that Lucinda got impatient. She'd expected her southern drifter to leave long before that. So she'd pushed open the door to the back parlor, and she'd seen Jeanne and she'd hoped that somehow the girl had lived through it, which was why she'd sent for Doc at the same time she'd sent for the sheriff.

Which was why she was willing to talk to me.

"This sort of thing got me closed down in St. Louis," she said. "I been real careful about it in Hope's Pass. I run a safe house and my girls get treated good. You catch this man, Will, and you make everyone know that what he did had nothing to do with me."

"You should check your clientele for weapons, Cinda," I said.

"I do. They have to leave their guns at the door." Then her eyes brightened and she held up one chubby finger. "Just a moment."

She walked toward the door, moved a picture and opened a wall safe. From inside, she pulled out a small pistol.

"I suppose all your clients know that's there," I said.

Lucinda nodded. "That's where we keep the guns. The real safe is somewhere else."

She studied the pistol for a moment, then came toward me. "I got this off him before he went into the back parlor.

Obviously, he didn't come back for it, although he should have."

"Should have?" I stood.

"I've never handled a gun quite like this one before." She extended the gun to me, and I froze.

It was a Remington-Elliot single-shot derringer, .41 rimfire caliber, with walnut grips and blue plating.

"You sure that was his?" I asked.

"Oh, yes." She frowned at it. "Pretty little thing, isn't it?"

It was. It was so small that it fit in the palm of her hand. I took the gun from her and examined the barrel. Etched into the plating were the initials V. L., exactly as I expected.

"What's there?" Lucinda asked.

"Hmm?" I looked at her. She was frowning at me. "Oh, nothing. Mind if I keep this?"

"I surely don't want it." She put her hands on her wide hips. "But it is a special gun. He might come back for it."

"He might at that. Where's Travis?" Travis worked as her security on busy nights.

"Probably drinking. He hasn't come back since he fetched you."

I checked the gun's chamber. It wasn't loaded. I slipped the gun into my pocket. "You get your own gun out, stay awake awhile. I'll make sure Sheriff Muller comes to keep an eye on this place, and I'll find Travis for you."

Lucinda smiled at me. "You always take good care of us, Will."

In the past, I would have leaned over and kissed her cheek. But I didn't dare get more perfume on me than had already leached into my clothes from this place. "You can tell Doc that it's all right to come downstairs again."

Lucinda's smile turned sly. "I'm sure he'll come down when he's ready."

"When he does," I said, "make sure he does something with Jeanne. Remind him that's his responsibility, not mine."

Her smile faded. "Of all my girls to end up like that, I'd've never imagined Jeanne."

"Why not?" I asked.

Lucinda's gaze met mine. "She never was one who liked it rough."

* * *

I FOUND TRAVIS and sent him back to Lucinda's, not that he would do much good considering the condition he was in. Then I slapped Muller awake and sent him as well. He, at least, was a little more sober than Travis, only because he'd had time to sleep it off.

All the while, I fingered the gun in my pocket, the cold metal sending shivers through me. It took all my strength to find the men, to get them back to Lucinda's, before heading home.

The sun was rising as I walked up Main. My house was dark, curtains closed, and the door locked. I opened the front door as quietly as I could and stepped inside. The early-morning brightness hadn't reached the interior of the house. Everything was in shadow. But the baby wasn't crying.

I made my way up the stairs. When I reached the bedroom door, I stared at my wife, asleep in our bed. She lay on her left side, one hand tucked beneath her cheek, her chest rising and falling with her even breathing. Even asleep she looked tired.

I walked toward her, never taking my gaze off her. She didn't stir. I crouched beside her and opened the top drawer of the dresser, and suddenly she was awake, reaching for the gun, the one I was covering with my right hand.

"Will?" she asked, as she blinked herself fully awake. "Everything all right?"

"I don't know." My voice sounded odd to my own ears, flat and emotionless. I pulled her gun out of the drawer and rested it on my left palm. The blue plating was nicked, the walnut grip scratched. But even from my angle, I could see the engraved initials.

V. L.

"Will?"

From my pocket, I pulled out the other gun and let it rest on my right palm. "Look what I found tonight."

All the color left her face. Her brown eyes were wide, and I could see her tamping down panic. "Where?"

"In a whorehouse safe."

"That what they called you out for? A gun?"

I had heard that kind of question before, and it made me sad. It was a stalling-for-time question, one that let the asker think about her story rather than try to obtain an answer.

"No," I said, not willing to tell her what had happened. "Tell me about your gun, Ginny."

"It's just a gun, Will." Another stall.

"Then there's nothing to stop you from telling me about it."

Her gaze hadn't left my face, but I could see that it took some effort. She was at a disadvantage. I was good at reading people, but I was best at reading her.

"I got it in a pawnshop in Kansas City, before I took the wagon train out here. I figured Sam and I needed protection."

"From a single-shot revolver?"

She shrugged. "It was all I could afford."

She was lying. God help me, I could tell she was lying. The slight twitch of her upper lip, the sweat forming at the hairline. Something about this was scaring her and she didn't want to tell me what.

"I thought the V. L. stood for Virginia Lysander," I said. "In fact, you told me that once."

"It's my gun," she said. "It can stand for anything I want. I don't know what it stood for before."

"It was just a bit of luck that you found a gun with your initials on it?"

"That's why I picked it out," she said.

"I thought you said it was all you could afford."

A spot of color formed in each cheek. She knew I'd caught her. "That too."

"Ginny," I said, almost pleading with her. "This is serious."

She pushed her lips together. She wasn't going to say any more.

"The man who owned this gun murdered Jeanne."

She blinked at me. "Jeanne?"

"She was a whore on D Street."

Ginny frowned as if she were trying to place the name. It was a small town and she had lived here nearly as long as Jeanne. I knew they had to know of each other. "You mean that coal-black girl who worked Shantytown?"

"Yeah."

"I thought you said you got the gun from a safe."

"It's a long story, Ginny. I just want to know how you fit in."

She flung back the covers and got out of bed. She was moving with great purpose. "Where's the man now?"

"I don't know. That's what I have to find out. I thought maybe you could help me."

"How can I help you?" She grabbed her dress off the chair that she had lain it on the night before.

"Tell me what the connection is between the guns."

She pulled the dress over her head, then keeping it bunched around her shoulders, stepped out of her nightdress. I couldn't see her face when she said, "How should I know?"

"The matching gun, Ginny."

"I told you. I bought it at a pawnshop." She slipped her head through the dress. Her hair was mussed. "You believe me, don't you?"

I stared at her, this woman I thought I knew well. I didn't believe her, and I didn't like the way I had started thinking. The way she woke up on edge, the fact that she always kept the gun near her, the difficulty she'd had initially trusting me or any man.

"Where'd you get the gun, Ginny?"

She blinked, looked away, then shook her head. "Don't ask me anymore. You're not going to like what I have to say."

"What I like and don't like doesn't matter, Ginny. Where'd you get the gun?"

She leaned against the wall, her head narrowly missing the crucifix she had put up there when we got married. "From a dead man."

Somehow that didn't surprise me. "Who?"

She swallowed, closed her eyes, and bowed her head. "Sam's father."

HE'D BEEN A decorated officer in the Confederate Army. He'd returned to Atlanta on a short leave around Christmas 1862. That was when he'd forcibly raped Ginny and left her pregnant with Sam. Sam was born in August 1863 and she found she didn't care how he was conceived. He was her boy. She made up a husband, a father for Sam—Russ Lysander, tragically killed at Gettysburg, the man she'd always told me about—and prepared to leave Atlanta as soon as she was healthy enough.

It took her some time to regain her strength after the birth. By November 1863, she was ready to leave. But as she was figuring out how best to travel with an infant, she ran into Sam's father again.

He had returned to Atlanta on Jefferson Davis's business. Somehow—Ginny wasn't real clear about this—Sam's father managed to overpower her and take her to his home where he tried to rape her again. Only this time, she managed to get his gun.

She shot him, point-blank range, through the heart. He was dead before he hit the floor.

Then, she said, her voice oddly emotionless, she robbed him—took his gold wedding band, the diamond earrings he'd given his wife, some pieces of silver—spoons, a small box, and napkin rings. She also took the Confederate banknotes from his pocket and the gold coins he'd stashed in his safe, and she used all of that to make her way west.

As she told me all of this, she met my gaze. It was as if she didn't care what I thought—she would always be proud of what she had done.

"Who's the man with the second gun?" I asked.

"His son."

I waited for her to tell me his name.

Her lips thinned. "Beau Lewis."

We stared at each other for a long moment. I could see the fear and hesitation behind her bravado. She wanted me to reassure her that I still loved her, even though she had killed someone, even though she'd been defiled. Neither of those things mattered to me.

What mattered was that she hadn't trusted me enough to tell me either of them until now.

"May I have my gun?" she asked.

"You don't need it," I said.

"And if he somehow finds out I'm in town?"

"You're not using the same name, are you?" That question was as much for me as it was for her.

She shook her head once.

"Then you'll be all right."

"I don't like to be without it, Will." A plaintive note to her voice, just the hint of begging.

I handed her the gun. "Stay inside. I'll be back soon."

"How're you going to find him?" she asked.

"If what you say is true, then this gun means something to him. He'll come back for it." I slipped the extra gun in my pocket. "And I'll be waiting for him."

WHOREHOUSES WERE QUIET places in the daytime. The girls usually slept long past noon, and no clients appeared before dark. Things began to become active in the afternoons at a well-run place like Lucinda's—people ate, cleaned, shopped, did all they needed to do.

I figured Lewis knew this, and would be back. I had only a few hours in which to catch him.

By the time I arrived back at Lucinda's, Travis had fallen asleep in the chair by the door. Muller for once was awake and alert, but hadn't seen anything out of the ordinary.

I relieved him, locked and jammed the back door, ordered Lucinda to keep the girls upstairs, and then I unlocked the front door. I positioned myself between the front door and the safe, my Colt resting on my leg with my hand covering it.

Sure enough, long about nine A.M., I heard rustling outside. My grip tightened on the Colt, and I fished in my pocket for the derringer. The door opened, and a man sidled inside.

He was gaunt and blond, his hair ragged, his face careworn. He wore a threadbare gray coat, his hands in its pockets, ruining its shape.

"Come back for this?" I asked, holding up the derringer.

He froze, one hand on the jamb of the open door. Sunlight framed him, making him look as if he were outlined in light. "I left in a hurry last night."

He had a soft southern accent, not as coarse as I had imagined from Elly's description. He sounded educated.

"I bet you did. A man usually doesn't stick around when he murders someone in cold blood."

To my surprise, he didn't even try to bolt. "You the sheriff?"

"I'm the mayor."

"Then you should know why I did what I did. That nigra girl, she murdered my daddy."

"Did she now?"

"Yes, sir. After the Devil Lincoln issued his illegal declaration freeing all the slaves in a country he no longer ruled, she let herself into the house, took one of my daddy's guns from his matched set, and shot him with it. Then she told all her people to run away. Thank the good Lord some of them stayed to tell me about it when I came home more'n a year ago."

I felt cold. "You're sure this was Jeanne?"

"Her name wasn't Jeanne. It was Jubilee. She took my dead momma's name when she pawned my family's silver in St. Louis and signed onto the wagon train. That's how I tracked her here."

"Your momma's name?" I had to brace my arm so that the hand holding the Colt didn't shake.

"Virginia Lysander."

I felt as if I were encased in a shell.

"I take it," I said flatly, "you never met the woman who murdered your father."

"Oh, I seen her," he said. "She was ours, after all."

"But you don't remember her," I said, "and you didn't ask for her by name when you came here."

"What is this?" He stepped further inside. "Why should I ask for her by name? She'd already changed it twice. I just asked where the town's nigra women were. I was told there was only one."

"And?" My throat was dry.

"She recognized me same time as I recognized her." He held out his hands. "I was telling you this because I thought you was a reasonable man. I wasn't willing to take her back to Georgia for trial. Laws've changed, and I didn't want to travel with a darkie, not in today's world. Surely, you can see that."

"I can."

"So you can give me my daddy's gun, I'll leave your fair city, and we'll pretend this conversation never happened."

I stood. "I'm afraid I can't do that."

"Whyever not?"

"You just reminded me," I said as I approached him. "Laws have changed."

"It's biblical. An eye for an eye. Justice has been done."

"No, it hasn't," I said, fishing for my handcuffs. "Murder's a hanging offense in Hope's Pass."

"She was a nigra, a murderess, and a whore. Ain't no one gonna miss her."

"I can think of at least two people who will," I said as I cuffed his hands behind his back.

I led him into the sunshine. As we stepped onto D Street, I wasn't surprised to see Ginny, standing alone in the dust, her derringer out and pointed at Lewis.

"Go home, honey," I said, feeling more weary than I'd ever felt in my life, hoping that Lewis wouldn't realize the mistake he'd made.

But his face flushed an angry red. "Ruby," he said in soft recognition. "Son of a bitch. You and Jubilee done this together."

"Step aside, Will," she said to me. "I don't want my shot to go wild and hit you."

"Ginny, honey, this isn't right."

Lewis gave me an odd sideways look.

"It's right that he killed Jube?" she asked.

"He's going to hang for that."

"He's gonna ruin our lives, Will."

"What the hell's she talking about?" Lewis asked me. "You got something with this woman?"

"She's my wife," I said softly.

"Tarnation, man, don't you know what she's done? She's been passin'. She was one of our house niggers from the time she was old enough to carry."

"Shut up!" Ginny waved the gun at him.

"She's been lying to you," he said in that sly voice. "All these years, making you think she's something she's not."

"Move aside, Will," she said again.

"She used you to make her greater than she was. And now you know what she is. A killer, an animal, no better than a snake."

That frozen feeling was still with me. All of this felt like it was happening to someone else.

"Will." Ginny sounded panicked. "I don't care what you

think of me. But what about Sam? The baby?"

Sam, with his gray, trusting eyes, and my daughter, whose black hair had more curl than I'd ever seen in a baby. Curly black hair and skin so white it made mine seem dark.

I reached into my pocket for the handcuff key. My hand was shaking. I wasn't thinking. I was just acting.

I unlocked his cuffs and walked away, leaving her with her single-shot pistol alone with him and his knife.

SHE HAD LEFT the children by themselves. The baby was crying in her crib, drool coming from her sore gums. Her diaper was wet. I changed it by rote, then cradled her against me and looked into her black, black eyes.

I could see it now, of course, now that I was looking. The curl of her hair, the darkness of her eyes, the twist of her features in a way that I had once thought particularly Ginny. Amazing that I'd missed it before.

Sam was tugging on me, his face splotchy. He'd been crying too, although, at three, he was too big a man to admit it. I crouched down and hugged him to me, and willed the numb feeling to go away.

I was afraid of what I'd find underneath it. Loathing for Ginny, for me. I'd always despised men who used their slave women, like my father had used his. I'd walked away from that life ten years before, wanting no part of it, content to sit out the war in the West and watch the casualties roll by.

I didn't figure I'd have some of its victims in my own house.

Sam was a bright little boy, full of pluck and energy. He didn't deserve half a life. And neither did the baby, her whole future ahead of her.

Maybe, on some level, I could understand what Ginny had done. And why she had to lie to me.

I could understand it, but I wasn't sure I could ever forgive her.

SHE CAME HOME about a half hour later, her eyes haunted. The blood that spattered the bottom of her skirt told me she'd had to use Lewis's knife to finish the job—her shot had only wounded him.

The baby was quiet. Sam was watching us from the doorway.

I led her into our bedroom, careful not to touch her, and closed the door.

"Where is he?" I asked.

"I left him on the street." Her voice was low. "Someone'll find him."

"And come get me."

She nodded. "But if you don't make something of it, no one else will."

She was right. No one would care, and everyone would have their own version of what happened. Some might even credit me.

In an odd way, they would be right. Because I wasn't going to speak up. As Lewis had said, justice had been done.

"You want to tell me the truth now?" I asked. "I deserve to know."

Ginny looked away, her expression sad. Then she closed her eyes, and took us both back to the past.

WHEN SHE WAS sixteen, Lewis's father visited her for the first time. When she was seventeen, she had his child. She had another child the next year, and the next, and when it became clear that she preferred motherhood to her duties, the children were sold as part of a package to a nearby plantation and she never saw them again.

She was pregnant with Sam when word of the Emancipation Proclamation hit. She stole the derringer, and waited, shooting Lewis's father as he pressed down on her in the dark.

Jeanne heard the shot, and was the one who thought of taking the money, the silver, the rings. Together the women left, making their way north, helping each other survive.

Sam was born in New York, the first free child in Ginny's family. It was there she realized that unless she was seen with Jeanne, everyone thought she and Sam were white.

She sold one of the spoons and left in the middle of the night for St. Louis, not telling Jeanne where she was going. She invented Russ Lysander and his untimely death, and received treatment beyond her dreams.

Everything went well, until Jeanne turned up in Hope's

Pass. She'd followed Ginny across country. Jeanne earned part of her living at Lucinda's and supplemented it by blackmailing my wife.

Which was why every time I saw them near each other, they looked at each other with such hate.

GINNY'S VOICE HAD trailed to nearly nothing. Her gaze met mine, and I saw the pleading. But Lewis's voice echoed in my mind.

She'd murdered two men. And she'd lied to me.

There was a knock on the door. I jumped, even though I'd expected it. In the next room, the baby started to wail.

"What do we do now?" Ginny asked.

"Will!" Travis yelled from the street. "Doc says we got another situation."

The baby's cries had grown piercing. Sam tapped on our door. "Mommy?" he said.

Ginny's gaze met mine and held it. I always prided myself on doing the right and honorable thing.

Only this time, I had no idea what the right and honorable thing was.

"Will!" Travis yelled.

I could see fear in her face, fear greater than any I'd seen before. I sighed.

"Change your clothes," I said, "and feed the children. I have no idea when I'll be back."

I pulled open the bedroom door. Sam launched himself at my leg, and held it so tight that he nearly cut off circulation. He would grow up slender like his brother. He'd have the same gray eyes, the same deep voice.

I slipped my hand on his head, feeling his thin straight hair.

Ginny was watching us, her hands clasped together.

"And make sure you're here when I get home," I said. "I want to have dinner with my family tonight."

Her breath caught. I could see her fighting to stay calm. "What happens next, Will?" she asked, her voice soft. "To us?"

I stroked Sam's hair. We had only one choice. "We put the past behind us, Ginny, like all people who come West."

Her smile was thin, but there was hope in her eyes. Maybe there was hope in mine as well.

"Will!" Travis yelled from below.

I nodded at her, kissed our son as I extracted him from my leg, and went downstairs to clean up Ginny's mess.

Lay My Money Down

Bill Crider

Bill Crider has written more than fifty western, mystery, and horror novels under both his own name and various pseudonyms. His mysteries have been nominated for both the Shamus and Anthony awards, and he won the latter for his first novel in the Sheriff Dan Rhodes series, *Too Late to Die.* The eleventh novel in the Rhodes series, *A Romantic Way to Die,* was published by St. Martin's Press in Fall 2001. His western stories have appeared in such anthologies as *The Mysterious West,* edited by Tony Hillerman, and *Great Stories of the American West,* edited by Martin H. Greenberg. His latest western novels are *Outrage at Blanco* and *Texas Vigilante.*

> "West of the Pecos, there is no law;
> and west of El Paso, there is no
> God."
>
> —old Texas saying

1

MY DADDY WAS a preacher, and when he walked into a saloon one day to bring a backsliding sinner into the fold, he never dreamed that he'd lose his only boy to what he called "the devil's playground."

But that's how it happened. I was with him that day, and

when I walked through those batwing doors, Satan got a hold on me that he never let loose. The way I figured it, the Devil was having a hell of a lot more fun than anybody else I knew, especially my daddy, and I wanted to have some of it myself. I wanted to spend the rest of my days where I could smell the smoke of the cheap cigars and sniff the sharp tang of even cheaper liquor. I wanted to watch the painted ladies smile their falsehearted smiles while the rinky-tink piano played all night and the ivory ball clacked 'round and 'round in the roulette wheel. I wanted to buy me a black broadcloth coat and a ruffled white vest and have a little black goatee like the one the Devil himself wore in the pictures of him I'd seen, all red and smirking, with a pitchfork in his hand and a long tail with a sharp point on the end of it.

Most of all, I wanted to lay my money down on one of those round green-topped tables and risk everything I had on one turn of the cards.

So as soon as I was old enough, I ran away from home. I guess my old daddy prayed for me every night for the next thirty years, right up until the day he died, but it never did him any good.

Oh, I never wore that broadcloth coat, and I never grew that black goatee, but I spent most of my nights at those tables, waiting for the next hand to bring me the big pot and make me the richest man around.

That never happened, either, mainly because there was enough of my daddy's teaching left in me to keep me honest. There were plenty of others who weren't, but I never shaved a deck or used a crooked deal. And while I never got rich, I did get to spend my time in some mighty interesting places, from Hayes to Deadwood, where I'd sat across the table from the cold-eyed killer they called Wild Bill. I'd been in Tombstone, too, where I met the Earp brothers not long before their little dust-up with the Clanton clan.

And I've laid my money down in plenty of places where the people were so bad that Hell wouldn't have 'em, and places where the Devil himself would have felt right at home. In places like that, just about anything can happen, and more often than not, it does.

And one of the worst of the lot was a little town called Vinegaroon.

2

THE VINEGAROON'S A scorpion, and no scorpion was ever meaner than the town that took its name. It was an end-of-track town on the Rio Grande when I went there, out west of the Pecos River. It was one of those places they called a hell-on-wheels, where there was damn little law and where God, if he'd ever been there in the first place, hadn't paid a visit in quite a spell.

The country all around was hard rock ground, and there wasn't much living there except for sheep and a few cattle. And scorpions, of course.

But that was before the Sunset Railroad started laying down tracks that way, headed west toward El Paso. When that happened, a town sprang up that was full of people from all over the country, with plenty of foreigners thrown in. There were even a few Chinese. It was a rough-and-tumble crowd, the kind that thought it had been a quiet day if there wasn't somebody killed every few hours. A crowd like that in a place like Vinegaroon just naturally attracts whores and cardsharps, men with dice and men with faro lay-outs, men with roulette wheels and men with nothing at all except a gleam in their eyes and a keen nose for a dollar.

And one of those men was me.

3

I RODE INTO Vinegaroon on a coolish day at the tail end of October, when a norther was blowing a stinging rain at my back and my horse and I needed something to eat and a warm place to sleep.

Finding a place for the horse was easier than finding one for me. The town was just about nothing but tents, most all of them thrown with nothing but the bare rock for a floor, and every one of them crowded unless you could find a place in one where somebody'd just been killed. There was always a chance of that.

The first place I went after seeing to my horse was a tent saloon called the Belle of the Rio. I guess the owner had a sense of humor.

It was getting on toward the latter part of the afternoon, so there was already plenty of trade in the saloon, especially if you counted the two men asleep with their heads down on the tables where they sat, snoring like hogs. Maybe they just didn't have any other place to sleep, like me, or maybe they just didn't want to go out in the rain. There was also something that looked like six or seven grapes scattered on the floor. One of them squished under my boot when I stepped on it by accident.

"Where'd those grapes come from?" I asked the bartender while I was pulling the cork out of the beer he'd brought me.

He leaned across the bar and took a look. "Hell, there ain't no grapes in these pasts. We had us a big fight in here last night. Them things are eyeballs."

I nodded and drank my beer, taking my time, like I saw eyeballs on the floor all the time. When I was done, I asked him if he knew where I could find a friendly game of cards.

"No such thing as friendly in this town, mister. You can find a game, though, just about anywhere you look."

"Not in here, though."

"Damn right. I got enough trouble with fightin' in here without that. There'd be more than eyeballs on the floor if there was gamblin' goin' on. These sonsabitches around here don't take lightly to losin'."

I accepted the implied warning, though maybe I didn't take it to heart the way I should have. I drank my beer and left, being careful this time not to step on any of the grapes. Or whatever they were. I was pretty sure they were grapes, but the light was bad, and I just wasn't taking any chances. I didn't want to step on anybody's eyeball if I could help it, even if I didn't know who it belonged to.

Before I got outside, the bartender called, "You be careful, young fella. There's been some mighty odd things goin' on around Vinegaroon lately."

"Like eyeballs in the floor?"

"Worse than that, a whole lot worse."

I turned back to him. "You want to tell me what?"

"Just watch your back, that's all."

"I always do," I said.

It was near about sundown when I left the Belle of the Rio, or it would've been if there'd been any sun. The sky was gray as slate, but the rain had let up to the point that it was just a mist hanging in the air, the kind of mist that clung to your clothes and seeped in wherever there was a loose seam or a little rip or tear. But that was all right. I didn't have to go far before I came to the kind of place I was looking for.

I could hear the music before I pushed through the tent flaps. It wasn't dark inside, with yellowish light coming from lanterns hung here and there, but it wasn't bright as day by any means. There were long shadows jumping on the canvas walls, and a haze of smoke hung in the air. There were men dancing with the fancy women in their ruffled dresses to the song a sad-looking man was plinking out on an out-of-tune piano, and there were men lined up at the bar with glasses in their hands. But I didn't care about them. The men I was interested in were sitting at a couple of tables near the piano. They were holding cards, and money was changing hands.

I walked on over for a closer look. They were as hard-looking a crew, as I'd ever seen, but then you didn't stay soft for long if you were laying tracks in the hard-rock country.

They looked like they'd been at the game for a while. Four of them had eyes as steely as brand-new railroad spikes and mouths as tight and thin as a rattler's. But the fifth one of them looked even meaner than the rest.

He was practically a giant, two heads taller than anybody else at the table, and he must've weighed over three hundred pounds. He was hairy, to boot. He was wearing one of those broadcloth coats, so I couldn't see much of him, but the backs of his hands were covered with thick brown hair. He wasn't wearing a hat, but he didn't need one, not with the shaggy head of hair he was sporting, and his face was almost covered with a beard so thick that I could hardly see his eyes and through which his long nose poked out like a rat from a thicket. There was a wild, rank, meaty smell to him that let me know he wasn't any too fond of taking a bath.

You wouldn't think a man that big would need much protection, but lying on the table in front of him was a Colt's Dragoon .44-caliber that must've been thirty years old or more. The walnut grips were worn thin, and the engraving on the cylinder was nearly rubbed away, as if the gun had seen a lot of hard use.

Now I don't carry a gun, myself, but if I did, it wouldn't be a Dragoon. It was fine for its time, but Mr. Colt makes a better gun these days. The Dragoon's big, heavy, and more than a foot long. It's hard to hold one steady and shoot it straight unless you're a big man. Which this one was. He was as big a man as I ever saw.

He looked up with yellow eyes when I got close to the table and said, "Want to sit in for a hand, stranger?"

His voice was a low rumble, almost a growl, and I couldn't see his mouth moving in the thicket of beard.

I looked around at the other players, who looked back without a word or a smile. If anything, their mouths got even thinner.

There was an empty chair at the table, though, and there were cards and money on the table, so I sat down and said, "Deal me in."

The big man said, "Ante up."

As soon as we all did, he said, "Cards to the gamblers," and started to deal.

His hands were big and they looked clumsy, but they weren't. He slid the cards across the table as slick as anybody I ever saw, and I've seen a few.

"Name's Bruno," he said when the dealing was done.

"Just call me Joe," I said, carefully fanning out my hand to have a look.

"OK, Joe. Whatever you say."

My hand wasn't much good. In fact, it was flat worthless, and I wondered about the deal. Something must've showed in my face because Bruno asked if anything was bothering me.

"You unhappy about something?" he rumbled, laying his hand on that big old Dragoon and sort of rubbing his fingers on the worn grips.

I looked around the table at four sets of eyes as flat and black as the steel rails being laid outside of town.

"Not a thing," I said, not being a complete fool.

Bruno nodded. "Right. Now let's get on with the game."

So we did. And as it turned out, there wasn't a thing wrong with the deal. Oh, I didn't win that hand, but the cards began to run my way right after that.

And they kept right on running. It was one of the best streaks I'd ever been on, and I was sorry to see it come to an end, but I could see that it was. I could see that it wasn't going to end with everybody smiling and shaking hands, too.

The four tight-mouthed men didn't complain much. They put in their money and they took their losses with barely a sigh or a cuss. But not Bruno. From the second hand on, he growled in his beard and looked at me with half-hidden eyes that glowed like coals.

He didn't say anything, though, not for a good long time. He just kept playing and drinking beer. I never saw a man that loved his beer so much. Maybe it was the beer that made him do what he did late in the game when I covered his three queens with three kings. As soon as I did that, he kicked back his chair and stood up, a lot quicker than you would've thought for a man that size.

The chair slapped into the wall of the tent like a shot. The piano stopped, and the place went dead quiet. Everybody in the saloon was looking our way, not that I blamed them. Bruno was quite a sight. His head was near to brushing the top of the tent, and he was swinging his arms wildly, and that Colt's Dragoon was in his right hand. It was a mighty big gun, but it didn't look any bigger than a derringer with Bruno holding it.

"You cheatin' son-of-a-bitch!" Bruno said.

There wasn't any use asking who he meant. He meant me. I looked him straight in the eye, though I had to look up a long way to do it.

"I never cheated a man in my life," I told him, which was God's own truth. "You can ask these other fellas here if they think I was cheating. They'll all tell you I wasn't."

I looked to them for confirmation, but it was too late. They'd slithered away into the crowd as if they'd never been at the table. They didn't have to worry about taking their money with them. I had most of it. Keeping it looked like it might be another matter.

Bruno brought that big pistol of his down on the tabletop, and the wood popped like breaking bones as the table shattered into flinders. Money scattered all around.

Bruno took a step toward me, and I was thinking that it'd be my eyeballs on the floor the next day, and my arms and legs, too, most likely, but it didn't work out that way.

Someone behind me said, "Hold it right there, you big bastard."

Bruno stopped and looked past me at whoever was standing back there.

"I can get you before you pull those triggers," he said, but he didn't bring his pistol up to fire it.

I sneaked a look behind me. The bartender was standing there with a Winchester rifle in his hands. The rifle was pointed right at Bruno's face, and it was steady and still. The bartender looked like he knew how to use it.

"Hand your pistol to your friend," he said.

Bruno didn't think of me as much of a friend, I'm sure, but he handed over the gun. It felt like it weighed a ton, but I held it as level as I could and pointed right at his belly.

"I don't need a gun for pipsqueaks like you," Bruno said.

"You could be right," the man said. "But I don't think you could get to me in time. What I think is that this fella in front of me'd slow you down enough so I could pull the trigger on this rifle and put a bullet right in your eye."

I wasn't going to slow Bruno down unless he had to pause to knock me aside, not even if I gut-shot him, but I didn't want him to think that. So I said to the bartender, "You got that right."

"You cheatin' horse turd," Bruno said.

I could tell he didn't like me.

"You just go on along," the bartender said. "And don't make any more trouble."

"I'll go," Bruno said to the bartender. "But you'll rue the day." He looked at me. "And you, too, horse turd."

He walked over what was left of the table and lumbered out of the tent.

When he was gone, I picked up my money and thanked

the bartender. There'd been no real reason for him to take my part, other than out of the goodness of his heart. He was a thick-bodied man with a trim gray beard. He was wearing a vest, and he had on sleeve garters, a pretty spruce gent for a place like that. He accepted my thanks, but he didn't smile.

"I didn't do it for you," he said. "My name's Roy Bean. I own this place, and I was just trying to keep the two of you from tearing my business apart. You should've let that big bastard win."

I told him that something like that would never have occurred to me.

"Well, it should've. He don't look like one to take his losses lightly."

Seemed like I'd already heard that about folks in Vinegaroon.

"You know him?" I asked.

"Hell, no. Never saw him before, and I wish I'd never seen him this time. But there's been some strange things happenin' around here lately, and I don't like the looks of him. You might not think it to look at me, but I'm the law around here. The Law West of the Pecos, some folks call me, and I don't like trouble."

I didn't either, but I didn't say so. What I said was, "You mind if I stick around, see if I can find another game?"

Bean lowered the rifle and looked around. Nobody looked back at him.

"I guess you can stay," he told me. "Long as there's no more trouble."

"There won't be," I said, hoping I was telling the truth.

As it turned out, I was. At least for a while. The piano started up playing again, the whores started working the crowd, and I found another game with some players who hoped I'd used up my quota of good luck for the night.

Turned out I pretty much had. But I didn't lose everything I'd won earlier, and at least this bunch was chattier than the others I'd hooked up with.

"That was a big son-of-a-bitch," one of them remarked about Bruno as we watched the deal.

"Big enough to tear a man limb from limb if the judge hadn't stopped him," another said. He spit on the floor when he said it.

"Wonder if he's the one been killin' folks?" a third chimed in.

They weren't making me feel any more comfortable, so I asked what they were talking about.

"Been some bad things goin' on around here. Besides the usual killin's, I mean. Coupla Chinamen was found in an alley the other day, tore up like rag dolls. Shot first, then just ripped apart."

"God damn," I said.

"Hell, it was just Chinamen," the dealer said. "Let's play cards."

So that's what we did.

4

I NEVER COUNT the hours when I'm at a gaming table. If others want to do that, it's fine by me, but what I care about is the turn of the cards.

So all I know is that it was getting on into the small hours of the morning, in that time between the dark and the day-light when the world outside the tent starts to get quiet and slow, even in a town like Vinegaroon. It's a time when the air gets heavy and the mist rises up out of the river valleys, a time when the scorpions burrow a little deeper in the cracks in the rocks, and the dogs whimper in their sleep. It's a time when some funny things can happen, things that men tell about around campfires and card tables for years to come. Nobody ever believes the stories, or so they claim, but you can see them sneak a glance over their shoulders when they think you're not looking, or touch the handles of their pistols to make sure they're still there. Or maybe shud-der a little and then try to pass it off with a laugh.

I'm not vouching for what happened that night in Vine-garoon. There might be other people who would tell the story differently if you could get them to talk about it at all. But I was there, and this is the way I saw it.

It started after I laid down a pair of deuces that I was hoping would steal a pot. I should've known better, and another fella was raking it in with a big grin that his two pair didn't really rate, when I heard a noise outside the tent.

It sounded a little like the low rumble of a train.

I wasn't the only one who heard it. Everyone at the table looked up.

"What the hell?" someone said.

"I'm checking it to you," another said, throwing his cards in the middle of the table.

He started to stand up, and he was halfway out of his chair when five claws popped through the tough canvas tent wall and ripped it right down to the ground like they were tearing through a spiderweb. Through the shreds of the canvas stepped the biggest, meanest-looking bear I'd ever seen, and it was coming straight for me. Standing behind him was Bruno, laughing like he'd never seen a funnier sight than the look on my face.

There were three or four tables between me and the bear, but that didn't bother him. He reached out and swiped the first one out of the way, flinging it clear across the tent. One of the card players sitting there didn't move, and the bear flung him after the table, half his chest ripped out by those lethal claws, and he streamed ribbons of blood until he hit a tent pole and cracked it in the middle.

The blood splattered on the tables and the floor and on the men and women who were yelling and running and trying to get away from that bear. They were falling over one another and not making much headway, and the cracked tent pole let the canvas sag so that a coal-oil lamp crashed down and splashed fire and fuel on the canvas, which started to burn here and there.

Black smoke swirled all around, but the bear didn't seem to mind it. He stood up, reached out, and raked his claws down the back of one of the whores, tearing her dress right off her and leaving red tracks and flaps of skin. She took one step and fell over on her face.

Two men ran across her, stepping right in the middle of her bloody back. The bear swiped at one of them and took his hat and the top of his head right off, peeling the scalp straight back, where it flopped around as he ran. He didn't even seem to notice.

As for me, I couldn't move. It was like I was rooted to the ground. I couldn't seem to take my eyes off that damned bear. But I did manage to get that old Colt's Dragoon up and into firing position just as the bear was about on top of me. I pulled the trigger, and the damned gun nearly jerked my arm off. It had a kick like a government mule. I was sure the ball hit the bear, but the bear didn't seem to mind. It didn't slow down any more than if a flea had bit it.

"Get outta the way, goddammit," someone yelled at me.

It was Roy Bean, and he had that rifle. I ducked down, and Bean fired a shot at the bear's head. It didn't bother the bear a bit as far as I could tell, and the next thing I knew I was looking up into its slavering mouth, which was wide open and hanging over my head. Needles didn't have a thing on that bear's teeth, and I could tell he'd like nothing better than to bite may face right off me.

He was about to do it, too, but first he slammed a paw into my hand and sent that Colt flying. I watched it hit the floor, and I noticed two other things besides. You'd think I wouldn't have had the time, but it seemed like everything had slowed down, like we were wrapped in molasses.

First, I noticed the bear's smell, which was wild and rank and meaty. It smelled just like Bruno, who obviously kept close company with it.

And then, out of the corner of my eye, I saw Bruno. He was standing off to the side of the bear, looking about as satisfied as any man I ever saw. I wished I could shoot that look off his face, but I had other things to worry about.

I felt the bear's hot breath on my face and smelled its stink. I was sure I'd laid down my last ante, but the bear growled and jerked his head up and away from me.

A piece of burning canvas had fallen on his back and set his hair on fire. Quick as you could say "Jack Robinson" Bruno was over there, swatting at the fire and putting it out.

I heard the click of a shell being chambered and then of the rifle firing somewhere above me. Bean loosed off a couple of rounds at Bruno, but he missed. Maybe the smoke got in his eyes. It got in mine, and I blinked. When I looked again, Bruno was gone.

But so was I. At least I was gone from the place where I'd been. I rolled over and over on the hard-rock floor trying to get to the bar. It was a makeshift job, but I thought that if I could get behind it, I might be all right.

I rolled up against the bar, got up on my knees and scuttled around behind it. Maybe you think that was a cowardly thing to do, but I couldn't get to the Colt, and I wouldn't have stood a chance against that bear even if I'd had a cannon.

I didn't stand a chance even behind the bar, because when I looked over the top of it, here came the bear, building up a pretty good head of steam. I knew what he was about to do, but I didn't see any way to stop him. I managed to jump for it, sliding on my belly for a few feet, just before he smashed head-first into the bar, splintering it the way he'd splintered that table. Pieces of it went flying everywhere, and bottles crashed all around me, glass and liquor spraying.

The liquor caught on fire, and I was afraid the whole tent was going up, which it probably would have if it hadn't been raining all day and soaking the canvas. Not that it would have mattered to the bear.

Even if we weren't going to burn up, the smoke was thick and biting. At least there wasn't quite as much milling around now because a lot of people had gotten out of the tent. The bear didn't care about them. He was interested in me.

Roy Bean hadn't gotten out, though. I guess he was still trying to protect his place of business, what was left of it. I heard the rifle fire again and again, but it might as well have been a pea-shooter for all the mind the bear paid it. I could hear him growling and snuffling around, trying to find me in the smoke and the fire.

I wrapped my hand around a piece of the bar that was lying nearby. I was pretty sure there wasn't any way I could hurt that bear with it, but I was going to give it a damn good try.

I changed my mind, though, when I heard a noise down at the end of the bar. It was Bruno. He opened his mouth and howled, and I knew for certain he was calling the bear to come get me. So instead of whacking the bear, I duck-walked down the bar and whacked Bruno.

He'd been looking at the bear and didn't see me coming, so I got in a good solid lick right on the side of his head. It hardly fazed him, but it did surprise him enough to let me get in two more whacks, one on top of his head, and another one right between the eyes when he turned around. I put everything I had into it, and that was the one that did it. Bruno fell on his face as if he'd been pole-axed, which in a way, he had.

With Bruno out of the picture, something happened to the bear. The growling and snuffling stopped, and all I could hear was the crackling of the fire and a rifle shot or two.

I stood up and tried to look around the smouldering tent. Bean was about ten feet away, aiming his gun right at the bear's left eyeball.

"I don't think you should kill him," I said.

Bean looked up at me, never moving the rifle, not even a quarter of an inch.

"Why the hell not?"

"I'd think a man in the saloon business might be able to use a trained bear," I said.

The bear didn't move, and Bean thought it over.

"You might have an idea there," he said.

The bear seemed docile now. He was looking this way and that, as if he'd lost something.

"You think I could control him?" Bean asked.

"Bruno'd probably teach you. He should have plenty of time while he's in your jail, considering that he's probably a killer, or at least that bear is."

"It's something to think about," Bean said.

5

THE NEXT DAY was bright and clear. The sky was blue as far as you could see, and that was a good long way. Roy Bean's tent saloon was badly burned, but there was enough left of it for him to open for business. I supposed the bodies had been disposed of, and I went by to see him before I left town. I wondered just for a second if there'd be any eyeballs on the floor.

"You sure you don't want to stick around?" he asked me.

"I'm sure," I told him. "I think I've had about enough of Vinegaroon."

"Can't say as I blame you. But it ain't everywhere that you can get into a fight with a bear."

"It's not everybody that would even want to," I said.

Bean laughed at that.

"Get down off that horse and come around back," he said. "I got something I want to show you."

I dismounted and walked with him to the back of the tent. Somehow he'd managed to get a thick pole set into the ground. The bear was fixed to it with a heavy chain that was long enough to let him wander around in a ten- or twelve-foot circle. He was sitting there staring at us.

"Mean-looking son-of-a-bitch, ain't he?" Bean said.

"Sure is."

"What you reckon I oughta call him?"

"Bruno," I said. "I think it's only fitting."

"Sounds about right," Bean said. "Wait here."

He disappeared inside the tent. When he came back, he was holding a bottle of beer.

"Watch this," he said, and threw the bottle in the bear's direction.

The bear reached up and caught the bottle out of the air between his paws. He worried the cork with his teeth for a minute, and when he got it out, he tilted the bottle into his mouth and sucked down the beer.

"Ain't that the damnedest thing you ever saw?" Bean said.

I agreed that it was.

"It's going to make me many a dollar," Bean said. "People will pay good money to see a bear that can do that. And I figure the son-of-a-bitch owes it to me after what he did to my saloon."

I didn't blame Bean for feeling that way.

"What about Bruno?" I asked.

"He'll stay in jail here until the trial, which I'll preside over this very afternoon. Most folks I've talked to think he and his bear killed some chinamen just for fun. You want to stick around for the hanging?"

I said I didn't think so and that I hoped he had a really strong rope. He told me I didn't have to worry about that.

We started to go back to the front of the tent when I noticed something I hadn't seen before. There was an extra length of chain fixed to the bear's pole.

"What's that for?" I asked.

"I figure I might want to let the old bear have a little sport now and again," Bean said. "That chain's a little longer than the bear's, so if a man was tied to it, he could stay out of its way by about a foot or so."

"Why would you do something like that to somebody?"

"Lawbreakers," Bean said, as if that explained everything. He saw I didn't get it, and continued. "You gotta teach 'em right from wrong, get their hearts right with the Lord so they'll pay their fines. Come to think of it, I might try it out on Bruno before the hanging. You want a beer before you leave?"

I thanked him, but I didn't want anything to drink. I had the Colt stuck in the waistband of my pants, and it was about to weigh me down. I pulled it out and handed it to Bean.

"Maybe you could find a use for this," I said.

He hefted it in one hand and said, "You sure you don't want it?"

"I never carry a gun. If I did, I might have to use it. It didn't do me much good against that bear."

"I'll hang onto it then. You sure about that beer?"

I was sure. I just wanted to ride out of Vinegaroon and find me the kind of place I always seemed to be looking for, some place where there weren't any bears, some place where I could sit and watch the deal and not have to worry about getting killed. Some place where I could lay my money down.

AUTHOR'S NOTE: It was in 1882 in the hell-on-wheels town of Eagle's Nest, and a few months later in Vinegaroon, that Roy Bean began his career as the Law West of the Pecos. Later still, he took up permanent residence in Langtry and opened the famous Jersey Lily Saloon, where he kept a veritable menagerie, including a very large beer-drinking bear named Bruno. People said it was almost human. At least once in Langtry, a man found himself chained to the pole with Bruno. Bean might not have had the bear in Vinegaroon. But then again, maybe he did.

Ladysmith

L. J. Washburn

L. J. Washburn won the Shamus Award for her first novel, *Wild Night*, and for more than a dozen years since then has chronicled the adventures of her character Lucas Hallam in both westerns and mysteries. She has written other critically acclaimed westerns including *Riders of the Monte*, *Epitaph*, and *Bandera Pass*. Her most recent novel, co-authored with her husband, James Reasoner, is *Tie a Black Ribbon*, which introduced her character Skeeter Barlow. She lives in Texas.

THE BAD NEWS—and the package—caught up to Hallam in El Paso.

He had a room in the Camino Real Hotel downtown, a pretty fancy place for a man like him to be staying, but the client was paying for it. The fella owned a silver mine across the border in Mexico, and he had paid the Pinkerton Agency to find out who was responsible for high-grading some of his ore. Hallam was the agent given the job. He'd spent a week ferreting out the thieves, then returned to El Paso and wired the head office in Chicago to inform the boss of his success. He was waiting for a return telegram letting him know what his next assignment was going to be, so in the meantime he staked out his claim on a table in the bar. He was sitting there nursing a beer, long legs stretched out in front of him, when one of the desk clerks from the hotel lobby came over to him.

"*Señor* Lucas Hallam?" the man asked. He carried a long

white envelope and a package wrapped in brown paper.

"That's me," Hallam said.

"These were delivered for you." The clerk placed the envelope and the parcel on the table.

Hallam handed the man a coin and said, "Much obliged." He waited until the clerk was gone before picking up the envelope. His name was typed neatly in the middle of it. Up in the corner, the name of a Santa Fe law firm was printed. Hallam had never heard of them before.

He frowned. Why would a lawyer be looking for him? Only one way to find out, he decided. He tore open the envelope and unfolded the sheet of paper inside. Enough afternoon sunlight came through the glass doors on the other side of the bar for him to read what was written on the paper.

It was a letter from one of the members of the law firm, informing him that one of their clients, a Mrs. Rose Taggart, had passed away. Hallam wasn't sure who that was until he noticed that the late Mrs. Taggart had resided in the town of Raton.

"Red Rosie?" Hallam muttered to himself. He thumbed back his hat. "Red Rosie's dead?"

It didn't seem possible. The last time he'd seen her, she had seemed perfectly healthy. She was in her thirties, about the same age as Hallam. Of course, she was in a line of work that didn't promote long lives, but she had managed to buy her own house so she wasn't just a soiled dove anymore. She was a madam.

That was like saying that just because he was a Pinkerton agent now, instead of a hired gun, his own life was safe as houses, Hallam thought.

There was more to the letter. The law firm was handling Rose Taggart's estate, and one of the bequests in her last will and testament had gone to her old friend Lucas Hallam. The item in question was enclosed in the package accompanying the letter.

Hallam set the letter aside. So whatever was in that package was his legacy from Red Rosie. He was surprised that she would have left him anything. They had enjoyed a few romps together, and he supposed she had considered him a friend. He slipped out his knife, cut the string around the package, and began to unwrap it.

Inside a couple of layers of paper, he found a hinged box of polished hardwood about eight inches long, six inches wide, and three inches deep. A simple catch kept the box closed. Hallam unfastened it and raised the lid.

Inside, nestled on a bed of red velvet, was the gun.

He recognized it as a Smith & Wesson .22-caliber revolver. A small brass plate on the inside of the box lid had the word *Ladysmith* engraved on it. The body of the gun had a nickel-plated finish on it, and the curved butt was made of ivory. Hallam took the gun out of the box, his big hand nearly swallowing it up.

He was accustomed to the heavy Colt .45 that he always carried. This little gun was nothing but a toy, a trinket. And yet there was a sleek, almost beautiful wickedness about it, a sense that if handled correctly, it could be dangerous indeed.

Sort of like its late owner, Hallam thought with a faint smile. Rose Taggart had been the same way.

Ladysmith was a good name for a gun like this. If ever there was a lady's gun, this was it. Hallam hefted the revolver. It felt very light as it lay on his palm.

Why in blue blazes had Rose left this gun to him? He had no use for it, and since he had never even seen it before, it held no sentimental value for him. Why leave him anything at all?

He turned the gun over, thumbed the cylinder release button on the left side of the frame. As the cylinder swung out, he saw that the gun was loaded. That was a damned foolish way to ship a weapon. It could have gone off if somebody had dropped that package. Hallam shook the cartridges from the chambers into the palm of his other hand.

Then he frowned, and his fingers closed slowly around the bullets. Something was wrong, and he was beginning to have an inkling of what it was.

HE SENT ANOTHER wire to Chicago, advising his superiors at the Pinkerton Agency that he was unavailable for further assignments until he let them know otherwise. That would probably ruffle a few feathers, but Hallam didn't care. There was something else he had to do.

The next day, he stepped off an Atchison, Topeka & Santa Fe Railroad car at the depot in Raton, New Mexico. Nestled between two arms of the rugged Sangre de Cristo Mountains, the town served the large ranches in the area and was also the last stop before the spectacular ascent of Raton Pass. The Colorado border was just on the other side of the pass.

Hallam walked through the railroad station and onto the main street of the town. The buildings along the street were made of either adobe or red brick. Raton was bustling, industrious. A few horseless carriages were parked along the street and one was even chugging along raising a cloud of dust, reminding Hallam that it was the twentieth century now. But the streets were still unpaved, and they knew a lot more wagon wheels and horses' hooves than they did hard rubber tires.

Though it was spring, the altitude was high enough so that the sheepskin jacket Hallam wore felt good against the chill in the air. He walked along the street, trying to remember from his last visit to Raton where Red Rosie's place had been. Following his instincts, he turned a corner into a cross street, and things started to look more familiar. He walked past a Spanish-style residence with a walled-in courtyard and red tiles on the roof, then came to a large frame structure with a long porch on its front. He went up the steps to the porch.

A large man was sitting in a straight-backed chair on the porch. He had the chair rocked back against the wall. Looking up at Hallam from under the brim of his hat, he said, "Howdy, hoss. Something I can do for you?"

"This is Rose Taggart's place, ain't it? I'm lookin' for her."

The man let the chair's front legs down with a thump. "Reckon you ain't heard the news, hoss. Miz Taggart's dead. This house belongs to Cap Baldwin now."

Hallam shook his head. "Never heard of him."

"Don't reckon there's any law says you have to've heard of him, but it's still his." The man jerked a thumb toward the door. "Go on in. Just 'cause there's been a change in ownership don't mean the gals won't treat you nice."

Hallam stayed where he was. "What happened to Mrs. Taggart?"

"I wouldn't know, hoss." The man tipped his chair back again, then reached inside his shirt pocket and took out the makin's. "Cap don't pay me to palaver. Go on in or don't, whatever you want. Suit yourself, hoss."

Hallam said, "My name's not hoss." He reached out with his right foot, hooked the toe of his boot under one of the chair legs, and jerked upward. The legs went out from under the chair and dumped its occupant on the porch with a crash. Tobacco from the pouch scattered around him.

The man came up off the porch with a roar of rage. He was big, no more than two inches shorter than Hallam and probably ten or fifteen pounds heavier. But his first punch was slow and looping, and Hallam had no trouble stepping inside it and slamming a hard right into the man's mouth. The man fell back against the wall behind him.

Hallam crowded him, hooking a left to the belly, then bringing up a right that jerked the man's head back. Hallam caught hold of the man's shirt with both hands and turned, hauling the man around so that he crashed into and over the railing along the front of the porch. The man tumbled to the ground and landed so hard that all the breath was knocked out of him. He lay there pale and gasping, his mouth moving like that of a fish.

The commotion had attracted some attention inside, as Hallam figured it would. He turned back toward the front door as it was flung open. A tall, thickset man with a shock of pale hair rushed onto the porch carrying a shotgun. Hallam stood still and kept his right hand well away from the butt of the Colt holstered on his hip. He didn't want to give the hombre with the scattergun an excuse to get trigger-happy.

"What the hell's goin' on out here?" the newcomer demanded in a heavily accented voice that Hallam pegged as coming from Arkansas. "Rooster, what're you doin' just layin' down there on the ground?"

The man Hallam had thrown off the porch sucked down some more air, then pointed a finger at him. "That son-of-a-bitch done it!"

"Bein' called a name like that riles me even more than bein' called hoss," Hallam said.

The shotgunner lowered the double barrels of his weapon slightly. "Rooster, you been annoyin' the payin' customers again?"

"I never . . . He come up and started askin' questions."

"Questions about what?"

"About Rose Taggart," Hallam said. "I heard she owned this place, and that she and her girls sure knew how to show a man a good time."

"Oh." The shotgun went down even more. "Well, then, hell, this is all just a misunderstandin'." The man tucked the Greener under his arm and stepped forward with his hand extended. "I'm Captain Patrick Henry Baldwin, the current owner of this establishment."

Hallam shook hands with him. "Name's Lucas."

"You just come right on inside, Lucas. The first drink is on the house, to make up for Rooster's boorish behavior. He just don't know how to act around quality folks, you understand?"

"Sure," Hallam said. He allowed Baldwin to draw him inside the building.

The place wasn't as opulent as some of the whorehouses Hallam had seen in his life, but it was well-furnished—in more ways than one. Crystal chandeliers lit the parlor, and their illumination was necessary because heavy red velvet drapes were drawn tight over the windows, shutting out the afternoon sun. The rug under Hallam's boots was thick. The walls were covered with fancy paper, and plushly upholstered armchairs and divans were scattered around the room. Several attractive young women in various stages of undress made use of the furniture, draping themselves over it in blatantly sensual poses. All of them smiled at Hallam and Baldwin as the two men came into the room.

Baldwin put a friendly hand on Hallam's arm and steered him across the parlor toward a bar. A man with a large bald spot on the back of his head stood behind the bar, polishing glasses. Baldwin said to him, "Quentin, a glass of our finest for Mr. Lucas here. On the house."

"Yes, sir." Quentin took a bottle from under the bar and poured the drink. He looked at Baldwin and raised an eyebrow, and Baldwin indicated that he wanted a drink, too. Quentin splashed liquor into another glass.

Baldwin clinked his glass against Hallam's. "To your health, sir."

Hallam grunted an acknowledgment, then tossed back the drink. It was good whiskey that actually matched the label on the bottle, instead of the bathtub-brewed panther piss he'd halfway been expecting.

"What do you think?" Baldwin asked with a grin.

"Good," Hallam said.

"Nothing but the best for Cap Baldwin's customers," the man said, pride in his voice. He waved a hand toward the waiting women. "As you can see for yourself. Anything that pleases your fancy, Lucas?"

Hallam turned and ran his eyes over the women. Most of them were young, either in their teens or barely out of them. But one of them, a slender ash-blonde who wore a short wrapper of white silk and stood behind a divan resting her hands on it, was older, probably in her late twenties. Hallam nodded toward her and said, "That lady right there."

"You're a man of refined tastes, sir," Baldwin said. "Angela, come over here."

The blonde came out from behind the divan. Her legs were long and clean and good. She smiled at Hallam and took his hand, said, "Hello."

Hallam nodded. "Ma'am."

"Angela, this is Lucas. You treat him right, you hear?"

"I certainly will."

Still holding his hand, she led him out of the parlor and up a staircase to the second floor. Close beside her like this, Hallam could smell her perfume. It smelled good. Instead of dousing herself in the stuff, the way most whores did, she had showed some restraint.

They reached the second-floor landing and went along a balcony to a room with an open door. Several other doors off the balcony were closed. Angela took Hallam into the room, which was furnished with a bed, a porcelain chamber pot, a single chair, and a small table with a basin of water on it. She closed the door and turned back to face him, her hand going to the belt that was knotted around her waist, keeping the wrapper closed. "I'm glad you picked me, Lucas," she said.

Hallam's hand went out and touched her hands, stopping her from untying the belt. "Hold on," he said. "Do you remember me?"

Angela frowned a little. "Well, I thought you looked familiar when I first saw you downstairs. You're a big man. Have you been here before?"

"About two years ago was the last time."

"That was when Rose still—" Angela stopped short and stared at Hallam, her eyes widening. "Lucas," she said in a hushed voice. "Not . . . Lucas Hallam?"

He nodded.

And the cracks that were starting to show in her carefully controlled composure split wide open. Her face twisted and tears began to roll down her cheeks and she stepped forward into Hallam's arms, burying her face against his broad chest as she cried.

LATER, WHEN ANGELA had calmed down a little, she and Hallam sat side by side on the edge of the bed and she said, "Nobody from the old days comes here anymore, Lucas. Even all the girls from that time are gone, except for me."

"Figured as much," Hallam said. "That's why I picked you downstairs. I thought maybe you could tell me what happened to Rose."

"Baldwin happened," Angela said, bitterness and anger in her voice. "He showed up in town and sweet-talked his way in here. He's a gambler, and Rose let him run a poker game here. You know some of the men like to play cards as well as . . . the other things they do here."

Hallam nodded.

"None of the girls liked him much," Angela went on. "He was rough with some of them. Never with me, but I heard about it from the others. I told them they ought to tell Rose, but we all knew how she felt about him, and they didn't want to hurt her."

"Seems like a lady as smart as Rose would've seen through a skunk like that."

"You'd think so. But you know how it is sometimes. You

fall in love with somebody, and you convince yourself that all their flaws aren't really there."

Hallam supposed that was true. He'd had his heart broken a few times because he hadn't wanted to see certain things that he should have.

"Anyway, Rose started to get sick, and she relied more and more on Baldwin to run things around here. Finally, after about six months, she . . . she died."

"From what?" Hallam asked. "What sickness did she have?"

Angela shook her head. "The doctor never could figure it out for sure. Rose just wasted away to nothing, and then she was gone."

Hallam's jaw tightened. He didn't like to think about Rose like that. Vital, beautiful Rose, as full of life as any woman he'd ever known.

"How'd Baldwin get his hands on the house?"

"She left it to him in her will. That didn't really surprise any of us, but we didn't like it. One by one, the girls who were here then all drifted away, rather than stay on and work for him. All but me."

"Why didn't you leave, too?"

She laughed. "I'm too old, Lucas. I don't want to have to start over somewhere else. And Baldwin doesn't bother me very often. He prefers the younger girls. I have to put up with Rooster and Quentin, but . . ."

"You said Rose left the house to Baldwin in her will. Who handled that?"

"There's a lawyer here in Raton who was a customer. Still is, for that matter. He works for a law firm down in Santa Fe, but he's the one who drew up the will. His name is Arthur McKagen."

Hallam nodded. He knew the name from the letter he'd gotten in El Paso, along with the Ladysmith revolver.

"I need to have a talk with the fella. You say his office is here in town?"

"Just down the block from the train station. Lucas . . ." She laid a hand on his arm. "Why are you here?"

"Rose left me something in her will, too."

"I'm guessing you don't want me to tell Baldwin who you really are."

"Let's leave him in the dark awhile longer," Hallam said.

Angela's hand went to the opening of the wrapper at her throat. "While we're here, do you want to . . ."

Hallam smiled. "Maybe when this is all over."

ARTHUR MCKAGEN WAS a short, stocky man who looked impatient when Hallam came up to him on the sidewalk in front of the building where his office was located.

"I'm closed for the day," the lawyer said. "You'll have to come back tomorrow."

Hallam shook his head. "Sorry, I have to talk to you today. It's about Rose Taggart."

"Rose . . . I'm sorry, I can't discuss a client's business."

"I'm Lucas Hallam. I got a letter from you. And a package."

McKagen knew the name. "Hallam? I sent that letter nearly two months ago."

"It took a while to find me. I move around a lot."

"Well, Mr. Hallam, obviously you were acquainted with Mrs. Taggart, and for that reason I offer you my condolences on her passing. But I really have to get home to my wife—"

"Does she know that you were one of Red Rosie's *clients?*"

McKagen stopped short and glared at Hallam. "What you are implying, sir, is nothing less than blackmail!"

"All I need is a few minutes of your time. There're some things I got to get straightened out."

McKagen sighed and said, "Very well, come in. But only for a few minutes. My wife would probably be more upset if I were late for dinner than if she found out I, ah, patronized Mrs. Taggart's establishment on occasion."

The lawyer sat down behind his desk but didn't take off his hat. Neither did Hallam as he lowered himself into a red leather chair in front of the desk. "Tell me about Mrs. Taggart's will," he said.

McKagen shrugged. "There's nothing much to tell. The document went through probate and is now a matter of public record. Mrs. Taggart made a few small bequests to individuals, personal items for the most part, such as that gun she left to you, but the bulk of her estate, including her house, went to Captain Patrick H. Baldwin."

"Why would she leave practically everything to Baldwin?"

"I didn't ask her," McKagen said. "That wasn't really my business. But I suppose they were . . . close friends."

"But not married."

"No. However, an estate does not have to be left to a spouse. In this case, Mrs. Taggart was a widow and never remarried, so that would be impossible."

"What do you know about Baldwin?"

McKagen frowned. "Really, Mr. Hallam, this conversation is quite inappropriate."

"Be easier if you just answer my question, so your wife don't have to wait supper any longer than necessary."

"Very well, if you insist. But I don't know a great deal at all about Mr. Baldwin. He arrived in Raton about a year ago, claiming to be a cattle buyer. I don't think he ever bought any cattle, however. He spent most of his time at Mrs. Taggart's, playing cards, and eventually he spent all his time there."

"What about Rooster and Quentin? Did they come to Raton with him?"

"Who? Oh, you mean the two men who work there at the house. No, he hired them after Mrs. Taggart passed away. I don't recall seeing them around town before that."

But Baldwin could have sent for them, Hallam thought. He had gotten the feeling that Baldwin had known Rooster and Quentin for quite a while.

"Is there anything else?" McKagen asked.

Hallam thought about it, then shook his head. "No, I reckon not." He stood up.

Before Hallam reached the door, McKagen said, "You know, it's odd."

Hallam looked back. "What's odd?"

"You don't strike me as the type to be sentimental about a gun, Mr. Hallam. No offense, but you seem more the sort who would regard a weapon simply as a tool."

Hallam turned that comment over in his mind, then said, "Rose told you I was attached to that gun she left me, did she?"

"She said it carried a great deal of importance to you, as well as to her."

"Let me guess," Hallam said. "She came in and added that part of the will after the rest of it was already drawn up."

McKagen coughed. "Well, actually, I was at her place one evening when she asked me to come into her office. We drew up the codicil right there, and she gave me the wooden box with the gun inside it. I brought it back here that night."

"How long after that was it she died?"

"Only a week," McKagen said. "You almost missed out on your inheritance, such as it is, Mr. Hallam."

"Yeah," Hallam said. "Reckon I'm lucky."

HE HAD LEFT his war bag at the Santa Fe Railroad station. He picked it up, then walked over to the Raton House and got a room for the night. After eating supper in the hotel dining room, he went outside and took a deep breath of the cold night air.

It was time.

Hallam patted his coat, feeling the shape of the wooden box containing the Ladysmith revolver, which he had taken from his war bag and slipped into an inner pocket before eating.

"I'll square it, Rose," he muttered.

Rooster was still on the porch of the big house, but he wasn't sitting now. He stood there near the door with his arms folded, a glare on his beard-stubbled face as Hallam came up the steps.

"What're you doin' back here?" Rooster demanded.

"A fella gets an itch, he's got to scratch it," Hallam said.

Rooster mumbled something obscene. Hallam ignored him and walked inside.

Baldwin was in the parlor, leaning on the bar and talking in low tones with Quentin. The place was much busier now than it had been in the middle of the afternoon. Several men were sitting around sipping drinks and talking to the scantily clad women. Hallam saw Angela and gave her a brief nod, then went across the room to the bar.

"Well, Lucas, I didn't expect to see you back so soon,"

Baldwin greeted him. The man chuckled. "Angela must have made an impression on you."

"She sure did," Hallam said.

"She's yours for the takin', if you'd like."

Hallam shook his head. "I had something else in mind first. I've heard that you like to play a game of cards now and then."

Baldwin laughed. "Card playing is one of my vices, sure enough. My poor old Baptist mama tried to beat it out of me, but she never succeeded, rest her soul."

"Reckon we could get up a game?"

"I think that could be arranged." Baldwin looked around the room. "I see a few gents in attendance tonight who favor a game of cards when they get the chance. I'll speak to them, find out if they're interested. In the meantime, Quentin, why don't you show Lucas to the card room and give him a drink?"

"Sure thing, Cap," Quentin said.

Hallam followed the bartender into a small room that opened off the parlor. It contained a baize-covered poker table surrounded by chairs, as well as a small bar in one corner. Quentin set out glasses around the table and produced a bottle of whiskey. Hallam took a seat with his back to a blank wall, and Quentin filled the glass in front of him. He put the cork back in the bottle and set it in the middle of the table.

Baldwin came in with four other men, three of them dressed in town clothes and looking prosperous, the fourth man in the boots and jeans and Stetson of a cattleman. "Lucas, meet Ed Gloster," Baldwin said, indicating the rancher.

Hallam stood up and shook hands. "Howdy, Gloster."

"Lucas is the handle, is it?"

"That's right."

Hallam thought he saw something in Gloster's eyes; recognition, maybe. He wasn't personally acquainted with the cattleman, but Gloster could have seen him somewhere, might even know his real name. But if that was the case, Gloster was going to keep it to himself. He just nodded and sat down.

Baldwin introduced the other men to Hallam: Frank

Randall, John Edwards, and Parley Barnett. "Parley's our mayor," Baldwin added.

The portly Barnett looked embarrassed. "Now, we don't need to be goin' on about things like that," he said. "I'm sure Mr. Lucas ain't interested in local politics."

"I've heard it said that when you come right down to it, all politics is local," Hallam said. "Me, I never paid much attention to such things."

"That's probably wise," Frank Randall said with a chuckle. "There are a lot more important things in life. Like poker."

Baldwin took a seat and began unwrapping a new deck of cards. "Spoken like a true card player, Frank," he said.

The game got under way. Hallam tilted his hat back on his head and concentrated on his cards. For the first few hands, the players were feeling each other out, although these locals probably had played together before and knew each other's habits. But Hallam was a stranger, and therefore something of a wild card.

Baldwin was a good player, and as far as Hallam could tell, he wasn't cheating. The pile of bills and coins in front of him grew steadily as the game progressed. He wasn't winning so much, though, as to offend the other men. That, as much as anything, was proof of his skill.

Hallam didn't have a lot of cash on him, but that was just as well. He didn't want to prolong this. When one of the pots began to grow, he stayed in when he might have dropped out otherwise. So did Baldwin, raising consistently. One by one, the other players folded as they sensed that something was developing between Hallam and Baldwin. When the bet came to him, Hallam saw it and raised, using the last of his money. Baldwin's expression had grown more intense. The competitive juices were flowing in him, Hallam knew. Baldwin smiled and said, "Well, Lucas, I'm just going to have to see that bet and bump it up a little more. I have faith in my cards."

Hallam glanced at his cards without really seeing them. He didn't give a damn whether he won the hand or not. All he'd been doing was leading up to this moment.

"Are you going to call?" Baldwin prodded.

"I'll do more than that," Hallam said. He laid his cards

facedown on the table in front of him and reached inside his coat. "I'll cover the bet and raise it." He brought out the polished wooden box and placed it on the table.

"What's that?" Mayor Barnett asked.

Baldwin's eyes narrowed to slits as he looked at the box. Hallam didn't know if he recognized it or not, but his instincts must have kicked in, warning him that something unusual was going on.

Hallam unfastened the catch and opened the lid of the box. "I figure this is worth enough, especially to you, Baldwin."

Ed Gloster leaned forward and looked at the gun lying in its bed of red velvet. "I've seen pistols like that before," he said. "It's called a Ladysmith, isn't it?"

"That's right," Hallam said. "It's a Smith & Wesson, .22 caliber."

Baldwin licked his lips. "That's a nice little gun, Lucas, but it's not hardly worth enough—"

"Oh, it's not the gun itself," Hallam said. "What I'm really bettin' are the bullets."

"The bullets?" Randall said. "How can bullets be worth anything?"

Hallam took the Ladysmith out of the box and opened the cylinder, turning the gun so that the men around the table could see that it was fully loaded. "This is the way the gun came to me," he said. "I inherited it from Rose Taggart."

"Red Rosie?" Gloster exclaimed. "You knew her?"

Hallam nodded, his eyes fixed on Baldwin now. "I did. Not as well as I might've liked, but we were pretty close."

Baldwin's pose of affability had vanished now. "I don't know what you're doin' here, but this game is over."

"Not until we finish this hand," Hallam said. He shook the bullets out into his palm. "I understand why you might not want to let me bet the gun, but these cartridges are mighty valuable."

He brought one of them to his mouth and bit the lead bullet, pulling it loose from the shell. Hallam spit out the bullet, then turned the shell upside down so that a tiny, tightly rolled piece of paper fell out of it.

"Every one of these cartridges has a message inside it,

Baldwin," Hallam went on. "They're in Rose Taggart's handwriting. I reckon there are people here in Raton who'll recognize it without any trouble. They tell the whole story of how you came here and fooled her into thinking you loved her, while all the time you planned to kill her and take over her place. She even found the poison you'd been feedin' to her in small doses for months, makin' her sicker and sicker. But by then it was too late, and she knew it. She knew she was goin' to die. All she could do was leave behind a last request. So she left me this gun, and these bullets, knowin' I'd settle the score for her."

The room was completely silent as Hallam finished talking. Several heartbeats went by with Baldwin staring across the table at Hallam. Then Ed Gloster said, "Can I see that?"

Hallam handed him the note he had taken from the opened cartridge. Gloster unrolled it, looked at the words written on it, and said, "That's Rose's hand, all right." He looked up at Hallam. "I know you now, Hallam. I was up in Pueblo a few years back when you caught up with the Wilson brothers. How did Rose know you'd look inside these bullets?"

"She knew I wouldn't leave a gun sitting around loaded like that when it wasn't going to be used," Hallam said. "And I reckon she was counting on the fact that I could tell something was wrong with them, just by the weight and feel of them."

"That was a risky bet."

"The way Baldwin kept her cooped up here in the house all the time, it was the only way she had to get in touch with me. She didn't want him to know she was on to what he was doin' to her." Hallam's mouth curved in a cold, humorless smile. "I reckon she wanted it to be a surprise when I came to see Baldwin."

"You can't prove any of this," Baldwin said, his voice hollow.

Hallam's left hand brushed the bullets, sent them rolling into the center of the table. "We've got Rose's own words to prove it," he said. "So how about it, Baldwin? Are you goin' to call the bet or not?"

Baldwin moved, his left arm coming up under the table and upsetting it while he surged to his feet and grabbed under his coat for a gun with his right hand. Hallam fell backward in his chair, away from the table, and the other four men dived for the corners of the room, getting as far out of the line of fire as they could. The revolver that appeared in Baldwin's hand blasted twice, but Hallam was already rolling to the side. As he came up on one knee, the Colt on his hip seemed to leap into his hand. He fired once, driving a slug into Baldwin's chest. Baldwin was thrown back against the wall behind him, but he stayed on his feet and tried to raise his gun for another shot. Hallam triggered again, and this time when Baldwin hit the wall, he bounced off and fell forward on his face.

The door into the card room burst open, and Quentin tried to bring a sawed-off shotgun to bear on Hallam. Off to the side, another pistol barked. Quentin jerked around, dropping the scattergun and clutching at his shoulder where a bullet had drilled it. Hallam looked over and saw Ed Gloster holding a gun. He nodded and said, "Much obliged."

The cattleman grunted. "Rose Taggart was my friend, too," he said.

The shots had set off quite a commotion elsewhere in the house. Men were shouting questions and curses, and somewhere a woman screamed in fear. Rooster's big figure suddenly loomed in the doorway of the card room, but he stopped in his tracks as he found himself facing the guns held by Hallam and Gloster.

"Your horse out back, Rooster?" Gloster asked.

"Uh, yeah." Rooster's stunned gaze was fastened on Baldwin's crumpled body.

"Well, then, if I was you, I'd saddle up and ride out of Raton, right now. And I wouldn't ever come back." Gloster glanced over at Hallam. "That all right with you?"

Hallam nodded. Rooster had probably known what Baldwin was doing to Rose Taggart, and a part of him wanted to kill the son-of-a-bitch, but Baldwin was dead and Hallam supposed that was enough.

Rooster backed out of the room, then turned tail and ran. Hallam holstered his Colt and looked down at the wounded Quentin. "When he's been patched up, I reckon he ought to leave, too."

Gloster nodded. "We'll see to it." He looked around at

the other men. "We'll make things right for Red Rosie, won't we, boys?"

The townsmen muttered their agreement. Chances were, they would hush up the whole thing, Hallam thought, especially the mayor. But he didn't care. Rose's death had been avenged, and that was all that mattered.

That, and one more thing.

"There's a lady who works here named Angela," Hallam said. "I reckon the place ought to go to her now. That lawyer, McKagen, can likely fix it up all legal-like."

"Sure," Gloster said. "What about you, Hallam?"

Hallam scooped up the cartridges and thumbed them back into the cylinder of the Ladysmith. He closed it, put the gun in the wooden box, and lowered the lid. "There's a train out of here in the morning," he said as he put the box in his coat. "Reckon I'll be on it."

Copyrights and Permissions